Losing Jane

When I look back at what happened, some things get swirled in a mist that clouds my memory. Although there are set markers of undisputable truths to plot the story, the distance between them is sometimes hazy. So as I reflect, I fill in the gaps with how I think it went, which is most probably, how I like to think it happened. Everyone has their own agenda.

I did worry that confusing facts with my introspective bias, might alter my perceived reality, making what really happened less important. However, on balance, I think this rose-tinting serves only to make it easier to tell. The story still starts and ends the same way, no matter how much I want it to be different.

As promised I told no one. I've kept the secrets for so long that they took on a life of their own and aged with me. They have been a heavy burden over the years but like all old secrets they did eventually die, yet still I wasn't rid of them. Their spirits have continued to torment and haunt me. This is my exorcism.

A.K.Biggins

Losing
Jane

A.K.Biggins

A.K.Biggins

ISBN:0995590508
ISBN-13:978-0-9955905-0-2

For Paul, Andrew, Emma and Sarah for giving me the encouragement, time and space to finally tell this story.

Chapter One

When she was ten years old my best friend Jane Schofield lost her mother. Actually to be specific her mother just vanished. There was quite a furore in the first few weeks immediately after that cold, dark Friday evening, back in February 1968, when Maggie Schofield pulled off her amazing disappearing trick. The last sighting of her was at ten past five when she went out to buy fish and chips, leaving Jane watching television. Don Schofield was well known around Bramley, the suburb of Leeds where they lived, as a drunken bully and wife beater. Maggie, being the wife in question was often seen sporting the evidence of her husband's 'manliness', with many a colourful bruise and a twice broken right arm. The police were called out by neighbours on various occasions but Maggie always sent them away claiming accidents and clumsiness and no charges were ever pressed. So when Don finally reported her missing, on the Sunday morning, 36 hours after the last known sighting of her, the police were suspicious. There was a communal nodding of heads and knowing looks from friends and neighbours as they speculated, not too discreetly, that he'd finally struck her a fatal blow and 'done her in'. The local police were in full agreement of this theory and were so certain of Don's foul deed that they failed to consider any other scenario. However, despite their continual searching of the house, digging up the garden and even dredging the beck at the bottom of the lane, no body was found. So by the time they finally accepted Don's cast iron alibi there was little left to investigate. The case went cold, Maggie

Schofield became just another missing person and Jane's fate was sealed.

Our first meeting was on a sunny September morning as we stood in line to enter our first day at secondary school. By then her mother had been gone seven months. We were two of the one hundred and sixty eleven-year-olds who happened to be standing next to each other in the queue, waiting to be processed into the beginning of our adolescent lives. I was instantly drawn to her and can still remember the frisson of excitement as she smiled and spoke to me.

"You don't have to wear that beret; everybody'll think you're a bit mental if you keep it on."

Despite my objections Mum had insisted on coming along in the car when Dad drove the mile and a half for my first day at the big school. I was horrified when she wanted to get out of the car and walk right up to the school gates with me, where all my soon to be new class mates were assembling. As if having your Mummy taking you to school at eleven wasn't bad enough, she had her hair in rollers covered only with a bright pink chiffon scarf, a coat over her night dress and her slippers on.

My parents were not like everyone else's. This was something I'd become painfully aware of. That morning Mum had been quite adamant that I should wear the full school uniform, including the beret. As we pulled up at the school gates, I could see only one other girl wearing one and no boys whatsoever donning the school cap, and tried to point this out. But Mum persisted with her insistence of my keeping mine on.

"Well it looks right smart and really suits you. Doesn't it Ray?"
She nudged Dad who was scrutinising the gathering assembly of children and giving special attention to the boys. Without moving his eyes he responded, on message.

"What, oh aye, she looks a right bobby dazzler." His intonation at complete odds with his words gave away his low level of interest in my headwear.

The growing throng of pre and post pubescent males had his full attention as he glared through the windscreen at the assembling masses. He hadn't been happy about me going to a mixed comprehensive and had been complaining to Mum about it constantly. But the decision was made by the local authority with no input or appeal from us; I was going to Hill Topp. I'd been a little alarmed at this prospect and would have much preferred to go to the all-girls school at the other side of town. I'd heard the term 'randy little bleeders' used by Dad on several occasions, describing the boys I'd be coming into contact with at a mixed school.

Afraid Mum would get out of the car, I gave in and pulling the beret over my shoulder length, mousey hair, I quickly got out saying,

"You can go now I'll be alright, I'll walk home, see you at half past four." There were no other cars around which heightened my embarrassment as clutching my satchel I rushed to join the line. All thoughts of my head attire forgotten until this very self-assured girl mentioned it. I glanced across to where our car was still parked and could clearly see my mother craning her neck to try and spot me. Looking back at my new companion with a grateful smile, I pulled it off, stuffed it into my bag saying, "Thanks."

"What's your name?" she asked.

"Kimberly. Well Kim, Kim Asquith."

My heart was beating wildly. This pretty and self assured girl seemed interested in me. Had I made a friend when I had only just got inside the school gates?

"Well Kim-Kim Asquith, I'm Jane Schofield." She nodded her head towards the road and asked, "Is that your Mam and Dad over there in that car?"

I nodded bending my knees so they wouldn't be able to pick me out.

"They wouldn't let me come on my own; I wish they'd get lost."

"You shouldn't wish that," casting her eyes down in a highly theatrical gesture she paused before looking back up at me and adding, "I've lost my Mum, well I suppose more likely she's lost herself."

"What? Oh sorry, I mean..., what do you mean?"

"She went out one night to fetch the fish and chips for our tea and never came back."

"What?" I said again, "Really? Blimey!" My mouth gawping, I asked "What happened then?"

"We had to make do with beans on toast." She laughed and nudged me before asking, "Did you just say 'blimey? God they're gonna make mincemeat out of you. You better stick with me or you won't survive till dinner time!"

Later I learned that the story of Jane's Mum's disappearance was a bit of local folklore. Most people had a view on what had happened. Surprisingly, few people had much concern for what life was like in the three bed-roomed council house for the four children left behind, especially the youngest. Jane had three older brothers. Iain, sixteen at the time, had left school and worked at the sheet metal works with his Dad. Kevin was thirteen and David just a year older than Jane. Both the younger boys were already established pupils at the school, although between the suspensions and truanting, they'd not had much presence. On the few occasions I saw any of her siblings I remember being absolutely terrified of them, particularly Kevin, who was a brutish and foul mouthed bully. Now, after all these years, it seems unfathomable to me that no one considered that there should have been a bit more concern about Jane once her mother was gone. But it was a different time and what went on behind closed doors back then was pretty much nothing to do with anybody else. Perhaps things aren't really all that different now.

I have an old school photograph taken just before Christmas that year and it still makes me smile seeing all those young faces, full of potential and infinite possibilities. A few were scowling or looking indifferent but most were smiling. There I am, second row, third from the left, standing next to Jane, both of us beaming widely at the camera. It's captioned –

'The class of 1968'- depicting thirty-seven innocent faced eleven-year-olds on the verge of starting their lives. Ready for what life was going to throw at us, well some more ready than others. We were form 1B, which meant we'd been judged B grade intelligence in the A to D grouping favoured by schools then. Four rows, the front row seated and three rows standing with the form teacher Mr Roundtree, proudly at the end of the back row. At the other side of Jane are Diane and Sharon, two other new friends. They'd known each other for years, living close to one another and they'd been at the same junior school as Jane, so knew her vaguely, but only really became friends throughout our first year. The foundation of this kinship was formed during the ritual of our first school dinner experience. Again chance played its part as we found ourselves thrust together for this initiation.

As an only child used to small village schools a long way from Leeds, I found the business of the 'not so orderly' queuing a lot more than daunting. The rules around first or second sittings and the Prefect control were terrifying. Jane's comment about me not lasting till dinner time rang in my ears as the authoritative older pupils circled us, performing a kettling manoeuvre while trying out their new-found power with spiteful glee.

The dinner routine had been explained to us that morning at registration. Once those of us who were not on free school meals had paid our one and six, we were taken in a crocodile of twos to see the dining hall. As we approached the double doors, the smell hit us. The sour odour of much boiled cabbage permeated the air and continued to prevail every dinner time throughout the years, whether or not it was on the menu. I'd taken Jane literally and stuck to her side throughout the morning, but once in the queue she started talking to two other girls who were just behind us and I began to panic. Standing quietly I marvelled at how easily she struck up a conversation with them but after a few shy smiles I started to allow myself to believe that these other girls could also want to be my friends too. Jane was confident and entertaining and her jokey quips and comments soon had us chatting away like we'd all known each other for years. Diane and Sharon were also only children but spent most of their evenings and weekends at each other's homes so were already really close. They actually looked a little alike too, with pageboy haircuts. At one point Jane said how great it was that all four of us were only children, which was why we would be best friends

"But haven't you got some brothers?" Sharon asked.

Jane just shrugged and said they didn't count as they were stupid, well David was alright sometimes but anyway she was the only girl so that was the same really. They were quite interested to hear that I lived in a pub and wanted to know all about how this worked and our living arrangements. Sharon particularly wanted to know if my bedroom smelled of beer and fags. I was just about to explain that the house was actually a separate building when the school secretary, a very stern looking woman, suddenly appeared at the front of the queue and shouted,

"Is there a Jane Schofield here?"

Jane's expression changed immediately, her lovely smile was replaced by sullen indifference. This was the first time I saw this change in her but soon came to recognise it as the mask she used to hide behind when she was frightened. She raised her hand and called back in a flat voice "Here Miss."

She was only gone for a few moments coming back with her smile back in place, she shook a brown paper envelope in front of us saying,

"Well this is good news. I got me dinner money back!"

"How come?" asked Sharon.

"Cos I'm a semi-orphan."

"What do you mean?" Both girls looked from her to me.

Later Jane told me she found their pretence of not knowing about her family hilarious but she enjoyed telling the story of when she last saw her mother and the drama of the weeks that followed. It was like she was talking about a film she'd seen. She was a detached narrator with the funny lines, making what was surely a terrible event into an entertaining tale. Without mentioning her Dad's physical violence, she left us in no doubt that her mother had no life other than cooking and cleaning, making her sound a bit like Cinderella. Her Dad on the other hand, although fearsome, was a bit of a lovable rogue.

In the afternoon break of that first day, we were sitting on the fire escape steps to the science labs on our own. I asked her what she thought had happened to her Mum. Her face lit up.

"You're the first person to ask me what I think."

"Honestly?" I was astounded. "Not the police or your Dad?"

"No, the police think me Dad's done her in and thrown her in the beck and me Dad thinks she's run off with someone so none of 'em care what I think."

"What about your brothers?"

"They think what Dad thinks."

"So what do you think?"

"I know she wouldn't have gone off an left me. Even though Dad did smack her about, it were only after he'd bin drinking an cos' he really loves her. He wouldn't have killed her, I know he wouldn't." She paused a second before leaning closer but looking down at her knees as she said,

"He's so fuckin' furious she's gone though and that's another reason she'd never have dared go off, cos' she knows he'll find her and fetch her back then he really would kill her, ring her neck probably."

My eyes must have been like saucers staring at her serious and pensive face. She glanced up at me and said,

"Somebody's taken her, I just know it. It's the only thing that could've happened an' one day she's gonna turn up dead cos whoever took her won't want to let her go once he's finished wi' her. I know this, cos I know that she would never have left me, she just wouldn't have!"

I saw the facade of her bravado crumble and instinctively, I pulled her towards me. I hugged her so that she could wipe her tears on the shoulder of my school jumper as I wiped mine away with the back of my hands.

Chapter Two

That first year at Hill Topp Secondary School was a steep learning curve and would have been even steeper for me, had it not been for Jane. There were so many new experiences and for practically all of them, she was by my side softening the impact. She became the best friend and confidante I'd longed for and arrived in my life at exactly the right time, steering me through the minefield of adolescence. But it took me a long time to work out what she got from our friendship. Probably the first big change was convincing my Mum that I needed a bra. She'd bought me some scallop-edged vests to wear under my white school shirt. As I'd started to develop around the chest area, I had suggested I should have a bra. *"You don't need one of them yet, you're way too young."* Age, not size or shape were the only criteria for supportive undergarments in Mum's eyes and I knew further discussion was pointless. I'd even convinced myself that my vests were quite pretty and being labelled ages eleven to thirteen they would be ok. Also my white school shirt was two sizes too big, providing growing room, so no one would be able to tell what I had on underneath. That was before Wednesday and my first experience of Games.

In my primary school PE lessons, I had perfected the art of quick changing, putting on my shorts before taking off my skirt and always wearing a t-shirt under my normal school top. I couldn't tell you how other children coped with this communal disrobing; I was always so intent on protecting my body against onlookers I never looked at anyone else. Modesty was something to be protected at all cost. This was just one of the confusing caveats of my upbringing. I am paraphrasing as what was generally said was '*you shouldn't let anybody see your underwear, it's not right.*' This quoted mainly by someone who was perfectly comfortable turning up at my school in her nightdress, slippers and curlers.

Having got through the first two and a half days of big school and already making friends, I'd been lulled into a sense of security as we walked round the outside of the school towards the gymnasium. I was probably smiling as I entered the girls' changing room. It was a stark, cold, communal bunker-like area with strip lighting and concrete floor. My smile would have dissolved completely as the terror hit me. We were to undress in full view of each other and the two games teachers. Fumbling in rows while standing in front of low benched seats, we took off our uniforms, hanging them on the pegs above, before putting our games kits on. I noticed that not every girl in my year was concerned about modesty. I was astonished to see some had shed their skirts and shirts and stood casually chatting to their neighbours, in their matching undergarments. I tried to keep my eyes down but my anxiety was growing fast as of course the girls that had this much self-assurance were the ones with slim bodies and clear complexions. My horrors increased. It was an hour and a half of netball which I was terrible at, never in the right place at the right time, never keeping up with play. But there was still worse to come. Once back in the changing rooms we were made to undress completely and walk naked through the open fronted showers leaving our towels on the hooks. Coming out the other end we passed the teacher, who marked us off on her register before we could collect our towels.

Miss Hanson took us for our double games slot every week and seemed to take great pleasure in the discomfort of this collective nudity. Her register would record periods, the only excuse accepted for not showering. Despite trying it on occasionally, no girl was allowed more than one period a month and no allowance was made for the unpredictability of prepubescent hormones. This occasionally had mortifying consequences. Once Sharon claimed she had a verruca after a morning games class. She was simply told to keep her sock on that foot. The rest of the day she had to slosh around with one wet sock. I know I wasn't alone in my embarrassment but the sheer humiliation of this experience was one that filled me with dread and despair. The barely stifled giggles and muttered comments designed to ridicule and hurt didn't make this weekly event any more pleasurable. But that first changing room experience remains deep in my psyche and can still make me shudder with mortification. The loud burst of laughter from a group of bra clad girls to the left of me following a comment about my 'fat saggy tits' and my 'granny's vest' made me burn with shame. But it was short-lived. Jane, stepped towards them and said,

"If you don't shut the fuck up and stop laughing at my friend I'll knock your teeth so far down your throat you'll have to stick yer finger up yer arse to bite yer nails.'

Although she said this quietly keeping her beautiful, butter-wouldn't-melt smile, there was no mistaking the menace in her voice. It was incredible; this ability she had to let someone know that she could and would hurt them, without ever having to prove it or even raise her voice. My tormentors withdrew immediately without any suggestion of comeback. Jane returned to folding her clothes, completely unfazed. She stood there in her pretty, lacy bra pants not caring who saw her petite and curvy, young body. I knew then just being her friend would not only help my credibility, it would stop me from being the target of that main clique of unpleasant and spiteful girls again. My cheeks still burned though when I heard them ridicule and humiliate other girls. The basis for this ridicule could be either having or not having breasts, having or not having pubic hair, being too fat, too thin or wearing the wrong underwear, which was just asking for stigmatisation and mockery.

Afterwards, as we walked back to our last lesson of the day, Jane told me I needed to make sure I had a bra before the next week. I explained that as far as Mum and Dad were concerned I was growing up fast enough without drawing attention to my developing female curves. Jane thought this was hilarious but told me what to say to convince them. I had to lay it on thick about the bitchy set in the changing rooms and to mention I was the only one who didn't have a bra. I should also say that the games teacher had said it was bad for my back and posture and I needed to have one by next week or I'd get detention. I was slightly sceptical about this plan as although there was some truth in it, there was also a bit of lying, something I'd never tried before, but I thought it might be worth a shot.

So, as Mum was doing her hair before work, I tried it out. I'd been rehearsing in my head since I'd got home from school. I was word perfect but nervous. However, once I started to recount the changing room scene the heat rushed to my face and before I knew what was happening, I was sobbing uncontrollably, hardly managing to get any words out at all let alone my prepared speech. Mum hugged me briefly, not wanting to get my snotty tears on her smart clean clothes and told me that, *"if it upset me so much of course you can have one"*. She would order me one out of her Burlington's catalogue the next day. I managed to pull myself together enough to push the point that I had to have one before the next games lesson and catalogue orders could sometimes take weeks. She breathed out loudly and as she filled the room with hairspray, she said,

"Right then we'll go to C&A on Saturday morning and get you sorted. I could do with some new tights for me self anyway so we can have a shopping day."

On Saturday afternoon I sat by myself in our living room, playing Dad's records on our radiogram. I was the happiest I had been for absolutely ages. Although I'd had to compromise slightly and hadn't got the pretty bra I'd wanted, I didn't have the ugly middle-aged woman's 'strap em up' one that Mum had chosen. So this still felt like my first real victory in my attempt at being the person I wanted to be. The communal changing rooms and showers still remained an ordeal for the rest of my school years but they were easier to bear. I felt more like one of the group and not the peculiar outsider who didn't have a clue.

There were lots of other firsts for me over the next few months when I did things I never thought possible. I discovered my love of English and could lose myself in my story writing, so much so that only a couple of weeks into that first term, I could stand up and read out my work in class when requested. Discovering that my shyness could be abated by pretending to be someone else gave me such a buzz and the exhilaration increased even more when the head of English, Mr Lloyd, asked me to join his school drama club. They met on Friday dinner break and Thursday after school. He'd already asked Jane but she had been reluctant saying she wasn't allowed to do after school stuff and she always had to go straight home. Mr Lloyd was having no excuses proclaiming it just what she needed; I'm sure he was fully aware of her recent family history. He sent a letter home to her Dad and after assurances on the timings of the club and supervision involved, Mr Schofield agreed, with a couple of stipulations.

In December, the end of the first term was marked by each form having a small Christmas party in their classroom. Mr Rowntree collected a thrupenny bit from all thirty-seven of us the week before to provide the usual party food of choice and he also brought in his record player and large box of records.

On the day of the party we had normal lessons in the morning but were allowed to bring a change of clothes for the afternoon. Sharon and Diane put on their new tie-dyed orange and green cheesecloth dresses. They'd bought these themselves from Leeds market the week before on one of their unsupervised Saturday shopping trips. This was a revelation to me that girls of my age were not only allowed to choose their own clothes but were allowed to shop for them without an adult. Jane had a purple mini-skirt with a pale pink turtle neck top which she'd also bought the previous weekend. Although her Dad had gone with her into Leeds, she'd been allowed to choose the clothes herself with his full approval. I looked around my class-mates in awe at the transformation out of their school uniforms. The girls nearly all looked like teenagers off to the disco while the boys all looked like scruffy kids off to play football. My party attire was a knee length flowery Crimplene dress the shape of which was difficult to see as, although it had a much defined waist, it wasn't where my waist was and so it made me look boxy and middle-aged.

"You all look great," I said with a sigh, confirming what my friends already knew.

"We'll take you shopping after Christmas to the New Year sales. There's loads of great stuff and it's right cheap in the market," Diane had said with a kind smile.

The rest of the afternoon was filled with talk about Christmas plans and a little bit of feet shuffling to the music while we chomped our way through the buffet. I knew there wasn't much chance of being allowed to go to the sales with my friends but when I got home I asked anyway.

"And just how old do you think you are?" Dad's raised voice asked, confirming that it wouldn't happen.

I tried again a couple of times once the New Year had got underway but to no avail. There was nothing wrong with the clothes I had, I was far too young to be getting a bus into Leeds on my own and it would break their hearts if anything happened to me, had I not thought of that? But encouraged by my three new friends to persist, I continued my pleading for this small slice of freedom. Eventually I wore them down and they agreed to let me go to the great metropolis of Leeds for a Saturday shopping trip.

It was March 1969 and I had just turned twelve. Jane had been applying the same pressure to her Dad, so she was also allowed to come and was given money to buy a new dress for herself. This was the first outing without a responsible adult I'd ever made, so I had to endure numerous lectures from Dad about not talking to strangers or getting into any trouble. I listened and nodded appropriately and promised I would be good, trying all the time to suppress the excitement that was practically bursting out of me.

The bus stop was right outside the front door of the pub and so the four of us arranged to meet there at nine-thirty. Mum stood on the step in her usual morning attire and waved us off. My introduction into the world of Woollies make-up counter, Leeds Market, the Headrow and Briggate was wonderful. All the time I kept thinking it was like being in a film. Sitting with my three buddies in a window seat booth in the Golden Egg cafe bar, pretending to like the coffee, in which we had to put copious spoonfuls of sugar in order to drink, I felt so grown up. I think we all would have preferred the milkshakes advertised behind the counter, but they wouldn't fit with the image we had of ourselves as we looked out on to Boar Lane and talked about our futures. This first taste of freedom was the start of my transformation from a plain, chubby and self-conscious misfit into a chrysalis, feeling the possibility of being able to transform into a butterfly. It was the first of many trips, although I had to catch my parents in the right mood to ensure my place. We probably had about half a dozen such days out in that year, before everything changed.

It was suggested, a few years later, that Jane was not always a good influence on me but I whole heartedly dispute that. She was the catalyst for some of the changes I made but only in the way she gave me the courage to be myself. I will concede it was Jane who first taught me how to lie convincingly to my parents, otherwise it would have taken me a lot longer to grow up. Jane always knew the right thing to say. I never understand how she did it but I was always impressed how she seemed to be able to get what she wanted. She could look so soft and sweet, saying the things grown-ups seemed to want to hear while all the time working to her own agenda; wearing an easy smile of gratitude as she got her way.

I learnt so much from her, starting with the drip-feed pleading approach that got me that first day of independence, through to the psychologies and strategies required to know what battles were worth fighting and when to keep my powder dry.

My parents loved me immensely. I was never in any doubt of that. However, that love was sometimes at odds with their lifestyle. They were both smothering and occasionally careless over my welfare, making my entire childhood a mass of contradictions. They had worked in the licensed trade, running pubs for most of their married life and were good at it, in fact they excelled. They were also totally devoted to each other, which was lucky as they were together twenty-four hours a day, every day. I have a wonderful memory of Mum sitting on my bed after a heavy night on the gin telling me just how important I was,

"I hope you realise just how much me an' your Dad love you. We're nothing without you. You make us a family and we bloody love you!"

We moved around a lot throughout my early childhood as my parents managed clubs and pubs around South Yorkshire. In January 1968 we moved to the Unicorn Public House in Bramley, the first pub they actually owned.

I was enrolled at the small church school just around the corner. As a new girl I was popular for about a week until my perceived shyness was recognised as dullness and I became invisible, as I had in every other school. I'd got used to this state of affairs and the transitional nature of it, but still longed for a feeling of belonging and acceptance. This was why starting secondary school was such a huge thing for me. I would be one of many new girls with a chance to be 'in' at the start of something.

My parents approached both the work and social aspects of their profession with equal enthusiasm. This meant that they worked to different clocks to everyone else. I would hear my friends talking about their days out or visiting relatives and soialising as a family and I would feel the stirrings of envy. Being an only child didn't help. I'm not really explaining this very well, let me elaborate; A normal weekday for me would entail getting up at seven thirty to wash, dress, eat my cornflakes, brush my teeth and leave at quarter past eight. I'd walk to school, meeting Jane on the way, to get there for ten to nine. Sometimes Dad would be coming down stairs just as I left but usually they'd still be asleep. They'd both got up to accompany me on that first day but I was desperate for that event never to be repeated.

Their day generally began at about nine fifteen when after a couple of mugs of tea and several cigarettes, Mum went through the large reinforced door at the back of our kitchen. Behind this door was the store room that separated the pub from our house. The second reinforced door brought her out in the bar of the pub. Dad would be left at the kitchen table restoring the deficit that a night's sleep had caused to his nicotine levels, while reading the Daily Express. Mum would take a bottle of milk with her to the bar and her first job would be to put the kettle on ready for when the cleaners arrived at half past. Her apparel for this morning ritual was always the same. One of her many long Bri-Nylon, pastel coloured nighties, covered by a bright blue quilted dressing gown. On her head was a pink chiffon scarf encircling the blue plastic curlers in her highly streaked, lightly permed hair. A pair of blue fur trimmed slippers on her feet completed her morning look. Not a natural fibre in sight, she was a massive fan of Bri-Nylon and Crimplene. The constant static shocks were just a minor nuisance to endure for the many desirable practicalities of the man-made material that made life so easy. At about ten Dad would come through washed and dressed and ready to start stocking the bar and Mum would go back to the house and get ready for the pub to open at eleven. Usually she would bring sandwiches back with her; bacon, sausage, egg or whatever else she found to fry up for their substantial breakfast. They closed and locked up at three o' clock, returning to the house for another bite to eat followed by an hour or so of sleep, depending on the previous night's excesses. By six they were back behind the bar for the evening until eleven thirty when, having seen off the last customers and all glasses cleaned, they locked up. They had one evening off a week together which they would spend in someone else's pub or occasionally at Batley Variety Club on an organised coach trip. Mum didn't work Saturday lunch times as this was her laundry and house-work day, even though we had a cleaner. Weekends differed only in that there was generally a lock-in after the Friday, Saturday and sometimes Sunday nights' openings.

The time these sessions ended would depend on who'd been invited to stay and also if Harry Henshaw, the local policeman happened to call in. Harry's visits usually signalled a really late night, as of course back in the late sixties, police cars could be cold and draughty places to hang out in. He turned up the first weekend we'd moved in, *"Just to go through a few things,"* with Dad about the area and let them know he was out there patrolling and keeping us safe. He arrived five minutes before closing time and Dad, not being any more green than he was cabbage-like, suggested that Harry and his sidekick might want to stay on, after they'd locked up, for a drink on the house. Harry accepted gratefully, it seemed that being on duty was no reason to refuse a drink. As it was a Saturday night, I was there washing glasses but was sent home to bed as soon as this invitation had been made. As I left, I heard him telling Mum he had a son around my age called Christopher. In fact Chris was a year older than me and although I did become aware of him soon after I'd started at Hill Topp, I didn't really get to know him until my second year. Our introduction was quite dramatic as fate placed him in the right place at the right time and he most probably saved my life. But I'm jumping ahead and need to fill in some of the foggy areas before we get to that significant marker, so I'll come back to Chris later.

Chapter Three

I'm always amazed by snowdrops, the way they come peeping through the frost or snowy winter debris, when you least expect it. Looking so dainty and fragile yet really they must be anything but. Poetically described as *'drops of winter cheer sent to stir the soul'*, they're impervious to the frosty winter damage as up they pop in the coldest of months. What is it that makes them thrive and keep coming back, breaking through the drab and greyness with the colour of peace and hope?

Even though it was February, I don't think there were any snowdrops in the aftermath of Jane's Mum's disappearance; even if there were they would have been trampled or dug up in the search for her. After the dust settled with no body found, people in the area fell into one of two camps; the ones that were convinced Don killed his wife and the ones who were sure she'd run off with some mysterious fancy man. No one shared Jane's belief that she'd been kidnapped by some bad man who was keeping her in worse slavery than her husband had. I'm not sure I was that certain of this theory either but I pretended to be, as I knew how much Jane wanted to believe it.

As the life my parents had chosen wasn't conducive to dealing with a strong and willful child, my upbringing had been ordered as such that I wasn't one. While never being in doubt of my parents' love, I knew that sometimes I was an inconvenience. They dealt with this by building a tower of overprotection around me, filled with lots of things to keep me happy. I had great toys and gadgets but these were the trade-off, for the time and patience they couldn't give me while they were working to provide a better future - and quite often too hung over. I suppose I was like Rapunzel without the hair. For them buying the pub was a massive deal. They had all their savings as well as some borrowed money invested in it, so it had to be successful. They'd learned their trade well and were an excellent team. However, they didn't get to be so good by assuming everyone was as straight and honest as they were; quite the opposite in fact. Trust was something that had to be earned and proved in their eyes. Their mantra was, *'Trust no bugger and assume nowt!'* Anyone they employed was vetted and watched and left alone in charge of the till reluctantly, which is why they had so little time off. They'd met in a small mining village near Sheffield where most of our family still lived. Mum had been fourteen and Dad eighteen and it had been love at first sight for them, or so Mum always said. They married a week after Mum's eighteenth birthday and apart from the two years of Dad's national service they never spent a night apart. Perhaps it was because their working life was so social that our home life was fiercely private and detached. Family visits either made or received were not high on their priorities and generally avoided. Playing mine hosts between licensing hours plus the late night lock-ins took up enough of their time so anything that encroached into their off-duty and recovery time was avoided at all costs.

As a solitary child I found it difficult to make friends, so after-school tea parties or play dates never happened. Once we moved to the Unicorn I realised it was unlikely that they ever would. Mum and Dad became even more wary of strangers in our home, even ten-year-olds. Their rationale based on two important facts; one - that there was generally a lot of money in the house and two - possibly the most important, that it would interfere with their resting time.

This isolated home life was something Jane and I had in common. The Schofields had never been particularly welcoming to anyone appearing at their door, even before Maggie disappeared. Don did his socialising in the clubs and other licensed premises and his home was his castle for which he alone held the keys. The only visitors that were tolerated were Don's parents who lived in Middlesbrough and came annually on Christmas Eve. This visit was reliant on public transport which took over two hours door to door, so they never stayed long. The week after Maggie's disappearance they did make an impromptu trip offering to stay for a few days but their offer was firmly refused by their unaccommodating son. I don't know if social services were aware of the Schofield's living arrangements but I do know, via my eavesdropping on late night lock-in conversations between Harry Henshaw and my parents, that the police were keeping an eye on the family. There was never any doubt in Harry's mind that Don Schofield was a *'wrong un'* and that he'd be caught out eventually and that he'd be the one to catch him.

Generally though, as the weeks passed, public opinion softened a little towards Don, which seemed to irritate Harry more. It was acknowledged in all the gossip mills that, outwardly anyway, Don had stepped up to the plate, cutting back on his drinking and keeping his kids in order. Initially he seemed very protective of Jane, certainly in the first year and was very strict about her being out of the house, other than for school but in general he was doing ok as a father, at last.

When I was telling Mum about my new friends, after my first day, I knew she'd only been half-listening. Backcombing her hair at the time she uttered the odd 'mm' and 'that's nice' between her smoking and tea drinking. I saw her physically start when I said,

"I was sitting next to a girl called Jane Schofield. Her Mum went out for fish'n'chips and never came back. The police have been searching for her for ages. Anyway, Jane's really nice and so funny."

She stopped her hairdressing, putting down the tail comb and turned to look at me. For a second I was filled with fear that she was going to tell me I wasn't allowed to be friends with Jane. I opened my eyes wide and looked back at her.

"She's really nice Mum, you'd like her," I blurted out.

She considered her response for just a second before saying,

"I'm sure she is but you'll probably make lots friends, so don't be tying yourself to one."

"Oh no, no I'm not, there's Sharon and Diane as well, they just live round on Summer Lane and there's lots of other girls as well who seem really nice."

"Right, well that's good then." She finished off her tea and picked up the hair lacquer.

I'd taken the warning from the initial look she'd given me and not mentioned Jane's name again but she'd obviously stored it away. A couple of weeks later, I overheard her conversation with one of the barmaids.

"Well, it's only natural in't it?" Betty was telling her. "I mean, if he didn't do her in an if she 'as run off, he'll be scared she's coming back to take 'er wont he, an you've only got to look at him with 'er to know she's favourite."

Mum obviously keeping up to date with local gossip on the family, which at this time, seemed to be positive. It was also commented on how nicely presented Jane seemed to be. Her hair always brushed and tied back and she was smarter and better dressed since her mother had gone. On another occasion, I heard Betty telling Mum that Don Schofield was probably spending more of his beer money on his daughter than he'd ever spent on his wife.

Back at school, Diane and Sharon joined the drama club. The first few weeks were spent doing group readings and discussing possible plays for the annual production. Mr Lloyd brought in three different suggestions and put it to the vote and the winner for that academic year was Pygmalion. All four of us loved the club but for different reasons. For Diane it was the whole idea of acting and drama that she enjoyed. She would have liked to be on stage but accepted her nerves would never allow this, so she volunteered for just about anything that wasn't under the spotlight. During Pygmalion she helped with props and was also stand-by for the prompt. Unfortunately, Wendy Shaw, the third year girl who was the prompt, remained healthy and well throughout the four day performance so, much to her disappointment she wasn't called upon.

Sharon was desperate to be an actress. She'd learnt the part of Eliza Doolittle and stood in the wings reciting the part throughout all the rehearsals, edging her way into Mr Lloyd's vision so he could see she was off the book a long time before our leading lady. She was hoping at least for understudy but had to settle for flower girl and lady at the races, both non-speaking parts, accepting that first years never got a speaking roles.

The drama club for Jane provided a source of escapism and it meant she had a little less time at home on a Thursday evening. The club finished at six thirty and she was collected at the school gates by her eldest brother Iain. Dad picked me up, leaving Mum in sole charge of the bar. I told Jane we could give her a lift home but she shrugged and said thanks but it was arranged. When I started to argue she held up her hand and said her Dad had already told her he wasn't having any of this getting in strangers' cars business. He'd only agreed to let her go on the condition that Iain brought her home and that was that.

For me the drama club provided the initial mechanics for the start of my personal development, enabling me to be someone else. For the first time I was doing something I'd chosen to do. I was part of something where I was allowed, in fact encouraged, to offer opinions and ideas along with my peers. This was an epiphany to me, highlighting what I was capable of and my shyness melted away. This was purely down to the brilliant way Mr Lloyd and Miss Tate, his able assistant, ran the club. Like Diane, I'd been nervous of acting, even though I'd been fizzing with excitement at the possibility. I was sure that when I walked on stage, I would freeze in fear. But when the moment came nothing could have been further from the truth. My confidence grew with every second in the limelight. As soon as I stepped on to the stage, my nerves evaporated and I transformed totally into my character. It was exhilarating and I became alive in my pretence. The whole dressing up, grease paint and spotlights got into my psyche and I was in my element.

The school production was always performed in March and even though I was only an extra, I could not have been happier to be a part of it. Consequently I was totally beside myself with disappointment once the four day run was over. There was no club the week following and even though there were other things going on in my life, I was bereft without it. When the club started up again after the Easter holidays we read through some one act plays. Mr Lloyd explained that this was his way of finding his cast for the following year's production, which started a whole new wave of excitement.

Suddenly before I knew where I was the school year was over and we were breaking up for summer and I was miserable at the prospect. As I walked home on the last day, all I could see was six weeks of emptiness ahead of me and I had no idea how I would get through it. Jane on the other hand was stoical about it, suggesting that we might be able to see each other, although not at her house and perhaps we could go into Leeds or even somewhere else on the bus. I brightened a bit at this, saying I'd ask Mum and Dad and she said she'd call for me on the Monday of the following week, after her Dad had gone to work. She didn't and it was nearly three weeks before I saw her again. Her Dad had made other plans and taken her on the three bus route to stay with her grandparents for the first half of the holidays. So I filled my time with my new-found hobby, reading and joined the library, providing me with days of wonderful distractions. Once Jane got back from her Granny's, she came to call for me. Reluctantly Mum agreed to me going out for a walk with her with a strict time limit of two hours. We walked up to Bramley Park and sat on the swings, talking endlessly about television programmes and singing along to the music on my transistor radio. I have a picture in my head of that morning. Two happy girls laughing as they kicked their legs out in front of them, faces to the blue sky and buoyant with all the life ahead of them. A marker set to music of the time, as Thunderclap Newman sang 'There's something in the Air'.

We had such a good time and I was back well within the curfew but wasn't allowed to repeat it until the following week when we called for Diane and Sharon. The weather wasn't so good this time and the swings didn't have the same appeal so we went back via the shop, where we bought chocolate bars. On the last week of the holidays the four of us had a trip to Leeds and spent hours hanging round Woolworth's make-up counter and record section. When we went into the Golden Egg, we pretended that our choice to have milkshakes instead of coffee was sardonic but we fooled no one. It was a relief to sit in our window seat sipping the sweet creamy liquid without having to endure the face pulling bitterness of the coffee. As I sucked noisily through the blue stripy straw, I smiled at the prospect of only having to get through four more days before I could go back to school.

In September 1969 I started my second year by arriving at the school gates under my own steam. Feeling fully embedded in life at Hill Topp, I was delighted to discover that Mr Lloyd was to be our form teacher. He continued to teach us English Literature and each of his lessons was a new discovery for me. He would stand in front of the class regaling us with anecdotes, stories and poems from secret lives and worlds, and invite us to go inside them. He taught with such passion it was impossible for me not to be captivated. He introduced us to a vast range of works and genres, to the classics and literary novels and witty observational essays and articles. He brought writers into our classroom and beguiled us with their words. Writers like Ray Bradbury, Dorothy Parker and James Thurber. One afternoon in that first term of year two he read 'The night the ghost got in' and he had the attention of every child in front of him. Although he didn't manage to create the same passion for English in everyone, he did evoke the possibility of where our imagination could take us.

As Mum and Dad didn't read anything other than newspapers, we didn't have books at home. There'd been children's books and fairy stories when I was much younger but apart from comics - The Dandy delivered on a Tuesday and The Beano on Thursdays - I hadn't read anything out of school. So when at the end of the first year, Mr Lloyd offered to loan 'To Kill a Mocking Bird', to take home and read over the summer holidays, I'd been the first up to his desk for a copy. This brilliant introduction to the pleasure of reading was the start of my lifelong love of books. I've read it countless times and it still gets to me every time. Not just because it is a beautifully written and superbly crafted novel but it also reminds me of the animated talks and discussions Jane, Sharon, Diane and I had after reading it. We all became obsessed with this essay on humanity and justice, perhaps because it was told from a child's perspective, but we raved about it. Unhappily, only a short time later, it became tangled up in a less inspirational memory for Jane and me.

A few weeks into the new term Mr Lloyd announced he'd arranged a class trip to the Hyde Park Picture Palace to see the film adaptation of this wonderful book. The four of us were convinced that the trip was arranged purely for our benefit, not even considering that such a brilliant novel might have been appreciated by zillions of others. As not many of our classmates were in drama club, we felt that we were closer to our form teacher and looked knowingly at each other when the excursion was announced. On the night of the trip, the week before half term, Sharon's Dad drove the four of us to the cinema for the six fifteen meet up with Mr Lloyd and Miss Tate. It was on the condition that we would be escorted door to door that Jane and I were allowed to go. It turned out we were the only ones not using public transport, even the teachers arrived on the bus. In total there were twenty-two of us and as Mr Lloyd had a reputation for not putting up with bad behaviour, it was twenty-two well behaved and truly interested pupils who filed in behind him.

I can still feel the emotion tingle behind my eyes as I remember the film and wonderful acting that made the characters I already knew, so real. It made me feel that I was there in Maycomb Alabama, watching the events unravel before me. Afterwards we were picked up by Diane's Dad and sat, un-belted in the back of his estate car, chatting continually. We were reiterating and repeating over and over the bits we found moving or brilliant and talking over each other in hyper-excitement. It was only when the car stopped at Jane's house that I realised she'd hardly spoken a word all the way home and looked unhappy.

"Hey Jane did you like the film?" I asked.

"Yeah it were really good. See you tomorrow," and she was out of the car and through her gate in seconds, the kitchen door beaming a shaft of light that swallowed her as the car drove off. I craned my neck to look back at her home as we drove on to my house while Scout and Atticus continued to dominate my thoughts.

Chapter Four

I didn't sleep well the night after the cinema trip. After telling Mum and Dad what a great film it was, I went straight up to my room. When Mum put her head round the bedroom door, much later, I was still wide awake. Laying with my back to the door, eyes tightly closed I pretended to be asleep. Even though I was tired sleep evaded me for most of the night. There was something wrong with Jane and I felt I'd let her down by not knowing what it was.

I went through the whole day in my head, starting from when we met at the footbridge on our walk to school. I'd been so full of it, bursting with excitement about the cinema trip and the half term holiday coming up. Mum had arranged for my cousin Alison from Sheffield to come and stay to keep me company during the half term. This had never happened before and I'd been animated at the prospect. Lying in the darkness I remembered talking constantly on the way to school. Once there, we were joined by Diane and Sharon who were equally as excited about the cinema trip. Jane, I realised had hardly said a word as I had ploughed on regardless with my self-obsessed chatter.

I continued to re-run the day in my head. Registration was normal, Mr Lloyd reminding us about homework before we formed an orderly line to walk down the corridor into the hall for morning assembly. First lesson was double science and a memory flashed forward. Something I should have noticed wasn't right. I was busy writing my headings for the experiment we were discussing when Mr Griffin's voice boomed across the lab making me jump.

"Jane Schofield, what are you doing?"

"Nothing Sir," Jane's voice low and her head bowed.

We were sitting on the high stools on the second row of work benches. Sharon, Diane, me and Jane on the end.

"Yes I can clearly see that you're doing nothing, you're certainly not listening to me or learning anything."

"Sorry Sir." This time her head raised for a second before looking back down at her hands on the bench.

This wasn't like her. Although she never liked the science lessons, even the practical sessions, she thought Mr Griffin was OK and would normally have made some jokey response, not disrespectful but certainly not the meek bowed head apology of that day.

Mr Griffin clearly thought it odd as he requested that she come down to the front to act as his 'able and willing assistant' in an effort to retain her interest in his lesson. She'd perked up a little after that but thinking it through she'd not been herself all day. Even when we saw that apple pie and custard was on the dinner menu, there was no elevation of her spirits. It wasn't so much that she was down, she was just not the buoyant and bubbly friend I'd been used to. After the dinner break we had history with Mr McDonald. Jane hadn't finished her homework, so she went to the form room straight after eating, to sort it. I'd walked across to the benches at the bottom of the boy's playing field with Diane and Sharon, with the pretence of stretching our legs but really it was to watch the third year boys' playing football.

Jane was already at her desk when the three of us went back inside for afternoon registration, her books packed in her bag ready for the next lesson.

"Did you get it finished?" I asked.

"Dunno," she shrugged. "But at least I've had a go so I won't get detention."

The homework was an essay on the Jacobite risings of 1715 and 1745. Jane had mentioned that her Dad had been interested in this; he had been born in Scotland. Even though he'd moved to Yorkshire when he was six, he still considered himself a Scot.

"Did your Dad help you?"

"Oh yeah he were loads of help!" she said standing up without looking at me and walking to the classroom door.

Following one of Mr McDonald's engaging and totally biased lessons, we had double needlework before home time. I really hated this hour and a half and only generally got through it because I knew drama club was straight afterwards. Miss Aveyard the needlework teacher didn't like me at all and the feeling was more than mutual. On our first meeting in the previous year, I'd got off to a terrible start with her. I accidently knocked her thermos flask off her desk as I walked into my very first lesson.

On my first day at Hill Topp, besides the beret, my uniform was also accessorised by a brown leather satchel that Mum had bought me. Yet another item that made me stand out from everyone else, it was soon banished to remain in my bedroom along with the hat. From the second day onwards, I'd used a wicker basket that had been given to me by Sally, one of the women who worked for Mum and Dad. Sally had a daughter four years older than me who had left school. She'd given it to me a couple of weeks before I started and I'd been using it to keep my comics in. After seeing that practically all the girls at school carried their books in one of these baskets, I reinstated it as a school bag.

By day four, I was confidently carrying it, arm looped through the handle and resting it on my hip, conforming to the accepted stance. On that fateful afternoon we were again segregated according to our sex. All the boys went to the crafts annexe for their woodwork lesson while we girls entered the cramped and messy needlework room, chattering and slightly excited about our induction in to the world of clothes making.

Miss Aveyard sat to the side of her heavily cluttered desk drinking coffee out of the plastic cup of her thermos, scowling at us. My previous experience of sewing was non-existent and I'd been looking forward to this lesson, day dreaming of being able to make my own clothes and imagining beautiful flowing dresses of the 'non-Crimplene' type.

Perhaps, if I hadn't turned slightly at the wrong moment, catching the flask with my basket and knocking it from the desk, I might have enjoyed a much better experience of Miss Aveyard's teaching. It fell to the floor with the depressing sound of the inside shattering, followed immediately by the screech of the teachers's chair being pushed back as she leapt to her feet. I was mortified and blurting out how sorry I was, while holding back tears. She was furious and holding back nothing. I was a careless, stupid and charmless child who needed to sit as far away from her as possible. It was possibly one of the very few moments she ever achieved silence in her classroom in her whole thirty years of teaching. I was made to sit at a small desk at the very back of the room in the opposite corner to the sewing machines, on my own. Her dislike of me did not abate even when I turned up to her next lesson with a brand new flask for her. Instead she took it, without grace or thanks, telling me to remove myself from her sight and sit again at the back, where I remained for every lesson for the whole of that year.

Twelve months on and she just about managed to tolerate my presence in her class. At the first lesson of the second year she didn't make me move when I sat next to Jane, but she never spoke a single word directly to me or gave me any help or instruction; clearly not a forgiving soul. Although this classroom experience didn't help, it soon became apparent, even to me, that I was not a natural at needlecraft. It would have been hard to describe any of my practical efforts in this subject as anything but poor, which is exactly what Miss Aveyard put on all my reports.

Conversely, Jane discovered that she did have the required dexterity and ability. Her flair showed right from the start and she became one of Miss Aveyard's favourites and so was treated to limitless patience and almost individual instruction throughout the lessons. She told me she was embarrassed by the difference in the way we were treated but I said not to worry about it. She couldn't be my champion in everything. However I did suggest that maybe she could give me a bit of help from time to time without Old Graveyard seeing. I knew how proud she was that she was so good at needlework.

The project of the second year was a skirt with waistband and zip and even though we were only six weeks in, I was already well behind. I'd pinned the pattern to the material but was too scared to start cutting without someone checking it. Therefore I was hugely relieved when, on the day of the cinema trip, Miss Aveyard was off ill.

"Something serious I hope," I muttered as Miss Morgan, the home economics, teacher told us.

My relief was palpable as Miss Morgan left us, saying we were to just get on with what we were doing and she would be back in a while to check how it was going. That was the first sign of a smile I remembered from Jane that day as she pulled my material towards her and started to cut out my skirt panels. Completely ignoring her own sewing, she proceeded to work on it for the entire lesson as I sat and gratefully watched.

Just before the four o'clock bell, Miss Morgan bustled back in telling us to pack away our stuff. Standing hands on hips looking flustered she also instructed us to make sure we took our pieces home to finish anything that we had not done in the lesson. With a look of distaste and shake of her head she added that we leave the workroom in the state we found it, which raised some semi-stifled giggles. As we walked to the school gates with Sharon and Diane, our conversation was of the evening ahead. After confirming what time Sharon's Dad was picking each of us up we parted and Jane and I walked down the hill towards the footbridge over the bypass. Jane went right here along the bottom of the Spring Valley estate while I went through it. Again throughout this journey I was full of my own news, telling her again about my cousin coming to stay.

"It's a shame we can't all go into Leeds on Saturday but she's not getting here till dinner time. Anyway Sharon and Diane said they're not off anyway."

Not noticing that the conversation was one-sided I went on.

"I'll probably be allowed to come out a lot more while she's staying. I don't like Ali that much but she makes me laugh sometimes and her Mum, my Aunty Shirley, lets her go out loads."

Although Alison was nearly a year younger than me, she was allowed a lot more freedom. According to Mum, her sister and husband just let her run wild and do what she wanted. Telling Jane about this I had prattled on about us doing stuff together, not picking up on her vague and non-committal responses. Not picking up on them because I wasn't listening, just wittering on about me and my stuff.

After my poor night's sleep, I left the house a good half an hour earlier than normal for my walk to school. Arriving at the footbridge I started to walk along the footpath by the bypass towards Jane's house, to meet her on her way.

It was a drizzly morning after a rainy night. I was walking almost on the grass verge to the side of the tarmac path, trying to avoid getting splashed from passing cars. As I got close to the old tannery building, I stopped and put my basket down on the ancient crumbly wall. Friday was a heavy bag day as we had all single lessons. My basket was pretty full and making my arm ache even more than normal without the usual distraction of chatting with Jane. I stood for a while, massaging my arm and shoulder, idly looking over the wall at the dilapidated structure in front of me. The old tannery had been deserted for years, after the last of a series of fires had bankrupted the business and it had been left to decompose. Looking over at the grey and bleak dereliction, a strange feeling came over me and the word lifeless came into my head. My eyes began to take in more of the building as I surveyed its austere and ruined exterior. I thought of the dangerous rotten floors, broken glass and crumbling walls inside. The building was originally a woollen mill in the early 1800s but was bought by the Gibson family and converted into a successful tannery business some years later. The two large towers, remnants of the dark satanic building, still stood majestically intact at the back of the disintegrating structure. There were also a number of large vats and pools scattered around the exterior. The whole site was a magnet for the kids in the area who had added to the dereliction with their graffiti and petty vandalism. I, of course, had been warned that I was never to go anywhere near the place. So my twelve-year-old imagination, vivid and dramatic according to Mr Lloyd, and overactive and nonsensical (although their actual word was rubbish) according to my parents, began to work overtime. The visual prompt in front of me and data from bits of overheard conversations, along with hours of Jane's suggestions and protestation, ballooned inside my head. Suddenly I was sure that Maggie Schofield's body was in there somewhere just waiting to be discovered.

I almost jumped out of my skin when Jane pushed her basket into my back to attract my attention. I have no idea how long I'd been standing there leaning on the wall and working out my theory but it seemed like hours since I'd left home.

"What doing here" she asked, looking at me like I'd grown another head.

"I were early so I thought I'd walk down towards your house."

"That's not my house." She nodded over the crumbling stone wall. "Although," and with the briefest suggestion of a smile, "I wouldn't mind having a look round it sometime."

I turned and was just about to tell her my newly formed theory when I noticed her eyes were red and puffy, remembering the reason I was there and why I'd slept so badly and I asked,

"What's up Jane? Have I done or said something to upset you? If I have I'm really sorry but please tell me."

She put her hand on the top of my forearm and her eyes filled with tears.

I stepped forward to embrace her but she shrugged me off saying,

"No don't hug me I can't ..." Her words trailed off as she bent down to put her basket on the floor and search her pockets for a hanky.

"Jane, please tell me....," I started but she cut me off.

"It's nowt to do with you, it's just stuff at home. It'll be ok, I'll sort it."

Picking up her basket, she said, "Come on we better get goin' or we'll be late and end up with detention."

The subject firmly closed. I picked up my bag and fell into step with her on a faster than normal walk to school. After a little while she asked me to tell her about my cousin again, which I did. Understanding that she didn't want a conversation, I just tried to regale her with stories of family discourse and feuds attempting to distract her. She managed the occasional smile but mainly focused on the journey. It was a relief to both of us that once inside the school gates the whistle went immediately.

Chapter Five

I was a well behaved child, never answering back and certainly never causing disruption at school, always obedient and compliant. Even as I started to find my confidence and establish my own identity, I remained amenable and respectful. My need to be liked and well thought of, along with my fear of confrontation, made me look for the middle ground. Jane managed her school life differently. Although she also wanted to be liked, she would never shy away from confrontations with fellow students. Despite her diminutive size, she was treated with a fearful respect, perhaps by family reputation. She had this knack of inciting a chill in her voice as she squared up to anyone causing her difficulty. But she also had an unreserved respect for her elders and keenness to please. So she was considered a good natured and well behaved child by all the teaching staff. This reinforced her revere and status as classmates knew any suggestion that she was capable of intimidation or threatening behaviour would be dismissed as ridiculous by our school guardians. On that Friday when we got to school, everything changed.

Although she was quiet, she did seem a bit more like her normal self until the lesson after the morning break when she completely lost it. Mr Roberts, a newly qualified teacher and devout Christian, taught us RE and English language and was being his normal ineffectual self. It was a timetabled English session and he was reading aloud to us, The Children of the New Forest. This he did in a monotonous drone which engaged no one. He was one of the few teachers with poor classroom control, allowing the disruptive element to take great advantage. Robbo's lessons were seen as their opportunity to play up and show off boorish behaviour in a way they thought witty and entertaining. Apart from lack of charisma or talent for reading aloud, Mr Roberts other failing as a teacher was that he was delusional. He believed that if he ignored the calling out, laughing and general loutish behaviour, it would eventually stop. He would walk around the classroom holding his book as he read aloud. His tediously dull and weedy voice was completely devoid of any emotion or expression, as if he were trying to say,

I will not be baited, I can do this and I don't care if you are listening or not. This is my planned lesson and this is how it will go.'

The protagonists for the disruption were a group of rowdy boys championed by Eric Moody. He and his three mates sat at the back slouching in their seats in a surly, rebellious manner. There were a couple of girls who didn't shout out or do anything directly but giggled loudly, providing encouragement to Eric and co. I sat with Diane, Sharon and Jane at the front and although we were equally bored, we tried to follow his words or just quietly zoned out. Occasionally, one of the teachers from a nearby classroom would open the door and ask, "Everything all right Mr Roberts?" to which he would reply, "Yes thank you, everything is fine." The interrupting teacher would throw a meaningful glance around the class, ending on Eric. If the noise level had been particularly high there would be an additional comment of, *'Eric Moody, go and wait for me outside the headmasters office now please!'* before they left, allowing Mr Roberts to continue. There was a joke in the class that Mr Wedaburn, the headmaster, was fixing a plaque with Eric Moody's name on it, above one of the chairs outside his office. Perhaps, if intervention had happened in that particular lesson on that eventful Friday in 1969, or maybe if Mr Roberts had not chosen that lesson to finally change his approach to classroom management, things might have turned out differently. Unfortunately, it was one of those freaky moments when the fates aligned and began a chain of events that imploded our little world.

I don't recall the particular heckle that started the outburst. I have an idea that it wasn't Eric but one of his cronies. Probably keen to raise his profile in the group of troublemakers. A voice on the verge of breaking called out through the teacher's dour monologue and created a wave of snickering around the room. There was the slightest of pauses as Mr Roberts took a breath mid-sentence but it was only a brief hesitation and he continued his monosyllabic recital of the text. Eric must have decided that the stakes were worth raising so he called out,

"What's up Robbo? Gettin' carried away there thinking about all them bucking stags?" This was quite an improvement in his normal barracking. Pleased with himself at the laughing encouragement Eric went on,

"Giving you a stiffy is it sir?"

There was an eruption of jeering and laughter from the back of the classroom and even we 'the goody two shoes' found ourselves trying to stifle our giggling. Mr Roberts was now bright red and incandescent with anger, Eric's crude comment had finally pushed him over the edge of his misguided tolerance limits.

"Eric Moody get out of this classroom right now, you disgusting foul mouthed child!" he yelled in decibels we'd never heard from him before. His whole being was transformed with such fury that it silenced everyone, except Jane who leaned towards me to say quietly,

"Bloody hell, Moody's gonna get us all detention. What a wanker!"

Mr Roberts's roaring at Eric had ended on Jane saying the word detention so her last three words were muttered in the utter silence of a shocked classroom. He'd been standing fairly close to us in the aisle and immediately spun round to look at our desk.

"Who said that?" he yelled his eyes and bulging with rage.

I quickly looked down at the book in front of me and sensed that Jane was doing the same.

"Who just used that foul word?" he yelled again slamming his hand on the desk and leaning forward. His purple face, just a foot or two above our bowed heads. That's when it happened. Quietly Jane said,

"I did."

He reached down and got hold of her jumper at the shoulder and pulled her to her feet. Having completely lost control of his temper and common sense, he was almost foaming at the mouth and shouting incoherently. Jane was struggling as he tried to grab hold of her other shoulder to pull her straight in front of him. He was still yelling about profanities and that he would not have that kind of language in his classroom, Eric standing like a statue next to his desk looking totally bewildered, when Mr Lloyd and Mr McDonald burst in. Jane was flailing her arms around in an effort to pull away, screaming and shouting between loud sobs,

"Get off me, stop it you're hurting me. Get off you fucking bastard, get your fucking hands off me!"

The two other teachers rushed across to our desk. I hadn't even realised I'd stood up until Mr Lloyd's booming stage voice said,

"Be quiet everyone!" Adding slightly quieter, "Sit down Kimberly."

Mr McDonald positioned himself between Mr Roberts and Jane, facing the teacher, and muttered something inaudible as he put his arm across him and led him out of the classroom. I glanced at his exiting back and saw he was shaking violently. Jane remained standing in the aisle, her sobbing subsiding slightly, head bowed. Mr Lloyd pulled a spotless white handkerchief from his pocket and handed it to her.

"Right!" he said, letting his gaze drift across the whole class who were still totally silent. His eyes finally rested on me as he said,

"Miss Asquith please accompany Miss Schofield to the lavatories to wash her face, then go with her to the headmaster's office where I will meet you shortly."

As we left the classroom, I noticed that Eric was back in his chair looking like butter wouldn't melt but Mr Lloyd was not fooled.

"This unfortunate incident has your name written all over it Moody. You will see me at the headmaster's office at the end of school today."

"Sir, this had nothing to do with me!" he said in mock astonishment.

"Four o'clock Moody, no discussion."

In the girls' toilets Jane was splashing her face with the icy cold water but her crying and choking sobs showed no sign of subsiding. Clutching a handful of paper towels, I went over and tried to hug her.

"Don't worry I'll tell Mr Wedaburn what happened. It's not your fault Robbo just lost it and Mr Lloyd already knows that it was Eric Moody that started it, it's gonna be alright honest, please don't cry."

She pushed me away and I felt my eyes starting to water. I knew she'd be in trouble over the swearing, but I was hoping we could plead mitigating circumstances. I tried again to hug and reassure her, but she pushed me away with more force this time.

"Shut up Kim, you've no idea. It's not all right, it's all wrong, it's all bloody wrong and you or me can't do anything so just shut up and leave me alone."

I stepped back feeling like she'd slapped me. The door opened and Miss Tempest the deputy head came in. Glancing briefly at me she said,

"Kimberly, you can go back to your class now, I'll deal with this."

Her voice brisk and authoritative left me in no doubt that she was dismissing me. With a last failed attempt to catch my friend's eye and let her see that I was there for her, I pulled open the door and went back down the corridor. Re- entering the English class, Mr McDonald was reading aloud. His narration held so much expression and animation; it was hard to believe it was the same book. Everyone looked up as I entered.

"Sit down Kimberly, you haven't missed much," the teacher said.

Taking my seat I was aware of several questioning eyes fixed on me. I allowed myself one sidelong glance towards Diane and Sharon and the briefest shake of my head before forcing my eyes to stare at the book in front of me. At the end of the lesson, I put Jane's copy back into her basket and asked Mr McDonald if I should take it back to our form room. Taking it from me he said there was no need for me to get involved with this. He would see that Jane got her things back.

We have no idea what happened to Mr Roberts after the meltdown but neither he nor Jane were seen anywhere around school. Eventually, I did find out what happened to Jane but how Robbo spent the rest of the day was never discovered.

The lunchtime drama club was cancelled, so I hung around with Sharon and Diane in the covered doorway to the dining room speculating. We decided unanimously that it was Eric Moody's fault and that Mr Roberts was a grade one knob. The remainder of the school day ticked by and at 4 o'clock I saw Jane's coat had already gone from the cloak-room. As I took mine, I felt the sadness whirl up inside me, threatening to come out of my eyes, so I left quickly just waving to Sharon and Diane as I ran for the gate. I was struggling with the sheer unfairness and frustration of what had happened and not knowing what to do as I hurried home. I thought about telling Mum but decided that would be pointless. Her thoughts on bad language were made clear to me, and everyone who knew her, on a regular basis. Also she believed, like most other parents of that time that the teachers were always right and would have sided with Robbo. So I said nothing remembering that children rarely have a voice in these matters. Jane would not be allowed a defense and there was nothing I could do to help her. Wrapping myself in a blanket of hopeless despair, I managed to get home and through our teatime ritual before I found the safety of my bedroom, finally allowing my frustration out in warm salty tears.

Chapter Six

It was still dark when I woke the next morning and after some lucid but intangible dreams it took me a few minutes to come round. As the events of the past two days came flooding back, I remembered there was no school for the next week and my wretchedness returned. Dad knocked on the bathroom door while I was getting washed to ask me if I wanted a bacon sandwich, which I didn't. Coming out a few moments later Mum rushed past me, her dishevelled manner and eagerness to get in confirming that there had been a late night lock-in. I took my time getting dressed and flicked through Jackie magazine, my new periodical of choice, while listening to Ed Stewpot Stewart on my radio. I was slightly unnerved hearing the downstairs radio on, as I cautiously descended. Pushing the door open, I was completely taken aback to see both parents sitting at the table drinking tea, smoking and fully dressed. Mum's hair was still in curlers but she'd put her foundation on and a suggestion of eyeliner and mascara.. She was engrossed in the newspaper while holding a cigarette between the fingers of her left hand, just inches from her face. I thought she looked like a glamorous film star waiting to be called to set.

"Why are you up and dressed, it's only just gone eight?"
I hadn't heard them come to bed the night before and I'd been awake well after midnight. Mum should not be this functional after such a late night.

"Aunty Shirley will be here at eleven with Alison and I've got a lot to do before then." She said flatly without any sense of irony, turning over the page of the Daily Express and taking another drag on her cigarette.

"Right," I said pouring myself a cup of tea, "Anything you want me to do?"

"Yes go and have a good clear out of your bedroom and get rid of all those old comics. Sally will be up in a bit to change the sheets and vac."

"But have some breakfast first though eh love?" Dad added, glancing up from the Racing Post he was reading.

Noticing the plate with the remnants of his sandwich and the smell of bacon in the air made my tummy growl with a sudden hunger but I knew better than to say I'd changed my mind. The frying pan was already in the sink, marinating in washing-up liquid and congealing fat. I poured myself a bowl of cornflakes and sat at the table, consuming my breakfast along with the secondary cigarette smoke which permeated the room; my parents keen to replenish their nicotine levels. Once I'd finished, I put my dish and spoon by the sink and went upstairs to begin my tidying.

Sally was a godsend to Mum and Dad. I heard them say so on many occasions and I thought so too. Not only did she do two regular shifts behind the bar, she could also come in at short notice when someone let them down and she was also one of the pub cleaners. She'd started the week Mum and Dad first took over the Unicorn and her reliability had made her trustworthy in their eyes. She was therefore given the honour of cleaning our living quarters every Saturday. When she'd finished mopping, vacuuming, wiping and ashtray empting in the pub, she came through the store-room to do the same for our living quarters. She changed the sheets and 'did' upstairs before giving the downstairs a really good 'going over'. Our ground floor accommodation consisted of a large room we used for cooking, eating and general living. It had a kitchen area with cooker, fridge and twin-tub washing machine. It was heavily furnished with a drop-leaf table and four chairs, a sofa and arm chair, a sideboard and television. All these items were placed on a large rug which in turn was placed on autumn leaves patterned linoleum, just visible around the edges. As everything we needed for our day-to-day living was in there, it truly was our living room. At the other side of the house was our 'best room' which had a dark red Dralon three-piece-suite, radiogram, newer television and a large glass cabinet containing the best china and assorted porcelain ornaments. This best room was used only for the rare occasions we had visitors. Now and again it would be used by Mum and Dad to watch a film. Back then, in that very different world, there wasn't a massive choice on TV. There were only two channels, both of which ended around midnight after a rousing play of the national anthem. A little later BBC 2 began its Midnight Movie slot on Saturday nights. So on the very rare occasion when they didn't have an after-hours session, they watched a film. I wasn't allowed to stay up to watch this with them, it was too late and not the right sort of programme for a child. But once I'd recognised the established routine, I discovered I could watch them on my own. When Harry Henshaw's police car was in the car park I knew they wouldn't be back through before it finished, so I would settle down, on the much more comfortable sofa, and watch films from the forties and fifties, keeping my ears open for the sounds of their unexpected return.

After brushing my teeth I decided I'd got plenty of time before Sally would be ready to start in the house, so lay back on my bed and picked up my magazine, trying to keep my worries about Jane at bay with the distraction of the Cathy and Claire problem page. I needed to see her and couldn't possibly wait a week to see if she was alright. Dare I go to her house to call for her? She'd always discouraged any of us from going there. We'd been there to drop her off or pick her up but hadn't been further than the garden gate and certainly not inside the house. *What's the worst that can happen if I knock on the door and her Dad or one of her brothers answered?* I asked myself, and deciding it couldn't be worse than waiting a week to find out how she was, resolved that I would do it today. Hearing someone coming upstairs I got off my bed quickly and started to put my magazines in order. Mum put her head round the door saying,

"I've made a list down-stairs of things I need from the shops. Your Dad will give you some money. I need you to go now as your Aunty Shirley will probably get here earlier than eleven, just to try and catch me out!"

"Catch you out at what?" I asked, knowing very well what she meant.

My Mum and her sister were always scoring points off one another. Aunty Shirley didn't approve of my parents choice of occupations and never missed an opportunity to say so. Mum, on the other hand, did not think much of Aunty Shirley's lazy work-shy husband. Although she was slightly subtler in her articulation of this, she was seldom reticent about making the point when they were together.

"Come on Kim, don't you start back-chatting, I'm wound up enough!" Waving her finger at me she added, "And for Christ's sake take off those horrible trousers and put on something a bit smarter." Before I could object she was gone.

My horrible trousers were in fact my treasured Wrangler jeans. These were hand-me-downs from Sally and part of a large bag of clothes that her daughter had grown out of. I heard Mum tell Dad that 'she obviously means well but most of it is rubbish'. I didn't agree. All of it was fabulous, proper teenage girl clothes and not a scrap of Crimplene in sight. The jeans had been put in the pile to be sent to the Salvation Army jumble sale when Mum had sorted through but I'd managed to salvage them, by sheer stealth. Her view on denim was that it was a material for working overalls to be worn by manual workers, not suitable for young girls and certainly not suitable for her only child. Once I'd liberated them, I only wore them in the bedroom while on my own. I loved the feel of them as in my head they made me look modern and trendy. They also helped me build up an imaginary social life that I could dip in and out of on my long evenings alone. I could re-create one of the stories from Jackie with me in the starring role. Of course it was hard to have secrets from my parents, as I discovered. Dad came through in the middle of one evening, probably about half past nine, to get some aspirin for Mum. I was dancing around the sitting room in my Wranglers to Daydream Believer, imagining I was on Top of the Pops and I hadn't heard the door. I nearly jumped out of my skin as I did a wobbly dancing spin and saw him standing, arms folded in the doorway. I had also liberated a skimpy red mini top, providing me with a full teenage outfit and exposed midriff. It clearly was not a look he approved of. I froze, locked in his displeasure, until he nodded his head towards the radiogram. I immediately turned it down to silent.

"Go upstairs and put your pyjamas on, I'll send your Mother through." His tone leaving me in no doubt that I was in trouble.

When Mum came through about half an hour later, she first wanted to know where I had got the money from to buy the clothes. Her relief when I told her they were from Sally's bag immediately made her shoulders relax and the tight line of her mouth softened. I went on to explain that I just wanted to have some clothes like all my friends, instead of the all-Crimplene wardrobe. After a few minutes of trying to get across how all I wanted was to fit in and dress like other girls my age, she relented with a compromise. The tiny tee-shirt was going to the next jumble as it was completely inappropriate for a girl of my age but the jeans could stay, on condition that I only wore them in the house.

I was wearing them on this Saturday morning hoping to keep them on so that Alison would think I was modern and trendy. I hadn't seen her for over a year and actually didn't really like her very much. The decision for her to come for the week was nothing to do with me, nor had I been consulted about her sharing my room. Aunty Shirley had asked Mum if she could come and stay as her and Uncle Bill wanted a week's holiday without the kids in tow. Their younger child, Mark was staying with Bill's sister's family but Alison had caused a fuss about going there. I found out afterwards, by eavesdropping, that the last time Ali had stayed with her

Aunty from that side of the family, she had been lippy and bad mannered and so they weren't that keen to have her anyway.

I took off my Wranglers and put on my black Bri-Nylon slacks Mum always said looked smart. Carefully, I folded my jeans before putting them in the big canvas bag hanging on the bedroom door. Smiling resignedly, I went down to get the shopping list to fulfill my errand, like the good obedient child I was.

"Dad, do you think I'll be able to take Alison to the park this afternoon, when Aunty Shirley's gone?"

I tried to make my voice sound casual.

"Mmm?"

He was polishing his shoes in a distracted manner but I knew he'd heard me so I just looked at him widening my eyes but saying nothing.

"The park? Yes, well I suppose that'd be alright so long as you're home before it starts to get dark."

"We'll be back well before then. I just thought it'd be something to do cos she's gonna be here for a week and I'm not that sure I like her very much."

Dad laughed.

"Well from what I hear she gets more like her Dad every day so I doubt that she'll be that popular with me an your Mam either!"

He passed me the list and taking a wad of paper money from his back pocket counted off four pound notes and handed them to me.

"That'll more than cover it."

Putting his money back he said,

"I'll have a think about somat for you to do with her while she's here, pictures maybe or swimmin' baths or there's a bowlin' alley in Leeds now in't there?"

He must have seen how my face lit up at the prospect of these outings as he added almost to himself,

"Yes, I'll talk to your mother, you should be out enjoying yourself while you've got your cousin here, and it might help to keep her out of our way." And we both went off on our separate errands smiling.

I'd hardly finished putting the shopping away when Aunty Shirley and Alison arrived. It was only just after ten o'clock. My mother ducked her head in a slight nod towards me saying *"Told you so,"* before fixing her face with the reproduction smile she reserved purely for her sister and got up to let them in.

"Ello Shirley, bus were early were it?" It was her normal type of sisterly greeting.

"Well we were up an' ready so we got an earlier one. I'm parched though; hope you've got the kettle on."

An equally cool response, lines drawn and intentions clear. Dad, a seasoned bit player in the long running sibling rivalry made himself scarce, muttering about changing barrels and cellar stock takes. I was therefore in charge of making the tea. Best china and milk in a jug, no milk bottle on the table when family are visiting. As I busied myself with the parlourmaid tasks Mum ushered them into the front room.

My cousin and I refused the offer of tea, fully aware that we were expected to make ourselves scarce. I was instructed to take Alison and her things up to my recently cleaned room; we were dismissed.

As we hadn't seen each other for some time, we skated tentatively around one another for a little while, chatting about school and friends, although I did most of the listening. It became apparent quite quickly that my younger cousin either lived a jet-set lifestyle with a full social calendar and exceptionally liberal parental control or, which was definitely more likely, she was a mendacious fantasist. Despite Mum's description of Aunty Shirley as a 'bloody terrible' mother, I didn't believe a word. Deciding that her tales were at the very least heavily exaggerated, I surmised that she'd never be allowed this much freedom. I recognised that most of her tales of hectic socialising came straight from the teenage magazines I avidly read. I decided not to go into too much detail on my recently acquired freedom and occasional day trips to Leeds but I did talk sketchily about my friends. I told her that there was a loose arrangement to meet up that afternoon but I wasn't sure she'd want to go. Alison was more than keen to go and meet my friends but mainly wanted to know if any of them had dishy brothers.

I left her lying on my bed listening to the radio while I went down to ask Mum if we could go to the park. Not only did she consent without question or conditions but she also opened her purse and gave me a ten shilling note, telling me to get some chips for our dinner, adding quietly, so her sister didn't hear, she'd be off back to bed soon as Aunty Shirley had gone, before her hairdressing appointment at 3 o'clock. I didn't need telling twice. Before she could change her mind I dashed back upstairs, put my jeans back on and stuffed the ten bob note in the pocket before rushing Alison out of the house. I doubt that Mum had time to close her purse before the front door banged behind us. Holding onto Ali's wrist to make her keep up, I sprinted down the road towards the ring road on the route to Jane's house.

Chapter Seven

The day wasn't cold and the previous day's drizzle had gone but the sky was overcast and grey. I wondered if we'd get to Jane's before the heavens opened. Maybe if we got soaked, Mr Schofield would ask us in to dry off. It normally took about twenty-five minutes to walk to the Armley Heights estate but on this occasion we did it in fifteen. At just after quarter to twelve I opened the little green gate to the Schofield's front garden and walked up the path. Alison was right behind me, excited and expectant as I'd mentioned that Jane had three older brothers. The door opened immediately after the most hesitant of knocks and Jane's Dad fixed me with a stare through narrowed eyes without a trace of welcome.

"Hello, Mr Schofield. Can Jane come out to play for a bit?" I blurted before my new found valour evaporated in the intensity of his gaze.

"No she can't," his voice deep and unfriendly. "She's goin' to her Granny's an' will be away all week, so don't you be comin' back here calling for her again."

He closed the door firmly and as I heard the mortice click loudly, I thought of Jane now locked in behind that door. I knew she was in a lot of trouble over the swearing at Robbo, even though he'd deserved it. I felt my eyes prickle at the indignation of it all. This was so unfair but there was worse. I was sure that there was something I should have done or said. I'd let her down. She had helped and protected me after instantly spotting my weakness and vulnerability. She'd made it her mission to guide me through the minefield of puberty and at a time when she was equally vulnerable and raw. She'd been a true friend to me and I'd done nothing in return.

"He was a bit scary!" Alison said as we quickly left the garden and walked away from the house without looking back. I didn't respond, so she just shrugged and asked when we were going to get some chips. Suddenly something occurred to me. I'd been so lost wallowing in my inadequacy and frustration that I didn't think of it until we joined the back of the queue at Charlie's Chippie. We had walked the route Jane's Mum was supposed to have made when she disappeared. As we sat on the wall outside, eating our salt and vinegar cooled chips out of last week's Yorkshire Post, I made a decision. I would go and find where Don Schofield had hidden his wife's body and the police would finally lock him up so Jane would be free of him. First though, I needed to get some reinforcements. After wiping our greasy fingers on the thighs of our trousers we shared a bottle of dandelion and burdock before setting off up the hill towards Sharon's house. The door was opened by a very concerned looking Mrs Weldon.

"Kimberly, what's happened? Where's Sharon?"

"I don't know where Sharon is; I've come to see if she wants to play out a bit," I said nervously wondering what Sharon had told her Mum.

"Oh, well she's gone in to Leeds with Diane and Jane. I thought you'd gone with them, I'm sure she said the four of you were going."

She was looking at me closely with an expression of alarm. I was confused. I was sure Jane was at home and knew there was no arrangement for the four of us to go into Leeds. The penny dropped. I had unwittingly highlighted that Sharon had lied to her mother and knew I shouldn't make it worse.

"I was gonna go but I forgot my cousin was coming," I pointed to Alison in an over theatrical way. "So I couldn't an' then I forgot that they were goin'. Sorry to disturb you, bye."

Turning quickly, I grabbed Ali's hand and pulled her down the path, feeling really fed up and even more frustrated. Sharon, or was it Diane, had definitely told me that they weren't going to Leeds today. They knew about Alison coming and that I might not be allowed to go but that was irrelevant, they'd lied to me and Sharon had told her Mum the four of us were going. This wasn't right. We were supposed to be friends and the Saturday Leeds trips were what we did together. I made up my mind right then that I wouldn't let them in on my theory about Jane's Mum and the tannery, I'd just go ahead and check it on my own. I'd have to take Alison but she didn't count as she didn't know Jane and it would probably be another year before I saw her again. I didn't voice any of this as we set off to walk back towards home. Instead I asked her about the sort of thing she did on a weekend. She was more than happy to tell me, needing no encouragement, or proof, that I was either interested or listening. All the time she was talking we were getting closer to the tannery and my belief that Maggie Schofield's body was hidden in there increased. Not wanting to share Jane's family history with Alison, I was trying to think of a way of getting her to go in with me. I made an abrupt stop as we neared the crumbling old building as if I'd suddenly thought of something.

"Hey, I know what we should do!"

"What?"

"We should go exploring in there!" I said, grabbing her arm and pulling her towards the lowest bit of wall where we could climb over.

Initially she wasn't keen but once I regaled her with my made-up-story of the missing fortune that was supposed to be hidden inside and threw in the ghost of a small boy protecting it for good measure, she was more than up for it.

The derelict tannery was a very dangerous place; there was no doubt in my mind of that. Neither was there any uncertainty of Mum and Dad's reaction if they found out I was taking Alison inside. Exploring the decomposing building with its damp and dark passages and rotten floors was not a sensible thing to do. Yet in my twelve-year-old head the building was perfectly navigable and safe for someone as capable and determined as me. I suspect there was an element of showing off but I was also bordering on a hysterical certainty of finding Maggie's body and putting an end to Jane's misery.

The afternoon had continued to be gloomy but the expected rain hadn't materialised and there were hints of the sun breaking through. We carefully picked our way through the vestiges of more industrious times strewn around the periphery of the structure. It took us a while to find an opening but eventually discovered some broken slats across a small door at the side of the building which was least visible from the road. The gap, although a little high up, was plenty big enough for us to climb through if we clambered up the door frame. As we did, I noticed that the opening was large enough to allow adult bodies through, but said nothing. I was so intent on this quest that neither logic or consideration had any chance of distracting me. Even if Ali had voiced any concern, which she didn't, I wouldn't have listened, as I led the way purposefully inside the decaying carcass.

The high, glass-gone windows and missing sections of roof created fissures of daylight throughout the cavernous hall we found ourselves in. The dim luminosity and dank odour highlighted the bleakness and decay as we looked around the rotten, fire damaged remains and subconsciously we moved closer together. There wasn't much to see or search in what must have been the main working area. The machinery was long gone for scrap or salvage, leaving only the odd corroded indistinguishable metal structure or rail fitted in the hard uneven concrete floor. There was a suggestion of some organised layout with remnants of a section of wall cordoning off a smaller section towards the back. As I started to move slowly toward this Alison took my hand.

"I'm not scared or anything but I think maybe we should be getting back now Kim." Her voice a half whisper revealing her unease.

"Yeah, ok, but let's just have a look over here first," I began continuing towards the back of the building. "Look, I think there's another way out over there."

I pointed towards a gaping hole in the stone wall hoping I sounded braver than I felt. My confidence was evaporating in the damp and putrid space around me as I stepped forward. We'd gone about three quarters of the way when we first heard the voices. There was someone over by the gap where we had come in. We stopped as our ears picked it up and simultaneously looked at each other. The voices began echoing around the cavernous structure as the bodies they belonged to climbed through the wooden struts to gain access. I put my finger to my lips and moved quickly towards the shelter of the sectioned off area. Alison was holding my hand so tightly it hurt. I led us behind what was left of the wooden dividing wall. It was slightly dimmer behind this charred screen but I could see that the hole in the stone we had seen was not a way out but access to a further room. I was moving towards the corner next to the gap when I heard the newcomer's drop, one by one, their landing thud resonating around the walls. There were three of them. I looked at my cousin, who was now visibly shaking, her eyes full of sparkling fear. I pointed at the dark corner and moved forward until I felt the damp stone of the wall on my fingers and crouched down. We were in so much shadow it was difficult to see but I could make out some contraption with a wheel and handle just slightly in front of us. I noticed the remnants of a window in the wooden wall, just above Alison's head. As we squatted in the smelly corner, I was swallowing hard and trying not to cry while trying to work out what we should do. The voices were male and loud, booming around in the emptiness, laughing and jokey. All the things my parents had warned me about, strange men, dark dangerous places; how could I have been so stupid. We remained crouched in the darkness, listening to their footsteps and broken words distorting around us. Noticing small streams of light, I realised they had a torch and were waving it around. This just heightened my fear as the light-beams swept above us. They'd obviously come much better prepared than us.

I wanted to try and get a look to see what they were doing so I let go of Alison's hand and started to stand up with my back against the cold damp wall. I needed to get in front of her slightly so I could see out of the gap but as I leaned forward my foot slipped on something slimy on the stone slabs. I tried to grab at the fire damaged wooden panel but only managed the briefest of purchase before I toppled sideward, my arms thrashing in panic, desperately trying to grab for something. I don't know who screamed first but I'm sure I was screaming the loudest as I realised there was no floor to break my fall. There was instead a deep pit that I had fallen in head first. I hadn't managed to grab hold of anything but a hard and biting pain told me that my leg was caught on something, leaving me dangling in mid, rancid air. There was noise, lots of shouting and Alison still screaming and sobbing but I'd stopped. Some sort of instinctive survival mode clicked in as I began trying to bend myself upwards. My right leg, from just below the thigh, was jammed in some fixed contraption and even though it hurt like hell it was the only thing stopping me from plunging straight into the pit. I tried again to bend upwards towards my trapped limb but was nowhere near strong enough and still quite dazed. Suddenly there was some light above me and hands were grabbing at my free leg as the torch beam moved out of my eyes I could see someone leaning towards me on the left side while someone else was holding onto me and a voice shouted,

"Grab my hand. Here come on just give me your hand!"

As the hand appeared I used every last ounce of energy I had to bend up against the gravity that was forcing me down and grasped it. I felt a firm hold, locking onto it in a vice-like grip that continued pulling me.

"Whatever happens, don't let go of my hand!"

The voice was calm and slightly familiar. As I was pulled up I saw the boy who had been holding my free leg but my vision blurred as I screamed out in pain. My right leg was being crushed by the machinery that was trapping it. The person holding my hand spoke again.

"Ok, we'll get you free in a minute don't worry."

Someone was standing slightly behind this person pointing the torch right in my face so I couldn't see who hand was holding me.

"Bloody hell you're so lucky your leg got caught!" The voice came from behind the beam of light. I was feeling dizzy and sick with the pain and probably in shock as I heard the first voice again speaking, this time to the person holding my leg.

"You can let go now, Kenny. You need to try and get the cogs to move a bit the other way." Then to someone else and quite sharply, "Paul, put the bloody torch down and help Kenny shift that will you!"

"Yeah, ok, but bloody hell did you see how far down that hole goes, she'd have been a definite goner if her leg wasn't caught."

He waved the torch once more across what I could now see was a large purpose-made hole about eight feet square before moving across to offer it to Alison.

"Here, you hold this an point it at the old mangle while us lads get your mate out of this mess."

The light moved to take in more of our little tableau and that was when I finally saw Chris Henshaw holding my hand. Robotically, Ali focused the light and after a few more minutes the boys dislodged my bleeding and dirty leg.

"Oh my God, thank goodness you were here. Thank you," I managed to say at last through my chattering teeth.

I'd been crying throughout my suspension and was trying to wipe away the tears and snot from my face with the sleeve of my jumper. Chris pulled a handkerchief out of the pocket of his jeans.

"Here," he smiled at me, "You're just rubbing grease or somat on your face."

I glanced down at my filthy clothes and the black oily patches on my top and jeans. Taking the hankie from him, I wobbled a bit and he put his arms out to steady me.

"Wow, steady. Are you ok?"

"Yeah, I think so, just a bit dizzy."

We all moved back into the main part of the building and Chris helped me sit down on his jumper near to where we'd come in. The others followed and sat down around us. Paul nudged Kenny and nodded towards his pocket. Kenny took a packet of cigarettes out of his pocket and handed them to him along with a box of matches. As Paul lit up he did the introductions and asked who we were. Alison immediately jumped in with her name before adding,

"And this is my cousin ..."

"Kimberly Asquith and her Mum and Dad own the Unicorn," Chris cut in.

I was amazed that he knew who I was and said so. He shrugged and looked a bit embarrassed before going on to tell us this was the second time the three lads had been in the tannery. He seemed suddenly quite nervous and asked me if my leg was alright and if I'd have to tell my parents about what had happened. He was relieved to hear that I had no intention of telling them as it would result in me being in a lot of trouble. He laughed, saying however much trouble I would be in was nothing to what would happen if his Dad got to know he'd been in the tannery. Harry, he told us, would come down hard on him and his friends for trespassing, which was against the law. But he would be furious for him going anywhere that he had specifically told him not to. This, he said, was against Harry's law, and a much worse crime. My leg was really hurting and although the bleeding had stopped, my jeans were soaked and I knew they were ruined. My hip was hurting a good deal too from where I'd been suspended and when I stood up the pain of putting my weight on it made my eyes water. Again, Chris was my knight in shining armour getting me out of the building. He kicked at the wooden slats to make a bigger hole and practically carried me out. I tried to play down the pain and focused on my need to get home and cleaned up before my parents saw me. Alison promised she wouldn't say anything and I was sure she wouldn't especially when I pointed out that any chance of us going to the cinema or bowling alley would be gone if she did.

Chapter Eight

Although I'd known of Chris via his Dad's regular late drinking sessions at the Unicorn and I'd seen him at school, I had no idea he knew who I was. He was in the year above me and wasn't in the drama club, so before the tannery, we'd never spoken. I had a mild curiosity about him but my fear of boys in general had kept me from talking to him. My parents had done a sterling job of their individual form of safeguarding. Their comments and warnings about the selfish and brutal nature of boys, which got worse as they entered their teens, made sure I kept my distance. This information was complemented with the odd anecdote about fast girls who ended up in trouble, poverty and terrible unhappiness. Although nothing specific was ever discussed regarding fornication I was left in no doubt about the sordid and unpleasant consequences of sex. Shortly after my twelfth birthday I had the 'facts of life' conversation with my Mum. It was an uncomfortable five minutes for both of us and happened only because of the arrival of my periods. This talk consisted of her telling me, now I had the curse, I had to keep well away from boys. If I didn't, I'd get myself into trouble. My wide-eyed and horrified silence at her remark prompted her to elucidate,

"If you let a boy touch you now, you'll get pregnant and disgrace the whole family and break me and your Dad's heart."

So it was a bit of a revelation to me, on that Saturday back in 1969, to discover that some boys could actually be alright and even quite nice. Chris was the younger son of our local bobby. His two friends were Kenny Welborne and Paul Turner and they all lived on the same street where they had grown up together. They had been an inseparable little gang playing together at home and school until Paul and Kenny passed their 11-plus and went to the Grammar school while Chris, unlike his older brother - the sainted Michael, failed. His Dad told my Mum that he had only just missed out, being just one point off passing.

"Hill Topps a good school though and it's only round the corner from where we live and he's in the A stream, of course."

PC and Mrs Henshaw lived on Hill Top Close, which was on an estate built in the late fifties just behind the school playing fields.

Chris had a different story to tell of his 11-plus attempt. He reckoned he'd missed it by a mile and really messed up. He'd been so confident he'd pass, everyone told him so, his parents, his teachers, his friends; he was just going to breeze through it. So he didn't bother to prepare for it, didn't need to, it would be a walk in the park. However, when the day came and he turned over the first paper he had the shock of his life and his ten and a half year old brain froze. As he struggled to find answers to the mental arithmetic questions, he became more and more alarmed and as the panic took hold of him, his confidence evaporated along with the time. His essay and general problem solving skills which probably could have saved him were lost in the swamp of terror that was clogging up his head. He knew with utter certainty, as he filed out of the hall, that he'd failed. Initially devastated, although not as much as his parents were, he did become quite philosophical about it. It was a lesson learnt and he'd never take anything for granted again. I pointed out that he was still put into the A stream and so he must have got quite a lot of it right, even in his panicked state.

I wasn't sure why they deemed me a B grade student, having not taken the selective exam - we were moving into the pub on the day it was scheduled at my old school in Sheffield and they'd already taken it at the new school when my parents finally got round to enrolling me.

Chris still hung out with his friends at weekends and holidays but through the week Kenny and Paul didn't get home from school until almost six and they had a lot more homework. Chris counted these things as his silver lining to the cloud of his failure. Kenny was quite similar to Chris in appearance, dark hair and brown eyes and with a similar personality. They were mostly serious, practical and sometimes self-conscious but generally good fun to be around. Paul differed in appearance; he had fair hair, sparkly blue eyes and was generally anything but serious. He was usually playing the joker and always had plenty to say for himself. I knew as soon as I met him he was what my parents would call a bit of a charmer and one to be very careful of. It was some years later that I learnt his outwardly and charismatic appeal covered a very different personality; however, I mustn't race ahead.

The three lads had gone to Gibson's tannery to smoke the cigarettes that Kenny had got from his older brother, as they had done the previous two Saturdays.

Alison was happy to join them claiming to be a regular smoker. She purloined her parents' supply when they foolishly left packets lying around. I refused the offer of one, perhaps something to thank my Mum's fear based childcare for. Hearing her constantly claiming that one cigarette and you're hooked and couldn't give them up even if you wanted to, had marked me for life. I quoted this mantra as the reason for my refusal and Chris responded that his mother had given up smoking two years ago and even though his Dad still smoked, she was never tempted to start again. I wouldn't be swayed in my abstention, although I filed this snippet of information away. I mentioned to Mum a week or two later that I'd heard that Harry's wife had managed to give up smoking. Her response was both cutting and dismissive.

"Sadie Henshaw's as big as a cart horse since she's packed in smoking, that's why Harry never wants to go home, poor sod!"

After leaving the tannery we walked to the ring road footbridge where we were to go our separate ways. Standing around awkwardly trying to keep the weight off my sore hip and leg, I noticed Chris seemed to be wittering about the school playing field being at the bottom of their garden. Paul impatiently cut into his ramblings and said that they were going to be at the park the next afternoon. If Ali and I had nothing else to do, we might want to hang around with them.

Alison was beside herself at this, insisting that Paul had been looking directly at her as he'd said it and so it was a sort of date. All the way back home, she talked about him. How good looking he was, how he fancied her and how she could make a long distance romance work. She could come and stay every weekend and all her friends would be so jealous. Paul's good looks were undeniable and he certainly had an entertaining way about him. I smiled as she prattled on knowing that her desire to see him again would stop her from telling tales about where we'd been. I was also smiling at the thought of Chris. His lovely dark eyes and the way he'd held my hand for a while even after he'd pulled me out of the pit. I stopped myself from telling Ali though, as it seemed incredulous that he might like me. He probably thought I was just some stupid girl who went skulking about in the tannery and was too scared to try smoking.

Once back home, I managed to tidy myself up and change my clothes before Mum came home from the hairdresser's. Although I needn't have rushed, apart from a call upstairs to check we were in, neither she nor Dad disturbed us. My beloved jeans were torn, bloody and filthy. I folded them up and put them back in the canvas bag with a plan to throw them out at the next opportunity. After cleaning myself up as best I could, I took stock of my injuries. There was a big cut above my right knee and massive bruising erupting round my thigh and running down past my calf and my hip was unbelievably painful.

The good thing about my parents' unusual working times and busy life meant that it wasn't difficult to hide my injuries and pain from them. In fact, the only adult to notice the damage was the P.E teacher, ten days later, when as I was grabbing for my towel after the dreaded weekly shower ordeal, she bellowed across the changing rooms at me,

"Kim Asquith, what happened to your leg?"

"Cut myself shaving Miss," I replied immediately, having already prepared for the question the night before. And of course, as was the way back then, that was that.

However it was sore and I struggled not to limp or cringe with pain for the first few days but was heartened at my acting ability. That evening as Alison and I were watching Bonanza, Mum uncharacteristically commented that I had a nice bit of colour to my cheeks and the trip to the park had done me good - I should get myself out more often. So the next day that's what we did.

Although nothing very exceptional happened on our first real outing to the park, it remains a wonderful memory that stands out in my childhood. We left the house at half past nine the next morning to the sound of Mum's call,

"Make sure you're back here by 1 o'clock at the latest to set table and help with dinner," echoing through the house.

Acknowledging this instruction we swept out of the back door and headed for the park. I was so excited. Inside my tummy was a kaleidoscope of butterflies and their flapping wings must have been causing major catastrophes at the other side of the world. We tried to run but once we realised that I could only hobble, we slowed to a more sociable pace, chatting and giggling all the way. Coatless, in complete denial of the cool drizzly weather, pink and breathless, we arrived at the park gates just before ten. The boys were already there, just by the swings and had come prepared with a tennis ball and cricket bat, a football and a transistor radio. I had five bags of crisps, having told Dad that Jane, Sharon and Diane might be there - a small untruth that I decided didn't really count as a lie as I had softened it with an added vagueness of a *might*.

Dad would have had some sort of an apoplectic fit if he'd realised we were meeting boys. Even though it was an innocent, uncomplicated fun-filled morning, playing hybrid games of rounder-cricket and foot-net-ball-rugby, not that I could join in too much but in between we laid around on coats, cardis and jumpers. There were defined divisions of space to avoid accidental touching of limbs or any other bodily parts as we listened to the end of Dave Lee Travis's show and sang along to Bad Moon Rising in a showy off adolescent way. The last record was It's getting better by Mamma Cass and I watched Ali fluttering her lashes and giving Paul her best cow eyes in a blatant display of flirting. I remember wondering if this was what Mum meant by being 'fast' but also thinking it looked fun. Paul stood and taking her hand, gave her a couple of twirls before holding and swaying her to the end of the song. We all looked on in awe at the easiness in which he did this, seemingly totally unaware of any awkwardness of boy girl contact; they danced with beaming faces and full eye contact. As the song finished he gave her a final twirl into a semi-dramatic hug before pushing her back on the coats where he sat down next to her. The spell was broken as the lunchtime slot of family favourites started at which point Paul switched off the radio and we got up to have a go on the swings before we had to go home.

As we walked back in the same direction together, Paul asked if we would be out again later, saying they could come round to call for us. I was mortified at the prospect, having a vision of Dad warning them off at the top of his voice. The disappointment was clear on Ali's face as I stumbled through my words of explanation about doing stuff with my parents but Paul just shrugged and said OK.

As the pub didn't shut until two, we didn't have our roast beef and Yorkshire puddings until around half past. Generally, my parents would then watch TV for an hour, before going to bed for an hour and a half. At six, they would get ready for the 7 o'clock opening time. This Sunday though, in honour of our family guest, we were going to play Cluedo, my favourite board game. Being able to play it with other people was so rare,

I'd been looking forward to it.

"Oh well maybe we'll see you on another day then?" Chris suggested.

"That would be great. Me an' Ali are going to the pictures tomorrow afternoon to see Oliver."

"Oh right where's that on at?" he asked eagerly.

I explained it was at the Pavilion in Stanningley which was 4 stops away on the number 14 bus from the Unicorn. Kenny said they could get the number 11 from the end of Hill Top to Stanningley Bottom and it was a few minutes' walk from there.

"Or," Paul cut in looking directly at Alison, "we could walk to the Unicorn and get on the number 14 and all go together."

I made a mental note to try and make sure Dad was nowhere near the window when we left for the bus stop. They walked us back as we made the arrangements for the next day and made it home just after the 1 o'clock curfew. Mum and Dad were too busy with the customers to notice the small group of boys who passed as Ali and I went into the side 'off sales' door. Alison was giddy with excitement.

"It's a shame we can't find someone to go out with Kenny," she whispered to me as we were washing our hands in the bathroom.

"What do you mean?"

"Well he must feel a bit funny what with me going out with Paul and you with Chris."

"What are you talking about?"

"Oh I know he hasn't asked you yet but it's obvious he fancies you."

We were stopped from discussing this any further as Mum's voice boomed up that we needed to hurry up. This didn't stop me thinking about it all afternoon. I was so lost in thoughts of being fancied that I failed to spot that it was Miss Scarlet in the ballroom with the lead piping.

After a fretful night worrying that Dad might change his mind about letting us go to the cinema, the next day went exactly as planned. Ali and

I dashed out of the side door into the heavy rain, just in time to catch the bus. We got on just behind the lads who had been standing at the stop for a while getting soaked. We followed them to the upstairs deck where Kenny and Chris sat on one double seat and Paul sat on the seat in front. Much to my embarrassment, Ali went and sat next to him. So I sat across the aisle her, sideways on. Consequently, I spent the whole of the bus ride wondering how the seating in the cinema would work. The boys got in before us and sat four rows from the front with Kenny in first, Paul in the middle and Chris on the third seat from the end. Ali went in next and asked Chris to swap her seats, which he did with a bashful smile to me as he sat down. Eyes front and sitting rigid in our seats, a surge of pleasure fizzed through my bloodstream, making me start to giggle nervously.

Apart from sitting next to each other there was no other contact between us, other than an occasional brushing of knees as we changed position so I was not wholly convinced that Alison's assessment of the whole fancying business was accurate. A million thoughts stopped me from watching much of the film. I sat there in the dark with my adolescent angst and hormones whirling around my head. I was longing for Jane, for her to bring some certainty back and share this new found autonomy but the memory of that terrible scene in the classroom and the fierceness of her Dad came to mind and I wanted to know that she was ok. But I knew there was nothing I could do until we were back at school.

Before leaving the lads at the bus stop - they were going a more direct route home - a trip to the bowling alley was planned for the day after next, meeting them there this time. On the point of departure Paul pulled my cousin towards him and gave her a hug and a quick kiss on the lips. So she was 'off with the fairies' for the whole journey home.

I slept well that night and woke up full of energy and keen to get out of the house again. Ali and I were just eating our cornflakes noisily at the table when Dad came down and started to make a pot of tea.

"Mornin' you two."

"Mornin' Dad," I muttered.

"Mornin' Uncle Ray," Alison spluttered with her mouth very full of milk, corn and sugar.

"So what you up to today then?"

"Dunno, we haven't thought about it yet but we might go to the park again."

I looked over at the window and registered the heavy raindrops pelting at it. Dad was oblivious; there was something on his mind.

"Harry called in last night for a chat," he said in an overly casual way and my heart skipped a beat. I couldn't move and hardly dared breathe. Had Chris told his Dad we'd been hanging around together?

"He was telling us about your friend Jane's Dad."

The noise of my exhaled breath of relief sounded so loud that I panicked more and forced a cough to cover it up.

"What about him?" I finally managed to ask.

"He's been locked up. He put his eldest lad in hospital on Friday night. Beat the livin' daylights out o' him and left him on the street."

I forgot about my breathing now. My heartbeat was so loud, I thought Mum would be able to hear it upstairs.

"Aye, he's in a bit of trouble this time, doctors thought lad weren't going pull through at first. He only came round on Sunday and told 'em who'd done it. Harry were beside himself over finally getting the chance to put him away."

Chuckling he picked up the two cups of tea and went back up to Mum. I remained where I was, sitting at the table and staring at my half full bowl of soggy cereal.

Chapter Nine

As soon as Dad left the room, I told Alison to hurry up as we had somewhere to go. I called upstairs that we were going to see Diane and Sharon and without waiting for a response, slammed the door as we stepped out into the pouring rain.

We went to Diane's house and were warmly greeted by her Mum who sent us up to her bedroom to find her lying on her bed reading a comic. She seemed pleased to see me and when I introduced her to Alison said that she didn't look twelve and could easy pass for fourteen and my cousin was delighted. Sharon was visiting family with her Mum so Diane had been expecting a dull day. I started to tell her about calling for Jane on Saturday and what her Dad had said.

"So we went to call for Sharon, cos her house was nearest," I paused to see if she would react in any way but she was just looking back at me waiting, "But you'd already gone off to Leeds."

Diane was wide-eyed and incredulous, shaking her head.

"Oh God! What on earth's going on?"

"Tell her about the lads we went to the flicks with yesterday!" Ali burst in jittery with excitement, not remotely interested about the 'Jane stuff'.

"What?"

Diane's eyes were like saucers. I gave Alison a look that I hoped conveyed that I was getting to that, sighed and started to explain about the tannery. I didn't mention my made-up story of the ghost and treasure, nor did I reveal my conjecture about Mrs Schofield's hidden body. Instead, I suggested we'd gone for something to do but I did tell her about my fall and narrow escape and Chris Henshaw pulling me out.

"Bloody hell he saved your life!" she exclaimed.

"Yes I know," I said emphatically.

"Yeah, Chris is alright but his mate, Paul, well he's just gorgeous. Me an' him are going out with each other. He's coming to Sheffield in a couple of weeks."

Her words poured out with a certainty of someone marking the claim she had staked. It was the first I'd heard about Paul going to Sheffield but I didn't say so. Alison's relationship with any boy either supposed or real, was nothing to do with what was important. I was just about to say that when she added,

"And Chris really fancies Kim. He's not asked her out yet cos he's a bit shy."

Diane looked from her to me but I just shook my head and said quickly,

"That's just rubbish!"

"No it's not, Paul told me. He's fancied you for ages."

"Who's this Paul then?"

"He's called Paul Turner. Him and Kenny Wellborn are Chris's mates but they go to the grammar school," I informed her.

"I think I might know him, he went to my junior school. He's in the year above us." Diane said vaguely.

Alison looked a little peeved and blurted out,

"Anyway we're going bowling in Leeds with 'em tomorra!"

"What, like on a date?" Diane asked, her eyes rounding up again.

"No, course not, they're just mates and I've never done bowling before so I reckon it'll be a laugh." I could feel my cheeks burning as I spoke.

She giggled but didn't say anything, so I continued.

"You and Sharon should come; we're meeting them there at about two."

"I'll see what Sharon thinks," she nodded and smiled. "It sounds like a date to me."

"Well it isn't! Anyway what are we gonna do to find out what's happened to Jane and if she's alright?"

"Well I certainly don't fancy going round her house after what her Dad said to you."

"No, well there wouldn't be any point as there's probably no one there."

I told her what Dad had said that morning about Don being in prison and Iain being in hospital.

"So I don't know how we'll find out anymore till we get back to school," I concluded.

"You could ask your boyfriend," Diane suggested mischievously. I opened my mouth to object but she raised her hand to stop me,

"Seriously Kim, you should ask Chris if he can find out anything from his Dad. My Dad says nobody has a pee in Bramley without Harry Henshaw knowing about it!"

"Ok, I'll try asking Dad if Harry said where Jane is."

"Anyway," she went on, "tell me more about your adventure and the fun you've been having."

Alison took over at this point going into great details, one or two of which were actually accurate, about my rescue form certain death, her dancing in the park and the cinema outing. She concluded that Chris was brilliant, the real strong silent type and that she and Paul were practically engaged. I added the odd comment from time to time but Alison's telling was really a monologue and Diane was so engrossed that I started to flick through the June and School Friend comic, although I was listening closely.

"Anyway, we'd better get off back home," I said as she started to recap yet again with further embellishments. She looked a bit disappointed at my interruption and moodily snatched up the comic I'd just put down.

"I've read all of them," Diane said gesturing over the scattered pile, "I was gonna throw them out so you can have 'em if you want."

She was talking to me but Alison immediately started gathering them together saying, "Great thanks!"

She tucked them under her arm as we went downstairs to put our shoes on. We reminded Diane again of the time and route to the bowling alley before saying goodbye and setting off for to the Unicorn.

Mum was in the kitchen when we got back home, tutting loudly and saying we must be 'bloody soft in the head' for going out in this 'bloody awful' weather and she would be 'bloody furious' if we came down with a cold. Giving us stern instructions to get out of our soaking clothes she went to sort us out some dinner. After we had eaten our middle of the day meal of ham, eggs and chips, Ali wanted to go to the park again but as it was still teeming with rain I knew it wasn't worth asking if we could. I didn't want Mum and Dad to start wondering what the sudden attraction was to a wet field at the top of the town. I also thought that there was little chance that the lads would be there anyway. Dad came through just as we were washing our plates and said that as the weather was so awful, if we wanted, we could help in the bar. Which meant washing glasses; in return we could sit in the snug with a bottle of pop and play dominoes.

The snug was a very small area to the left of the tap room bar. It was partitioned off with a three-quarter, wood and clouded glass screen. There were two small round tables, each with two chairs positioned by them. The majority of regulars were men who only ever occupied the tap room where they played cards, darts or dominos. These games played as a backdrop to putting the world to rights and talking about what they'd read in the papers. The snug was generally only used on a Sunday evening or very occasionally when one or two of the regular customers treated their wives to a night out. On these rare instances, the ladies were placed in the snug with a half of mild or sweet sherry and then abandoned. The couples, or very occasionally small groups of women that frequented the establishment, went to sit in the lounge bar with its thick red carpet, padded seats and flock wallpaper. This mid-week lunchtime, the lounge bar was empty and the tap room had only a handful of regular drinkers, the ones drawing dole or sick money or the retired.

We drank our pop, ate crisps and played dominos. I taught Ali to play fives and threes which I'd been playing with my Dad since I'd learnt to count. He'd taught me how to play darts and although my playing was rubbish, I was good at scoring. Pub games taught me more mental arithmetic than any school I attended. The dart board was occupied by customers, so I promised to teach Ali when the pub was shut. We had a good time clicking the dominos into different lines of crazy paving, occasionally knocking and using match sticks to score how much I beat her by. Even the washing-up of glasses and emptying ashtrays at closing time was fun. Mum and Dad were happy having us around, probably because they could see where we were and what we were up to.

Mum hadn't revised her opinion of Alison but my view had softened. I couldn't see what she was doing to annoy Mum so much but I noticed the hardening of her expression and narrowing of her eyes every time Ali said 'Yes, Aunty Pam' or 'No, Aunty Pam'.

It was as if just calling her Aunty Pam was a massive insult. At the end of the week after she'd gone back home, I asked Mum why she didn't like her. She made no effort to pretend or deny otherwise,

"There's too much of her father in that girl and she's bloody sly, with her 'Yes, Aunty Pam, course I will, Aunty Pam!'

She said this in a high and childlike voice mocking her niece.

"Any road, it'll be a long time afore we have her back here!" she concluded.

It wasn't raining on the Wednesday afternoon as we caught the bus towards Leeds but it was still grey and the showers didn't look far away. I couldn't help smiling at Alison as she talked constantly throughout our ride on the top deck. She only needed me to nod and say 'yes' or 'course' from time to time as she planned how her 'relationship' with Paul was going to pan out. She would, obviously, come back and stay during the Christmas holidays, so they could spend time together as she knew Paul would want this. She would probably meet all his family as well; in fact she would need to find out who she would need to buy presents for. I was mesmerised by how she could lose herself so completely in this imaginary world and wasn't afraid of doing it out loud.

We got to the Top Rank Bowling Alley just before two and were high on the anticipation. Ali had been bowling before with her mother and brother in Sheffield and wasn't holding back at telling me how good she was. She was trying to explain the scoring as we made our way to the shoe exchange, scanning the existing groups of customers as we walked. We handed over our shoes and waited for the woman behind the counter to find us each a pair of bowling footwear. There seemed to be no attempts on the part of the shoe lady to correlate sizes and I was just handing back the second pair I'd tried when Alison squealed with delight. Paul had come up behind her and put his arms around her giving her a hug. Chris and Kenny were more restrained with their hellos and after finally getting shoes that fit, we were told there was a ten minute wait for a lane.

"Let's go and wait in the cafe," Paul suggested pointing at the metal tables and benches. Having found a table, I sat down quickly before anyone else and Ali sat opposite me. Paul said he was going to get a coke and walked off towards the bar. Chris touched my shoulder and asked me if I wanted a drink. I was flustered and a bit embarrassed, so I refused a little abruptly. Chris flinched slightly at my 'No' without a thank you and followed Paul to the counter. Kenny sat down next to me and asked what we got up to yesterday. Alison immediately launched into a detailed narrative and knowing I'd struggle to get a word in, I glanced around. Alison was deeply engrossed in explaining how to play five and threes when I caught sight of Sharon and Diane and waved across at them. Once they'd got their shoes sorted, they came over to the table just as Paul and

Chris came back with their cokes. I managed to introduce my cousin to Sharon before she stood up and started to introduce everyone else.

The actual bowling was, at best, average for the four of us girls. Alison's declared expertise was not evident, which I mentioned. She claimed a sore wrist was hindering her swing. I found the bowling balls cumbersome and heavy and my aim was hopeless but it was fun and I enjoyed the games. The lads were all good and mainly playing to beat each other. Kenny and Chris were better than Paul, both taking time to line up and aim the ball while Paul did a lot of posing and playing to the crowd. At one point halfway through the first game, I found myself sitting next to Chris as we waited for our turns.

"So what's it like then living in a pub?" he asked the first question everyone asked me.

"We don't actually live in the pub; we've a perfectly ordinary house."

"Yes, sorry I know. I was just wondering how it was for you, with your Mum and Dad working every night."

"I don't remember it ever being any different. What it's like for you to be a policeman's son?"

"Well it can be a nightmare at times." Smiling he went on to tell me about everyone knowing who he was and how folk were only too keen to tell his Dad when he'd been seen somewhere he shouldn't be. In between our goes we gravitated back to the same seats and chatted throughout. This was when he told me about Michael, his perfect elder brother who did everything right, and exceptionally well. He was just about to take his O Levels and was planning, not unrealistically, to be the first person in the family to go to University.

"I always knew he was cleverer than me but it wasn't a problem till I ballsed up my 11 plus and since then I can't seem to do owt right."

He shrugged to pretend an indifference it was clear he didn't have.

"Your Dad told my Mum that both his lads are a brain boxes."

I wanted to try and cheer him up with this particular piece of gossip and he smiled appreciatively as he got up for his go.

When he sat down again, I asked him if he'd heard anything about Jane. I saw the change in him as the newly found relaxed manner evaporated and he said his Dad never talked about work stuff at home, on the rare occasions he was there. Overhearing this Paul leaned in towards us and said that he'd heard the full story. Chris bowed his head slightly and seemed to find something interesting on the floor by his feet as Paul continued to speak. Bowling was paused as he told what he had heard.

The story was that Iain, Jane's eldest brother, had gone on some sort of a bender on Friday night after work. His Dad had gone to look for him and found him in the working men's club. He'd grabbed him and dragged him outside before laying into him in the car park like he wanted to kill him. Nobody dared try and stop him other than shouting at him and saying they'd called the police. It was only when Iain had stopped moving that he just walked off without saying a word. When the police came no one wanted to grass Don up cos they were all scared of him finding out so they claimed it was too dark to get a proper look. It was only when Iain came round in hospital that he told them who'd done it. Harry Henshaw had gone round to arrest him on Sunday afternoon.

"Bloody hell, he sounds like a right nutter!" Kenny said.

"He's a lot more than that," Chris muttered, not taking his eyes off his feet and I knew that his Dad was no more discreet at home than he was after hours in the Unicorn.

"Do you know what's happened to Jane?"

"Oh yeah, she's your mate in't she? "I think she's been shipped off to her grandparents' in Middlesbrough and their Kev and Dave have been sent to a kid's home at Chapel Allerton."

Chapter Ten

Towards the end of the last game, the enthusiasm for bowling had waned somewhat amongst the girls. I asked Sharon what she and Diane got up to on Saturday when they'd gone to Leeds. Diane definitely blushed a little but Sharon just said it had been great and they'd be going again on the coming Saturday. Overhearing this Paul said,

"We're off to the Pavilion on Saturday, it's only thrupence to get in an' it's a great laugh."

"What time's it start?" I asked.

"Half ten while half twelve, Saturday morning cinema they call it. Are you coming then?" his sparkly baby-blue eyes, full beam towards Alison.

"That'd be ace!" She looked like she was about to explode with pleasure.

"We might give that a try for a change." Sharon quickly changed her mind and nodded at Diane, who just shrugged.

It was raining when we came out; Kenny had beaten Chris by ten points. We got soaked as we walked, not particularly fast, along the road to the bus stop but none of us seemed to mind. Reaching the cover of the bus shelter en masse we huddled in out of the rain. Through the back of the Perspex wall of our refuge, we could see the huge building site of the new Yorkshire Post offices emerging from the muddy half fenced site. In a slight lull in the conversation, Paul announced he was going to work there when he left school.

"Wow are you going to be a newspaper writer then?" Alison asked squeezing in next to him on the long bench, almost pushing Kenny off the end in the process.

"Journalist," Sharon said, quite pointedly.

"Maybe," Paul shrugged, "I've not decided yet but I just know I'm gonna work there."

Diane moved across to stand by Kenny and asked,

"What about you Kenny? What you gonna do when you leave school?"

"Dunno really haven't thought about it."

He looked generally puzzled, like he'd never considered life after school and that he had only just realised he might need to have some idea of a future plan. Although it could also have been that somebody, a girl, had asked him. After a few seconds he said,

"I'll probably work for the council like me Dad." He nodded his head as if he'd just made up his mind right there and then, that was what he was going to do.

I was just about to ask Chris when Sharon got there first.

"You gonna be a policeman then Chris, like your Dad?"

"I'm gonna join the police force and become a policeman but definitely not like my Dad. How about you Kim, what do you want to do?"

"She wants to be a barmaid like her Mam."

Sharon answered for me and I felt a flush of anger that I just about managed to quell as I corrected her.

"No I don't! I'd like to go to university but I'll have to see how I do with my O Levels and," I was suddenly quite cross, "my Mum's not a barmaid, she's the landlady."

Further conversation was prevented as our bus came round the corner. I gave what I hope was an encouraging smile and nod at Chris and stepped out of the shelter. Sharon and Diane did the same but I was aware that Alison hadn't stood up. The bus stopped and I turned around to tell her to get up, letting Sharon and Diane on first. Alison and Paul were in an exceptionally close embrace, kissing fully on the lips in a slightly frenzied way. I was so taken aback having never seen this sort of physical display before, I froze on the spot until the bus driver brought me back to reality asking if we were getting on or not.

Finally on board, the four of us made our way to the top deck and all sat on our own seat with backs to the window and legs stretched out. Alison talked at length, much encouraged by Sharon about what a great kisser Paul was and she should know cos she'd kissed lots of boys. I had the feeling that Sharon was making fun of her but wasn't entirely sure. She seemed to suddenly have become Ali's best friend and wanted to know all about where she lived and what sort of things she did at weekends. I didn't say much at all. Sharon asked me what I was looking so miserable about. I told her I was worrying about Jane.

"Well there's nothing we can do about that till we see her next week," she said dismissively before going back to her interrogation of my cousin.

"So are you seeing Paul again before the flicks on Saturday?"

Having extracted from Ali that Paul had told her they'd be at the park the next day, Diane and Sharon called round for us, eager to be part of the newly formed gang, and the four of us trundled off to meet them.

This time the fun in the park was ok but not as good as our last outing when it had been just the five of us. Alison, Paul and Sharon were quite animated and lively. Their interactions were tactile, Sharon still being Ali's new best friend with lots of shared giggling and whispering. But there was a slight awkwardness in the rest of us and something I didn't fully understand at the time. In later years I would look back and see that this was the day that Paul fully realised his appeal to the opposite sex and the power it gave him. It was obvious that Sharon fancied him and as he knew that Alison was only around for a few more days, he wanted to keep her interest warm; which is more or less what happened.

I was surprised to discover that Saturday morning cinema had nothing to do with watching a film, it was just a place for kids to congregate in cinema-rowed seating. The main purpose seemed to be to chat loudly, calling and shouting to people, throwing screwed up paper, sweets or lolly sticks up and down the stalls and occasionally climbing over the seats to change location. I've no idea what film was showing that morning, although I have a vague idea it featured pirates. I do remember there were a series of cartoons on first followed by a brief interval when we could stock up on lollies and other types of sugar substances. Once inside, I again found myself sitting next to Chris who asked me if I'd like a choc-ice which I refused, this time with a little more grace, saying I wasn't hungry and remembered to say thank you. Chris bought himself one, which he ate while telling me about how he was learning to play the guitar and showing me the calluses developing on the ends of his fingers from the strings. During this discussion, I passed the tip of my index finger across these hard mounds as he held out his right hand. I felt a jolt of electricity surge through me on connection and pulled my hand away quickly, as the lights went down again for the main feature. I glanced across at the others who were sitting Ali: Paul, Sharon, Diane and Kenny. Paul was holding Ali's hand but talking to Sharon. Ali was just sitting there smiling and stroking Paul's fingers. I kept my arms folded in front of me and tried, in vain, to concentrate on the screen. I was wondering if Mum and Dad would be alright about me having a boyfriend if it was Harry's son. I'd moved on to wonder what it might be like to be kissed by him when he nudged me and asked,

"When's your cousin goin'home?

"Tomorrow morning," my eyes still on the screen and body fully forward.

"Right, so do you think you'll be at the park then?"

"No, I'll have to be home when her Mum comes to collect her. Ali's Mum is my Mum's sister and they can't be in a room on their own without fighting,"

Laughing he said,

"Well I'll see you on Monday anyway."

I looked across at him and he smiled.

"At school?" he reminded me.

I smiled back but tightened my arms across my chest and turned my gaze back to the front. It seems so strange now remembering this scene but I was absolutely terrified of the situation, terrified and delighted. Having had all boys demonised by Dad for the last few years I had no idea how I should be behaving towards this one who really seemed nice. I wanted him to hold my hand but was terrified at the prospect. Also there was this odd but fairly pleasant sensation I could feel in my stomach. It was like the swarm of butterflies I normally experience when nervous, flapping their wings with such ferocity they had reached turbine level, creating electric currents. This had started with our brief touch of fingertips and had flooded my bloodstream with adrenalin. In my confusion, I was trying to balance up my elation and fear. Consequently my perceived but not intended, off-hand behaviour was enough to thwart the nervous advances of a very shy Chris. *'If only Jane were here'* I thought.

On Monday morning, I waited at the footbridge for as long as I could before giving up and racing up through the Swinnow estate to get to school just before the whistle. Jane's name was not answered at that morning registration or any other morning that week. In fact, she didn't come back to school at all that term. My school days seemed strange without her but I think they would have been strange anyway, so much happened in those next few weeks leading up to Christmas.

My initial sadness at her not being there was forgotten briefly when Mr Lloyd announced the news about the school play which was scheduled to be in March the following year. It was a play called 'The Grey Angel' about Elizabeth Fry and her campaign for prison reform. As we'd missed the last drama club meeting before half term, we had an additional meeting on the second day back where we all had a read round of various parts. Much to my amazement, at the next meeting I was given the title role. It was unprecedented that a second year got a leading part but Mr Lloyd said that after the initial readings it was clear that I understood how it needed to be played. Even though I was delighted, I was aware that a few people in the group weren't so happy, particularly Sharon, who became very agitated after the announcement.

"I don't think it's right. I mean you were good an' all that but he should have chosen a third year."

She was a bit off with me for a couple of days, which was annoying. I knew that if she'd been picked she wouldn't have given the third years a second thought. Her coolness didn't last long though and by Friday we were making plans for the weekend. The following Monday, Sharon wrote Paul's name all over her pencil case and lesson diary. This following our second Saturday morning cinema trip when he had kissed her at the bus stop. She was very keen that everyone should know she was going out with him. This time I didn't sit next to Chris and found myself instead in the middle of Diane and Sharon. I chatted to him a bit at the bus stop but it was all very awkward. Now Alison had gone, the group dynamic seemed to have changed and the bit of confidence I'd felt was nowhere to be found.

Although I didn't talk to Chris much at school, or any other boy for that matter, we smiled and said hello when we passed. I wasn't allowed out on the dark evenings after school but my new found freedom at weekends was not withdrawn after Alison had gone home. So we continued to hang around together on Saturdays and Sundays. This hanging around was mainly at the park on Saturdays after the cinema and again on Sunday mornings, although we did progress to sitting on the wall outside the local chippy as it was a bit warmer there over the Saturday lunchtime openings.

The next big thing was Chris's 14th birthday party which was on the 23rd of November. He'd invited me two weeks before and at first, I was really excited but I reminded him and myself of my Dad's stance on my contact with boys. I also told him I'd only been to two parties before in my life. These had both been in the middle of the day and involved jelly, ice cream and pass the parcel. He looked a bit fed up, so I promised I'd try and get Mum on my side before asking Dad.

"If you come, we won't play pass the parcel but I'll see if we can have jelly."

I asked Mum first with the most insistent pleading voice I could muster. She said that she'd have a talk to Dad about it, which she did that evening before they went to open the bar. I was in my room and heard my Dad's booming voice proclaiming, *"She's bloody well not going!"*

Sighing hard, I flopped onto my bed and picked up that week's Jackie. I was composing, in my head, a letter to Cathy and Clare about my over-protective parents and stopped listening to the voices below. So I almost jumped out of my skin when the bedroom door opened and Mum strode in unannounced.

"Right!" she began hands on hips. "You can go on condition that your Dad takes you and fetches you home, dead on half past nine."

I opened my mouth to object that the party was 7 until 10 but she put her hand up to stop me and continued,

"And you need to be at the gate at this time or he will come in and get you. Also, you so much as sniff any alcohol while you are there you will not be allowed to go anywhere else again - ever!"

She paused, giving me a second to take in what she had said. I said nothing, knowing it was useless to push for further concessions and actually it was a blooming miracle that I was being allowed to go at all, so I allowed myself a smile.

"So, are we clear on that?" she asked.

"Yes." My smile widened.

"Don't you let me down Kimberly. It's taken a lot to convince your Dad on this."

"I won't, thanks Mum." And I got up and kissed her.

Even though it was the busiest night of the week in the pub and there was an offer of a lift home from Sharon's Mum, Dad was intent that he would collect me from the party. Although he did relent about taking me, so I went with my friends, in Diane's Dad's car. They picked me up en route at quarter to seven. Getting into the car, I was giddy with the pleasure of my first teenage party. Despite the restrictions - I was the only one there who didn't partake in the cider - I had a good time. I wore my new Midi dress that was another cast-off from Sally's daughter and managed to get out of the house wearing a hint of mascara and eye shadow. I'd also slept with my newly washed hair in rags the night before and kept them in until tea time. This transformed my normally heavy straight hair into soft curls, framing my face.

Harry was there when we arrived and said hello to everyone and made a joke about not wanting to arrest any of us but would do just that, if anyone spoilt the party. Chris had his *"not impressed"* look the whole time his Dad was in the room. Finally though, he took the hint and left, saying he had villains to catch. Once Harry had gone Chris visibly relaxed. Smiling he turned up the sound on the reel to reel tape player where he had his recording from the hit parade. There were about twenty of us standing, a little cramped, in the Henshaw's sitting room as he came and stood by me.

"Do you want some cider?"

"No thanks," still refusing him, but at least remembering my manners.

"We'll have some!" Sharon was quick to accept for herself and Diane.

Chris smiled at her and went in to the kitchen. I sat down on the sofa next to a girl called Maureen who was new to the school having just moved to the area in September. Even though she was in our class, I didn't know her very well so thought I'd chat to her, remembering all the times I'd been a new girl. It was a very stilted conversation only partly due to the loud music but I did learn that her family came from near York and she lived round the corner. I was asking her what she thought of the school when she stood up abruptly as Chris came back into the room and took one of the three plastic cups from him. The music changed and a couple of the older girls got up and started dancing. Maureen and Sharon joined them enthusiastically while continuing to sip cider. Diane came over and, putting her drink down on the fireplace, held out her hand to me, gesturing for me to get up too.

It took a couple of songs for me to smooth down the self-conscious barbs pricking at my psyche before I could move my body weight around, struggling to try and move with the confidence the others seemed to have or even being somewhere close to being in time with the music. Mick Jagger started to sing about meeting a gin soaked bar-room queen in Memphis and knowing the words to this song, I managed to relax a bit. As the song ended, Chris appeared at my side with a dish full of orange jelly with a dollop of yellow ice cream on top, saying gallantly,

"As promised my lady!"

I sat on the sofa to eat it and he sat next to me.

"I'm glad you could come."

"Me too. Thanks for the jelly, it's lovely. Aren't you having any?"

"Yeah, in a bit. Sorry about my Dad. He's such a tosser!"

"He's alright. At least he let you have the party. I'd never be allowed all these friends round."

"Yeah, I suppose you're right. I just wish everybody in the world didn't know I was his son. Anyway, well done for getting the starring role in the school play."

"Thanks. It was such a surprise but I'm really excited."

"I'll definitely be buying a ticket."

We smiled at each other and I felt the butterflies start to swoop.

"Kim, I wanted to ask you....."

I didn't find out what he wanted to ask me as Maureen came and pulled him to his feet.

"Come on Chris, you need to dance with us."

I finished my jelly as one of the third year girls took the empty seat and started to talk to me about the school play. A little later all the girls were dancing while the boys stood around watching and drinking cider. The music started to get a bit slower and Sharon and Paul, then Diane and Kenny joined the other two couples smooching on the shag pile rug. I watched as they all seemed to be getting scandalously close, arms locked around each other moving in a circle, while shifting their weigh in time to the music. I became so scared at this vision that I went into the kitchen muttering that I was going to get a drink of water. Chris's Mum was sitting at the small Formica table eating chocolate and reading her copy of Woman's Weekly. She looked up as I came through the door.

"You that lass from the Unicorn?"

Mrs Henshaw's tone was cool and unfriendly and left me in no doubt that she would not be impressed with my affirmative. I nodded anyway.

"Yes I am." Adding my best smile I tried, "Please can I get a drink of water?" as I took a step towards the sink.

She looked me up and down before purposefully closing her magazine and raising herself slowly. Noisily pushing back her chair, she walked towards me. Still giving me the disapproving stare, she took a cup off the draining board, filled it with cold water and handed it to me, all this done without saying a word. I thanked her with what I hoped was my humblest smile and drank it all in two massive gulps as quickly as I could, so I could escape her hostile glare.

As I returned to the hormone laced, darkened living room, I checked my watch. It was nearly twenty past nine and so I went over to Chris who was sitting on the arm of the settee talking to two boys I recognised but didn't know. His face lit up as I walked over to stand in front of him.

"Kim, there you are. Are you having a good time?"

"Yes thanks. I've had a great time but I've got to go now cos my Dad will be here in a minute to pick me up."

He stood up quickly, his smile fading and I could smell the cider on his breath as he leaned towards me.

"Aw, you can't go yet. We haven't had a dance."

He leaned closer with his arm about to circle my waist. I stepped back and he stumbled forward, caught slightly off balance, causing a snigger from his friends on the sofa.

"We'll have a dance another time, I've got to go now. Thanks for inviting me."

I fled from the room, said a quick goodbye and thank you for having me to a very unimpressed Mrs Henshaw and let myself out of the kitchen door. As I walked round the side of the house towards the gate, I could still hear the music and glancing again at my watch, I clocked the time as 9.25. I walked through the gate to the sound of The Family Dogg singing *'it's just a way of life.'* I smiled at Dad as I got in to the car which was already parked and waiting, directly outside the gate.

Chapter Eleven

The day after his party, Chris finally plucked up the courage to ask me to go out with him and I said no. Well, it wasn't quite as brutal as that and I was the one who ended up bruised.

It was teeming with rain that morning and I wasn't expecting Diane and Sharon to call for me so was surprised when they did. I got my coat and set off with them to the park. Our anoraks doing little to protect us, Diane suggested waiting in the doorway of the Thrift stores until it stopped. I'd felt there was something a bit out of kilter from the moment I'd seen them on the doorstep and now my senses were screaming for me to brace myself.

"Shame you had to leave so early last night." Sharon said in a tone suggesting she didn't think anything of the sort. "Still, Maureen was well pleased when you went!"

There it was, the reason they'd called for me. She wanted to tell me that as soon as I'd gone, Chris had started slow dancing with the new girl, till his Mum came in, switched on the light and sent everyone home.

"They were doing a bit more than slow dancing an' all!"

Sharon added with relish and an exaggerated nod of the head to make sure I got the message.

"Right," was all I managed to say, trying to smile but my mouth and eyes seemed to be working independently.

"Maureen's had a thing about Chris ever since she moved here in the summer," she continued. "Anyway, she's coming to the park today so we said we'd wait for her. She'll be here in a bit."

"Right."

My eyes firmly focused on the closed sign on the shop door in front of me. A cheery voice behind me saved me from further comment.

"Hello, hello fancy seeing you here!"

"Paul!" Sharon stepped out into the rain and grabbed him. He gave her a huge grin before planting a real smacker of a theatrical kiss on her cheek.

"It's not really a day for the park," Kenny added striding into the doorway and shuffling up towards Diane.

Chris seemed to be hovering a bit behind them still in the deluge. I avoided any eye contact but felt his reluctance to join the group.

"We could go to the bowling green and sit in that long porch thingy," Paul suggested. Maureen arrived and agreed the bowling green was a better place to hang out and we set off back down the hill, absorbing more rain into our already sodden clothes. I hadn't said much more than hello to anyone and was desperately trying to keep a smile on my face but knowing I couldn't keep it up for much longer. We were moving as a group but I got the distinct impression I was the odd one out, the spare amongst three couples. When we got to the gate of the bowling green, I stopped.

"I'm really cold and wet; I think I'll get off home."

"Oh alright, bye then, see you at school tomorrow," Sharon turned her head briefly towards me as she and Paul led the others through the gate.

"I'll walk some of the way with you," Chris said, and was quickly at my side. I didn't look back and couldn't hear if anyone else said anything. My heart was beating so loudly inside my anorak hood and I kept on walking. After a bit he said,

"I'm glad you came last night."

"Thanks for asking me."

"Thanks for my record token."

"What you going to get with it?"

"Dunno yet, maybe a record!"

We both laughed and he suddenly pulled at my arm to turn me towards him and blurted out,

"Will you go out with me Kim?"

My immediate response was to pretend I hadn't heard him and just run off. I was so full of conflicting emotions, Sharon's words playing in my head, *'They were doing a bit more than slow dancing an all'.* I just stood there looking anywhere but at his eager face and finally managed,

"I really like you but I don't think it'd be a good idea for me to go out with anybody just now. My Dad would go mental. He's always said he'll lock me in the beer cellar if I start any of that boyfriend malarkey before I'm thirteen."

"So when are you thirteen?"

"March, just after the school play and that's another reason why it's not a good idea just now."

He reached across and lightly flicked the end of my nose with his fingertip.

"I forgot you were just a toddler."

"Cheeky!"

What I'd said about Dad was absolutely true even if the going out with someone malarkey only consisted of hanging around together, holding hands and a brief kiss on the lips, not that we'd done either of those but he'd still go mental. I said I just wanted us to carry on being friends until after the play and maybe then we might start going out, if we both still wanted to. I felt very grown up after this conversation and Chris seemed ok too. We said goodbye and he turned to go back to the Bowling Green; we were just a hundred yards from the pub. I smiled thinking it was all actually going to be alright but I couldn't help but notice when I turned around to check a couple of times that he didn't look back.

I found out the next day that Kenny asked Diane to go out with him that afternoon as he walked her all the way home. She enthusiastically agreed and invited him in to dry off, where he also had a cup of tea before her Dad drove him home. I also discovered that there was a communication breakdown in the conversation I'd had with Chris. He didn't seem to have the same perception of how our chat had gone as I had. As he walked home with Maureen he asked her to go out with him and she happily said 'Yes'.

So choices were made. It had been my choice to say not now when Chris asked me to go out with him and it was his choice to interpret that as a no and then ask someone else, who chose to say yes. It was Sharon and Diane's choice to forget that we were friends and give me the cold shoulder and it was my choice to be devastated by this.

I have a memory here of a new kind of loneliness for the rest of that term which even seeped into my habitual solitary home life, making me desolate. I was so miserable that even Mum noticed something was wrong but in fine old Asquith family tradition didn't speak to me about it. She would never ask a question that she thought she might not like the answer to.

On the following Saturday morning when I would normally be getting ready to go off to the pictures, I got dressed as normal but stayed in my bedroom looking out of the net curtains on yet another damp day. Mum barged in but just stood in the doorway without saying anything.

"What?"

"You off to pictures this morning?"

Making my mind up quickly I nodded.

"Mm yes, course."

She produced three pound notes from her purse and said,

"Why don't you go to Leeds after with your mates like you did afore? Here, get yourself somat nice."

"Thanks Mum, yeah I'll see if they wanna go."

I managed a smile for the effort she'd made and got my things together to go out. I put the money in the small glass jar I used to keep marbles in, before Mum had thrown them out on our last move. Grabbing my bag I called out a goodbye and left. Checking that they weren't near the window, I didn't wait for the bus but walked towards the high street, making for the library. Once inside, I spent over an hour choosing a book before taking the long route home via St Peters church. I had a bit of a walk around the churchyard reading the gravestones before going to sit in the shelter of the back porch. I thought of going inside as it was getting pretty chilly but the door was locked. I sat on the stone slab of the portico for a further hour, reading until I was almost blue with cold. I managed to get home and into my room without either seeing or being seen by anyone and wrapped myself in the shiny blue eiderdown, making a little nest for myself, and went back to reading my book.

Feeling friendless at school, I immersed myself in the lessons and the rehearsals for the play. Sharon and Diane still turned up for drama club which was mostly rehearsals but hardly ever spoke to me. On the odd occasion they did, it was definitely not as friends. Sharon was still irked that I'd got the lead role and felt at liberty to express this. One of the third year girls told me that she'd said I'd only got it because Mr Lloyd drank in the Unicorn and was friendly with my parents. As far as I knew he'd never been in the pub. Dad would definitely have mentioned it if he'd had one of our teachers in the bar. As my two ex-friends had parts as extras with only a couple of lines each to learn, they were generally not on stage, choosing instead to sit at the back of the hall. There they remained, heads close together whispering their plans of double dates with occasional unfriendly glances in my direction. I was relieved that Chris and Maureen weren't in the drama club. I don't think I could have survived that particular awkwardness. The classroom situation was difficult at first but after the first couple of days I started sitting next to a girl called Suzanne. She was fairly quiet and very bright and used the break time to read Enid Blyton's 'Malory Towers' books that she started to lend me. Maureen just completely ignored me and although Diane did offer me the occasional smile, Sharon would either blank me or very pointedly make comments about there being a smell of fags and beer in the air. Anyone who didn't know would never have guessed that we'd been friends.

I saw Chris rarely at school, so rarely in fact that I suspected he was purposely avoiding me. On the times our paths crossed, I felt my cheeks burn and I lowered my eyes. He never spoke. So all in all it was with great relief when school ended that term for the two week Christmas break. I managed to convince Mum I was unwell on the last day in order to avoid the classroom party but spent the day mooning around my bedroom imagining everyone having a brilliant time and making myself more miserable.

The day before Christmas Eve, I was in my room wrapping some presents when Mum called up to me,

"Kimberly, phone."

As I came down she put her hand over the mouthpiece of the handset and said quietly,

"Don't be long," before removing it and saying in a loud and friendly voice, "Here she is Alison, I'll put her on."

Giving me a very pointed look, she handed me the receiver and went back into the living room. I sat on the stairs to hear a very excited Alison telling me all her news. Paul had phoned her the evening before to tell her that he was supposed to be going to Newcastle to see Leeds United play on Boxing Day but he'd sold his ticket so he thought he'd have a trip to Sheffield instead.

"So he's coming to see me!" she squealed.

I felt awful having to tell her about him and Sharon but I knew I had to. I'd only just started when she told me she knew all about it. He'd told her how Sharon had thrown herself at him and as his friend Kenny wanted to go out with her friend, he'd played along. I was just taking that in when she added,

"Anyway he's dumped her now, said he didn't want to have to buy her a Christmas present." This said with a hearty laugh.

He also said, according to a delighted Alison, that she was clingy and had apparently called her, to her face, an irritating limpet! Although this sounded really cruel, I couldn't help smiling and hoped it was true.

I told Ali all about the Chris saga and how miserable I'd been at school, although I had to keep my voice quite low as I was sure the radio had been switched off in the other room. She told me that Paul had phoned her a couple of times over the last few months. All her friends were planning on hanging around when she met him just to get a look.

When I came off the phone Mum called for me to give her a hand getting the dinner ready. As I peeled the potatoes for the chips she said very casually,

"You can help behind bar tonight and tomorrow if you like, after your telly programs have finished."

"What an' stay up till Santa comes?" I asked with a laugh.

"Aye, you can stop up till he's been an' open your presents afore we go to bed then we can all have a lay in next day," she smiled back adding, "An' if you behaves yourself and don't get in the way maybe's you can have a snowball after we close."

I helped Dad open up that evening and stayed washing and putting away glasses for most of the night. The time passed quickly and I slept a lot better that night than I had for a few weeks.

The following day, Christmas Eve, at 9pm when the 'Cilla Black Show' finished, I went through the storeroom into the bar to help again. The pub was heaving with people and the air thick with smoke. Dad put a stool in front of the sink with a piece of red tinsel wound round the legs and there was already a large collection of glasses waiting to be washed. It was a really busy night and Mum and Dad were in excellent form, as were the two bar staff who, even though they were definitely earning their money, were doing well for *"have one yourselves"*. There was no extension to the licensing hours that night so Dad called last orders at ten to eleven. As most of the customers, mainly male, had been drinking steadily since opening time, there was no massive rush at the bar and the custom was already thinning out. It was at this point, after a brief word with Mum, I saw him go back through the store room door, knowing instantly he'd gone to get my Christmas presents from wherever they'd been hidden and put them on my bed. The only bit of normal Christmas we had.

Harry arrived, in uniform, with a very young looking police constable, at exactly 11pm as Dad rang the bell calling "Time gentlemen please!" The sight of the two uniformed officers helped the remaining customers finish their drinks and make a speedy exit, especially the ones intending to drive home. The husbands of the two barmaids stayed where they were, nursing the last few mouthfuls of their beer knowing that free drinks and a late night was on the cards. As Harry came round to the hatch he saw me at the sink and grinned.

"Well if it isn't the little lass who broke my son's heart!"

I felt the blood rush to my face and knew I'd turned scarlet. I was just about to say I was tired and wanted to go to bed, all hopes of a snowball abandoned. But Dad wanted to know what Harry was on about so a discussion began about me with no regard for the fact that I was standing right there, deeply embarrassed. Harry, as if telling some funny joke, explained that I had given his son the brush-off at his party and how he'd been *'Right torn up about it'* for about a couple of days till he'd taken a shine to some other lass who *"weren't so choosy!"*

I was mortified and looked over at Mum hoping for some female solidarity or at least a change of subject. She didn't let me down.

"Well she's only a bairn yet Harry, far too young for boyfriends!"

Making it clear that the conversation was over she asked loudly,

"How many cherries do you want in your snowball Kimberly?"

I was glad I hadn't rushed off to bed and did indeed have an advocaat and lemonades, with three cherries on top. I also learned, once everyone had forgotten I was there, that Jane's Dad had not been charged over the attack on his son. Iain had withdrawn his claim saying he'd been confused before but it was definitely not his Dad who'd beaten him up. It was a stranger who he'd never seen before. No matter how many times the police told him there were witnesses he was adamant that they were wrong. So the charges were dropped much to Harry's annoyance.

"There's somat right fishy going on in that family."

When Iain had been discharged from hospital he had not gone home. Instead, he'd left his job and moved away, somewhere way down south, Leicester maybe. I was desperate to ask about Jane but knew if I raised attention to my presence I'd be sent to bed and hear no more. So I sat quietly in the corner, out of my parents' eye line and prayed someone else would ask. It was Mum.

"What about the other kids, where are they now?"

Harry responded. Jane was in Middlesbrough with her grandparents and the other two lads,

"Savages, both of 'em have been split up and put in care on t'other side of Leeds, although they'll probably come back home now. But if anybody's got any bloody sense, that little lass will be left where she is."

The conversation moved on after this to that bloody idiot Harold Wilson, who couldn't run a piss-up in a brewery let alone the country. I chose that moment to announce that I needed to go and see if Santa had been. Dad said he was sure he'd heard sleigh bells a bit ago so he probably had and I could open all my presents now if I wanted. They wouldn't be through for a bit yet so there was no point me stopping up.

"Ok, I'll see you in the morning."

"Oh aye, but not too early eh love? Night-night."

So off I went to wish myself a merry Christmas and see what Dad in his role as Santa had put in the pillow case at the bottom of my bed.

Chapter Twelve

The Christmas of 1969 came and went and we saw in the New Year with some busy nights at the Unicorn. The new decade looked like being a prosperous one for Mum and Dad and I spent most of the school holidays helping out with the glass collection and washing. The times I wasn't doing that, I was either lying on my bed reading old copies of Jackie or June and School Friend or watching telly while lying on the sofa in the front room. Safely in my little bubble, I could ignore the passing of time and inevitable return to school.

The morning of Monday 5th January started off with a small but pleasant surprise. I came downstairs to find Dad standing in front of the worktop making a pot of tea.

"Thought I'd give you a lift to school this mornin' so you don't have to rush." Lighting the gas on the eye level grill he went on to ask, "Do you want some toast? I'm havin' some."

With my first smile of the day, I replied, yes please I would.

"Do you want some of this lovely beef drippin'? That's what I'm havin' on mine." He stuck a knife into the dish of solidified animal fat and exposed the dark brown jelly underneath it.

"Look at that, bloody lovely!" he exclaimed.

After our breakfast, accompanied for Dad by a cup of strong builder's tea with four sugars and three cigarettes and a glass of orange squash for me, we got in the car to drive to school. Without looking at me, Dad asked,

"You looin' forward to seein' your mates again then?"

I mumbled what I hoped was a non committal 'mm... .' and just looked out of the window.

As most pupils used the back gate, when Dad dropped me off at the front of the school, there were very few people around, just a small group of first years. Pulling up the handbrake but not turning off the engine, he asked,

"Do you want me to pick you up at four o'clock love?"

"No thanks, I'll be alright." I knew he would really prefer to be having his afternoon catch-up nap at that time.

"Right then darlin', have a nice day and we'll see you for your tea then."

We both smiled at each other as, clutching my heavy basket, I got out of the car, took a deep breath and walked determinedly towards the school gates.

The whistle went as I walked around to the playground, so I didn't see any of the usual suspects until I got into the cloakroom. As I hung up my coat, I felt someone come and stand close behind me, just a split second before I heard her voice.

"Hi ya Kim, did you have a nice Christmas?"

Turning round and mustering as much joviality as I could, I replied,

"Yes thanks Diane, did you?"

"Oh it was really good thanks." I picked up my basket and turned to see she was on her own. We started walking towards the form room for registration and she continued talking to me, seeming eager to tell me about her Christmas.

"I got a new record player and loads of good presents and I went to Kenny's house and met his Mum and Dad!"

"Great!"

I tried to enthuse back. I had to admire her guile, she had barely spoken to me for most of the last term and had made no secret of whispering about me behind my back.

"Where's Sharon?" I asked.

"Oh she's about somewhere, we walked in together. Did your cousin come and stay with you over Christmas?" she asked quite quickly as we got to the classroom door.

"No," I smiled at her, "I was all on my own, why?"

"Oh just wondered, you know."

And yes I did know. Spotting Sharon, she scuttled off over to her. I looked across briefly to see the two of them and Maureen, heads together deep in conversation. I had almost forgotten about Ali's phone call and hadn't spoken to her since Christmas to find out if Paul had gone to Sheffield but guessed, from that little exchange, that he had. Sharon didn't look too happy, so maybe he had dumped her. I had my second smile of the day.

After registration and dinner money collection, I was asked by Mr Lloyd to go to the headmaster's office straight away and take my bag with me. Instantly concerned that I was in trouble with no idea why but also with a surge of relief at missing the start of the maths lesson, I was unsure of what facial expression to wear. I felt thirty-six pairs of eyes on me as I left the classroom and walked down the corridor to the offices. The school secretary sat at her desk clacking away on her Olivetti typewriter. She looked up as I stood in the open doorway.

"Kimberly Asquith?" She raised her eyebrows to confirm it was a question.

"Yes Miss."

"Take a seat outside Mr Wedaburn's office and he'll call you in when he's ready."

Following her instructions, I sat down. The door opened almost straight away and Jane's Dad, Don, came out. After shaking hands with the headmaster and aiming a brief nod in my direction, he marched off down the corridor.

"Come on in Kimberly." Mr Wedaburn's voice seemed slightly warmer than normal and even though I was confused, I started to feel a little less scared as I stood up and went into his office.

There were three other people already in there, sitting to the side of the large and almost empty desk. I felt my face break into a smile at the sight of Jane who sat in the middle of Miss Tempest, the deputy head, and another woman who I had never seen before. Indicated a single chair in front of the desk.

"Sit down please."

As I sat, I stole a glance across at Jane who was looking down at her American tan tights and my first thought was that she must have grown as her skirt looked a bit short. Mr Wedaburn sat in his big important chair and took a deep breath. He informed me that Jane would be coming back to school as of today, brushing over the reason for her absence and referring to her stay with her grandparents as a holiday. Miss Tempest, after a pause in his narrative and nod from him, went on to inform me that it was important that Jane should feel supported and for this they were relying on me. As her friend, I could make sure that she would be able to slip back into life at Hill Topp seamlessly. The word 'seamlessly' made me think of needlework lessons and my complete lack of ability. I said nothing but was wondering if I was the right person to perform anything seamlessly. I tried to take a quick peek at my friend from the corner of my eye. I thought I caught a fleeting conspiratorial smile touch her lips before her face regained its serious expression. She seemed to be scrutinising the thick nylon denier covering her legs. I nodded my agreement to absolutely step up to the plate and mumbled the 'Yes Miss' and 'Yes Sir' when required which seemed to satisfy them. I was dismissed to wait outside while Mrs Harding, who was the other woman, had a few more things to say to Jane before we could go back to class. Mrs Harding obviously had a great deal to say as it was another fifteen minutes before Jane was led out by Miss Tempest. We were told to go and sit in the hall until the bell went for the next lesson and then to continue as normal. The day just seemed to be getting better and better. Toast and dripping for breakfast, completely missing Monday morning maths and getting my friend back.

We had ten minutes before the bell to start to catch up, after a big hug. She told me that the time with her grandparents was awful. She'd been made to go to the local school at the end of the road from her granny's house and she had hated it. Kevin and David had been sent to different children's homes in an effort to control them. She'd heard that David was now with foster parents but Kevin was still in the home and really playing up. There was no chance of them coming home just yet as her Dad couldn't cope with them. Mrs Harding was a social worker. She was ok and meant well but didn't have a clue. I told her what I'd heard about her Dad beating up Iain and putting him in hospital and the police being annoyed that Iain insisted it wasn't his Dad. Her face went pink with a flush of anger as she said,

"You mean Harry fuckin' Henshaw was annoyed. God, I hate that bastard!"

I must have flushed too at her words as her laugh washed away her anger.

"There's so much I need to tell you but it'll have to wait. It's all a bit of a mess still."

We hugged again and I told her I'd got a fair bit to tell her too, although my stuff was nowhere near as important as hers. I'd missed her so much, I thought I was going to start blubbing.

"Well I'm back now and not intending to get sent away again so you don't have to worry. So just give me the need to know stuff till we can talk properly later."

So I blurted out,

"Diane and Sharon are not my friends anymore, I went to Chris Henshaw's birthday party, he asked me out and I said no, he's now going out with a new girl in our class called Maureen who is best friends with

Diane and Sharon, my parents are letting me go out a bit more at weekends and I've got the lead in the school play."

"Bloody hell Kim, I've only been gone eleven weeks. I thought you'd 'ave been sitting at home pining for me to come back not causing all this havoc!"

Her friendly sarcasm was like a soothing balm to my ears as I concluded, to her astonishment,

"Oh yes, and I got to know Chris when he saved my life, during half term in Gibson's tannery."

"Well, we really have got some catching up to do."

The bell sounded.

"We'll have to wait till break, although I know that's not going to be long enough. Tell me what's happened with Shaz and Di though and what lesson is it now?"

We stood up and started making our way along the corridor back into the main school.

"It's science. I'm not really sure why they've fallen out with me but I think it's something to do with this friend of Chris's that she's been going out with, but I think he's just dumped her for my cousin Alison."

"Honestly Kim, I can't leave you for two minutes without a drama unfolding around you," she laughed. "Well let's see if they're still friends with me then."

As we walked through the cloak room passing a huddle of first years on their way to their next lesson, I noticed her skirt again.

"Your skirt is really short; I'm surprised Miss Tempest didn't say anything."

"She will, don't worry. I could see her staring at my legs all the time I was in Weddo's office. She was dying to get her tape measure out to give her a chance to touch my legs!" she laughed. "I've got it rolled up, see."

She lifted her jumper to show the thick rolled up waistband.

"I'm just testing the boundaries today; see how far I can go before they stop *'supportin''* me!"

We'd just arrived at the science lab, so I didn't have a chance to answer. I was totally distracted by the look on Sharon's face as we walked in together smiling. She was sitting at the bench where we all used to sit but Maureen had taken my place, leaving a seat spare. For a split second I though Jane was going to sit with them but she stopped at the end of the row and looked at me, a question in her eyes. I moved my eyes to two rows behind, where Suzanne sat alone. Jane nodded her approval and walked smiling to sit next to my new classmate leaving me the seat on the end next to her. As I sat down, she whispered,

"Seamless!"

We both smiled as we took our books out of our baskets.

After the lesson it was morning break and as we filed out, Sharon waited by the door to step into line between Jane and me.

"Hi Jane, it's great that you're back!"

She turned her back on me, blocking the doorway completely as she went on,

"There's loads to tell you and I'm havin' a party on Saturday night. If you can come, it'd be ace!"

"I hear there's been a lot goin' on," Jane said, then asked "Is it your birthday then?"

"Yes, it's on Sunday."

"Right, well I'll let you know."

Putting her arm out to push Sharon to one side she looked at me and raised her voice slightly,

"You goin' Kim?"

"Goin' where?" I asked with the pretence of not having heard what had been said.

"To Shazza's birthday party on Saturday night." She smiled innocently at Sharon.

"Not been invited," I said suddenly feeling brave as I edged past

Sharon with a polite excuse me and started to walk off. I was aware that Sharon was speaking but didn't wait around to hear what she was saying. Jane was beside me a few seconds later.

"I think you'd better start telling me what's been happening while I've been locked up at me grannies, my stuff can wait," she said as we collected our coats and went outside.

The fifteen minute morning break was nowhere near long enough to tell her everything but I made a start, attempting to be as succinct as possible. I started by telling her about calling for her on that Saturday, briefly mentioning Alison. She said she was sitting on the sofa when I'd come to the door. Her Dad had just been telling her that she was going to stay at her Gran's and was annoyed that he was interrupted. He didn't have anything against me, so I shouldn't take it personally. I didn't mention his lie that she'd already gone and I left out going to Charlie's for chips. I did tell her about calling for Sharon and discovering that she'd gone to Leeds with Diane and that I'd been peeved by this.

"Well Shaz has never really liked you, you must have noticed that?" she said.

I told her I'd no idea and asked her why she didn't like me. She shrugged and said she was jealous of me being Mr Lloyd's favourite. I started to say I wasn't his favourite but decided against it as we both knew I clearly was. I got to the bit about taking Ali into the tannery to have a look round. Forgetting totally about being succinct I explained about my fall and getting lodged upside down in the mechanism of the washing pit. I'd just got as far as the next day at the park when the whistle went to signify the end of break. We had an hour and fifteen minutes of home economics to get through before dinnertime. I was still apprehensive of how Sharon would behave but determined not to be cowed by her. We joined the back of the queue outside the locked classroom and Jane leaned towards me and whispered,

"That Maureen girl really doesn't like you either does she? Look at the daggers she's giving you!"

I looked down the line to see Maureen staring at me while Sharon was saying something in her ear. I could see something close to hatred in her face as she glared at me. I looked away quickly feeling the blood rush up to my face.

"Don't worry," Jane said softly, pushing her way forward while holding on to my wrist and pulling me behind her. "She just needs to learn some manners."

She stopped just in front of the new girl, her face so close to hers that she must have been standing on her toes. Maureen flinched slightly and leaned back a little but as Sharon was right behind her there was nowhere for her to go. Jane spoke in a tone so chilling I drew in my breath.

"Didn't your mother ever tell you it's rude to stare?"

There was silence in the corridor as everyone stopped chatting and watched to see what would happen next. What did happen was the door opened and we were ushered in by Mrs Morgan. Still holding on to my wrist, Jane pulled me past Maureen and Sharon so that we entered the room first.

"Ah Jane."

The warm and friendly voice exuding the message '*I want to be your friend as well as your teacher.*'

"Seamless," she whispered again in my ear.

Mrs Morgan came up close to her and gave her the full force of her welcoming smile.

"I heard you were back, good to see you." Turning to the class, smile back on low to medium, "Now class, today we will be talking about the different food groups so please get yourselves into groups of three."

Jane and I left the home economics class quickly as the dinnertime bell went and Suzanne, who had been in our group, hurried along with us to get in for first sitting. The rest of our table of ten were first years and so of course we took no notice of them. Jane was asking Suzanne about her pet budgerigars and telling her that her grandmother had one but she'd never had a pet of her own.

"They're great company and so loving," Suzanne enthused.

Concentrating on my plastic-plated meal while I tried to chew the overcooked chicken helped me to dispel all thoughts of Suzanne's budgie. All the time she was talking at length about how her budgie, Joey, would sit on the side of her plate and peck at her food which she seemed to think was not only acceptable but also cute. Jane, however, was really involved in this conversation.

"Lucy, my Gran's budgie was the only one what talked any sense in that house!"

"Kim's scared of birds," Suzanne informed Jane, "She nearly let our Joey escape, running out of the room when she came round to meet him."

She looked across at me with a mix of pity and accusation.

"I've never had a bird land on my head before with its spiky claws," I began in my defense, "and as they are the only living creature still directly descended from dinosaurs I think I'm absolutely right to be scared of them!"

After dinner Suzanne went back to the form room as she always did, to catch up on her homework. Jane and I went round to the fire escape by the science labs. Sitting on the damp and cold steps next to each other, I got a surge of emotion and before I could stop myself blurted out,

"I'm so glad you're back!"

She smiled and nodded.

"So am I and it looks like I'm back in the nick of time to save you from being turned into a budgie lover."

"I don't think there is any danger of that and anyway what about you and your new best friend Lucy?"

"I was just sayin' that. Sooz is alright an she doesn't have many friends or people to talk to does she? See I was just playin' nice, I can do that you know. I actually bloody hated that bird of me grannies. I think Lucy is short for Lucifer!"

"Do you want to talk about what happened with you?" I asked.

"No, not yet."

"Okay then, I'll finish telling you about my brief experience of having a social life then."

I spent the remaining forty-five minutes telling her about the half term excursions, Chris's party and Sharon turning on me. She listened, nodding her head occasionally and narrowing her eyes but said nothing until I told her about Ali's phone-call and her telling me about Paul dumping Sharon.

"Well, you have to phone your cousin tonight and find out if he went to meet her."

I nodded my agreement and she asked,

"If she invited you, would you go to her party on Saturday?"

"Oh! I don't know!" I was flustered. "Will you be allowed to go?"

"Not a problem, I'll be allowed to do what I want from now on!"

"Oh, really? Right, well if you were there, yeah, I'd go but she'll not invite me."

"Oh I think she will."

"Ok then but I'm not getting her a present!"

"Right then, let's get this sorted," she said, standing up as the whistle went for afternoon classes.

Chapter Thirteen

I don't remember all our afternoon classes that day but I remember we had Religious Education with Mr Roberts for last lesson. As we walked between classrooms, I asked Jane,

"Did they make you apologise to him for swearing?"

"They tried to at first but gave up when I showed them the bruises on my arms where he grabbed hold of me. I said my Dad would call the police when he saw them."

She spoke quite matter-of-factly and I was suddenly stopped in my tracks.

"Oh God, I hadn't realised he'd hurt you so much, oh Jane!"

"Yeah, well he did!" she said defensively but was stopped from saying anything else by Eric Moody pushing past us.

"I bet Robbo's really looking forward to seein' you again Skofey!"

His words were shouted for the benefit of his guffawing mates and undoubtedly with the hope that Mr Roberts was sitting at his desk. He wasn't. Walking into the empty classroom behind Jane, I was surprised to see her sit down at a front desk and sat next to her. When Mr Roberts came in a few minutes later, the whole class held its breath. He must have felt the atmosphere as he walked in but it was probably the never before experienced silent class that unnerved him the most. Walking through the charged anticipation, without looking at the assembled class, he put his books on his desk and he spoke without focus, in a low monotonous voice,

"Right 2B open your text books on page 28 and read the passages A and B, to yourselves, not out loud, and answer all the questions in that section in your exercise book."

Having avoided any eye contact whatsoever, he turned his back on us and began writing on the blackboard. The sound of rustling and chairs scraping as we got out our books only seemed to enhance the silence. Mr Roberts' hand moved carefully across the blackboard as he confirmed in large white letters what we were expected to do. As he finished chalking he turned around and Jane's hand shot up in the air.

"Sir!"

Everyone froze, Robbo in mid stride back to his desk. Jane's voice again with arm raised higher, hand waving now to amplify her presence.

"Please Sir!"

"Yes, Jane?"

His voice was sharp and suspicious, as if he'd been waiting for her to ambush him.

"Sir, I haven't got a text book."

"What?"

His voice raised and his face flushed, it was clear for all to see that he was fighting to remain calm. I quickly realised he thought she had deliberately not brought her book so I shouted out,

"Jane wasn't here when you gave them out sir. She can share mine if you don't have a spare one."

His fear was palpable. He was afraid of losing control and was visibly shaking.

"Right, well yes, you can you share with Kimberly for now. I'll get you a copy of your own for next week."

The rest of the class went without issue but I noticed during the whole forty-five minutes of the lesson that Mr Lloyd and Mr Macdonald hovered around outside in tag team fashion.

When we walked across the playground to go home that evening Suzanne was again talking to Jane about her Joey and saying that she could call in anytime after school if she wanted to see him. I was silent, thinking of the devil budgie at her Gran's and imagining a pair of red horns on top of his green feathered head. I didn't notice the little huddle of people chatting by the gates until we were almost next to them. It was Maureen, Chris and Diane. My heart sank with heavy expectancy of unpleasantness. Maureen said something to Chris, obviously about us, and nudged him forward slightly. Jane was still laughing about some budgie antic as she quickened her pace to forge slightly ahead and veered towards them.

"Christopher Henshaw!"

This in her cheery matey voice but giving him time only to nod a response before going on, "What have you and your mean-faced girlfriend got against my friend Kim then? Starting some spiteful vendetta against her, like your Dad did with my family?"

"No!" He looked panicked. "I've got nothing against Kim."

I saw the softness around his eyes as he shot me a glance.

"Nothing at all," he repeated "Kim's my friend as well."

It was like he'd just made up his mind, saying it like a declaration but he immediately lowered his eyes after speaking.

"That's all alright then cos we're all getting together on Saturday night at Sharon's party and I'd hate for anything to spoil it for her."

"Are you and Kim going?"

Chris's face lit up with the question, Maureen's face darkened. Diane and Suzanne were smiling, probably just enjoying the show. I tried to keep my face without emotion. Jane was beaming,

"Yeah course we are, the old gang back together again."

Chris and I exchanged the briefest of eye contact as I moved away with Jane and Suzanne to start walking down the hill. Suzanne lived just round the corner from the school and I'd got into the habit of walking with her during Jane's absence. Now I was really pleased that it seemed we would continue to do this. As we got to her gate she said,

"You know everything was all right without boys but as soon as they come along everybody starts to fall out with everybody else. They're nowt but trouble. Anyway see you both tomorrow, don't forget it's needlework Kim, so bring your magnet as old Aveyard will probably have you on the floor picking up pins again."

Suzanne was always so much wiser than her years.

That night I phoned Alison and the next morning as we walked to school, I relayed what I'd learned to Jane. Paul had been to see her. He'd bought her a milkshake in the Wimpy bar and told her he'd never stopped thinking about her. He'd also written to her since and so, according to my hopelessly romantic cousin, they were now going steady.

"So what's he like then this Paul?"

"Well he's quite good looking an a bit cocky but he's really funny."

"Right."

She seemed to be somewhere else for a few seconds, staring into space, before changing the subject, asking me how my skirt was coming on in needlework.

As we got into our form room for registration, Sharon came over to my desk and with her crocodile smile invited me to her party. I accepted although I still had mixed feelings. Jane was in a buoyant mood and kept telling me it was going to be brilliant. She was so upbeat and happy, I couldn't help but feel the same. Even the dreaded double needlework that afternoon passed without too much trauma, so as we walked home we talked about what we would wear. I had a new, well new to me, purple maxi dress with a lace-up bodice that Sally had brought round after Christmas. I'd been swirling in it in my bedroom wondering if I'd get a chance to wear it. Jane said she'd got a few new things so I suggested she could come round on Saturday morning to show me and let me help her choose what to wear.

"Will that be ok? I mean, your parents won't think I've come to rob their safe?"

"Yeah, it'll be fine," I said in a tone more confident than I felt adding, "I think they've been worried about me not going out and being so fed up lately. They're trying a bit harder to be normal and help me fit in."

Knowing about how Dad always insisted that I leave well before the end of parties, she suggested I say the party finished at eleven and not half past ten as Sharon had previously informed us. As it transpired, because Sharon only lived a short walk away, it was agreed that Jane and I would walk back to the Unicorn together for half past ten where Jane's Dad would be waiting to take her home. They were fine about Jane coming round on Saturday too, in fact Mum even asked if she'd like to stay and have a *'bit of dinner'* with us as her Dad was no doubt in the pub.

Mum called us down for dinner at about half past twelve and we had tinned ham sandwiches on white bread with tomato sauce. Pretending it was normal and we did it every day, she produced tinned peaches with carnation milk for a pudding, served in her best glass bowls.

"Thank you Mrs. Asquith, this is lovely."

As she said this, I was instantly panicked and looked quickly at Mum for her reaction to these polite words of thanks. Jane's appreciation had been sincere but I wondered if Mum would find this objectionable, as she had with Alison.

"You're very welcome flower," was her response and she beamed with an air of someone who had just produced a banquet and not just opened a couple of tins and spread some bread with butter. "Glad you enjoyed it."

After the feast, we returned to my room for a further hour until Jane had to go home.

We agreed that she should wear a lovely orange psychedelic midi dress she'd bought in a post-Christmas shopping trip with her Dad. She had a choice of three dresses all new and equally lovely and offered to let me borrow one of them. Given her petite and slim frame, I raised my eyebrows at her to highlight the impossibility of my taller and slightly chubby body fitting into any of her clothes. Telling me that my chosen purple outfit was lovely and I looked lovely, she left me some of her lilac eye-shadow. After she'd gone I was lounging around in my room daydreaming when Mum came in. She started to move things round on my dressing table as if that was the reason she'd come up before starting the conversation she wanted,

"How is she copin' being back home with her Dad then?"

"Alright."

I was instantly suspicious and picked up a copy of Jackie to give me something to focus on.

"Has she said anything about what happened with 'er Dad an' 'er brother?"

I didn't take my eyes from the magazine as I answered.

"No. She doesn't want to talk about it."

"Aye, well I don't blame 'er,"

She was hovering round the door now realising I either knew nothing or wasn't going to share if I did.

"Well any road she's a nice lass and me an' your Dad are glad she's back an' you've got your smile back again."

And with that proclamation of approval she went back downstairs.

We'd arranged to meet at the end of Sharon's street at seven, so just before, I hurried along in my black patent boots, holding up my dress and a card with a ten shilling record token. Mum had insisted that I couldn't go to someone's birthday party without a gift. As I turned into the road I could see a group of people on the entrance to the cul-de-sac where Sharon lived. Getting closer I could see Jane, Chris, Kenny and Paul.

"Aye up Kimbo. Long time no see!"

Paul's jovial voice rang out with friendly amusement.

"Hello Paul, has Sharon invited you to her party?"

My voice betraying the incredulity of this. He just laughed and said,

"I'm surprised she's invited you!"

"He's not been invited but he seems to think Sharon will be okay with him coming anyway," Chris said, in a tone displaying his annoyance.

"It's her birthday and she really wants me here, you'll see," Paul beamed.

"I spoke to Alison the other day!" I blurted out, thinking he was way too sure of himself but he just laughed.

"Ah your pretty little cousin. What a lovely lass!"

"Are you going out with her?" I demanded.

"Ali is more of a pen pal. I'm not going out with anyone just now." Looking briefly over at Chris, he added, "In case you're interested!"

Jane who seemed to have been finding this interaction quite amusing broke in,

"Come on then let's get inside, I'm freezing here."

"Do you know Paul and Kenny?" I whispered as we followed them up the drive.

"They were at my junior school and Paul used to go to football with our David." Pausing for a second for me to absorb that, she chuckled. "Before they got arrested that is. Paul's Mam's not a big fan of our family."

"They got arrested?" I exclaimed in a loud whisper. Jane shushed even louder, so I asked again as quietly as I could,

"Your David and Paul, this Paul, got arrested?"

"Yeah, it were at Elland Road. Criminal damage or somat like that. They damaged a road sign, it weren't anything really bad but they had to go to court. Paul's Mam gave him hell and said he wasn't to go near our David again."

She chuckled again as if this was a really funny story and stepped up the pace down the garden path. Sharon's parents opened the door, both wearing their coats and smiling.

"Come in, come in," Mr Weldon chimed drawing us into their large tidy kitchen. "The birthday girl is just finishing her beautification and will be down in a minute."

Beaming at us, he ushered us through to the sitting room where a couple of people from our class were already standing.

"So, hello everyone, I'm Geoff and this is Barbara, Sharon's Mum."

His introduction of his wife was accompanied by a flourishing hand gesture and the words were still on his lips as a very flushed and heavily made-up Sharon burst into the room with Maureen and Diane in her wake.

"Haven't you gone out yet?" she asked rudely.

She was clearly cross and embarrassed at her father's attempts to welcome us. His wife immediately turned to give her daughter a *just who d'you think you're talking to young lady?'* look as she answered,

"We're just off and as discussed, we're trusting you to behave like sensible teenagers. There's cider over by the sink but it is the only alcohol allowed in the house and no one is to get silly or sick with it!" Her eyes swept the room but went back to settle on the birthday girl as she concluded, "We'll be back at ten thirty and expect the house to be in the same condition we are leaving it in. Clear?" Mrs. Weldon was clearly not as happy about the party as her husband seemed to be.

"Yes Mum, course. Have a nice time."

There seemed no question that Sharon's Mum was the boss. We all smiled and nodded our agreement as Mr Weldon moved to the front door with an air of reluctance. Opening it, he was clearly delighted to see three more guests.

"Welcome!" he boomed, clearly not able to resist the role of greeter. Waving his arms flamboyantly he looked like he was about to start introducing himself again. His wife pushed him aside allowing Julie, Wendy and Peter from the drama group across the threshold muttering sharply,

"Come on Geoff, let's get to the pub, I need a drink."

As the door shut behind them Sharon immediately burst into life saying hi, taking her cards and presents and firing instructions to Maureen and Diane to put on music and pour some cider. The rest of us were instructed to remove our coats, which she took and dumped on a chair in the kitchen. Her eyes had an excited twinkle as she clocked Paul and she seemed a little giddy. I wondered if she'd started on the cider already.

Julie, Peter and Wendy produced a bottle of sherry which they proceeded to pour into cups and topped up with cider and lemonade. Jane and I were the only ones that refused the cocktail and the cider, pouring ourselves a cup of dandelion and burdock from the kitchen bar. After an awkward half an hour or so of Diane, Maureen and Sharon trying to get everyone to dance, Paul suggested a game of charades and my eagerness to play masked my relief as Paul took to the floor. We played for about an hour and the effects of the alcohol increased the volume and animation as everyone threw themselves into the game. Maureen stayed close to Chris throughout, using the excuse of getting more crisps to get up and take a seat or position next to him after either of them had had a turn.

Sharon was beaming openly and loudly calling out encouragement to Paul, each time he had a turn. Half an hour into the game, I noticed him whispering with Jane, their heads close and felt a panic as I saw Sharon notice this. The constant swapping of seats as people got up for their turn finally gave Sharon the chance to squeeze next to him on the sofa, midway through my mime of *The Sound of Music*. The sherry and cider mix must have made her quite brave as I saw her nuzzle up to him and try to take hold of his hand. Paul guessed my charade and stood up letting Sharon fall sideways into the middle of the settee. Undaunted, she rolled forward on to the floor laughing quite loudly before going to the kitchen and coming back with a very full cup. Jane guessed Paul's mime of '*Frankenstein Must be Destroyed*', much to everyone's amazement.

She stood up to have her turn and Paul sat in her place next to me. Sharon finished her drink and pushing her way through the room made a quite dramatic exit through the door to the upstairs. Glaring at me, Maureen got up and went after her. Jane ignored these activities and proceeded to do some very elaborate gestures to her mime of 'Lady Chatterley's Lover'. Lots of loud shouting and laughing and general enjoyment was in the room so it took a few minutes before anyone realised Maureen was leaning round the door calling to Diane to come up stairs. Wendy eventually guessed correctly but didn't get up, she just asked,

"Is there any more punch left Pete?"

"There's a bit, shall I get you some?"

"Yeah, I'll have some. Shall we put a record on now?"

Jane suggested that she and I go in the kitchen and finish off the fabulous beef and onion crisps that had been put in a big bowl on the table. As we stood munching this new flavour, we decided unanimously that although it was only twenty past nine, it might be a good idea for us to leave. So grabbing our coats we opened the door as quietly as we could to set off back to the Unicorn.

I took Jane via our house through the store-room and into the pub where Dad was leaning on the bar chatting to Don who was nursing a pint. Dad offered to give them a lift home but Don declined saying it 'weren't rainin' and so they'd be fine.

After they'd gone I went back into the house to get ready for bed, thinking about what we'd talked about on the way home. We'd linked arms as we walked along the frosty pavement and I started the conversation with,

"I don't know what that Maureen's problem is."

"It's you; you're a boyfriend stealer, first Chris and now Paul!" My friend laughed.

"Me! It's you that Paul fancies not me."

She seemed to find this really funny.

"Paul dun't fancy me. He'd be too scared to even think about it and for two very good reasons."

"Which are what?"

"Firstly his mother, the stuck up, spiteful old bitch would go mental at him if he went out with me, he's not supposed to even look at anybody in my family." She paused and with a throaty chuckle added,

"And secondly, he's met my Dad!"

Chapter Fourteen

Going back to school on the Monday after the party, I was worried how it would be. When I expressed my concern to Jane as we walked up the hill that morning, she said she'd a feeling there wouldn't be a problem. I told her how nasty Sharon had been while she was away and wondered if the way we'd left the party would start her off again. Stopping and putting down her heavy basket she said,

"Maybe she'll be a bit funny with us for a day or two but what does it matter? She's not a good friend anyway. She's actually a bit like a wasp, buzzing around and being annoying. So stop worrying." Picking up her things she smiled and we set off again, adding, "Anyway how come you never told me Mr Lloyd drinks in the Unicorn and is best mates with your Dad?" The grin on her face highlighted her teasing and started our conversation about the school play.

Spotting Sharon at the school gates, I took a deep breath. She was standing with Diane and looking in our direction. As we got closer she smiled broadly calling,

"Hi ya!"

"You waiting for us?" Jane wanted to know, head on one side.

"Oh no, not really. It was a good party on Saturday wasn't it?" Sharon spoke but both of them were smiling at us like their life depended on it.

"Yeah, it was great, thanks for inviting us."

"Did you enjoy it Kim?"

"Yeah, thanks, it were ace."

"Shame you had to leave early, it really got going after you'd gone."

"Oh well, I'm glad you had a nice time," I said feebly and Jane nodded.

"Yeah, see you later."

She nudged me as we walked towards the playground and away from them.

"There you go. She needs us to think the party really got going after we'd gone. She doesn't want us to know that everybody except Diane went home about ten minutes after us. Silly cow!"

"What! How do you know that?"

"Me an' Dad passed them all at the end of Town Street waiting for the bus. Thought Paul was gonna shit his self when Dad nodded at him as we passed."

We never let on to Sharon that we knew and were surprised that Maureen, who was also was at the bus stop, had chosen not to tell her either. Instead, we just raised our eyebrows and smiled when she mentioned it from time to time over the next few days.

Mr Lloyd gave Jane a part as an extra in the play and much to Sharon's annoyance, he gave her a line to say. On the first rehearsal she attended, Jane pointedly announced,

"Course, I only got the line cos me Dad's big mates with Mr Lloyd."

That week's drama club was rehearsals and I was on stage for most of it. Sharon and Diane were backstage involved in the set arrangement and costumes. Diane was doing this because she much preferred the stage management part but Sharon just wanted to big-up her involvement. I was in my element, especially now Jane was back and I was completely word perfect with still six weeks before the performance.

I was whizzing through my lines, basking in Mr Lloyd's smiles and nods when, just outside my peripheral vision, I noticed Jane at the back of the hall deep in conversation with Chris. This threw me momentarily and I forgot my line. Seeing Mr Lloyd's frown I stammered the next line, freezing again. I could still see them talking quite animatedly in what looked like an argument. My concentration completely gone, I missed my prompt and Mr Lloyd asked if I was ok. I nodded but he suggested a few minutes break. He came on stage to ask if I was getting nervous and I said I was a bit but I just needed a drink. All the time, I was trying to see behind him but Jane and Chris had disappeared. I went down to sit next to Wendy Shaw, who was the prompt, to pretend to check my lines and drink my squash. It was a good five minutes before Jane came back in to the hall and sat beside me.

"What have I missed?"

"Kim's just had her first bout of nerves."

Wendy stated her perspective on what had occurred. I looked to the back of the hall and back at my friend before asking,

"Where've you been?"

"Just to the loo. Are we havin' a break then?"

And that was it. She didn't mention Chris that evening either as we walked home, or the next day as we walked back. So I filed it away, trying not to worry about what might be happening and why she didn't tell me.

At the end of the dinner break the next day, Sharon came over to us in the cloakroom. She was keen to tell us that she'd decided not to get back with Paul. He wanted to of course, he'd begged her, but she really wasn't interested. She'd met someone at the Pavilion a couple of weeks ago called Wayne. He lived in Pudsey and went to a different school and was absolutely gorgeous, much better looking than Paul.

"You two should come along this Saturday, he's got loads of mates."

Jane shrugged and was about to speak when Sharon added that Diane and Maureen were going and probably Kenny and Chris, as if this might make it more appealing to us. I was about to say we'd got other plans but Jane got there first.

"That would be good but Kim and me have something on tomorrow. Mebbe another week." She walked off towards the form room with me scurrying after her, whispering my question.

"Are we going into Leeds?"

"No, but you should tell your Mum and Dad we are."

"Ok, but where are we off to?"

She leaned forward to whisper her reply, her face lighting up with the promise of something exciting.

"Rodley canal but don't tell anybody!"

"Oh no, god I can't go there, I'm not allowed. My Mum will go mad."

"That's why you should tell her we're going to Leeds!"

Taking her seat at her desk she started to swap her books for the afternoon lessons while giving me one of her *for goodness sake Kim stop being such a wuss'* looks.

"Why are we going to the canal?"

"We're off fishing. You'll need to bring your radio."

"Fishing?" I exclaimed a little louder than I intended.

"Shhh! I don't suppose we'll do any fishing, but we'll definitely have a laugh!"

For the rest of the day she refused to enlighten me any further, just telling me to meet her at ten the next day and not to forget the radio.

The day was dry and quite bright for January but incredibly cold. Wearing my anorak, gloves and scarf I left home just before ten, carrying my canvas bag containing money, crisps and my transistor radio and allowing my parents to believe I was going into Leeds. I walked briskly towards the bus stop by the catholic school where Jane was waiting. I could see she was visibly excited and smiley. Still refusing to say why we were going, she paid my fare on the bus down to Rodley Bottom and we got off at the terminus in front of the Barge pub. My parents seemed to know every other pub landlord within a twenty mile radius, so I was keen to get past that establishment quickly. Dashing down the road and up the steps on to the canal towpath, we walked towards Horsforth Bridge. Jane was almost skipping as we got closer to the bridge and I was about to ask her what was going on when I saw them. A group of four lads with bags and fishing gear stood smoking just a way ahead of us. She'd already clocked them. One of them stepped forward, away from the group to meet us.

"Aye up our kid, how you doing?"

"David!"

Their delight at seeing each other was obvious but they were guarded in their physical contact, choosing to stand grinning at each other, respecting personal space. Glancing back to the group, I saw Paul and the two others boys shuffling their feet awkwardly as they observed this family reunion. Noticing me looking at him, he grinned and his self-assured poise returned.

"Kimbo! Come here and meet some great lads!"

Jane's assertion that we'd have a laugh was spot on and her brother wasn't half as scary as I'd thought. The other lads were Keith and Andy who were at the Grammar school with Paul. The meet-up had been arranged by Paul. Keith's parents did short term foster care and David had been placed with them since before Christmas. He'd not been allowed contact with any of his family since being removed from home when Don was arrested. Jane was already at her grandparents' by then and they'd told her that her brothers had been *shipped off to Borstal* as they were uncontrollable. She'd only learned the truth once she was back home. Both boys had been placed in two different children's homes in North Leeds that specialised in disruptive adolescents. David said the staff were heavy handed and didn't take any shit and so he'd knuckled down and behaved. He'd even started to enjoy the new school he'd been sent to and in a matter of weeks was fostered out to Mr and Mrs Wood. He'd continued to flourish in this household and had a good friendship with Keith. He'd heard that Kevin had a different coping strategy. The regimented and at times brutal form of discipline had the opposite effect on him and he was permanently in trouble for fighting and causing trouble, when he wasn't absconding, and soon deemed completely out of control. David had no idea where he was now and said he didn't really care. Jane asked him quietly as we walked along the bank if he knew where Iain was. I glanced across at them as David just shook his head and muttered something I didn't catch. She nodded and they continued to walk in silence until Keith stopped and started to unpack his bag.

"Right, this is the place."

Two rugs, four small stools and a large umbrella were assembled close to the edge of the bank and we made our little camp.

"How do you know this is the place?" I wanted to know.

"Cos we needed to be well away from the road noise of the bridge and somewhere where there's not a lot of weed. This is defo the place."

Keith had a lovely twinkle in his eyes as he spoke with friendly authority. While they erected our fishing base, Jane and I stood back on the path to keep out of their way. I asked her how Paul had sorted out this arrangement.

"He came round to our house and told me Dad our David wanted to see me," she said and, seeing my incredulity, just burst out laughing.

"Course he didn't, he's not that soft. He got Chris to tell me on Thursday while you were being all Lizzy Fry up on stage. He was right narky about it though and said he won't pass on any more messages."

"Ah right."

I smiled my relief at the incident being explained.

"I'm really glad you told him to get lost when he asked you to go out with him," she said giving me a big smile before biting her bottom lip and looking across at her brother.

"It would be hard for us to be friends if you went out with him."

"Really?"

"Harry bloody Henshaw hates my Dad and will do anything to get at him."

She stated succinctly without raising her voice.

"But that's nothing to do with Chris," I began, "Chris doesn't like his

Dad either."

"You can be so dense sometimes Kim. Chris is desperate for his old man to like him. No offence but wanting to go out with you is all part of his pleasing his Dad plan and I don't fully trust him not to split on us about today either."

I was stunned.

"Look, I'm not saying he doesn't like you or anything, I just think he knows his Dad would love it if his son was going out with the lass from his favourite pub."

"But why would that make us not friends?"

"Think about it Kim, it just wouldn't work." She reached for my radio, adding a little more lightly, "Anyway, he's going out with Maureen, so it's not a problem now is it?"

We stayed on the bank watching the boys catching nothing for nearly four hours and mostly it was fun. Shortly before we left Jane and David went for a short walk on their own and when they came back they were both a little subdued. A few minutes later Paul walked some of the way back to the bus stop with us and said in a pretend matter of fact way, that didn't even lightly mask his anxiety,

"It's probably better if you don't let on you were here today Kimbo."

"Well I wasn't planning on writing an essay about it!" I answered.

"No, well Chris knew Jane were coming to see Dave and he sort of asked if you were coming and I might have said you weren't."

"Why?"

"Dunno, just dint want him to come and he might have if he knew you were coming. He wasn't happy about passing the message to Jane, somat to do with his Dad."

"He wouldn't have come anyway, he's at the pictures with Maureen."

"Yeah but he's only goin' out with her for a couple more weeks then he's gonna dump her."

"Why?"

"Cos you said you'd go out with him after your birthday and when the play were finished. He's only going out with her to make you jealous any road. "

"What!"

This time it wasn't a question. Paul looked a bit shifty and grinned,

"Probably better if you don't tell him I told you that either."

Jane grabbed my arm and started to pull me along as we had to run for the bus, leaving the four of them to continue to not catch any fish.

I asked Jane when she thought David would be coming back home; she'd been so happy about seeing him.

"I hope he never comes back," she replied. "He's so much better off with Keith's Mam and Dad. He's even liking school and talking about stopping on for his O Levels!" There was pride in her voice and seeing my look of surprise she added, "He was always the cleverest of us and probably would have done much better at Hill Topp if it weren't for our Kevin."

She looked out of the window as if processing her memories.

"Kevin and Iain were always causing trouble an fighting. Our David just went along with it so they wouldn't pick on him."

Thinking that her mood was being spoilt by her memories, I changed the subject.

"My Mam and Dad don't want me to stop on. They want me to go into hairdressing so they can buy me a shop."

"Do you want to be a hairdresser?"

"No. I think I'd like an office job or somat like that. I want to do me O Levels and then decide."

"You should do that then. I'm leaving as soon as I can. I'm gonna be a nanny."

"Really?"

It seemed this was a day full of revelations. She'd never shown the slightest hint of being interested in children.

"Do you like kids then?"

"Not really but nanny's are mostly live-in which is what I need. Our David wants to work in a bank; our Kevin will probably end up robbing one!"

Mum and Dad were shutting up for the afternoon as I got home. The night before, there'd been a very late lock-in so all they wanted to do was have an hours sleep before the Saturday night session. I made a sandwich and ate it front of the telly processing what I had learnt when something occurred to me. In the two weeks she'd been back at school Jane hadn't mentioned her Mum once. I wondered if she'd started to accept that she wasn't coming back. As I munched my potted meat sandwich, I speculated on what David might have told her when they'd gone for a short walk on their own. Maybe he knew something about her Mum's disappearance. He'd told her something that had upset her. We could all see that she'd been crying, her lovely long eyelashes still glistening and the hint of mascara she'd been wearing had made dark shadows under her eyes. I started thinking about Chris and in particular what Paul had said. I found myself thinking about him differently and admitting to myself that Jane had a point. I became annoyed thinking about the way he'd been blanking me for the last couple of months and how I'd been struggling to be his friend, let alone his girlfriend. And what if it was true that he only wanted to go out with me to please his Dad?

Sandwich finished, I wiped my hands on my trousers and reached for my latest copy of Jackie. I read through the problem pages to find other people's tales of woe and gave up worrying about mine.

Chapter Fifteen

Next on that year's event calendar was Maureen's birthday. Having not learnt the lessons from Sharon's disaster night, she decided to have a party. She invited almost everybody, with the exception of Jane and me, and was full of it for weeks, going to great lengths to make sure we knew the guest list was massive. Watching her hamming up her concern about how all these people would actually fit in her house made me realise just how lucky we were she wasn't in the drama club.

Diane and Sharon kept up their friendly pretence while remaining firmly in the Maureen camp. Chris now smiled at me whenever we passed and occasionally stopped to ask how the play was going. As he was no longer involved in the passing of information between David and Jane, she always seemed to find something much more interesting in the other direction, walking off the minute she saw him. The new go between for them was Lorraine Brookes, a first year, who lived next door to the Woods family. David and Keith asked her to seek Jane out the week after the fishing trip and she began delivering notes and messages weekly, mainly on a Friday during the morning break. I stayed in the form room during these assignations and chatted to Suzanne.

I continued to be impressed with Suzy. She was at ease with who she was and completely self-reliant. Party invites were of no interest either way, citing these gatherings as the cause of so much stress and unhappiness. On the day Maureen flitted around the form room issuing her largess, Suzy shuffled uncomfortably in her seat in total confusion, looking at the envelope in front of her. Maureen beamed at her and said,

"I hope you can come Suzanne, it's gonna be a great night!"

The day before the party, we were finishing our maths homework in the form room during the dinnertime break when I asked her if she'd decided what she was wearing for the party.

"I'm not going," she said without looking up from her trigonometry.

"Really. Why not?"

"Well she only asked me to get at you and I reckon it'll be rubbish anyway."

Her voice full of grown-up certainty, I was even more in awe of her.

"There's a teenagers' disco at Pudsey baths tomorrow night so all the third an' forth years she's invited will be off there."

Back then, in the winter months, a few of the local swimming baths closed for the season and to retain an income occasionally held dances on Saturday nights. This was achieved by placing a sprung maple floor on to beams laid across the empty pool. Run by the local youth club, the age range was 13 to 19 and they were massively popular.

"Have you ever been?"

"No but our Denise has, she went to 'em all last year. She's goin' with Wendy Shaw and that lot, so I know that they won't be off to Maureen's *big party.*"

Suzanne's cousin Denise was in the year above us and one of the Very Popular Gang. The requirements for this group, for a girl was to be pretty, curvy and wear clothes that made you look a lot older. An abundance of self-confidence was also a given. Denise also had a bit of a reputation for being *'one for the lads'* or *'red hot'* as my Mum would have called it.

"You and Jane should go," she stated while drawing an almost perfect isosceles triangle free hand.

I told her that there was no chance of me being allowed to go but I'd ask. That afternoon I mentioned it to Jane. She agreed it sounded great but that it would be unlikely either of us would be allowed to go. We considered lying about it for a while, claiming we were going to

Maureen's party but decided the fallout from getting caught lying wasn't worth it. Jane didn't need the social worker poking her nose in again. So instead we just delighted in the fact that Maureen's party would probably be a flop.

My request to be allowed to go was only half-hearted but I made it anyway that tea-time as I ate my egg, bacon and tinned tomatoes. Dad was standing with his foot on the sofa arm as he polished his shoes while Mum was finishing her make-up in the mirror above the fire place.

"There's a teenage disco at Pudsey baths tomorrow night, can I go?"

"You're not a teenager." Dad continued his buffering not taking his eyes from the task.

"I will be next month."

"Well ask again next month."

"There won't be one then. They only do them in November and February."

Blotting her lipstick on a piece of toilet paper, her eyes fixed on the mirror, Mum said,

"Well ask in November then."

I hadn't meant to ask for anything else but neither of them looked at me or seemed to be aware of my growing pains. An anger I didn't know I had came from nowhere. I slammed down my knife and folk yelling,

"Great, I'll just sit here on my own again then, watching telly while all my friends either go to the disco or do stuff with their Mum and Dads!"

Even I was surprised at the petulance of my voice and without even looking up I knew I'd caught their attention but the anger hadn't finished.

"Or, if I get fed up being totally on my own AGAIN, I could come and wash glasses for you instead as long as I remember to be quiet and invisible."

I got up and left the table, something I'd never done before without asking, and stomped upstairs. I was both appalled and proud of my outburst but also preparing myself for the consequences. A few minutes later Mum shouted from the bottom of the stairs,

"Kimberly, get yourself down here now!"

She was sitting at the table, ashtray in front of her and cigarette poised between her fingers. Dad still buffing his shoes, the leather now so shiny it looked like patent. I stood just inside the doorway waiting to be chastised. My outburst had been a shock to them and it was quite a surprise to me but they were further shocked that I was making no effort to say sorry. Instead I stood there with a defiantly truculent expression, waiting to be told off and looking like I didn't care. Mum began to grind out the cigarette she had only recently lit before taking a long inhalation of breath through her nose and saying,

"Me and your Dad's been talking."

She used this opening quite frequently and it was generally meant for Dad's benefit as well as mine. I caught him give my Mum a quick questioning glance before attempting to arrange his face in an '*I know all about this and am in total agreement with your mother*' look.

"We were sayin' that it might be nice for you to have Jane round to stop one night if you wanted."

Dad looked slightly alarmed at this, confirming he had no previous knowledge of this suggestion.

"So your Dad's gonna ask her Dad if she can stop over tomorra night."

He was even more alarmed at this prospect.

"He's been coming in on a Friday night for the last couple of weeks, only has a couple or three pints all night an he's not as bad as folk make out," she told her reflection, as she stood to check her appearance, before lighting up another cigarette.

"Aye, well he doesn't drink as much as he used to since what 'appened with is lad," Dad said, nodding his agreement but still looking unsure.

"Any road if he comes in tonight, your Dad'll ask him an' if not, he'll drive you round to their house tomorra afore we open up." My mother had proclaimed it and so it was going to happen.

"Now sit down and finish your tea."

I did as I was told even though it was cold. My family practiced the empty plate rule and a girl can only rebel so much in one day. Mum and Dad quickly finished their preparations and went through to the bar as I was finishing and I allowed myself a little smile. Settling down to watch television a bit later, I laid on the rug instead of the sofa. I felt sure Jane would be doing the same in their living room. She'd told me she never sat on the furniture, so she would be lying on the rug, or maybe leaning back against the front of the armchair, but she'd be watching Crackerjack, as she always did on a Friday, waiting for her Dad to get home from the chippie with their tea. He didn't have his couple of pints after work anymore but the Friday night fish n' chip tea had been reinstated into their weekly ritual. I wondered if she would bother to ask about being allowed to go to the baths.

That night, I fell asleep as soon as I'd gone to bed but became semi-awake when Mum came in to straighten my covers. This was her way of checking if I really was asleep or just pretending. On this occasion it was a vague awareness of her touching my hair and the smell of gin and tonic on her breath. Drifting in and out of my nocturnal musings, I was suddenly woken fully by hearing her and Dad yelling at each other. I looked at my alarm clock to see it was two thirty in the morning.

When they'd had a drink or five, Mum and Dad could argue over everything or anything. Their rows were always loud and enraged, hurling furious and hurtful words at each other but these scenes were always private, behind closed and locked doors and only ever verbal. To an outsider these quarrels could have portrayed a loveless and mismatched couple on the verge of breaking up. This could not have been further from the truth. My parents absolutely worshiped each other and these occasional but voluble outbursts were purely a result of spending all day and everyday together, living and working side by side.

The eruption this particular night had been instigated by a conversation an hour earlier at the lock-in with our local bobby on the beat. The gist of this argument, from what I could hear, seemed to about Jane's Dad. Mum was of the opinion that Don Schofield wasn't such a bad lot after all and had apparently said as much to Harry. Harry had gone on at length about what a wrong un he was and his kids were no better. He'd been only too happy to tell them about *'the eldest one, the one that had got the shit kicked out of him by his lovin Dad'* having been arrested for burglary in Sheffield. There was the other one who'd been sent to Borstal for assaulting one of the female workers at the home he had been living in. Apparently this was just one of a string of offences. Harry's opinion was that kids learn how to behave from their parents. Don Schofield had taught his kids how to fight, swear, steal and have absolutely no respect for 'any bugger' and he had most certainly murdered his wife.

I heard Dad yelling quite clearly that Harry knew things they didn't and they should take in what he'd told them. Mum replied that Harry Henshaw was full of shit and would make his mouth say anything to prove himself right. I was sitting half way down the stairs at this point. She went on,

"Jane's a decent little lass and any road, she'd been asked to stop over, so she's stopping over!"

I missed the next bit as they lowered the decibels a bit but Dad shouted,

"Well our Kim's not stopping at their house. And if we have to have her here it's a one-off an' I'll be up all night making sure she's not letting her thieving family in to rob us blind."

Suddenly ignited by indignation and anger, I marched down stairs and into the living room and yelled at both of them.

"Stop it, just stop it now!"

Both stunned into silence, they looked at me in astonishment.

"Jane is my friend and she's nice and kind and has been brilliant to me ever since the first day I met her. What her Dad an' brothers do is nothing to do with her and you should stop listening to Harry Henshaw. He's got it in for her Dad and will say anything to turn you against him. So stop all this drunken shouting and go to bed and sleep it off."

My anger had built as I spoke and given my words such certainty they remained frozen and silent. Not wanting to push my luck, I turned round and stormed back up to my bedroom slamming the door. Throwing myself back into my bed while wiping away fat salty tears, I lay on my back listening to see if there was any further discussion but heard nothing. I must have fallen asleep because suddenly it was morning and I could hear Dad in the bathroom. I went down stairs and put the kettle on and was just pouring the boiled water on to the tealeaves when he came into the room.

"Your mate's Dad came in last night so your Mam asked him if their Jane can come an' stop over tonight."

I didn't dare turn round or say anything as I bent down to get the milk bottle out of the fridge.

"Any road, he says she can come but we've all said it's not happenin' regular, so that's it."

He picked up the packet of Benson and Hedges and his lighter off the mantelpiece and went down the passage to go into the bar.

"Dad!" I called after him. He stopped and turned round.

"Don't go without your tea." I put the milk into the waiting mugs and reached for the strainer as he walked back.

"Thanks love, you make a grand cuppa." He ruffled my hair as he watched me pour. Picking up the biggest one, he turned and walked away whistling as he went.

Chapter Sixteen

After Dad had gone to check the cleaners had arrived, I poured myself a bowl of cereal and sat at the table, smiling and munching. He came back a few minutes later and embarked on a further act of reconciliation; making us bacon sandwiches.

My memories of this day are clouded with a pinkish rose colour, I was so happy. I went to call for Jane as soon as I'd wiped the grease from my hands and brushed my teeth. The door opened before I knocked, she'd been watching for me and was ready to leave straight away. No sign of her Dad or of any goodbyes as she hoisted a canvas bag onto her shoulder and we walked back up the hill. We decided to go to the Pavilion, so Jane could see what it was like, after putting her stuff in my room we dashed to catch the bus. Walking into the auditorium, the scene that greeted us was more anarchic than I'd remembered and the noise level was riotous. The cartoons were just starting but the side lights stayed on to help the ushers identify the troublemakers and evict them if they got too lairy. Well that was the theory. In practice the ushers were well out of the way in a back room smoking and drinking tea.

We found some seats at the back and had a good look around. Sharon and Diane were sitting very close to the front amidst a group of boys but we couldn't see Maureen, Chris or Kenny. There were still a lot of kids moving around, so it was hard to tell if they were there or not. As our class mates didn't notice us, we made no effort to attract their attention. Two boys from our school we knew vaguely swapped seats so they could come and sit just in front of us. Kneeling on their seats they attempted to engage us in conversation.

"Well if it isn't the famous Jane Schofield and her funny looking mate!

Didn't know you two came here."

"And we didn't know that stupid, ugly knob-heads like you were allowed in or we wouldn't have bothered. Now fuck off you pair of spazzers." Jane didn't mince her words.

Responding to the rejection, the lads muttered something that sounded like 'fuckin lezzers' and shuffled off down the row of seats.

"This is a bit shit Kim."

We watched sweets, lolly sticks and all sorts of other debris being hurled around while the noise levels increased and reverberated around us.

"Yeah I know," I confirmed nodding my head.

The cartoon ended and the main lights came up as three usherettes with trays of choc-ices and ice lollies appeared at the front. I had this mounting feeling that the day was about to be spoilt and was just about to suggest we left when Jane stood up and started waving to a group of lads a couple of rows in front. One of them waved back and said something to the others who smiled and nodded. Jane was out of her seat and, shoving past the two people on the end of the row, making her way to the aisle. I followed uttering pointless 'excuse me's.

I didn't recognise any of the three boys she was talking to although one of them did look slightly familiar.

"This is a real dump. Didn't expect to see you lot here."

"Tweedy's after getting off with some lass and he wanted help from the professionals."

The largest of the three was pointing at a fourth boy who had remained seated and was deep in conversation with two girls who were looking at him intently.

"Looks like he's doing alright without your help," Jane laughed. Glancing at me she said, "Kim this is Russell Turner he's Paul's brother."

"Wow, is this the famous Kimbo?"

He grinned giving me a good look up and down.

"Dunno 'bout famous," I muttered.

"You live in a pub and your Mam and Dad have wild parties that go on all night," Russell informed me. A smiling admiration in his voice.

"Well one of those facts is true," I admitted.

"So where's your Paul then, is there a match on?

"NO!" he yelled partly over the noise around us and partly out of incredulity that Jane might not know the fixture list of Leeds United.

"They're playin' Man U. on Monday, no game today." A little calmer he added, "He's down at the canal again with some lads from school. Suddenly he's into this fishin' lark!"

I saw the disappointment wash across her face briefly but was replaced with a fixed smile.

"I dunt think your brother's gone this time though. He's helping Keith's Dad build a shed. He's ok your Dave, he's a good laugh!"

His last statement made as if to counter a previously held belief about David Schofield and I found myself nodding.

"Yeah?" Jane raised her eyebrows at him. "So your Mam'll be askin' him round your house for tea then?"

They both laughed at this, so I joined in not really sure why as an overweight and sweaty official walked past us telling us to *get sat down*.

"Come an sit with us so I can make our kid jealous when he gets home." Russell said.

Again I have no memory of the film but I do remember thinking I'd been right about Paul fancying Jane and adding it to my mental list of things to talk to her about that night. As we left the picture house Sharon called out as she caught sight of us,

"Hi ya, didn't see you were here, who are you with?"

She was craning her head round to see the lads just ahead of us.

"Oh just some mates. You with that Wayne lad then?"

Jane's answer was dismissive and the question a deflection.

"Yeah, he's coming to Maureen's party with me tonight. You're not goin' are you?"

It was quite a nasty little smirk she had and I thought of her again as a wasp and wanted to slap her away. A lad who I guessed was Wayne came up behind her grinning, a couple of other boys at either side of him.

"Aye up, who's these gorgeous lasses then?"

His eyes specifically on Jane and she responded with one of her laser beam smiles accompanied by a flutter of her long dark eyelashes. Answering with the slightest suggestion of a step forward, nudging Sharon out of way,

"Hi ya, I'm Jane. Shaza was just telling me you're off to some kid's party tonight. I thought you'd be going to the Pudsey baths disco."

"Kids party?" He glanced at Sharon but only for a second, his eyes straight back on Jane.

She was very close to him now, laughing as she touched his arm slightly for full effect.

"Yeah, pass the parcel and musical chairs and if you're lucky her Mam and Dad might let her have a bottle or two of shandy. We're off to the baths for a proper night out."

I could see both panic and anger in Sharon's face as she watched Wayne take this in but Jane wasn't letting up. Another smile and lowering of her eyelids giving him the full power of her charms and a further small tap on his forearm as she concluded,

"Anyway, we've got to get off, enjoy the party games but if you change your mind, we'll see you at the baths." With a provocative pout, she tossed her hair back, linked arms with me and we walked off to get the bus.

Before going home we called in at the Thrift stores to buy essentials for our sleep over. These consisted of a box of Smarties, some sherbet lemons and teenage magazines. Mum had just got home from the hairdressers and was in one of her cheery and smiley moods. She made us a 'bit of dinner', egg, chips and tinned tomatoes, which was made even more delicious with lots of brown sauce and soft white bread and butter.

A bit later we walked up to the phone box. This was a common gathering place for kids in the evening but not generally inhabited in the afternoons so we had it to ourselves. As we sucked our sherbet lemons we discussed Sharon and Maureen and wondered who would actually turn up for the party. Once we'd exhausted this topic we spent half an hour or so listening to dial-a-disc in the phone box before being told to get out by an angry looking woman who needed to call her mother. The song was Raindrops Keep Falling on my Head from the film Butch Cassidy and the Sundance Kid.

"Do you know what would be brilliant?" Jane exclaimed as we huddled round the receiver for the fourth or fifth time.

"What?"

"For us to go to the flicks an see this."

I agreed completely. The day was turning out just as I'd imagined it. Having Jane sleep over wasn't going to be like when Alison came to stay. This was my very best friend staying in my room with me and we would be able to talk freely and for as long as we wanted. Even though our Dads had said it was a one-off, I was convinced it was just the start of many such nights; all at our house of course. It was also a prelude to when we eventually rented a flat together like in the Liver Birds or some of the other TV programmes I'd seen.

After we'd watched Dr Who, which we both agreed wasn't as good now that John Pertwee was the Doctor, we went to tell Mum we were going to the chip shop which was a couple of hundred yards from the pub. She replied without a trace of irony, blowing her cigarette smoke just between our faces,

"Well get them open and eat them outside. I don't want them stinking the house out."

We ate them leaning on the pub wall before going in to watch the telly with large glasses of dandelion and burdock. Just after nine o'clock we were sitting at each end of the sofa with our feet up in the best room, magazines strewn about us, when I asked her what she would be doing if she was at home.

"I'd probably be sitting on the rug watching whatever's on telly an' thinking how much I'd like to have some Smarties!"

I laughed and tossed the box of Smarties over to her.

"So why don't you sit on the sofa?" I asked. "I mean, if you're in on your own you can spread out and watch telly."

She didn't answer straight away and although she was concentrating on the cellophane wrapper, I saw her expression cloud. I immediately regretted asking and started to dig my nails into my palms as I balled my hands tight. Finally she spoke,

"Do you really want to know?"

"Well yeah, course I do," I said but was wondering if I really did.

"You have to promise not to tell anyone."

"Course I won't if you don't want me to."

"Can we go up and get in bed first though; it'll be easier to tell you if we're in the dark."

So we packed up our stuff and went upstairs. After using the bathroom we shuffled down under the blankets into my three-quarter sized bed and I switched off the small reading lamp. We lay on our backs, allowing our eyes to adjust to the semi-darkness of the room. Only the orange street light just outside my window illuminated us as she started to speak.

"I'm gonna tell you all of it but you've got to be quiet and not say anything 'til I've stopped."

"Ok."

"And you have to say out loud that you promise you will never tell anybody."

"I promise I'll never tell anybody anything if you don't want me to."

A small silence and then she began,

"Dad's really not as scary as everybody thinks and he dunt go round beating folk up for no reason. He did smack Mam about I know, and that were wrong and he knows it an' all. He knows he treated her bad but it was cos he loved her and he thought she were too good for him."

I said nothing, as requested, but wondered how punching someone in the face giving them a black eye and breaking their nose could ever be an indication of love.

"He's never hit me!"

Her words insistent, a declaration she had obviously made before.

"He did give our David a smack round the head a couple o' times an' our Kev was always getting a crack but he were always asking for one. Him an Iain wanted to be hard men, like me Dad. They were always pushing it."

My eyes were getting used to the dark and I could make out the ornaments on my dressing table.

"It were cos of our Kev that David got into trouble with the police, you know when they were at the football with Paul. It were our Kev he smashed a shop window cos they wouldn't serve him, cos they were with him they were blamed. Dad went mental when the cops came round."

I was focusing back on the ceiling, examining a large crack around the top of the chimney breast.

"Police had only just stopped coming round and giving Dad grief after Mam was took. It was just after I'd started at Hill Topp an' we were trying to get back to normal. Then that Harry Henshaw starts coming round again being all high 'n' mighty sayin' we're all a bunch of savages and he knows what really happened to me Mam AND he's watching us!"

Her voice wavered a bit with emotion. I moved my hand across to her and felt for hers. There was a long pause as we both laid there, eyes open and focused on the darkened Aertex above us, holding hands.

"I never sat in the chair, its Dad's chair, always were. I remember him grabbing hold of me Mam's hair and pulling her out of it once. I were only little, it were well before I started school. There was some row;

probably over money it usually were and she thought he'd gone out but he came back in. She was sitting in the chair with her purse on her knee. I remember that because all this money went flying all over as he pulled her up. Any road I knew never to sit in his chair after that."

She took a deep breath and swallowed before going on,

"The sofa, that were different, that were our Iain's."

Her voice had got softer, she was almost whispering now as she continued,

"It were only after Mam had gone, well not straight away but a month or two after, Iain started cuddling me, sayin' he was gonna look after me but - I didn't like it. He'd start to tickle me but his hands would be all over, you know, so I tried to keep out of his way but then..."

She stopped and I heard her sniffing a little. I squeezed her hand.

"You don't have to say anymore if you don't want," I whispered.

"No, I do, I have to. I want to tell - but just you."

She brought her other arm up and wiped her nose on the sleeve of her nightie.

"Thing is that after Mam were took, Dad really missed her. That's why I know he didn't hurt her like Harry bloody Henshaw keeps sayin'. He's heartbroken that she's gone. He dunt drink like he used to, you can probably ask your Mam and Dad, they'll tell you he hardly has half what he used to."

Another big sniff as the emotion made her voice raise a little. "It started about a week after she'd gone. Dad would come to my bedroom and sit on the edge of my bed, crying. I pretended to be asleep at first but he just kept on crying, so I sat up an' asked him what were wrong. He said he was stupid and he'd lost Mam but he wouldn't lose me. Kept telling me I was his princess and he'd make sure I was safe."

I lay totally still trying to absorb her words. I realised I was holding my breath and so exhaled loudly. Her head moved a little towards me as she said,

"It weren't like that, he never touched me. He'd just come in most nights and sat on me bed crying. Couple of times he laid down, on the blankets and fell asleep. But it weren't mucky. He just wanted to be with me. Said I was so much like Mam."

Pride in her voice and genuine affection for her Dad and his broken heart.

"Iain must have known he was coming in me bedroom but he thought it were somat else. So that night after we'd been to pictures and Diane's Dad dropped us off, I knew Dad were out. He'd gone into Leeds to meet some bloke from work an' wasn't gonna be home till late. That's why he'd told Iain he had to be in for ten o'clock when I got home. I'd been dreading it. Soon as I got in he told me he'd sent our Kev and David out, given 'em some money and told them not to come home till after eleven. I'd been worrying all night about what he'd be like and I knew he'd been drinking soon as he opened door."

She took a deep breath but I could hear the strain of her control.

"He said he wanted to make me his special princess like Dad had an' he picked me up an' put me on sofa." The first sob burst out with these words.

"Oh Jane..."

"It were awful, really awful. I tried to get him off me, I were crying and screaming so he put his hand over me mouth and I bit him. He lifted his hand up and I though he were gonna hit me but then he stopped and started kissing me instead. I tried to stop him, I did, I really did but it were no use. He hurt me so much."

Her last few words barely audible and we were both crying now.

"After he'd finished, he panicked a bit and said I'd better not tell Dad or he'd be jealous and wouldn't believe me anyway. He gave me two quid to get me self somat nice and told me to get to bed."

We leaned into each other, holding tight as we cried into each other's hair. After a few more minutes like this she pulled away and gaining some control again, she went on,

"So the next day when Robbo started yelling at me and then grabbed my arms, which were really sore and already covered in bruises, I just lost it. When they took me into Wedaburn's office, I told 'em Robbo had hurt me and rolled me sleeves up to show them the bruises. That freaked 'em out so they took me home. Dad told Old Mother Tempest to get the bloody hell out on his house. He told her that he'd sort Robbo out. The bastard wasn't going to get away with hurting his little lass and he didn't care what I'd said or done." She laughed. "He would have an' all so I had to tell him what had happened."

I squeezed her hand and tried to smile. She squeezed back.

"He sat there shaking while I told him, not saying anything, just staring at the sofa. Then he stood up and went upstairs and ran a bath for me and told me to take as long as I wanted. I heard our Kev and David come in, I don't know what he told 'em but they'd gone out again when I came downstairs. He'd been to the shop and bought me a big bar of fruit and nut chocolate and told me to watch telly for a bit cos he had to go out. He was out ages and when he came back, I knew he'd been fighting. He said nothing but I heard him crying in his bedroom that night after we'd all gone to bed and he didn't come into mine. Our Iain never came home again." Sniffing loudly and let go of my hand to wipe her face on her sleeve. "Next day he took me to Gran's and said I needed to stop there for a bit while he sorted somat out."

"Did you know he was arrested for beating Iain up?"

"Yeah, me Gran told me but Iain said it weren't him so they had to let him go."

"Oh Jane, I don't know what to say!"

"There's nothing you can say 'cept promise that you'll never tell anybody about this!"

"I promise I won't tell a soul!" I agreed and I meant it.

It's a promise I've kept for 44 years.

Chapter Seventeen

It was getting light when I woke up. I opened my eyes to see Jane lying wide awake on her back, staring at the ceiling. Although I'm sure the only bit of me that moved were my eyelids, she sensed my wakening.

"Do you know you talk in your sleep?" she spoke to the ceiling.

"Did I say anything interesting?"

"Not really, just the normal rubbish you spout." A smile lit her face as she turned to face me. "I think you were mumbling something about wanting to bring me breakfast in bed."

I went downstairs to fetch us heavily sugared, milky cornflakes, tea and toast. We munched our way through this feast sitting up in bed reading magazines with the radio on low, so as not to wake Mum and Dad. The previous night's revelations were not mentioned. Without any discussion we'd agreed a detachment. I needed time to process what had been disclosed. Jane needed to see if our relationship was damaged by it. In a slightly subdued mood, I digested the consequences of the shared secret, along with my breakfast.

It had been agreed that she could stay until 11.30; she had to be home to have her Sunday dinner with her Dad. We got ourselves dressed around eight and passed a bleary-eyed Dad on the landing.

"Where are you two off to at this time in the mornin'?"

"We're off for a walk before Jane goes home."

Giving him no time to respond, we left the house and set off to park.

Although there'd been an early morning frost, I don't remember feeling cold. The sun was struggling to emit some warmth through the grey and misty skies, suggesting some later relief to the chill of morning. It all seemed a bit dream-like as we walked briskly up the hill, speculating how Maureen's party had gone and who'd turned up, our breath vaporising as we marched quickly but sociably linking arms. Once in the park, we went over to the seats by the football pitch where the local Sunday morning teams were warming up. The easy silence prevailed for only a few moments after we sat down. Once sure we couldn't be overheard, we needed no prompting for what we wanted to talk about. Jane filled in the blanks for me as I asked the questions.

Her grandparents hadn't been told by their son the reason why he'd beaten his eldest child, their grandson, to within an inch of his life. He just told them what he'd done and was expecting to be arrested. Their attitude, it seemed to Jane, was very much *'he must have done something to deserve it and it was none of their business.'*

"They probably think it's somert to do with me Mam," she surmised.

Their indifference to the circumstances meant that the information of the incestuous rape remained contained to Jane, her Dad and Iain. Don told her that the fewer people knew the better and that if anybody found out what happened, she'd be taken away and he'd lose her completely. He didn't think Iain would tell the police why his Dad had attacked him as he'd be too ashamed but he'd probably be charged with assault or GBH and he might be sent down for a couple of years. He'd said that if that happened, it didn't matter just as long as no one got to know what that bastard had done.

The Grandparents refused point-blank to take the other two boys and so when Don was arrested, they had to be taken into care and were dispatched to separate children's homes. She'd learnt recently from David that Kevin went wild when they came to get them insisting that the police had fitted his Dad up and telling Harry Henshaw that he was a dead man. David had seen no point in resisting the arrangements and the first night in the children's home, he'd felt relief. She didn't think he knew what Iain had done, he might have suspected something but would be too scared to ask.

All the time she was in Middlesbrough, she had no contact with what was going on in Leeds and was told by her Granny that she'd be with them for the duration. Not wanting to ask exactly how long the duration might be, being terrified of the answer, she decided the prospect of this being her life from now on was untenable and so had started planning to run away.

Her grandparents would be described as good respectable people but their home reflected their way of life; stringent, cold and bordering on austere. They were not a warm and welcoming couple and they saw no need for emotion or sentiment. It was not that they were cruel or unkind, they just had no idea how to look after a young girl struggling through adolescence. Even without the emotional and physical traumas she'd experienced, this wouldn't have been a good place for her to be. As she described it to me I said it sounded like something out of a Dickens novel. She agreed saying,

"The only thing missing was the gruel although there was porridge!"

They didn't tell her that after three weeks on remand, the charges against her Dad were dropped, or that West Yorkshire police had raised concerns about Jane returning home - something Jane claimed Harry Henshaw had done out of spite. The first she knew about any of this was when, returning from her new school one day, she found a strange woman sitting on the sofa and drinking tea from her granny's best china. Her eyes glistened a little bit as she explained, with some pride, that she'd since discovered that her Dad had been fighting for weeks to get her back home.

The social worker, Mrs. Cooper, wanted to know all about her home life since her Mum had disappeared, mainly focusing on her father's drinking and temper. She was smart enough to know how to manage this conversation and knew what she needed to say to get back to her life. What we both thought was interesting was that the school hadn't reported the classroom incident. Instead, they had actually supported her

Dad's claims of a stable home life.

"They think Robbo made those bruises on my arms an' are probably scared shitless that it might come out."

She opened out the hanky that she'd been balling up in her hand and blew her nose.

"That's why he's so nervous round me now; he thinks he did it as well poor sod!"

She looked unhappy at this but shrugged her shoulders.

"But if they knew what really happened, it'd be so much worse. They wouldn't have let me back home and Harry Henshaw would have found some way to say it were Dad's fault."

I knew she was right on both counts.

"Yeah, and it'd mean your Dad had a reason to beat up Iain."

It was Don's decision not to have his sons back, agreeing with all parties that they were unruly and needed better structured parenting than he could provide. Jane said that this would probably have been the news that had made Kevin flip and attack the social worker. Being 15 now, he would have officially been able to leave school in July and had probably been looking forward to continuing the family tradition with a job at the factory. The fact that his Dad had turned his back on him would do nothing for his belligerent and aggressive view of life, seeing himself as a victim who had been mistreated. David, on the other hand, seemed to have benefited from the separation from his family. Having just turned 14 there was time for him to turn around his life and by choosing to stay on at school and do his O Levels, he'd impressed his foster family. Again, pride in her voice as she said that according to Keith, her brother was really bright and would do well in his exams. So was she, I said, but she shook her head and sighed deeply before changing the subject.

"What do you think about Paul Turner?"

I remembered what his brother had said at the pictures the day before.

"Never mind what I think about him, what do you think? He obviously fancies you!"

She narrowed her eyes at me, tipped her head to one side and tutting loudly said,

"You really are dense sometimes, Kim."

"What do you mean? His brother said yesterday that he fancies you."

"No he didn't. Anyway do you reckon he went to Maureen's last night? I know she asked him. Sharon still thinks she's in with a chance of getting back with him."

"What about that Wayne she was at the flicks with yesterday?"

"She only wants him to go cos she thinks it will make Paul jealous, silly cow!"

"Really?" I considered this for a moment, "Well I suppose it depends on if Kenny went. Chris will have gone, and Diane and Sharon, but it might have ended up with being just the four of them."

We both laughed again at this and as the few family members and supporters were growing and edging closer to us, we got up and started to stroll around the pitch.

"Your Mam 'n' Dad should get a Unicorn football team going. There's loads of other pubs got them in this league."

"Yeah, I'll tell them. The darts team does well and is great for trade."

We got back to the pub just after eleven and collected her bag. I walked to the footbridge with her where we said our goodbyes before returning to our separate homes for the traditional Sunday dinner; over-cooked meat and boiled to a pulp vegetables swimming in gravy. Thank goodness for Yorkshire puddings as high as top hats.

The next day at school, we heard that Maureen's party ended up as a very small gathering. Chris and Kenny and a handful of others from our year had put in an appearance but much to Sharon's annoyance and frustration, Paul and Wayne did not. They, along with most of the other invited guests, had gone to the baths. Suzanne was our source of this information as she'd gone to the disco with her cousin. Although while she wasn't much impressed with the event itself, she enjoyed her surveillance on who was there and who they were with, proving to be an excellent witness and informant.

Knowing Paul from primary school and also knowing that we'd be really interested in who he was with, she'd given him particular attention. He spent most of the night with a group of boys she didn't know but parted from them when the slow songs came on. He danced mostly with two girls, neither of which she knew, and she clocked him at the bus stop having 'a rite good snog' with one of them as she walked home. She also knew what had happened at Maureen's house, having walked to school with June, a girl from our year who went. Sharon had spent most of the night in the kitchen on her own waiting for her boyfriend who just didn't turn up.

"Sharon must be well embarrassed at neither of 'em turning up!" I giggled as we were sorting our books in the form room just before registration.

"Embarrassed? More likely she's bloody furious and she's not here yet," Jane exclaimed and the three of us turned round to see Diane and Maureen sitting, heads together whispering.

Sharon didn't appear that day or for the rest of the week. According to the note from her Mum, she'd had a really bad cold and temperature. It seems the disappointment of the previous Saturday night had taken its toll on her. Maureen was also a little subdued that week although we didn't find out why until sometime later.

The following week, at the Thursday drama club, with just over a week to go before opening night, I saw Chris hanging around the corridor as we came out.. I smiled and he gave me a brief up-turn of his mouth before focusing on Jane.

"You got a minute?"

Jane nodded and stepping aside I could see the flush in her neck as she turned to me.

"You go in Kim, I'll catch you up."

I was on the stage by the time she came in. Mr. Lloyd was *'completely despairing'* about some of the performances and not in any mood to suffer interruptions, so I had to wait for the ten minute break before finding out what he'd wanted. Having declared categorically that he didn't want to be involved in the forbidden correspondence, she was surprised that he had a note from David. It was in a sealed envelope which she hadn't opened, planning instead to read it as we walked home, before giving it to me to keep safe for her.

"But the real reason he'd agreed was he wants me to pass on some information to you." She smiled.

Chris wanted to me to know that Monday after her party, he'd told Maureen that he wasn't going out with her anymore.

"She's been phoning his house and sending him letters but he's ignoring her. Apparently, she's completely broken hearted and doesn't know what to do. Pathetic!"

"Really?"

Nodding and confirming her contempt and complete lack of sympathy she added,

"I'll have a word with her tomorrow and tell her she should write to Cathy and Claire and give the whole school a laugh."

Chapter Eighteen

The nerves kicked in at the dress rehearsal but it wasn't stage fright, quite the opposite. It was the despair that it would soon be over. I was encased in full Georgian garb which was dark and heavy but I felt amazing as I swished around backstage. My outfit included a large flattering bonnet which was completely impractical as its large brim muffled my voice, so Mr. Lloyd decided I should be hatless. I thought the bonnet was magnificent and decided to ignore him. On opening night I swept onto stage, in full costume, certain that the bonnet would add to the stage presence of the great woman. I began to remove it, taking my time and surveying the appalling prison conditions before handing it to the prison governor confidently, emphasising my authority. This part was played by Peter Brooke, a third year and, as this hadn't been scripted, he was genuinely taken aback as he took it while confusedly looking around before regaining his composure and delivering his lines. After the final curtain call Mr. Lloyd nodded at me smiling and although Peter didn't manage to recapture the look of intimidation in the corresponding performances, we kept it in for all three nights.

During this first scene there had been a split second of distraction as I'd glanced briefly at the audience. The front row mainly consisted of a large contingent from the boy's grammar school and perhaps it was their presence that egged on my flagrant scene stealing feat. I know it was on that night that I realised I could be strong and self-assured, even in a spotlight, when I was being someone else. It was just being me that I struggled with. After the applause of the first night was over, I hurried along to the girl's dressing room. As I started wiping off the stage makeup, I glanced across the room to see Sharon chatting to Wendy Shaw. As she saw me looking she raised her voice just to make sure I could hear.

"I know, that's just what I was thinking, completely over the top but then she's never happy unless she's centre of attention."

I felt my cheeks burn as I stepped into my flared trousers keeping my head bowed.

"Oh for God's sake Shaza, she's got the lead role, she is supposed to be the centre of attention and she was ace. You're just jealous cos you couldn't act your way out of a paper bag! You're a pathetic loser!" Jane called across the room which immediately fell silent.

"Well at least I didn't get my parents to bribe Mr. Lloyd into giving me a part with free beer!" Sharon shouted back just as Miss Tate walked in.

It was Sharon's turn to blush and lower her gaze as Miss Tate looked directly at her with narrowed eyes.

"Would you like to explain that remark Sharon?"

"No Miss."

"Right well hurry up all of you, Mr. Lloyd wants to speak to the whole cast before you leave."

I noticed Sharon edge her way to the back of the assembled players as we were all congratulated on our performance, not only by the director but also by the headmaster. We were a credit to the school and to all Mr. Lloyd's hard work and all in all – well done us! Jane and I had been allowed to walk back to the Unicorn together even though it was dark. Don would be waiting there to take her home and we were expected by ten thirty. So we dashed out of the side door and were just about to hare it across the playground when a familiar voice called out,

"You took your bloody time comin' out!"

Paul was leaning on the handrail of the side door steps. I couldn't help but smile even before he held out a pen and paper and asked,

"Can I have your autograph?"

The rest of them were a bit further down the path. David called out,

"All right our kid?"

He nodded and Jane smiled back before informing him,

"We can't hang around David, Dad's at Kim's pub waiting for me."

"Yeah I know. It don't matter, I just wanted to tell you I liked the play and you were good."

"I dint have much of a part, you know, thought I'd give the rest of 'em a chance this year."

Grinning his agreement he nodded towards me,

"Your mate was a bit scary though, I wouldn't wanna mess with her!"

I laughed and blushed at what I hoped was a complement.

"Come on, we'll walk through the estate with you and catch our bus down by the ring road."

Our entourage crossed the playground and I found Chris at my side.

"You were really good, Kim," he proclaimed.

"Thanks."

He touched my arm to get me to stop.. The others kept walking as if they hadn't noticed but I was sure Jane had seen his manoeuvre. He said my name and I felt my face start to burn again as blood flushed my face. He swallowed hard before saying,

"I really like you."

Looking right at me our faces only inches apart.

"So will you come skating with me on Saturday?"

"Skating?"

"Yeah, at the Rollerena on Kirkstall Road."

"Who else is going?"

"No one, just you and me."

"What, you mean on a date?"

"Yeah. You said before that when the play was finished you'd go out with me."

Even though Paul had told me that this was what Chris had thought, I hadn't truly believed him. I glanced over his shoulder and saw the others had stopped. They were about fifty or so yards away. Jane was the only one looking back at us.

I tilted my head and looked back at him with incredulity.

"You have to be kidding. What about Maureen?"

"I've finished with her!" His response was quick and a little truculent. "I only went out with her cos she went on about how much she'd fancied me and cos Kenny was with Diane."

He smiled at his explanation and in my confusion I smiled back, which he took as encouragement.

"You know I've fancied you for ages and it's nearly your birthday and as your Dad's mates with my Dad I reckon he'll be alright about it."

I started to shake my head slowly. All the things Jane and Paul had told me seemed to be true. He was smiling and I saw that he fully expected me to say yes. He moved forward slightly and I realised he was going to kiss me. I stepped back and in my best Elizabeth Fry commanding voice proclaimed,

"No! I will not go roller skating with you on Saturday or any other time and please don't ever ask me to go out with you again. I think you're despicable!"

I stepped round him and ran down the street to catch up with Jane and the others. Chris didn't follow and no one said anything as we started down the hill.

"Despicable, nice touch!" Jane said just under her breath.

Squeezing my hand briefly before pointing up at the full moon and saying very matter-of-factly,

"Looks like a good night for werewolves."

It was only after we'd parted from the lads, walking across the footbridge on our own that she said,

"So you turned him down then?"

"Did you hear it all?"

"Not really but Paul told me he was gonna ask you and I had a feelin' you wouldn't let me down." Linking arms she said, "I was a bit worried as I thought you liked him, so I wasn't sure which way it would go."

"I do like him, well I did and bloody hell he saved my life!" I could feel tears forming just behind my eyes as I tried to get a handle on my emotions, "And he was a good mate till he started going out with that cow Maureen."

"Yeah, but he's a tosser and he's Harry Henshaw's son."

She confirmed as we walked in step.

"Paul said he only went out with her to make me jealous!"

My anger bubbling through my words was pushing tears forward and down my cheeks. She pulled me to a stop while she got a tissue out of her pocket and passed it to me.

"Look, apart from the using Maureen thing, which I know is pretty piss poor, even though she is a right cow, AND he's Harry fuckin' Henshaw's son, he practically ignored you and joined in with Sharon in making your life rubbish. He's just a loser who doesn't have a bloody clue. You've done the right thing telling him where to get off."

We both laughed.

"And maybe he did save you from possible death in the black lagoon thingy but all that said and done; the most important thing here is that I don't think you actually fancy him. Otherwise you wouldn't have turned him down when he asked you the first time, let alone just now."

We walked on for a bit in silence as I tried to weigh up my feelings.

"I don't know if I fancy him or not," I conceded, "I know I like him and I thought he was alright, oh I don't know!"

"Yeah, but don't forget he's despicable as well," she started to laugh with a mild hysteria.

"What is so funny?"

"You are. Oh Kimmy, you are such a one-off." She gave me a hug and still laughing said, "Please don't ever change!"

"I won't." And I blinked away my tears.

My parents didn't come to see me in the play but I didn't mind. I knew they wouldn't enjoy it and it would mean them paying someone to cover the bar. Also it meant that Jane and I could walk home together afterwards, on our own in the dark. Although the play was finished by nine thirty each night, it still took a while to get changed and walk home, so it was quite something for us to be allowed to be out on our own that late. On the final night, Mr Lloyd gave us a lift, saying it was about time he sampled my Dad's ales, which he'd apparently been bribed with, or so he'd heard. Miss Tate came along too and I was incredibly nervous as I led them into the pub where I introduced them to Mum, Dad and a broodily watchful Don Schofield. Because we were earlier than expected, Jane and I went through to the house with a bottle of pop and bag of crisps, although we would have preferred to stay and listen to the grown up's conversation. Mum came to tell Jane that her Dad was ready to go after about fifteen minutes but my teachers were settling down for another drink.

I had to wait until the next morning to hear about how long they stayed and what my parents thought of them. There'd been three parent's evenings since I'd been at Hill Topp and my parents hadn't been to any of them. Their ambitions were for me to leave school at fifteen and train as a hairdresser, so they saw no reason to waste their valuable time hearing about my schoolwork. As a girl, any job I had was only considered transitional until I got married and had babies. Although given my Dad's attitude to me having any interaction with the opposite sex, I'm not sure how they thought that would happen. There was absolutely no value in leaving the pub to sit in front of teachers telling them about my academic capabilities.

"And any road they send a report home at the end of the year so that'll tell us what we want to know."

So they'd not met any of my teachers before. They knew of some of them, from the Sunday dinner ritual, when they asked me about school, not that I was convinced that they actually listened to my answers. So I was absolutely desperate to know what they thought about my two favourite teachers and more importantly what *they'd* said about me. When I woke up the next morning, I could hear Dad whistling along to the radio downstairs, so I raced through my ablutions to give myself more time to chat to him over my cornflakes.

"Mornin' love." He smiled at me lowering his newspaper slightly as he picked up his cigarette from the overflowing ashtray. "You're up early, want a bacon sarnie?"

He asked before taking a deep drag on his nicotine stick.

"No thanks, I'll just have me cornflakes," I said pouring a large portion into a bowl. "So did Mr Lloyd tell you about the play?"

"Yes, he did and as me and your Mam had known you would be, he said you was brilliant!"

"Really! Did he really say brilliant?"

"Yeah course he did, said you are top of the class in English and that other one said same, that Judith lass."

"Miss Tate?"

"Aye, if that were who she was, says you're a right little smarty pants and a pleasure to teach. Mind you, they'd both had a few when they told us that!" He laughed heartily at his own joke.

"Very funny. Did they stay till closing time?"

"Just about. Good customers they were an all, they can come again."

"They didn't get free drinks then?" I asked with a chuckle.

"They might 'ave got one round on the house but that was only after he'd put his hand in his pocket a couple of times already. He said somat about not wanting folk to think he'd been bribed. Any road, I better get that kettle on or yer Mam'll be on the war path."

He stubbed out his cigarette and went over to the sink.

"Did they talk to Mr Schofield before he went?"

"Oh aye, he came out on his shell a bit while they were there. He dunt normally say much when he comes in these days, mind you he dunt drink half as much as he used to." He'd been filling the kettle with water as he spoke and as he switched it on he said, "Bit of a double-edged sword for us really. I mean he dunt help me takings now he nurses his pints over a couple of hours but he dunt cause no trouble."

I thought his words were probably just him musing, so I kept quiet and got on with my breakfast. As he put the tea leaves in the teapot, he muttered again.

"Well, I suppose he's had a lot to put up with, his Mrs running off and his lads thieving and the likes."

I finished my cereal and put my bowl in the sink as he changed the subject,

"Me an your Mam were talkin' about holidays yesterday."

"Me and Mum goin' to Butlins with Aunty Shirley and Alison again?"

This had been my only experience of a holiday and had happened three years previously. It was not an experience I was keen to repeat.

"No love, we were thinkin' of getting a relief in to look after the pub, so we can have a proper family holiday, for a week mebbe. What do you reckon?"

"Where would we go?" I asked with suspicion.

A family holiday was a complete anathema, we didn't even have days out together let alone a whole week.

"Blackpool!" he exclaimed, "You liked it there dint yer?"

I'd been on a day trip to Blackpool with Mum when I was eight. It was a children's trip with the local Working Men's Club when we'd lived in South Yorkshire. Aunty Shirley came along with both her offspring, as did a whole gang of other adults. By adults on this occasion I mean drinking buddies. The trip consisted of a coach journey where all the kids, who just outnumbered the adults, were given a ten shilling note as spending money as we boarded the coach. We were supplied with a bottle of pop and bag of crisps for the journey and sent to sit at the back. The grown-ups took their seats at the front where they had a couple of crates of ale to help them while away the two-hour journey. Arriving around eleven, we had half an hour in the arcades losing some of our money on machines before we were rushed along so our chaperones could get a proper drink from the pumps of a 'nice pub'. This was a time long before children were allowed into licensed premises to spoil the grown-up's drinking, so we were deposited on a wall outside the back, again supplied with pop and crisps. As the eldest of our group, I was told to watch my two cousins and a couple of other kids I'd never seen before, while their Mum, Aunty Shirley, and one of the committee members joined my Mum in the lounge bar. This proper drink lasted till around 2pm, after which we went to eat our egg sandwiches on the sands. Luckily, it was warm and sunny so we made a little camp of deck-chairs for the grown-ups and a couple of bathroom towels that came out of Mum's shopping bag. We stayed there long enough to build a sandcastle, which Mark trampled down in a fit of boyish peak before being sent for a paddle in the sea to cool down. There was time for a donkey ride and ice cream before we hurried back to the prom to find a 'decent cup of tea', before getting back on the bus at 6pm for the trip home.

So for Dad to say I'd liked Blackpool was a bit of a stretch. My immediate thought was that I'd end up spending every day sitting on a pub wall on my own. Not my idea of a holiday.

"I don't really remember much about it," I responded flatly.

"Any road do you think your friend Jane might want to come, be a bit of company for you? I was thinkin' of askin' her Dad next time he comes in if he'd be alright about it."

Chapter Nineteen

After needing a night to sleep on it, Don agreed, with certain caveats, to Jane coming to Blackpool with us. Dad assured him that we'd be under constant supervision which I think he believed when he said it but absolutely didn't happen. A week later I discovered the real reason for my parents' desire for a holiday and their willingness to pay a relief manager. Their good friends, Joan and Barry Skelton, had recently become owners of the Bunch of Grapes public house in the English seaside resort, famous for its tower. This establishment, it transpired, was the very same pub that I had sat outside as eight-year-old child minder. It was also quite an iconic watering hole for serious drinkers. My parents, it seemed, were looking forward to a busman's holiday. Jane and I were beyond excitement and felt that the four months until we went would drag by.

On March 16th, Jane became a teenager and four days later so did I. Although there was no party for either of us, we were allowed two unescorted cinema trips to the big Odeon on the Headrow in Leeds. We went on the two non-school nights, between our birthdays. We saw Anne of a Thousand Days on the Friday and Paint Your Wagon on the Saturday. There was a suggestion that Jane might be able to stay at our house again on one of these nights but her Dad quashed the idea immediately. Instead, he met us at the bus stop by the Unicorn on both nights.

The Easter holidays followed our birthdays and Don booked some time off work. His plan was for Jane and him to spend a week with his parents in Middlesbrough. So we didn't see much of each other that holiday. I passed the time daydreaming in my room, a bit sulky, imagining Jane having a brilliant time. It was only after she got back I heard how it really panned out. They went on the Wednesday of the first week on the two bus journey. The plan for them both to stay a week fell apart after only the one night. Don claimed he'd suddenly remembered something he needed to get back home for and, giving Jane a Smarties Easter egg in a mug and instructions not to eat it until Sunday, left her alone with his parents.

She'd initially been furious with him for this. The prospect of another six days and nights alone with her Grandparents seemed unbearable. She'd been convinced she would be bored to tears staying on her own with them so sat sulking on the sofa, plotting to kill the budgerigar and silently cursing her Dad.

"So young lady, what are we to do with you to get that smile back?" Her Grandma asked. In response, she'd suggested going to the shop to buy a comic at which her granny's face had lit up. Saying she could do much better than that, she sent her husband to get the step-ladders.

Half an hour later, while he was closing the loft and putting his ladders away, Jane and her Granny sat at the kitchen table in front of two large cardboard boxes. The elderly woman seemed transformed as she spoke with passion about her love for detective novels. The boxes contained works from Conan-Doyle, Willkie Collins and Dorothy L. Sayers amongst others but her real favourites were the Agatha Christie's. Proudly, she told Jane she had all 82 of her books.

"I started collecting 'em when I were just a lass," a suddenly more talkative and amicable grandmother confided in Jane.

"I heard her on t' radio readin' out one of her stories. It were so good I thought to me self I should try and get some of her books."

Jane stared at her wide-eyed and pensive, absorbing this new information.

"It were while I was expecting your Dad. I already had me first bairn, your uncle Jimmy that would have been, if Diphtheria hadn't taken him."

Her face softened as she recalled her lost child and her eyes acquired a glassy front.

"Oh Granny, that's really sad. I dint know me Dad had a brother."

"Aye well," the old woman began, regaining her practical and slightly detached composure, "I dare say there's a lot you don't know and what you don't know won't hurt you."

Seeing the disappointment in her granddaughter's face she added, a little softer,

"Any road, it were all a long time ago. These books will be just the job to keep you occupied. I might start reading 'em again me self an' all."

A huge smile revealed the pleasure she would take from that.

"I don't think I can read all these in a week." Jane said.

"No love, I don't think you can either so you'll have to take some home with you, then every time you come to see us, you can get a couple more."

That was the start of Jane's obsession with the queen of crime fiction and all things Agatha. It also led to more regular trips to see her grandparents and discussions about the plots with this person she had found hiding inside her granny.

A week after abandoning her, Don returned to take her home. As they sat side by side on the bus, he confessed that he'd made up his stuff he needed to do and had actually taken some extra shifts at the factory.

"I knew if I spend one more night with them two and their bloody funny ways, I'd be back to drinking me self stupid again!"

So Jane agreed that he'd done the right thing and said it hadn't been that bad all in all and she was happy to visit regularly but just for the day in future.

We had another family visit at the Unicorn over the Easter holidays when Aunty Shirley and her husband came over to show off their new mark II Ford Cortina. Mum had gone into her usual overdrive on preparation for their arrival while Dad found some urgent work in the cellar. On appearance at the front door, my Aunt and Uncle were ushered into the front room where a massive display of cakes and sandwiches awaited them along with the best china. I had been instructed to entertain my cousins in the back room, where the table had been set for us. Our feast consisted of two large bottles of fizzy pop, six bags of crisps, bread and butter, and a large almost defrosted Black Forest Gateau. Alison seemed happy to be there and was keen to hear news of my friends, well one in particular, and Mark was as pleased to have been brought visiting as Mum and Dad were to have them visit. He munched his way through four of the bags of crisps and a very large piece of the cake while watching Billy Smart's circus on the telly. Alison whispered and giggled at me with all the news about her whiz of a social life back in Sheffield. She asked me about Paul and I said I hadn't seen him since the school play but told her about Chris asking me out.

"I thought you liked him?" she squealed.

"I do, well I did!" I exclaimed, "But now I think he's a knob."

Mark smirked at this proving my suspicion that he wasn't that engrossed in the circus.

"Aww, our Kim said Knob, better not let your Mam hear you or she'll wash your mouth out with soap and water."

I told her about the Pudsey baths discos and how I'd heard Paul had a new girlfriend from there. I thought she might have been cut up about it but she just shrugged and said it was never going to work with her and him.

"These long distance romances never really survive."

I smiled unable to comment without laughing. Later I told her the news that had gone round our school like wildfire, just as we broke up for Easter. The Pavilion was closing down as a cinema and was to be a bingo hall and next week was its final session. I told her that Jane and I had decided to go as we had heard that just about everybody was going.

"Well next time you see Paul, tell him I send him my love but it just wasn't meant to be."

I didn't have to worry about laughing this time as Mark threw a cushion at her from the sofa.

"Who do you think you are you stupid cow? You sound like you're in one of our Kim's stupid plays. This Paul lad probably dunt even remember who you are!"

I had time to stifle my laugh with a pretend cough and muttered I would certainly pass it on if I saw him. Needless to say I didn't, well actually I didn't get the chance.

Back at school the following Monday and we were plunged into preparation for the end of year exams, which would determine the following year's academic division. This system of catering for the educational needs was, I believed, taken from the English football league. The two highest marked girls and ditto boys in the B to D sets were moved up while the lowest achievers in A to C were moved down.

"We'll still be friends next year when you're in 3A wont we?" Jane asked as we walked home at the end of the first week, "

"What are you talking about? I'm nowhere near clever enough to go up!" I exclaimed, "But thanks for thinking I am."

"Well who else is there that would go up beside you an Suzanne?"

"Diane and Sharon?" I suggested.

"We couldn't be that lucky," she laughed.

Up to this point, I hadn't considered this scenario. I badly wanted to do well in the exams. Last year I'd been seventh in the girls and tenth overall in our class. I wanted to show Mum and Dad I was clever and should stay on and go to college. Whenever I thought of my future life, I imagined myself in an office, typing and moving files and bits of paper around. I knew the only way to get that sort of job was to convince my parents to let me go to college but I really didn't fancy going up into the A stream. There weren't any advantages I could see other than being declared a swot. Starting again to learn all the classroom politics, fitting in and being made to do French? No, I definitely didn't want to go up. When I'd said out loud that I wasn't clever enough, I'd been secretly hoping that I might be top five but now with the point raised, I was terrified. What if I was smarter than I thought? Two of the girls who were higher than me last year had gone up; what if the others hadn't worked as hard as me this year? Who, other than Suzanne, did I know that took school work as seriously as me?

These thoughts stayed with me as an unaddressed worry, until at the end of May when the testing time arrived. We spent three days filing in and out of the main hall at various times of the day to sit our *'let's see what you've learned this year'* yardstick examinations. After that, there was nothing to do but wait for the results.

Throughout those last few weeks of term, Jane and I reinstated our Saturday trips to Leeds, wandering around Woolworths and sitting in the window of the Golden Egg. Although now we accepted that neither of us liked coffee, drinking strawberry or banana milkshakes instead, slowly through long straws, eeking out our time playing at grown-ups. We occasionally saw Diane and Sharon on the bus and managed to be civil with one another but only said hello before moving swiftly past. I saw Chris at school but was spared the embarrassment of wondering what to say to him as he kept his distance. On the very rare occasions we passed in the corridors, he looked the other way. Jane and I had one more clandestine trip to Rodley Bottom and a walk along the canal to meet up with David, Paul and Keith and again we watched them not catch any fish. They were revising for their exams and working hard to impress their teachers and live up to expectations. Although in David's case, the greatest pressure of expectation came from himself. Keith made a joke about Paul not having to work too hard in biology as he was having private tuition. I asked innocently if he had a teacher coming to his house, much to Keith and David's amusement.

"He's getting his leg over with a fourth year from the girls' grammar is what Keith means," David informed me.

"Oh right," I said, embarrassed.

"Hey come on Lads, we're just good mates that's all!"

Paul laughed but that twinkle in his eyes belied his words and showed off the pride in the suggestion of his sexual prowess. The boys had brought a blanket as well as their fishing stools, so Jane and I took advantage of the weather and sun-bathed while they got on with the fishing rod posturing. It started to get quite hot after a while and I reached across to the large umbrella which was up and resting to the side of the stools, I positioned it just behind our heads as we lay down on the blanket and chatted. After a while, I noticed the nice little cloth drawstring bag that hung from the inside veins of the brolly.

"Oh what's in this pretty bag?" I asked reaching up and touching the bag that swung just above my face.

The answer came just as my finger felt the slight movement.

"Maggots!"

We got the bus home shortly after that giving the umbrella a wide bearth.

I remember being so nervous on the day the exam results were being announced, I felt sick. As we took our places in the hall, I really worried that I was going to throw up. I needn't have. I was fifth behind Julie Eden, Linda Mitten, Deborah Thorn, and Suzanne. The boys had worked a bit harder that year so in the class as a whole I was ninth but still a result I was happy with. At dinner break, Suzanne favoured us with one of her rare visits to the playground.

"I was really expecting you to be top you know Suzy," I said.

"Were you?" she responded raising her eyebrows and smiling, "Didn't you think I was smart enough to get enough wrong so I could stay where I was?"

I looked at her with disbelief. Here was a girl who worked hard all the time. Dinner times and breaks were used to swot up in order that she could do well, and she really wanted to learn French, yet now she was saying she'd deliberately dumbed-down in order not to progress. This was crazy.

Jane, who was twelfth, rolled her eyes and said,

"Well you weren't that smart. You only need to be third and you got fourth."

"Part of the plan," she said breezily, "Next year I'll be third so I can show some improvement without going up then either."

And I had no doubt that she would do just that.

"Anyway," she added, "what would you two do without me to keep an eye on you and advise you on all this pesky boyfriend stuff?"

"That's a fair point," Jane said with a smile.

"What about French though?" I asked.

"They're running some night school classes here from September and it's free for under sixteen's. My Dad says it'll be better as well as we'll concentrate more on speaking it rather than just the grammar."

Three days later the school year finished and we broke up for summer.

Chapter Twenty

A week later Jane and I packed our suitcases ready for our holiday. It was a warm but cloudy morning, mid July, and filled with exhilarated anticipation, we put our cases in Dad's car and set off towards the West coast.

We arrived in the back streets of Blackpool in brilliant sunshine after a three hour drive which had been on occasions, a little fraught. There had been a fair bit of swearing from Dad at both the traffic and Mum's map reading abilities and we'd eaten our egg sandwiches en route, Mum feeding Dad as he drove, so he didn't have to stop, so we were more than ready to get out of the smelly hot car.

Our vacation week had to be Monday to Monday, on Dad's insistence. This was so he could bank the previous week's takings in the morning before handing over the keys to the relief manager. Dad's trip to the bank meant that, despite Jane being at our house at eight that morning and both of us having our cases by the front door minutes later, we hadn't left until almost ten. The last thing Dad had done before we set off was securely double lock and bolt the door between the living quarters and the pub. Accommodation was not offered as part of the deal for the job. The stand-in manager and his wife were to sleep in their caravan, which was already moored safely in the pub car park. Even though Terry and Margaret were old friends of my parents, I'd heard Dad ask Sally to keep an eye on them. He gave her the phone number of where we were staying, telling her to let him know if she thought 'there were owt dodgy goin' on'. Interestingly, I'd also heard him say much the same to Terry about the three regular barmaids, of which Sally was one, and give him the number as well. Trust didn't come easy to my Dad.

Our accommodation was a four storey B&B called, very unimaginatively, Sea View, which it didn't have. It had a lounge, dining room and reception on the ground floor and bedrooms over the other three. These all had a washbasin and there was a shared bathroom on each floor. Mum and Dad's double room was on the second floor and Jane and I had our twin abode under eaves in the attic. It had two single beds with a small set of drawers between them, a wardrobe and dressing table with triple mirror. It matched perfectly with my fantasy of our future flat share. Mum and Dad came up briefly to inspect the room.

"Bloody hell, that beam's a bit low, you could knock your sen out if you got out of bed too quick!" was Dad's pronouncement.

"No kettle!" Mum declared in horror but once she saw our delight she nodded and with a small smile said, "I suppose it'll do alright for you two. Right we're off to sort ourselves out. You two get yourselves unpacked an we'll see you in the lounge in half an hour."

We did this quickly and as we hung up our clothes, bought especially for the holiday, I noticed Jane had some very trendy stuff. Right at the bottom of her suitcase, she had a new make-up bag, cotton wool balls and a bottle of Johnson's baby lotion. I laughed with happiness at the prospect of us getting ready together and going out in the evenings. Dad had already said we would go to all the shows on the piers and the Winter gardens and maybe the Tower Circus. We were delighted at the prospect of such a hectic week of social engagements and keen to start them as soon as possible. We raced down stairs to wait for Mum and Dad in the lounge and just after two-thirty the four of us went for a look around and ride on a tram. As we left, the landlady told us we needed to be back by four forty-five as high tea was five o'clock on the dot!

We crossed the road and the tram tracks to get to the seaside front and breathed in coastal air. A light breeze carried the mixed aroma of candy floss, fish and chips and the sea air and as it washed over me, I was so happy I thought I might cry. We were just a short walk from the south pier where the David Nixon magic show was on and Dad said we should definitely go to that. I said yes and maybe even that night but Mum said there was plenty of time. Dad went on to tell us how he really liked *that Anita Harris* who was in it with him.

"Lovely she is, aye we should definitely see that."

Mum told him he was soft in the head and to get a move on as there was a tram coming. We boarded with the intention of going right up to the north pier, sitting on the top deck so we could take in the golden mile, and walk back. This was a good plan and I'm sure it had been their intention when we actually got on, but when we got off at Grand Metropole, it seemed they'd changed their mind.

"Me an' your Dad are getting the tram straight back."

Mum was opening her purse.

"Here's a couple of ten bob notes to have a go on the slot machines and pay for your tram ride if you don't want to walk back."

She hardly paused for breath, let alone to allow me make any objections before continuing,

"We're gonna say hello to Jean and Frank at the Grapes for an hour or so. See you back at the lodge at quarter to five. Bye luv."

And they climbed on the south-bound tram and were gone.

We were back at Sea View just after four-thirty, so were sitting all angelic and well behaved in the lounge when they got back and on the dot of five, our landlady hit the gong in reception and ushered us and two other couples into the dining room.

We hadn't known what to expect for high tea but were delighted with the spread put before us. A large plate of small triangular sandwiches of potted meat, boiled ham and tinned salmon (vegetarians hadn't been invented then so were not catered for), cheese and fruit scones with small dishes of jam and cream. Four large pieces from a Victoria sandwich all presented on beautiful fine china and accompanied by gallons of strong tea, orange squash and lemonade. Drinking alcohol in the afternoon always made Mum and Dad mellow and affable, so I chose that moment to ask if we were going to see a show that night.

"Well we were thinking that it might be better to do that later on in the week."

Dad said just before putting a whole sandwich in his mouth and picking up a cheese scone.

"Oh right," I said, looking down at my plate with what I hoped was a disappointed expression.

"So what shall we do tonight then?" I asked looking directly at him.

Putting the scone on his plate, Dad gingerly picked up the delicate china cup with both hands. It looked so incongruous, I couldn't take my eyes off him as he took a sip of his tea but I could see he was avoiding my eyes. Mum leapt to answer,

"Well there's a darts match round at the Grapes and your Dad really fancies a game." She was spreading jam on to a scone. She was far more practiced at managing my expectations and dealing with my disappointments. "So we thought we'd go round there."

"Right," I said with voice that couldn't sound more miserable. "Will me and Jane be allowed in or will we have to wait outside?"

She looked up sharply as if I'd suggested something completely ridiculous.

"Don't you want to stop here and watch telly?"

"Not really," I whined.

"Well we can ask Jean if you can mebbe sit in the snug or somat."

Dad was thinking out loud and looking to Mum for a solution. It was obvious that they hadn't really thought this through and had only just realised that they were responsible for two non-adults.

"Can me and Jane go to the Pleasure Beach first then?"

I actually had tears in my eyes, which I knew would help my cause, but they had come unbidden along with my frustration at their inability to remember our existence.

Mum had been about to take a bite of her scone but paused and said,

"Why don't you and Jane go for a bit after tea while me and your Dad have an hour?"

I widened my eyes as I stared across the table at her.

"It's not dark till after nine so as long as you're back here by then, you can go on your own."

This was a better result than I had hoped for and later Jane complemented me on my performance at the table.

"If you don't win an Oscar one day there's no justice in this world."

As Jean and Frank's pub was only three streets away from the guest house, Mum said she'd pop back at nine and check we were in and safe. What she actually did was telephone the guest house at half past nine to be told by our landlady that we were sitting in the lounge watching the High Chaparral.

Mum and Dad didn't go back to the Grapes for a dinnertime session again but did go every evening. So they never took us to any of the shows but we did all go to the Winter Gardens, up the Tower and for another trip to the Pleasure Beach which was really good fun. I could see they enjoyed these little jaunts as much as Jane and I, but they didn't let them get in the way of a lunchtime drink in one bar or another. This was purely for research, Dad assured us, tasting the beer in the other establishments to let Joan and Frank know what they were up against. His firm opinion was none of them were anywhere near as good as Frank's and they were all over-priced an' all!

We weren't required to sit on any backyard walls during these taster sessions but deposited in the nearest slot arcade with a bag of pennies. They did generally only have a couple of drinks so it wasn't too bad and we discovered Bingo. More accurately, I discovered a dark-haired good looking boy who happened to be running a bingo stall. He was in his late teens, with masses of self-confidence and a warm cheeky voice. His name was John and he flirted outrageously with all the females that queued up to play his game. There were the occasional male players but they didn't tend to stay long, being edged out generally after one game by a constant flow of women and girls. Age was no barrier to his charm as grannies and schoolgirls alike were all caught in his welcoming smile. Although most of us ignored his instructions when he said 'eyes down' at the start of a game, preferring to look at him. It was hard to get a seat as quite a few of his clientele seemed to be there all day.

At high tea on the day we'd first stumbled on that particular arcade, Mum asked what we'd been up to and Jane told her,

"We played bingo and it were brilliant. I think we're going to play it again tomorrow."

And we did. We played every lunchtime drinking session for the rest of the holiday and although there was no direct interaction between us, I knew I'd fallen in love.

We even ventured there one evening but discovering he wasn't there quickly moved on. Jane said I had cow eyes when I looked at him and she'd never seen me so soppy and suggested,

"Shall we give him a note asking him where he goes in the evening?"

I was mortified at this prospect, looking round at the array of attractive girls and women hanging on his every word.

"I couldn't bear it if he told me to get lost cos I'm fat and spotty. I think I'd rather, if he's noticed me at all, he'll remember me as the one that got away. It will be his deathbed regret that he never asked me out."

Jane narrowed her eyes and told me I was neither fat or spotty and I was talking like an idiot, before giving me a hug.

Our routine established the days began with a full English breakfast followed by a wander around, a quick drink for them and a bingo fix for us, then something with chips which was eaten on the beach in deckchairs, except for on Saturday when it wasn't so nice. That day, dinner was inside a greasy spoon cafe with a big sign on the door barring admission to dogs, travellers and prams. Afternoons were a tram ride to one or other of the piers where we lost more money in the amusements, before setting off back for our tea at five. These teatime feasts were all fairly similar, although the appearance of chicken and the inevitable egg sandwich varied the savouries a little, and on the Sunday we were offered toasted crumpets with butter or honey which was a revelation to us all.

Having proved ourselves trustworthy on the first evening, we were allowed to go out by ourselves after tea but had to be back by nine. We'd taken Jane's make-up bag out with us each night and applied liberal amounts of eye shadow in the public toilets down the road. After realising Mum wasn't going to see us when we got in, we didn't bother calling in on the way home to remove it. The landlady smiled at us and gave us a conspiratorial nod when she let us in the next two nights at nine on the dot. Our evenings out were really very innocent, all we did was walk around the Pleasure Beach, linking arms, giggling and posing in our new modern outfits and make-up. On the Thursday night there was a teenage disco in the ballroom at the end of the north pier. We did the right thing by asking for permission to go, although I think I might possibly have described it as a dancing class. So when Dad said ok, we calmly went to our room before jumping up and down in delight.

That night the eyeliner came out as well as the shadow and mascara and although it was applied rather shakily it made us feel really grown-up. We hardly spoke to anyone once we got inside except for a couple of boys near the bar as we queued to buy a cola. They were quite good looking and seemed keen to chat to us but Jane was unimpressed, so once we got our drinks we went to the other side of the room. The hall was dark and smelly and we got quite hot practicing our disco moves in our teenage disguise. Singing along as we danced around our handbags, the evening grew dark and time became fluid. I noticed the clock and confidence and joy were suddenly displaced by panic; it was gone ten. We made a Cinderella type exit, running from the pier all the way back to Sea View. The landlady opened the door with her usual smile and our relief was palpable as she told us not to worry as Mum hadn't rung yet. With pretend serious face, she added that when she did call, she wouldn't split on us as long as we promised her we hadn't been up to no good. We had no trouble with this promise blurting out where we had been and what we had been doing.

"Right, well you best get up to your room and don't you be getting any of that make-up on my towels!"

By Friday, my parents were feeling a bit guilty at abandoning us every night although still not prepared to give up their plans, they bought us tickets for shows for the last three nights. They were the Tower Circus, Ken Dodd and his Diddy men on the central pier and the David Nixon magic show. I think Dad would have liked to have come to with us to the last one but the Grapes had a bigger pull than Anita Harris when push came to shove.

It was the last night of our holiday and the show finished quite late, so we didn't get back to the guest house until almost eleven. Not that it mattered as Mum had given up calling to check on us. We were actually back a good hour and a half before them as their farewells took a bit longer than planned and Dad treated the whole guest house to his rendition of 'Danny Boy' as Mum ushered him upstairs.

It was raining the next morning as Dad put our bags in the car after settling up with the landlady, telling her what a grand place she had and that we'd be back next year. She nodded and smiled, said we would be very welcome and also added what well behaved and well mannered teenagers we were. With a glance over at Jane and me and the merest suggestion of a wink she said,

"They're a credit to how you've brought them up."

"She thinks we're sisters Dad," I said.

"Yeah, like in Cinderella an' I'm your fairy god mother," he laughed as he shut the boot asking "Where the bloody 'ell has your mother gone? I want to be off."

Mum was stocking up on cigarettes for the journey from the newsagents round the corner. She'd also bought a couple of packets of opal fruits. I'd asked if we could have sherbet lemons.

"No you cannot!" she'd exclaimed, "Sucking boiled sweets in the back of a car is dangerous. If your Dad goes over a bump you could choke!"

So we chewed our way through the assorted flavours as she and Dad filled the car with nicotine smoke, window only opened a crack so as not to mess up her hair.

When we got home, it was agreed the holiday had been a success and as far as my parents were concerned Jane could come round whenever she wanted to, she'd always be welcome. For the rest of the school holidays normal service was resumed. We spent our days at the park or in my bedroom with my transistor radio and teenage magazines. Over two very rainy days towards the end of August, we decided to decorate my bedroom by completely covering all the walls with posters. It was lovely to fall asleep looking deep into the eyes of Donny Osmond.

Chapter Twenty-one

Even though the summer was lovely, Jane and I were both ready to go back to school in September. On our first day we were surprised to find Sharon, Diane and Maureen standing just outside the school gates waiting for us. They wanted to be friends, Sharon informed us, like we used to be. It seemed all animosity, real and imagined, had evaporated over the summer break and so for the whole of that first term, things were good. Suzanne wasn't convinced of this turn around in behaviour and shook her head in her quiet and knowledgeable way.

"Some people can make their mouths say anything but that's not what they're thinking. It's just a load of old rubbish to help them get what they want. Don't trust 'em Kim, they'll always be trouble them three."

Filing away this observation I cautiously tried to enjoy the return of friendliness.

We hung around together at school and sometimes at weekends. There were trips to the Rollerena, pictures and bowling alley but it wasn't as friendly as it had been and as far as I was concerned my real friends were Jane and Suzanne. The other three were just classmates. Once, when we were coming out of the bowling alley we saw Keith and David just arriving. Jane brushed my arm saying she'd catch me up and as none of the others had noticed, we kept on walking. She came running up to the bus stop just as the bus arrived, looking pink and flushed. Something had happened but she just bit down a smile and shook her head at my raised eyebrows. It wasn't till we got off the bus at the Unicorn that I found out what was going on. David had told her that arrangements were being made for a meeting with him and Don. This was to talk about the possibility of the three of them spending time together over the Christmas holiday.

The following week a social worker went round to her house to talk about David spending time at home. The meeting went well and it was agreed that the three of them would spend Christmas day together and Jane would be helping her Dad cook the dinner.

"It'll be like the blind leading the blind." She laughed.

"It'll be great," I said.

"Yes it will!" she beamed back at me.

A little later than normal, on the last week of that term, the drama club announced the school production was to be Billy Liar and would be performed just before breaking up for Easter the following year. We were all given a copy of it to read over the Christmas holidays and auditions would start on the first week of term.

Breaking up on the Wednesday before Christmas, we were excited to learn there was another teenage disco at Pudsey Baths that weekend. Jane and I had been told that, on condition we were outside at ten o clock for Dad to pick us up, we could go.

It was a magical time. We'd been having so much fun and since turning 13, it seemed I was being allowed more and more freedom. I remember thinking, as we climbed the steps that evening, my teenage years were going to be so great and things just kept getting better.

Walking in through the double doors, past the machine that served hot chocolate and Bovril, we paid our money to the lady at the trestle table and joined the throng of our contemporaries. The amount of adolescents mulling around on top of the boarded pool confirmed that there was little else to do for teenagers on Friday evenings. Some were swaying, self-consciously while others, mostly girls, embraced the loud, bass heavy music as they'd seen on Top of the Pops. The boys mostly stood around the edges in their packs, looking on. We walked over to the far corner to find Suzanne. She was with her cousin Denise who looked amazing in her sparkly eye shadow and false eye-lashes. She was very talkative and friendly but was soon whisked off to the dance floor by two of her class mates.

Jane was a little distant, scanning the faces around us in the dimly lit room, but after a while suggested we have a dance. While we gyrated to the music we waved and shouted to people we knew including Maureen who was talking to Chris. We spotted Sharon and Diane but before we could catch their eye, they were lost in the mêlée. It was all very amicable and everyone was having a really good time. We'd probably been there about an hour and Jane had gone to get us some squash while I was dancing with Suzy. The music slowed down a little and so we left the floor to stand and watch as people started to pair up for the close hold, stepping in circle ritual. Suzy was pointing out her cousin who was dancing with a really good looking boy who I thought looked familiar.

"It's Peter Ford," she said.

"Peter Ford off the telly?"

"Yeah, his Mam and Dad run the post office but he lives in London most of the time now." Just in case I wasn't impressed enough she added, "He's seventeen!"

Peter Ford had been a child actor since the age of eight when he'd got a small part in Coronation Street. Since then he'd had several bigger roles and rumour had it he was about to make a film.

"I can't believe he's here."

"He always comes when he's home. Our Denise really fancies him. She's been trying to get off with him for ages."

Watching the way they were grinding their bodies together I was just about to say that I thought she had probably succeeded, when I felt a hand on my shoulder and a voice in my ear said,

"Hello Kimbo, fancy seeing you here."

As I turned round, something bizarre happened. The swarm of butterflies was back, flapping around my stomach, causing heat, confusion and an overwhelming giddiness. It clearly showed on my face as Paul put his hands on my shoulders, leaned towards me and with his eyes locked onto mine asked,

"Do you wanna dance?"

Hypnotically, I nodded and with his arm around me, we moved a few feet on to the dancing area. Finding a tiny space, he turned and put his arms around me holding me so close it made me dizzy. The feeling of euphoria was so intense that everything and everybody around me melted away, it was just Paul and me. My head naturally tilted on to his shoulder and with his beautiful blonde curls brushing my cheek, I was totally relaxed. It felt as if I'd done this a million times before, it just felt right. Onlookers would have seen two teenagers standing very close, arms wrapped around each other and moving from foot to foot, round and round in a circle to the beat of the Jackson five singing 'I'll be there'. What they couldn't see was that for me it was a life changing three minutes and fifty seven seconds.

As Michael and his brothers completed their declaration of constancy we moved slightly apart. Mathew Southern comfort began to sing about Woodstock and he pulled me close again as we resumed our sway. This time my head didn't go on his shoulder and still smiling, he leaned forward and kissed me gently on the lips. I thought I would melt.

"I've wanted to do that for ages," his voice husky with emotion.

He brushed his lips over mine again and kissing me for a little longer this time, our lips parted but our foreheads were still touching and he lifted his hand to stroke my cheek. Unable to speak but still smiling, I gazed into his eyes as he started to lean in again. Our lips were less than centimeters away from touching when an arm forced its way between us, followed by Chris's very angry head wedging us apart and yelling,

"What the fuck do you think you're doing you fuckin' piece of shit?"

Things moved a little fast after that. The dancers parted as Chris and Paul fell to the floor, fists flailing into each other. From nowhere two burley looking men appeared and hoisted them back to their feet, dragged them to the doors and threw them outside on to the steps. I hadn't moved from the spot. I was in some sort of shock induced inertia, so I almost jumped out of my skin when Suzanne touched my arm.

"Kim," she said quite forcefully as if I had been ignoring her, "Come on you need to come and help me sort Jane out!"

Turning to look at her I started to recover my wits.

"What do you mean, sort Jane out?"

"I think she might have had somat stronger than squash, and I don't mean Bovril!"

Taking my arm, Suzy led me to the very back of the seating area. As we approached, I could clearly hear Jane's voice, overloud and slurry saying that this place was amazing and she'd had a really good time and that nobody had any idea how lucky she was. Some of her words were running into one another and she was giggling and hiccupping as she held forth her proclamations.

"Oh god!" I hissed to Suzy. "Who are those boys she's with?"

"No idea. They're not from our school and I think they're fourth years. They've got vodka."

As we got closer, Jane saw us and stood up on very shaky legs that made her fall straight back on her chair calling out,

"This is my lovely friend Kim, Kimmy, Kimberly, Kimbo, Kimmy-Kins, oh she's just lovely my friend Kim is and so nice oh so very nice and good, oh yes she a very nice and good girl Kim is."

Three pairs of eyes looked at me, one of them proffered a paper cup,

"Hello Kim, come and have some of our special punch?"

"No thanks," I said, swerving past them to get to Jane.

I thought there was going to be another altercation as Suzanne and I got Jane to her feet and manoeuvred her toward the girls' changing room and toilet. The lads seemed to think she should stay chatting to them and started to get leery. But some of the adrenalin that had been flying around that high glass ceilinged and redbrick building must have found its way into my bloodstream. I elbowed them out of the way telling them,

"You'd better just fuck off or I'll get the bouncers over! "My words set Jane off giggling and saying quite loudly,

"Aw Kimmy, you swore, I heard you, you said the F word. Your Mam will have to wash your mouth out now!"

"What time is it Suzy?" I asked

"Nearly quarter to nine, I'll go and get some crisps. If we can get her to eat somat that might sober her up," she replied, walking back across the dance floor towards the reception and the tuck shop. I continued into the changing room with Jane wondering how we could sober her up. We needed to get her into a less animated state before we all got into Dad's car for the lift home. The sight of Maureen being comforted by Sharon and Diane in the far side of the dressing rooms was something I hadn't bargained for and so I quickly turned Jane around, walked her back around the dance floor and met with Suzanne in the doorway to the reception.

"Change of plan," I said steering Jane to the door, "I'm taking her out to get some chips. The fresh air will help."

For a 13 year-old, I was very knowledgeable about over indulgence in alcohol. Nodding towards the bouncers who were looking curiously at us, she linked Jane's other arm and said, "I'll come with you."
Aware of the scrutiny we were under, we walked as steadily as Jane's state would allow as we left the building.

There was no sign of Paul or Chris when we got outside, so we bought three bags of chips and sat on the park wall by the bus stop eating them. Jane said she didn't want any but proceeded to eat hers in record time after which she threw up behind the bus shelter. After fully empting her stomach and telling us how she felt *'Bloody awful!'*, she was a lot quieter. We made her drink most of a big bottle of fizzy orange, bought from the off-licence, and we walked her up and down the high street until it was nearly ten. After using the last bit of pop and hem of my dress, I wiped her face free of the vomit smears and smudged makeup as she sat compliant in front of me. We got back to stand in front of the baths just as people started to come out. Dad arrived within seconds and smiled to see us waiting.

"You must have been first out," he said as I opened the back door.

"Well we didn't want to keep you waiting. Is it ok to give Suzy a lift home?"

"Course it is, jump in."

Without further bidding, Suzy got in next to him and I got in the back where I could keep hold of Jane's hand. I ignored Dad's puzzled expression at Suzy taking the front seat. Glancing at Jane and me in the mirror he asked,

"So did you all have a good time?"

"Well I thought it was a bit dull really," Suzanne began quite matter-of-factly before I had a chance to reply. She went on in a frank and older than her years voice. "Most of the people there were childish and really didn't know how to behave."

"Oh really?" Dad raised his eyebrows as he put the car in gear and pulled and away from the kerb. Having not met Suzanne before, her turn of phrase was a bit of a surprise.

"Yes," she went on, "that's why we came out early, not really our cup of tea at all was it Kim?" She turned round to look at me with this question.

"It certainly wasn't how I thought it would be," I admitted.

Thinking of my first kiss had set the nectar feeding creatures fluttering around again.

We dropped Suzanne off first and as she walked up her path, Dad commented rhetorically, "Well, she's an old fashion lass int she?"

My fears about my Dad realising Jane had been drinking were unfounded as she remained silent the whole ride home. Suzanne's star turn had distracted him enough for him not to notice her slightly dishevelled appearance or the slight aroma of a fruity sick smell that was prevalent in the back. She squeezed my hand as we pulled up outside her house and watching her walk towards her house, I smiled, feeling a huge surge of relief as she looked absolutely fine.

As soon as I got into bed that night, I switched off my bedside lamp and just lay there thinking about what had occurred and inevitably, about Paul. With my eyes shut, I could conjure him up before me, his beautiful blue eyes, his blonde curly hair and his cheeky smile. I could replay all the scenes when we'd met and the way he always seemed happy and upbeat. I could hear his voice playful and warm calling me Kimbo. As the images of our dance filled my head, I felt tingly inside thinking of his arms around me and I fell asleep imagining his warm moist lips on mine.

Chapter Twenty-two

The next day was one of those unusual ones where Mum was up early and ready to go out, with me in tow, to complete our Christmas food shopping. Aunty Shirley and Uncle Bill were due to visit the following day so she was having one of her rare housewife and mother weekends. She and I would be spending the whole day together, starting with the food shopping, followed by the afternoon in Leeds. Our groceries were bought in the shops along Stanningley Road, planned to the last detail. Our method was to divide and conquer which meant I went into the fish mongers and the bakers while she went to the green grocers and the butchers and we met up in the Thrift to buy the cereal, sauces and tinned stuff. This final meeting, timed to coincide with Dad arriving in the car at exactly ten thirty to pick us up and get home before opening up the pub. It all went precisely to plan but left me no time to dwell any further on the previous nights dance floor incident. Carrying the bags from the car, I was wondering when I would see Paul again. I'd been looking forward to going shopping with Mum in Leeds but now there was something far more important I wanted to do. I'd just gone through the door with a heavy bag of fruit when I heard a familiar voice addressing Dad on the doorstep.

"Hello Mr. Asquith, is your Kimberly in?"

"She is, aye, but she's going out with her Mam." he answered.

I put the bag down on the table and glanced across at Mum who had thrown herself in the armchair and was having a cigarette to help recover from her exertions. Taking advantage of the nicotine break I dashed back outside. Sharon and Maureen were just walking away so I ran to catch them up. Hearing my footsteps they turned round.

"We're getting the half eleven bus to Leeds so I've got to go and get ready in a minute, where are you two off?" I asked in my friendliest tone.

"Not sure yet," began Sharon cagily. "We just wanted to come and ask you what was goin' on with you and Paul."

"Nothing as far as I know. We had a dance and then him and Chris had a fight and got thrown out."

"And you and Jane went after them!" Maureen barked.

"We most certainly did not!" I countered decisively.

"You left at the same time as they were chucked out," Sharon challenged.

"We went to get some chips and to get away from some stupid lads that were trying to get us to drink vodka."

I began explaining but knew I was wasting my time.

"You were snoggin' Paul!" A fine mist of saliva sprayed from Sharon's mouth as she literally spat the words at me.

"He kissed me," I replied trying to suppress a smile that was forcing itself to my face.

"Twice!" Sharon hissed with another spray of spittle.

I couldn't help myself. I felt a huge smile erupt across my face as I nodded my head eagerly and confirmed,

"Yes, twice, and it was lovely."

I turned round and started walking back towards the house.

"So are you goin' out with him or what?" Sharon yelled after me but I didn't turn round.

The afternoon wasn't so bad and Mum in an exceptionally good mood let me pick two new frocks, neither of them Crimplene, although the stipulation was that I'd be ironing them myself. The memory of my slow dance and first kiss, playing on a loop in my mind in any spare moment. I'd edited a new bit on to the end now of seeing the look on Sharon and

Maureen's faces as I told them I'd liked it.

That night I washed glasses until being sent to bed at ten thirty. Dad said they wouldn't be too long themselves as they'd a lot to do the next day before Aunty Shirley and her gormless husband and spoilt kids arrived. In fact, it was ten past two when I heard them come upstairs and nosily use the bathroom. Any plans they'd had for Sunday morning had dissolved in the electronically produced froth on top of the beers they'd supped at their lock-in.

At half past eight the next morning, I was munching my cornflakes as I looked across the table at my parents. They sat, looking tired and hung over in a fug of their creation. Mum, in her head-to-toe encasement of nylon and Dad in his old dark shirt and cellar trousers, held up with brown and white striped braces.

"Did Harry pop in last night then?" I asked.

"He bloody well did and we couldn't get rid of him!" Mum said.

"Aye, and he were telling us about that bloody hooligan brother of your mate. He's only gone and stabbed some poor bugger!" Dad looked up from his reading of the newspaper and nodded his head at me to add weight to this statement.

I spluttered over my soggy mouthful. Covering my mouth with my hand so as not to spit, I managed to ask,

"Which brother?"

"Young un weren't it, Pam?"

"I dunt know, one of them, any road he'll be locked up a while which is no bad thing. Kim put kettle on I need some more tea afore I go and get me self sorted."

As she spoke she stubbed out one cigarette before immediately lighting another. I filled the electric kettle and switched it on. Realising I would get no further information from them I asked,

"What time's Aunty Shirley coming?"

"They're due at half past two just after we shut but I'll put money on 'em getting here before as that bloody Bill will expect a couple o' free pints," Mum answered.

"Well he can bloody well expect!" Dad exclaimed.

Although we knew he would be the genial mine host when his in-laws arrived.

"Is it ok if I go out for half an hour now then?" I asked, "Me and Jane are gonna swap presents."

"You've got plenty of time to do that tomorrow or later in the week. I need you to give the front room a goin' over and straighten your bedroom."

Mum's words were an end to any hopes I had to get down to see Jane. I didn't bother to argue that the front room and my bedroom had been cleaned thoroughly by Sally the day before. I went upstairs to brush my teeth and potter around until it was time to help Mum shell some eggs and prepare the spread for our visitors.

Uncle Bill did indeed make good time on his journey over, getting his family to the Unicorn in record time. He and Aunty Shirley were sat on barstools with a drink in front of them by half past one. Alison and Mark installed in the kitchen with me after being instructed to keep out of trouble. I was tasked with clearing the table for two thirty and covering it with the best white cloth. This so Mum could bring in the guest refreshments, which looked very much like a copy of the Blackpool guest-house high tea.

Alison was full of talk about her new boyfriend while Mark just mooched around the kitchen chewing pink gum with his mouth open and occasionally blowing bubbles which popped noisily. After telling me at great length about her exploits, none of which I believed, she finally asked me,

"So what's happening with you, are you going out with anybody yet?"

"Well I sort of am, I think."

And I told her about what had happened on the dance floor.

"Well that's a bit rubbish Kim, you can't go out with Paul!" she snapped.

"Why can't I?"

"Because I went out with him and he still likes me and," her voice rising with anger, "if he does want to go out with you it's probably only to try and get back with me!"

"Right," I began with a laugh "I'll bear that in mind. Anyway what are you getting for Christmas?"

Before she could answer me, the so-called responsible adults came in through the store-room. It was evident from Uncle Bill's joviality and slightly slurry voice that he had sampled more that one of Dad's excellent beers. Mum must have commented on him driving home as he was saying,

"I'll be fine Pammy love; I've driven home after six pints no trouble afore now ant I Shirl?"

Mum hated being called Pammy and Bill knew this very well.

The rest of the afternoon passed without incident although Alison was definitely off with me, hardly speaking and shooting me dirty looks. It was only when we were waving them off at quarter past five that she addressed me directly. Leaning forward she shouted out of the car window,

"Have a lovely Christmas with your new boyfriend Kim!"

Mum and Dad both looked at me,

"Kim?" Dad spoke first.

"She's just on about Chris Henshaw," I lied quite easily these days, "I told her that he keeps asking me to go out with him."

Dad looked relieved.

"You don't want to start any of that malarkey 'til you've left school," Mum said.

"Lads your age are just trouble!" Dad stated his firm belief, "Any road Pam, come on love, we've got time to have half an hour's kip afore we have to get ready to open up."

I went back to mop up the leftovers, eating so much jam and cream I started to feel sick. I tidied everything away and washed up before going into the front room to watch telly.

Finally, Monday morning came and I was up and dressed so early that I was walking past the old tannery by eight thirty on my way to Jane's house. I could have been there earlier but wanted to wait until Don had gone to work before I knocked on the door. I'd seen the curtains move at the front as I went through the gate so I was surprised when she didn't open the door straight away. I knocked again harder. I was desperate to tell her all about Paul and ask her to help me see him again. As she opened the door all these thoughts and ideas dispersed as I saw her blotched and tear-stained face.

"Jane!" I exclaimed "What's up?"

She said nothing, shaking her head slightly as she let me in. She led me into the living room where we sat on the rug. She was leaning on the chair by the telly, hugging her bent knees, I had my back on the sofa leg.

"What's happened?" I asked.

After a few minutes she told me. Her Dad had been out when she had got in from the disco. She was still feeling the after-effects of the vodka and was massively thirsty but after drinking two glasses of water she was sick again. This was when he got in.

Staring straight ahead she began to cry, making no attempt to stop the tears or snot, between sobs she managed to tell me what happened. After weeks of moderation he had well and truly fallen off the wagon and had burst into the bathroom in a drunken rage. He had pulled her up off the floor where she had been sitting with her head over the toilet and for a moment she thought he was going to slap or punch her. She watched as he drew back his hand, as she'd seen him do to her Mum, but as she cowered, waiting for the blow, he seemed to come to his senses and let her go. He stormed out of the bathroom yelling she was just like her mother and he was fed up of her games. She was shakily pulling herself up when he came back in and grabbing her began to shout,

"You think you're so grown up, goin' out letting lads touch and maul you!" He pulled her into his bedroom saying,

"Well you can sleep in here tonight where I can keep an eye on you," and he pushed her on his bed.

I was frozen as the images she was creating played out in my head. I knew what was coming. I didn't speak, what could I say? She was choking on her gulping sobs, head bent towards her knees and her hands over the back of her crown pressing it down. I managed to move towards her and put my arms round her. I managed to get some words out but couldn't utter the whole question.

"Oh god, he...did he...?"

A few seconds passed with my words hanging as her sobs subsided. She lifted her head looking directly at me, our heads inches apart, she wiped her eyes and nose on her cardigan sleeve,

"No, he didn't fuck me."

I tried to hug her but she shrugged me off.

"But he touched me. His hands were all over me and he kissed me and pressed his self against me."

She had stopped sobbing but big fat tears ran silently down her cheeks as she whispered the words.

"I didn't try to stop him, didn't even struggle. I just laid there and let him. He kept telling me that he loved me and he'd never hurt me and that I had show him how much I loved him."

I stood up quickly.

"Come on," I started, "Go and get some clothes and stuff, you can come to our house. My Mum will know what to do."

Startled she looked up at me sharply,

"What are you talking about? I have to stay here!"

I looked at her incredulously.

"I'm all he's got left." She was looking at me with a new expression of fear as she added, "And you can't tell anybody."

"What! You can't stay here now."

She stood up and fished a handkerchief out of her pocket and blew her nose before saying again, "I have to stay here. If anybody finds out about this I'll end up like our Kev."

I tried to argue with her but she wouldn't listen. She just kept saying she had to stay. He hadn't touched her again on either of the two nights since Friday and he'd not been out. He hadn't mentioned what happened but kept repeating that he didn't know what he'd do without her. I asked her if she was going to tell David. She looked horrified.

"Course not. No one must know and if you really are my friend you'll promise me that you won't tell anyone!"

I had to swear on my Mum's life before she calmed down.

She went to get us both a glass of pop and we started to talk about the disco. I stayed for about an hour as we swapped our stories of the evening. She remembered chatting to the group of lads and that they had offered her vodka.

"I've drunk it before," she said casually. "After Mum left, I found the bottle in the kitchen behind the sink. I'd seen her drinking it loads of times when Dad wasn't around. I asked her what it was once; she told me it was medicine for Mums."

She gave a mocking laugh.

"Anyway, I tried tasting it myself when I first came back from me Gran's last year. It made me feel a bit funny but sort of nice."

Her brown eyes were again sparkling behind tears waiting to fall.

"But I only had a little bit every now and again, there wasn't much left and there's not much else left of her."

A quick wipe away of the newly formed tears before she continued,

"So when these lads said they had some and did I want a drop or two in me squash, I thought yeah, that would be great."

She'd felt quite grown-up and liked the feeling as it had surged through her senses. She'd drunk it quickly 'a *bit like pop*' she recalled.

"One thing's for sure, I am never going to drink alcohol again. It ruins everything!" she declared.

She asked me what I thought of the disco. I told her about Paul and the dance and the kiss and for the first time that morning I saw a proper smile appear on her face.

"Finally the penny drops," she said, "Now you know why Sharon is so horrible to you. Anybody with eyes in their head could see he really fancied you."

"But he went after Alison and then Sharon," I argued

"Well that's because he knew his mate had a thing about you and there was that whole saving your life crap, so he had to back off."

She laughed out loud when I told her about Chris coming over shouting over a song about peace and love and how they were brawling on the floor in front of me before being picked up and thrown out.

"Well that's just typical!" Another real smile, "I missed the whole bloody lot. So what's happened since?"

I told her about Sharon and Maureen coming round and she was impressed that I'd finally stood up for myself and hadn't let them intimidate me. I explained that I hadn't been out anywhere so didn't know what happened with Paul and Chris.

"We'll have to find out what's going on then," she stated quite decidedly, "Not today though. I'll come round tomorrow morning after Dad's gone to work and we'll go up to Hill Top and see who's around."

"What!" I exclaimed, "Do you mean call for him?"

Another burst of laughter.

"Oh that would be priceless. Old Ma Turner opening the door to me and you calling for her darling son!"

I smiled but didn't think it was that funny. Still shrieking with laughter she went on, "It'd give her a heart attack, bloody hell yeah, we should do it!"

"She doesn't know me," I stated.

"Course she knows you. She's best mates with Chris's Mam, the two of them will have been muttering about you round their cauldrons. Pair of old witches!"

The laughter was tinged with bitterness, exposing her deep and strong dislike of the two women. Her features contorted a little as she continued, "It's the pair of them spreadin' lies about our David, trying to get him in trouble!"

Suddenly, I remembered what Dad had told me, so I reported what Harry had said. She went quiet for a moment glancing at the clock on top of the mantelpiece. There was a chance her Dad might come home for his dinner, we both stood up. I didn't need any further prompting to leave. I didn't run out of the house but I did leave remarkably swiftly. Once out of the door I walked at a brisk pace, hardly stopping to get my breath until I was home.

The afternoon was spent helping Mum wrap the Christmas presents for the staff. She was in an exceptionally good mood, chain-smoking her way through her Benson and Hedges, watching me covering bath salts and soaps in festive paper. We joked a bit about the present Aunty Shirley had brought for me. A slipper shaped package identical to what she'd bought me the previous three years. When she paused in her smoking to get up to fill the kettle, I asked casually what Harry had told them about Jane's brother.

"Oh it were somat about him fightin' in Leeds an stabbin' some lad."

I carried on with the gift wrapping, waiting to see if she would go on. She did. It was Kevin and he was now locked up while the lad he'd stabbed was in hospital, fighting for his life. He was lucky he was still classed as a juvenile otherwise he'd go to prison, although that was where he'd probably end up.

Chapter Twenty-three

The aftermath of the teenage Christmas dance turned out to be much worse than two adolescent boys falling out over a girl. They'd both thrown some heavy and angry punches, most of which had been on target, before being pulled apart but their fight had continued outside. It only stopped when a passer-by intervened and a resident shouted from her window that she was calling the police. They'd gone off to their separate homes and been cleaned up by two concerned mothers. Bloody noses, cut lips and blackening eyes told of the ferocity of their battle but neither of them would say what had led to their violent fall out other than admitting who the fight had been with.

Jane and I knew nothing of this as we walked up towards the Hill Top Estate at 9.30am on the Tuesday before Christmas. It was a bright frosty morning and Jane was back to her old self, making jokes about how she and her Dad would cope cooking their Christmas dinner.

"Gran and Grandad are comin' on Thursday. She's made us a cake."

"Did your Mum used to make cakes?

I don't know what had prompted me to ask this. She didn't look at me as she said,

"She made buns," her face smiling, "Butterfly buns and she let me help a couple of times an all."

A small sadness threatened to cloud her memory but she managed to shake it off and her smile returned.

"First time, I remember, we went to collect our David and Kevin from school and I kept telling them all the way home we had a surprise for them. She'd hidden some of them in tin at the back of the pantry cos she

knew they'd want to eat them all, but she let them have two each."
Our strides shortened and pace slowed as she described this treasured memory. She was narrating in detail, to give it substance and make it tangible.

"Iain were still at school then but he came home on his own. She'd put his two on a plate for when he came in. He told her they were the best buns he'd ever had."

This scenario sounded unlikely but I said nothing.

"When Dad got in she gave him his straight away, while she finished getting tea ready. He didn't say anything but he nodded at her, like he does when he's happy. She'd saved two at the back of the pantry for me and her to have the next day when we were on our own."

"You should make some for your Dad," I suggested.

"I don't think that'd be a good idea. Dad probably won't remember it like I do."

The sadness was clouding in again, taking a deep breath she went on,

"Anyway, you know how completely disastrous my cooking is. Remember the Victoria sandwich we made at the start of term?"

Laughing at the memory of the thin unrisen, slightly burnt sponge she'd produced in a home economics lesson, our spirits lifted. Mrs Morgan had glanced to the heavens in despair at the sight of it, before regaining her normal, optimistic composure. She'd spent the rest of the lesson helping her disguise the wreckage with jam and butter cream.

"Mm, but buns are easier to get right, they're smaller," I said.

"Have you made some?"

"No but I bet we could. After Christmas, come round and I'll ask Mum to get us the ingredients and we'll make butterfly buns."

As we turned the corner of Harley Road we saw Russell Turner and another boy walking towards us.

"Ay up, what're you two doing up here?"

"We're off to Pudsey, Christmas shopping," Jane lied, "What you up to?"

"We're off to see who we can round up for a game of soccer, wanna come?"

We declined.

"Did you go to the baths last Friday?" he asked.

"Yeah, we did, why?"

"Did you see our Paul and Chris Henshaw knocking ten bells out of each other?"

We feigned surprise saying we'd seen nothing. Jane asked what the fight was about and if they'd made friends yet.

"Not a chance!" Russell laughed, "It's like they're sworn enemies now and Mum and Mrs Henshaw have fallen out as well. Our Paul's in a right state, his nose is bust."

"Is he in?"

"Yeah, he's in his bedroom. Shall I go and tell him you're here?"

"Why not, let's see what the damage is. Best not let your Mum know though." Jane winked at him.

"She's at the shops. Hang on, I'll go and get him."

He and his friend went back along the road and we waited on the corner. He came back alone after a few minutes.

"Soz Jane, he said to tell you it wouldn't be a good idea him coming out talk to you. He's promised Mum he wouldn't leave the house."

I was gutted but managed to keep smiling, even when he added,

"He's just a complete wuss. He thinks somebody might see him with you an Kimbo. Mum would go spare if she though he was hanging around with you two."

"Charming!" Jane said with a laugh, "Oh well never mind, we'll get off then."

We turned to continue to walk towards Pudsey, giving credence to our alibi. Linking arms, she sad,

"Beryl bloody Turner is one of the biggest stuck-up cows you'll ever meet," she stated, "Don't be bothered about what she thinks, she's just a sad old bag who doesn't like anybody and no girl will ever be good enough for her precious Paul."

When we got to Lowtown, we decided a trip to Woolworths was required, so spent an hour milling around the makeup counter before buying a bag of pick and mix to eat on the bus back to Bramley. Jane pragmatically weighed up the situation, which was that if Old Ma Turner found out that I'd been the cause of the fight, she would definitely tell Old Ma Henshaw and it would almost certainly get back to my Mum and Dad, who wouldn't be too happy to hear that I'd snogged Paul. So all in all it was probably best to let the dust settle for a while.

I spent the remainder of the holidays sitting or laying on the sofa, watching TV on my own, with the occasional sojourn into the bar to help out with the glass washing. The brief spell of happy anticipation I'd felt the previous week was completely gone, leaving me miserable. Christmas Day was the standard norm, more or less, with only a slight deviation. There was no lock-in on Christmas Eve. So even with the thirty minute extension to normal licensing hours, Mum and Dad were back in our living room just before midnight. We opened our presents over a cup of tea; some buttered Jacobs cream crackers and Red Leicester cheese. It was an oasis in my adolescent angst and I even managed a genuine smile of gratitude when I opened my big present. They'd bought me a very expensive sewing machine. By their usual logic, if I had a top of the range machine I'd automatically be better at sewing. The all singing all dancing electric stitcher was no surprise but it was an acknowledgement that they'd listened to me. I had the idea that if I could improve my needlework skills, Miss Aveyard might not hate me quite so much, making that double lesson a bit less horrid.

I spent some time during my seclusion, considering the unfairness of not being liked by people who didn't know me. Miss Aveyard's angry and spiteful face immediately loomed into my thoughts. She'd made no effort to get to know anything about me other than the fact that I'd accidently broken her flask. For her, that was it, no second chances. Then there was Chris's Mum. Her dislike of me seemed to stem solely from my parent's career choice and probably her husband spending so much time at the Unicorn. Now it seemed that Paul's Mum disliked me too, even though she'd never clapped eyes on me. She disliked me purely by association and I was not going to be given a chance. I was Jane's friend and I lived in a pub, so was not the sort of girl her son should be associating with. The unfairness of this stung me sharply leaving a cloud of helpless despair, festering away in my head.

It wasn't till Tuesday, 29th December that I saw Jane again. We'd planned to make the fairy cakes that afternoon, so I'd been mooning around my room not rushing to get up. It was half past nine when I opened my bedroom curtains having just got dressed. I had to look twice at the figure leaning against the car park wall. I moved the nets aside and waved to her before running downstairs.

"How long have you been here?" I started to ask but seeing her face I didn't wait for an answer. "Come on."

I could see she was freezing so I led her back inside and straight up to my bedroom. Mum shouted from the living room as we'd stomped upstairs.

"What the bloody hell you up to Kim?"

I went back down and told her Jane had come round to show me her Christmas presents. I poured us both a cup of tea and collected a packet of fig biscuits from the pantry on my way back upstairs. It was only after we'd heard Mum go through to the bar that Jane started to tell me why she had been hanging around our car park since half past eight.

"It all went wrong," she began, "He just went mental at our David. It were awful."

I have gone over what Jane told me so many times that I feel like I was actually there. She spoke in such detail about the events of her

Christmas Eve and the big day itself that her words created a visual memory that I couldn't possibly have, but all the same it is scorched into the back of my conscious. This is what she told me.

The visit from her Grandparents went well. They'd brought a present for David, as well as a large box-shaped one for Jane and a spirit bottle shaped one for Don. In return Jane gave them the gifts from her and her father. Soap and bath salts for Grandma and garden gloves and seeds for Grandad. All wrapped in a Santa themed paper.

"You can open them now if you want," Jane had suggested, eyeing her own present hopefully.

"Certainly not!" her grandma had exclaimed sharply, "We'll open them tomorrow morning when you open yours!"

Her smile returned as she produced a beautifully iced cake with a robin and holly on the top from her cavernous shopping bag. Still marvelling over this baked masterpiece, Jane was doubly astounded when a large glass dish containing a trifle was lifted out of the second bag. This was for Boxing Day and they were not to even think about having any before then. Don was on his best behaviour, taking the cue from his father, who remained virtually silent throughout the visit. There was a sticky moment when Iain was mentioned. She'd been in the kitchen putting the kettle on when she'd heard her Granny say,

"You must have some idea why he took off. Do you think he's gone after her?"

She'd frozen in anticipation of his reply.

"How the bloody hell should I know." No attempt to disguise his anger. "An' why should I care? Far as I'm concerned they're both dead. And good bloody riddance to 'em!"

Coming back into the room with the only two un-chipped cups she could find, she was relieved as her Granny broke the brittle silence. In a warm and enthusiastic voice she began to talk to her about what was on television over Christmas. She pulled a copy of the Radio Times out of her magic bag. Passing it to her, she began to talk about a film of an Agatha Christie book which was scheduled for Boxing Day and asking her if she'd read that one yet. They stayed for a further half an hour, just long enough for the second cup of tea before saying they must get off home. Jane walked them to the bus stop asking for cooking tips for the next day's dinner. When she got back she found her Dad sitting at the kitchen table tucking into the trifle. An unopened bottle of whiskey with screwed up wrapping paper in front of him.

He'd gone out that night saying that he needed a drink but would just go for one. Jane said nothing, praying that he meant it. After she'd peeled the carrots, potatoes and sprouts, she took the cushions from the sofa and made herself a nest on the rug where she watched telly. She stayed up till ten thirty before scurrying off upstairs, hoping to be asleep before he came in. He'd woken her, slumping drunkenly on her bed and stroking her hair. Trying initially to feign sleep she kept as still as she could with her eyes closed. It was only when he leaned in to start kissing her that she moved and pushed him away.

"Please Dad let me go back to sleep."

He'd stopped and she felt him tense. Seconds seemed like hours to her as she waited to see what he would do. Sitting up again, his hand went back to her hair and giving her one last stroke he said softly,

"Night, night my little princess."

He went back downstairs. She heard the clink of glass and knew he'd started on the whiskey.

The next morning she found him asleep on the sofa, over half of the bottle consumed. She made him a mug of tea and switched the emersion heater on for him to get a bath, before trying to wake him. It was half past seven and David was due to be there at ten. She switched on the telly to see Anita Harris visiting sick children in hospital and smiled, remembering the show on the pier. Severely hung over and probably stressed at the prospect of the day ahead, it took Don an hour to come round properly. Jane made him more tea and tried to cajole him to have a bath before David arrived. She knew that Mrs Wood would be bringing him and they would need to ask her in.

"Bloody busy body nosey parker, she's not stepping foot in my house," he'd muttered to Jane as she passed him the glass of Andrews liver salts.

Finally, he went to get in the bath so she could get back to checking everything in the kitchen. They'd decided on a big chicken rather than a turkey and had a large packet of sage and onion stuffing. Checking her notes that Mrs. Morgan had given her, she switched on the oven, putting a little tick next to the instruction. They were having roast as well as mashed potatoes to accompany the vegetables and the inevitable Yorkshire puddings with the necessary three pints of gravy, a perfect feast for the family reunion.

Don came downstairs washed, shaved and wearing an almost clean shirt just as the Wood's car pulled up outside the house. He sat down in his arm chair and stared at the television, a Tom and Jerry Christmas caper cartoon taking his full attention.

Chapter Twenty-four

It was odd for Jane, opening the door to her brother and a strange woman but she hid her unease with a smile and asked them in. Don didn't acknowledge them; remaining in his chair, eyes fixed on the television. Jane offered tea but Mrs Wood declined before commenting on how organised they were and that something smelt good. With a bright confident smile she moved past Jane towards Don's seated muteness and held out her hand saying,

"You must be Mr Schofield. Hello I'm Rona Wood, good to meet you at last."

To her amazement Jane watched him stand and shake her hand although he said nothing, just nodded at her.

"Well I'll leave you to get on with your celebrations. I'll be back at around four to collect David. Is that alright?"

Don nodded as David shuffled his feet and addressed him with a hesitant smile,

"Hello Dad, Merry Christmas."

Relieved to see Don's face soften, Jane believed, at that moment, it would be ok. She was smiling as she showed Mrs Wood to the door but it didn't last. She began to realise it wasn't just Don's hangover affecting his mood. Seeing the hardness of his features as he turned up the TV and sensing danger, Jane asked her brother to help her with the dinner. David looked at her searchingly but all she could do was shrug, aware that their father was listening to them and watching them out of the corner of his eye. Their chat was stilted as they went about their tasks, until at eleven, Don stood up and announced he was going to the club for a pint and expected his dinner to be on the table when he got back at twelve thirty. Jane was relieved to get him out of the house and take his dark cloud with him as she struggled to understand what was going on.

"He's not improved with age then?" David's disappointment was obvious as he sat down heavily on the sofa.

She sat on the rug, facing him, her back leaning on Don's recently vacated chair and tried to explain her confusion. She told him the safe and highlighted versions of Don's behaviour since she'd been returned home.

"And he's not been drinking so much, well apart from last night but that's just cos it's Christmas."

"Has he ever hit you?" His words were as direct as his stare.

"No!" she gasped, "and he never would either. Oh David he's really not like everybody thinks. He'll come round to you coming home in a bit, I'm sure he will."

"Bloody hell Jane, that's the last thing I want! I couldn't come back here!" His eyes were wide with incredulity. "I'm doing really well at school, I live in a nice house with people that are interested in me and want me to do well. Why would I want to come back to this?"

It was as if he'd punched her. She couldn't speak and sat frozen in the moment staring back at him. He filled the silence.

"I only came today cos this meant a lot to you. You said he'd changed, that he wasn't such a twat, so I thought it'd be ok." Suddenly noticing the effect of his words he tried to back track a little, "and cos I wanted to spend Christmas day with you."

She'd not even felt the tears, her trance-like state had created a catatonic immobility. He was suddenly at the side of her and offering her a well laundered white handkerchief. When she just stared at it, he started to dab at her tears.

"I'm sorry our Kid," he began, "but it wouldn't work."

When she didn't respond he moved to put his arm around her and she shot to her feet as if she'd been electrocuted, jumping to the other side of the room. Seeing his expression, a mixture of shock, fear and sadness, she swallowed hard.

"Sorry. Yes I got it wrong. Why would you give up all that? Stupid me!"

David stood up.

"Oh come on, you've seen how he is with me. He doesn't want me back here either!"

"He does he just finds it hard to cope with all these other folk poking their noses in his business, but he's changed. It's not like before."

"Come on stop trying to play happy families. He's an alcoholic bully and he's never going to change. The sooner you get away from here the better!"

"Oh right yeah that would be great. Dumped in some home and forgot, till I end up either on the streets or in jail." She didnt shout but her bitterness was clear.

"They'd find you a foster home," he began, "then you'd...."

"Just shut up David! It wouldn't happen like that for me. Nobody would want to take me on," she rubbed her eyes with her knuckles before pulling herself together, "and I'm not leaving him. I'm staying here, so just shut up about it now."

She strode into the kitchen and after swilling away her tears quickly in the kitchen sink she turned her attention back to the dinner preparation. This tableau was like an echo from the past, Jane playing her mother in a reconstructed misery.

Don came back just before the time he'd said. The table was set; David was on the sofa and Jane in the kitchen. Having had his hair of the dog he seemed more sociable as the three of them gathered around the small kitchen table. Plates full and knives and forks busy, after a few platitudes from David about the beautifully risen Yorkshire puddings, a *silence fell. Both offspring saw their father's expression change and as if he were a hammy actor in a badly written stage play, he placed his utensils down and picked up his glass of beer.*

"I saw Harry Henshaw in the club."

They'd initially carried on with their dinner but when they saw him put his glass down and fold his arms they stopped. His measured tone, barely containing his rage.

"He were telling me, well telling the whole bloody club actually, about what a bunch of fucking animals my kids are."

Harry had walked up to him like an old friend smiling from ear to ear before letting him and everyone in earshot know how his eldest two sons were getting on. Iain it seems had appeared back on the radar. He had been arrested for aggravated burglary in Leicester and was remanded without bail. As if breaking and entering into the home of a seventy-four-year-old widow wasn't bad enough, he'd tied her to a chair and threatened her with an air rifle. This showed the lad wasn't human, in Harry's very experienced opinion. As for the other lad, who folks had bent over backwards to help, he'd repaid this kindness with a feral savagery that left Harry almost speechless, he'd declared. Far from speechless, he went on to describe how Kevin had head-butted a female carer before absconding with her purse, only hours after being returned to the children's home. He'd spent six months in borstal before escaping. He was now in a young offender high security wing.

"You have to wonder about the home life," Harry had commented.

Don had stood silently not looking at the off duty policeman, just staring ahead and taking occasional mouthfuls of his beer. Finishing his second pint, he caught the barman's eye and ordered another. Still not rising to the blatant provocation, he leaned on the bar, eyes forward. Harry continued his loud one-sided conversation.

"Then there's the other two. Sneaking around together down at the canal and in Gibson's tannery, meeting up at all hours of the day and night. Christ knows what they're getting up to. Better check your locks, Terry," he nodded to the club steward who was nervously watching Don's reaction. "Course it might not be thieving, the way that lass of his dresses, she might just be looking for an easier way to make some money. What do you think Don?

Taking his money out to pay for the pint and handing it across the bar, he turned slightly to look at Harry who was still grinning at him with eyebrows raised at his question.

"I just come in here for a quiet drink. I'm minding my own business. Mebbe you should do the same."

He turned back to his beer, studying the row of optics behind the bar. Harry laughed sensing that he had found the perfect needle point.

"Jane she's called int she, your lass? Looks like her mother, I've heard. Well her and that lass from Unicorn are red-hot. Smoking, swearing and getting up to who knows what with lads from here and abouts. Still, they say the apple never falls far from the tree."

He finished his drink and put his glass down next to Don's. With a nasty smile, he wished him a merry Christmas and left the club, safe in his knowledge that he'd lit the fuse, no matter how much Don had tried to pretend otherwise.

Don shared his new-found knowledge over the dinner table in an amazingly calm way to begin with. Jane and David said nothing as he told them the fates of their older siblings. Speaking in a dismissive way, his voice suggesting he'd always known where they'd end up. As they sat silently digesting this information, the room darkened along with their Dad's expression. Banging his fists on the flimsy Formica table, he demanded to know what the bloody hell had been going on with the pair of them. David tried to speak but was shouted down as his fury grew. His beer stimulated rage fuelled his supposition as the possibilities of what, 'sneaking around together' meant.

"You bloody whore, just like your mother! Not content with fucking one brother. Did you let our Kev have a go as well?"

"Dad!" she screamed, "Dad, please don't ......"

He cut her off as he pushed himself to his feet, unable to contain the ferocity of his anger, lunging towards her. David shot to his feet knocking the table over, providing a barrier between siblings and father. Don glanced down at the mess of broken plywood and crockery and his rage dissipated suddenly, leaving him looking confused and uncertain. With a small glance up at them he physically deflated, collapsing into himself. He turned and walked through the living room towards the stairs. They remained motionless as they heard his footsteps above them. The sound of his bedroom door closing broke their trance. Jane stood up as David spoke.

"What he just said...." He was unable to find the words to ask what he wanted to know.

"He's drunk and Harry Henshaw has wound him up. It's the beer talking." She bent down and started picking through the wreckage. "Are you going to help me?"

They weren't able to salvage much and ended up sweeping most of it into the bin. David tried to make what was left of the table useable while Jane mopped the floor. They worked in a silence until he said,

"You can't stay here. You have to come with me to the Wood's house."

"The Wood's have got no room for me and you heard what Harry Henshaw's saying about me. There's no way I'm going to get a nice family home. I'm staying here 'til I leave school and can get a live-in job."

He tried to get her to change her mind, coming up with all sorts of chocolate box scenarios but she remained resolute. She told him to go while Don was asleep, saying that any further father and son moments would only make things worse. Even though David couldn't see how *things could be any worse, he accepted her conjecture and left. It was only after he'd gone that Jane had allowed herself to cry, silently huddled up on the pantry floor. She let the tears flow freely, knowing that they washed away any hope she'd had of family life.*

After his sleep Don was in a better mood but didn't ask after David or mention anything that had happened or been said. Instead they watched TV in silence until he asked her to make him a chicken sandwich for his tea. After explaining all the food from dinner was now in the bin, she flinched, as for a second it looked like his temper was about to flare again. However, as his memory caught up with him, his face softened and he said he'd just have some cheese on toast then. After this, he sat on the floor with her and got out the old board games. They played snakes and ladders and then ludo before settling down, Don back in his chair, Jane still on the rug, to watch TV while he finished off his bottle of whiskey and fell asleep in the chair. She had a fitful night's sleep but was left alone and undisturbed and woke early to a rainy but mild Boxing Day morning. Hearing him snoring in his own room, she crept downstairs as soon as it was light. Don didn't get up until almost eleven and after some more toast, went to 'see who's about' at the club. Jane engaged her coping mechanism and escaped into the book her grandma had bought her, Jane Eyre.

The day after being a Bank Holiday, Don was not back at work but instead took Jane into Leeds in the morning to have a look round the sales. As an added treat they had their dinner in the Wimpy bar before buying some new plates and cups and a few groceries. All the time, Don kept up his perfect parenting routine and even talked about giving the kitchen a lick of paint and smartening up the house. Jane nodded and answered, taking his cue, trying for best supporting actress. That night although he hadn't been drinking, he again came into her room.

I'd been silent as she'd recounted this unhappy tale and it was only after she'd finished that it occurred to me that our bobby on the beat hadn't been drinking in the Unicorn over the festive period. Now I knew why. He'd been in the Working Men's Club bear baiting. I was sad and angry at what had transpired and seeing her desolation was even more heartbroken at my inability to help. But I had been paying attention so I asked,

"How did Harry know about us going to the canal?"

She looked at me, knowing that I already knew the answer and shrugged lightly.

"Chris," I said simply. It could only have come from him.

"But why would he do that and why mention the tannery? We've not been there and I haven't been there since I nearly fell in that pit thing."

"This is his way of getting at all of us. He is seriously pissed off with Paul and you. Chances are he's hoping his Dad will tell your Dad as well."

"Jesus, my Dad will go mental!"

"Yeah, and he'll stop us being friends," her voice brimming with emotion.

"No he won't!" Trying to sound more confident than I felt. "I'll tell them that none of its true and what a shit faced liar Chris Henshaw is."

"Anyway, that explains why Paul didn't want to be seen with us. Chris must have laid it on thick about what a pair of slags we are," her voice full of dejection.

I asked her again to tell someone about her Dad but she just shook her head saying that I just didn't get it, telling anyone about what he did would just get her taken into care. Staying at home and telling no one was her only option. She made me renew my promise not to tell either. I nodded and whispered the words. She hugged me and brightened a little as she said,

"I've promised him that I won't see our David again, so he'll be alright now. I can deal with it."

When I got home Mum gave me money to buy the ingredients we

needed to make our fairy cakes. Her friendly cheeriness confirmed that Harry's malicious Chinese whispers hadn't reached the Unicorn yet.

That afternoon Jane came round and we made two dozen butterfly buns and even coloured some of the butter-cream pink. This window of normality, two young girls creating pretty things from butter, sugar, flour and eggs was a welcome sanctuary from the other events that were unfolding around us.

The repercussions of my first kiss were far-reaching. My initial thrill and excitement was replaced by dark foreboding. My over-stimulated imagination played havoc with my downtime, creating disturbing visions and scenarios. The night of butterfly buns, I woke up my parents, and probably the whole street, according to my Mum, screaming in a terrified panic. One minute I was wrapped in Paul's arms, looking in his eyes and swaying, the next a giant black octopus with long suckered tentacles began to loop and lash at familiar faces around me as I fell sideways into a pulsating black hole. The internal teenage angst and frustration, coupled with high sugar levels, did their worst. The filing cabinet in my brain fell over, allowing the night demons to scoop up the spilled memories, fears and suspicions and swirl me into a deep dark pit of horror.

Mum detected a temperature in the night as she tried to sooth me back to sleep. The next day I was still a bit warm as well as having a runny nose and sore throat. An eiderdown and pillow were used to make me a haven on the sofa where I spent the next two days, reading and watching TV. I left this sick bed only to use the bathroom and was waited on with a great deal of care and attention by Mum and Dad. I was given copious amounts of lemon barley squash and ate body weight in rice pudding. Dad carried me up to bed on the evening of the first night and agreed to me keeping the light on. The second day of convalescence was New Year's Eve and my puffy face and fitfulness caused Mum to ring for the doctor. I didn't object even though I was convinced my anxiety and pained appearance was down to worrying about a lock-in that night. Having calculated the odds of the laughing policeman turning up that night, I felt it was a certainty. As it happened I needn't have worried. The doctor came and didn't take long to make an accurate diagnosis. There was no lock-in that night, even though Harry and his sidekick appeared just after the extended hour's last orders. Dad told him they couldn't hang around that night as I was poorly. I don't know what his reaction to this was; I was too scared to ask but was so relieved that I started blubbering. The Unicorn was cleared of patrons by a quarter past midnight and Dad locked up while Mum came through to put the kettle on. Five minutes later the three of us welcomed in the New Year with a cup of tea and I began 1971 with mumps.

Chapter Twenty-five

The doctor's pronouncement of my condition was made with disdain. At almost 14 years of age, I was old to be coming down with such an infectious illness. I could tell Mum felt she was being chastised for failing in her motherly duty for not getting me to catch it earlier. This type of illness, we were informed by our GP, was much easier fought off and less likely to leave lasting effects, if contracted at a pre-school age. Neither of them could remember having had mumps themselves, so the doctor briefed them on the dangers to adults in catching this infirmity. But they chose to throw caution to the wind and spend every spare moment with me, either together or in relay. This self-inflicted penance helped them with the guilt they felt for their lack of forethought to expose me to enough viral infections as I grew up. We played dominos, cards, Cluedo, and Monopoly (where I was always allowed to be the banker) and I was given meals on a tray on the sofa. Every now and then, I caught Mum looking in horror at my elephantine face which took the edge off the special treatment. I looked dreadful and recoiled myself when I looked in the mirror. Our family trinity was only broken up by the occasional visit from Sally who brought me more precious cast-off clothing, magazines and homemade lemonade. The day after my diagnosis, one of the other barmaids came round with her two young children. They were an eighteen-month-old boy who screamed and held on ferociously to his mother and a snotty nosed three-year-old girl who tore my most recent copy of Jackie and tried to put my new pink sparkly hair brush in her pocket. I had to try to give them both a hug in order to pass on the virus.

Something neither they nor I wanted. As soon as they'd gone, I asked if I could have a bath as I felt so grotty.

I missed the start of the new school term. I'd worried about Jane waiting for me at the bridge on the first day back. As there was no phone in the Schofield household, there was no way of letting her know. Mum said her Dad would probably be in over the next couple of days so not to worry but I wasn't so sure. I wasn't sure if I wanted him to come in to the Unicorn, still worried about what he might tell them. All the trust and extended boundaries would disappear in an instant if they heard I'd been at the tannery or the canal. The other stuff too, smoking and swearing and going with boys, although it wasn't true, I would be guilty as charged especially when Harry Henshaw told the same story. But there was nothing I could do. I had to just lounge around the house feeling utterly miserable, looking like the elephant man. Mum rang up school on Monday to tell them I had mumps and would be off for a fortnight, so I figured that once Jane found this out she would come round to see me but she didn't. I was wretched with not knowing what was going on and worried constantly about what was being said or done in my absence.

On the first weekend of the New Year, I heard Dad mention Harry's name. He said to Mum that he must have taken umbrage when they'd turned him away on New Year's Eve, as he'd not been near since. Mum supposed that he could've found some other mugs to provide his free ale and Dad conceded this was a possibility. They both agreed though that his non-appearance was unlikely to be because he was spending more time at home with his Mrs. This seemed a hilarious suggestion that amused then for ages.

I knew immediately when Harry had been in. It was the Friday at the end of my second week off school. Feeling much better and the swelling almost gone, I'd stayed up late watching TV. When Mum and Dad hadn't come through at half past eleven, I'd gone to bed and fallen asleep almost straight away. I woke startled and confused as I heard a door slam.

Sitting up, I pulled the string above my head to switch on the light. It was half past one in the morning and I could hear raised voices. Hearing Jane's name, I knew without any doubt that Harry had been round. This time I didn't dare go down and put them right. Instead, I turned off the light and lay there in the dark, yearning for sleep or to wake again and find it was just a dream. They quietened down after about half an hour or so and my heartbeat increased as I heard them making their way upstairs. I lay with my back to the door and eyes screwed tight, waiting for one or both of them to come in and confront me. But they didn't. After a few moments, I registered the sound of them going about their normal night-time ablutions. Finally, breathing normally and allowing the rhythm of the blood pumping in my ears to regulate, I guessed they were sleeping on the new revelations.

I considered getting up and clearing off for a bit, so I wouldn't be around when they got up but accepted that this would only be putting off the inevitable. I considered the whole running away scenario, cramming some clothes in a bag along with my tin of saved glass washing money but my cloistered upbringing and ingrained fear of the unknown didn't equip me for this type of bravery. So I decided the best policy was shock, ignorance and denial over whatever I was accused of. As it happens, I wasn't in a position to do either. After the early hours' disturbance, I didn't wake up until gone half past eight. I could hear the radio on downstairs as I went into the bathroom and I saw Mum and Dad's bedroom door was open. They were both up.

The fallout wasn't as bad as I'd imagined it would be. Not wanting to antagonise them in the same way he had Don Schofield, Harry had changed the story slightly when he'd recounted it to them. He was the concerned local bobby who felt it his duty to inform Ray and Pam who their little lass was hanging about with. In short, I was being led astray by Jane and one of her brothers and they should put a stop to it. I was sitting at the table as Mum confronted me with Harry's statement.

"Have you been smoking?"

"No I haven't and neither has Jane and I've only met her brother once and he's alright."

I saw a quick look between them at my mention of a boy. Seeing their surprise at my defense of David I decided that I should continue on the offensive and let them have some proper facts.

"This is all rubbish and it's made up by Harry and his son Chris, just cos I told him I wouldn't go out with him. And you know he hates Jane's Dad. He's just making trouble. "

I could see they were undecided. Dad said,

"Harry said he saw you and Jane going into Gibson's tannery with a gang of lads."

"That's just a lie!" I yelled as the anger bubbled up inside me. "I have never been in Gibson's tannery with Jane or any lads so he's a big liar."

I could feel my face burning with indignation and I could also see my Dad's anger rising. Both he and Mum must have been alarmed at the ferocity of my denial. This was not how their quiet and obedient daughter behaved. I saw my advantage.

"And anyway, if he did see me going in, why didn't he arrest me and this gang for trespassing?"

Again I saw the doubt as they glanced at each other, so I continued,

"I'll tell you why, cos it's not true. God he's supposed to be reliable and trustworthy. You know what he's like, coming here for his free beer when he's supposed to be working, spreading rumours and lies...."

"That's enough Kimberly!" Mum cut me off and reached out for the packet of Benson and Hedges. "Get yourself some breakfast."

She nodded at Dad, giving him his cue to leave the room and go through to the bar. I got some bread out and lit the grill on the cooker as she lit her cigarette.

"I will give you the hiding of your life if I find out you've been smoking," she said before sucking in a mouthful of the nicotine.

As I looked back at her, I saw her narrowed eyes suddenly take on a different expression.

"Are you feeling alright? You still look really pasty and you're as thin as a rake," her head on one side as she looked me up and down.

" I'm just a bit tired and upset that you'd believe Harry over me."
I was looking at the box of cornflakes and thinking I really wasn't hungry.

"You need a proper breakfast in you not that cereal rubbish. Let me do you a nice big fry-up. Build you up a bit before you go back to school."

"I'm not sure I'm hungry enough for a fry-up. I'll just have some toast."

"Rubbish! Go and ask your Dad if he wants one while I get the frying pan out."

Sensing dissention would be futile, I went through to the bar to ask the question. *'Is the Pope catholic?' was Dad's response,* so Mum got frying. I used my sore throat as excuse for not eating much of the coagulating egg and bacon on my plate, so Mum didn't make too much fuss. In truth, it would have choked me to swallow any of it so I just cut it up and moved it around my plate. It was Saturday morning and in just two days' time I was going back to school and I was worried sick about what to expect.

My uniform felt loose and looked baggy as I got ready on Monday morning. Looking in the mirror, I saw how pale I was with dark circles under my eyes; I didn't look better at all. Mum said as much adding her own thoughts that my eyes looked yellow and perhaps I needed another week at home. Even though I was scared of the reception I might get, I was more anxious of being away any longer. On my insistence, she agreed but only on condition that Dad would take me in the car. I didn't bother to argue and was actually relieved. When I went downstairs to try and have some breakfast, Mum was already up and making porridge.

"I don't like porridge," I tried.

"You have to have something to eat before you go to school and porridge won't hurt your sore throat."

I gave in and sat down as she poured the hot, thick and lumpy mixture into a bowl. Covering it in sugar, I managed to eat a couple of spoonfuls between gags, all the time willing her to leave the room so I could put it in the bin. I noticed she was putting her make-up on.

"What you getting ready this early for?"

She didn't have a chance to answer as Dad was yelling from upstairs asking where his trousers were. With a loud tut, she wiped her hands on the tea towel and went upstairs. I took the opportunity to scrape the solidifying paste into the bin and put my dish in the sink. I went to brush my teeth as it dawned on me why she was up and dressed. She was coming to school with us. Thankfully this time she was without the curlers and headscarf. In fact, she was in full make-up and her best coat was getting a run out. Dad drove through the front gates and pulled up right in front of the entrance to the school offices and Mum and I got out. I am sure I looked both truculent and wary as I followed her down the corridor.

"Can I help you?" the school secretary asked in a tone suggesting it was the last thing she wanted to do.

"Yes, you can show me where I can find the headmaster," Mum replied in her 'don't mess with me' tone.

"Do you have an appointment?"

I felt my shoulders sag at this question, knowing that this was the wrong way to deal with my Mother. The blue touch-paper had now been most definitely lit. I glanced up at her to see one of her widest and coldest smiles. Her eyes a bright and steely blue, locked on the head teacher's gate keeper. She took in a deep breath as she reached out her arm to push the smaller twin-set clad woman aside,

"No I don't and I don't need one either," she said as she marched past her.

I followed, my mortification contained by keeping my eyes on the floor. Hearing steps ahead, I looked up.

"That's Mr. Wedaburn, Mum," I whispered.

Mum's smile became a little friendlier as she stepped towards him and introduced herself to a very smiley headmaster.

"I've brought Kimberly to school personally. She's better but as you can see she's still not hundred per cent so I want to be sure you'll be keeping an eye on her and making sure she's alright."

Talking in her vowel softened voice, she put her arm around me briefly. His face took on the required concern as he nodded before gesturing down the corridor.

"But of course Mrs Asquith, let's go to my office so we can talk about what we can do to make sure Kimberly is alright. There is actually another matter I'd like to discuss with you so if you'd follow me."

He led us to his office as the secretary scurried behind us muttering that he had a very busy timetable on Monday mornings. Mr Wedaburn asked her to ask Miss Tempest to join us before offering Mum a cup of tea. Mum beamed at this, mainly because of the obvious annoyance it caused the secretary, and accepted immediately. The deputy head arrived before the tea and, after being informed of my delicate state, was asked to escort me to my form room for registration. I glanced at Mum with what I hoped was a *'please stay on my side'* look as I left the room but was disheartened by her returned expression of *'what else am I going to hear!'*

As I stepped into the classroom, I heard Mr Lloyd's voice saying 'Joyce Chambers?' as he sat, head over the class register and pen at the ready. Instinctively, my eyes went to a desk near the front where Joyce Chambers sat, her eyes fixed on me as I stood just inside the door, next to Miss Tempest. Mr Lloyd repeated her name raising his head to look at her.

"Sorry Sir, here Sir," she muttered her eyes still fixed on me. Eyebrows raised, he turned to acknowledge us.

"Ah Kimberly, good to have you back with us, take your seat while I amend the register." Standing up he addressed my escort, "Miss Tempest?"

"A word outside please Mr Lloyd," she responded, exiting the room.

I went to my desk and sat down, giving Jane a quick smile and nod, aware that everyone was looking at me, except her. She looked to be concentrating on a doodle she was creating on the cover of her exercise book. As soon as both teachers were at the other side of the door, Jane stated more than asked,

"You're better then?"

I nodded and said, "I thought you might have come round to see me while I was off."

"I've been a bit busy; anyway I didn't think I'd be very welcome." Looking at me properly for the first time, she added, a little friendlier,

"You don't look better."

There was no time for further chat as Mr Lloyd came back in to finish registration before we trailed off for the Monday morning assembly. But I knew something had happened and something more was brewing.

It wasn't until morning break that we got a chance to speak properly. We were sitting on the steps at the back of the science labs, shivering in the biting cold of the January morning. The adrenalin that had been coursing through me all morning had drained my already weak body making me wobbly and emotional. So as she told me that she was now in temporary foster care but was probably going to end up in a children's home, I crumpled. There wasn't time for her to tell me all of it and my snuffling didn't help, so I had to wait until the dinner break to hear the full story.

Chapter Twenty-six

Harry Henshaw had really gone to Town this time. He'd filed such a convincing report about his concern over Jane's home life that Social Services had immediately become involved. On 2nd January, she had been woken up by loud hard knocking at the front door. Her Dad jumped up and went to the window. Cursing, he started to pull on his trousers and told Jane to stay where she was before he thundered downstairs. Everything happened quickly then. There was shouting and banging followed by heavy footsteps coming through the house and upstairs. She pulled the sheet and blanket up as the bedroom door burst open. Harry led the charge, followed by a social worker, a policewoman and two other policemen. They took in the scene, noticing Don's shirt on the floor by her bed. Harry was smiling a righteous victory as he stepped across the landing and kicked open the other doors. This revealed an empty room with a double and single bed stripped of sheets, the soiled mattress and the musty smell of damp confirming it unused. The other bedroom had a double bed made up and clearly not slept in. They had taken her away there and then. She spent most of the day at Leeds Infirmary being prodded and poked by doctors before some posh middle-aged women looking down their noses asked her how long her father had been abusing her. Knowing the futility of insisting he had done no such thing, she just refused to speak. This was put down to trauma and she was shunted back to the social worker. She sat mute in a messy cold office, warmed only by a one-bar electric heater, while phone calls were made, eventually securing her three weeks foster care with a family in Pudsey.

Three days later in yet another session with social workers, she was told that her Dad had been charged with statutory rape. She tried again to tell them that he'd only slept in her room because she had nightmares and that he had never touched her in that way. At this point they got cross with her.

"You've got to stop this now! The hospital examination proves to us what he's done to you. You're not helping yourself here by continuing to lie like this, you're not stupid, you know what he did to you was wrong, so you need to start telling the truth."

So again she shut down and sat sulkily staring at the floor.

"You must realise that by not telling us the truth we have to wonder about you."

They told her the police believed that her father gave her alcohol and encouraged her to have sex with boys for cash. There was information that she'd been drunk at the Christmas disco and had been heard offering to go outside with a group of older lads for money. She'd pressed her lips together firmly and completely disengaged with them, so they gave up and took her back to the foster home.

"Why is Harry doing this now? What's made him go for your Dad again?" I asked.

But I already knew the answer and I burned with shame. This was all my fault. I tried to hug her but she pushed me away saying,

"Chris fuckin' Henshaw started blabbing to his Dad. Bastard!" Looking me in the eye she went on, "Look, no point in going over this now. I'll get him back for this one day, so help me I will. But now I need you to promise me again, on your life, that you won't tell anyone what I told you, either about Iain or my Dad."

I nodded.

"No Kim, I need to hear you say it. They will ask you, they were going on about what we did on our holidays and what me and you did on weekends."

"Oh god, that must have been what Wedaburn meant this morning."

I told her about Mum bringing me in and what had happened at home after Harry's visit. I reassured her that I was sure it was only smoking we'd been accused of and what my response had been.

"So, promise me?"

"I promise."

A forced smile and a nod before the dark cloud came back to her eyes. She told me that David had backed up Harry's claims that Jane was being abused by her father. He'd been interviewed and had told in detail of Don's violent outburst on Christmas Day, compounding the damage. This was the most hurtful thing of all; she'd been betrayed by the only member of her family she'd trusted.

"Why won't they let you go to your Granny's again?"

"Apparently, they think that they knew what was going on. They aren't even allowed to visit me."

Walking back to the form room for afternoon registration Jane fixed her carefree smile to her face. I walked down the corridor alongside, trying to exude a similar confidence while quelling the fear bubbling up inside. Just before the end of last lesson of the day Miss Tempest walked into the art room.

"Kimberly Asquith, please go to Mr Wedaburn's office once you have your coat. Your parents will meet you there."

We'd been copying a picture of York Minster and my usual poor drawing skills were even worse than normal. As the bell went, I leaned forward and whispered in my friend's ear as I stood up, "I promise."

I sat in Mr. Wedaburn's office with Mum and Dad, Miss Webster the social worker, a policewoman and Miss Tempest. It was very crowded in the small office and I remember feeling hot and scared. It was mostly Miss Webster who spoke. I noticed that Dad wasn't sure what to do with his hands as he fidgeted next to a very straight backed Mum. She was looking at me with an expression that I couldn't work out. Was it anger, fear, annoyance? I had no clue. Miss Webster started by telling me I wasn't in any trouble, they just needed to talk to me and that it was important for me to be truthful with my answers. Did I understand that? I nodded my response. Miss Webster first referred to when we had met before, when Jane had returned to school. She knew what good friends we were but how long had we been friends?

"Since the first day we started here."

Did I know about her Mum disappearing?

"Yes, Miss."

And what had Jane told me about that.

"Nothing really, Miss."

She must have told me something. What did Jane think happened to her Mum?

"We didn't talk about it Miss, she just said...."

I trailed off scared of saying the wrong thing. They were trying to trick me, I had to be careful. I dropped my gaze and stared at my knees.

"What did she say Kimberly? It's important. Tell us what she said."

I was terrified of saying anything. Why on earth were they asking me about her Mum? Was this all still about Harry proving he'd been right all along about Don killing Maggie? Are they trying to say that Jane knew what had happened to her Mum? My hands were clenched at my sides and I was digging my fingernails in to the palms as I tried to think what I should say.

"Kim!" Mum began sharply, "answer the question. What did she tell you about her Mam going missing?"

I raised my head quickly to look at her and with horror, I could see the fear in her eyes. My mother was also terrified of what I was going to say. This was too much. Swallowing hard and blinking back tears I spoke quietly.

"She just said that she'd gone out to get the fish and chips and never came back."

"And then what happened?" It was Miss Webster again.

I thought about it for a split second. I thought about just saying it to lighten the mood and stop my suffocation in their discernment.

"They opened a tin of beans instead!"

But of course, I didn't. I wasn't Jane. I wasn't even a close imitation.

"Nothing happened. The police came and dug up their garden and asked some questions but they couldn't find her."

"And what does Jane think happened to her Mum?"

"She has no idea. I've told you she just went out to the chip shop and never came back." A burst of anger came from nowhere as I asked suddenly and fiercely, "Why are you asking me this now?"

There seemed to be some fire in me after all. I saw Mum lean forward, about to speak again but Miss Webster waved her hand. Mum won't like that, I thought, but she sat back in her seat.

"Was Jane drinking alcohol at the children's disco just before Christmas?"

"No." My eyes focusing back on my knees.

"Was she talking to some older boys from a different school that night?

"No. We danced for a bit but didn't think it was very good so we came out a bit early and bought some chips while we waited for Dad to come and collect us."

"You didn't leave the Baths with anyone else?"

"Suzanne was there too, Suzanne Ruston."

There were some glances exchanged before Dad cleared his throat and confirmed.

"I picked up all three of 'em.. They were sitting on the wall in front of the baths, on their own and they'd NOT been drinking, none of 'em!"

I daren't look at him. I could feel his rage and indignation but I also knew there was something else too. In the back of his mind was nagging doubt. Was I lying, did I know what had been going on and was I

227

somehow involved? It was tearing him apart sitting there listening to this informal interrogation. Miss Webster smiled at him coldly and changed tack slightly.

"Jane went on holiday with you and your parents in the summer," she stated looking directly at me with a smile.

I nodded.

"I'll bet you had a good time."

I nodded again. This was another trap. I wasn't going to be fooled that easily.

"And you shared a room."

Another statement from a false smiling Miss Webster. I responded with a sullen nod.

"Oh for goodness sake!" Mum burst out, "Kimberly, has Jane ever talked to you about her Dad touching her and doing things to her he shouldn't?"

"No!" I yelled in horror. "No, she hasn't because he hasn't. This is all just a pack of lies!"

My voice high and shaking with emotion, I caught the laser beam glare of Mum's eyes as she examined my face. It was the end of my control as a massive sob racked my body and the dam of tears burst. There was a mumbling between the policewoman and social worker and Dad stood up.

"Right that's enough, she dunt know nothing about any of this and we're taking her home."

This is another marker. An undisputable fact which I am sure was recorded. When questioned in the headmaster's office, without the headmaster present, Kimberly Asquith broke down and cried.

We drove home in silence that evening and as soon as I got in the house, I went straight to my room. They didn't try to stop me or follow me up but I heard them mumbling along with the normal teatime sound. Mum called me down for my tea just after six. One plate of egg, bacon and tinned tomatoes sat on the table with a knife and fork and two slices of unplated, buttered bread next to it. I turned to look at Mum who was busying herself washing the frying pan, her back to me.

"Where's yours?"

"We've had ours. I need to get ready then give your Dad a hand in the bar. We're running late."

She didn't look at me, just wiped her hands on her pinny and left the room. As I heard her go upstairs, I picked up one of the slices of bread and started to ball it up in my hand. I enjoyed the feeling as the softened butter and doughy whiteness combined. Dropping it into the tomatoes, I did the same with the other slice before scraping the lot of it in the bin. I put the unused fork back in the drawer, washed the plate and knife and put them away then took myself to bed. When they came in that night Mum didn't look in on me.

Their cold and brittle silence continued while they came to terms with what they thought they'd learned. I knew they wouldn't ask me again if I had known what Don was doing to Jane, they didn't want to hear the answer. It was easier instead to let the silence frost over the gap between us, making a bridge, albeit slippery, back to some sort of normality. It took over a week for things to get any sort of semblance of how they'd been. Mum and Dad had difficulty being in the same room as me, let alone actually looking me in the eye. Their disappointment was palpable but never spoken of again. Slowly, things started to become bearable and finally we settled into an easy avoidance of the awkwardness. But the elephant remained in the room.

At school it was a bit easier, although I was manifestly aware of the whispering and funny looks from the other pupils and the watchfulness of the teaching staff. Over the rest of that week, Jane told me about the family she'd been housed with. They were a couple of churchy types (her words) who had two daughters of their own. They regularly offered short-term fostering and were kind but the girls, one twelve and one fifteen, were resentful and secretly spiteful. They hated that their parents' desire to help young people in difficulty meant they had to share a room, while the reject child (their words) got one to herself. Both the girls went to a school in Pudsey, so thankfully Jane had the school hours away from their indignation and meanness. The evenings however were full of malicious jibes and hurtful comments, mostly out of the parents hearing, but not all.

"It won't be long before I get moved on," she'd said on the Friday.

In fact it was just a couple of days later Mr and Mrs Kind Foster parents, as she called them, chose to believe their devious and lying youngest daughter when she claimed that Jane had stolen money out of her piggy bank. The money was found in Jane's room in her underwear drawer.

"I suppose they had to believe I'd done it cos if they didn't, they'd have to accept what a sly little cow she was," she said pragmatically. "The only thing I regret is not smacking her one when I had the chance."

As this move was sudden, she was sent to a Lodge House, a children's home in Armley until another placement could be found. It was meant to be a temporary arrangement. It happened on Monday 15th February 1971. A date that has gone down in British history as the day our monetary system lost its shillings and we became decimalised. Jane's new living arrangement still allowed her to stay at Hill Topp but she was driven to school each day, arriving just before the whistle and collected at four o'clock on the dot. She was also now under a strict care order and not allowed out in the evenings, even to attend the afterschool drama club. This meant that she couldn't be in the play. As I'd missed the first two weeks of the group I'd missed the casting and was given the job of props and stage setting. Sharon had finally secured a good part and was in her element. She was even happier that I was relegated to back stage. I didn't mind, I was just happy to have something else to think about and I did learn all the main female parts, just in case.

I walked to and from school on my own every day, calling for Suzanne to walk into the playground with. These journeys seemed so much longer on my own and I missed my friend's jokey conversation and outrageous observations. We still sat next to each other in class and spent our break times reminiscing about Blackpool and our Saturday trips to Leeds. She'd made it clear that she wouldn't talk about her family. After my initial question, even her grandparents were out of bounds and I was careful to avoid topics where Chris or Paul might come up. We were both tiptoeing over eggshells. She was often moody and easily irritated and spoke to no one else other than Suzanne and me.

She'd also started to be disruptive in class. Nothing too bad, she chose her battles. Her aim, she told me, was to have a detention every week but not get sent to the headmaster. She no longer did her homework; even English and art were abandoned. Her claim that she wasn't given time or space to do it in the home was met only with a sigh or a click of the tongue. Sharon, Diane and Maureen pretty much kept clear, trying their best not to even look at us.

We saw Chris asometimes but he was quick to get out of our way, so sightings of him were rare. This intensified the deep and burning hatred I felt for him. What he'd done by telling his Dad lies about Jane had started this whole nightmare. I'd no idea if he and Paul had made friends again as we didn't see hide nor hair of him. As the months went on, I stopped thinking of that moment on the dance floor. The euphoria of a teenage fantasy was replaced with a hormonal flood of insecurity.

So that was how our school year continued. There was the odd bit of light relief, for me at least, with the school play. It went well without any need for last minute substitutions but I still enjoyed my backstage role. The distraction of pleasurable farce and fiction, Billy Liar, seemed to have been a prophetic choice.

Our birthdays were very low key, Jane's more so than mine. There was a birthday tea for her at Lodge House and a book token from the staff. Her grandparents were allowed a short visit and bought her a new nightie, dressing gown and book. I bought her a zodiac sign necklace in a box from Woolworths. Mum had taken me into Leeds the Saturday before for new shoes. I told her I was buying Jane's birthday present and she offered no comment. I actually bought two, both with our sign, Pisces, the two fishes swimming away from each other but still connected by a cord. I wrote a soppy letter about how she was the most wonderful person I'd ever met and that no matter what, we would always be friends. I gave it to her at school and we both had a bit of a blub. She'd no money or chance to go shopping and so gave me the book token. I didn't want to take it but she said she didn't need it as her Granny had given her the rest of the Agatha Christies so she was sorted.

It was just before we broke up for the Easter holidays when she told me that one of the male supervisors was giving her a hard time. He'd started off being all pally with her but she knew what he was after, so she'd tried to keep her distance. Then he'd changed tack. The morning of the last day of term he'd done the school run and made sure she was the last to be dropped off. She was in the back of the car and she tried to jump out as soon as the car stopped but he'd leaned behind and grabbed her arm. His exact words were,

"I know what you are, you little cock teaser, so don't think you can play all coy with me."

I said she should tell someone, he couldn't behave like that, it was wrong. She shook her head and with a flash of anger said,

"You've really got no idea have you? In your world there's right and wrong but in my world wrong is all there is!"

She was off with me for the rest of the day and when the bell went at the end of school, she gathered up her stuff quickly. As she left, I called after her to wait. She didn't turn round just called over her shoulder,

"No time. Got to go, can't be late for my lift."

And she was gone.

Chapter Twenty-seven

Things were still uncomfortable at home, the three of us going through the motions of what we took for normality but with no conviction that any of it was forgotten. Harry's first visit to the Unicorn was on a Friday night around mid-March at his regular time of on-the-dot last orders. I'd been back at school a couple of weeks and the rawness of it all was still smarting. I'm sure the lack of geniality wasn't lost on our laughing policeman. Mum and Dad had stopped looking for truths, deciding to trust their instincts, and accepting that Harry also carried some blame. Whatever happened behind our closed doors, blood would always be much thicker than water and Harry was now recast as a villain; some of my protestations had registered. Although Dad was perfectly civil and offered him the customary drink on the house, there was a distinct absence of warmth or welcome.

I was washing glasses. Mum instantly ushered me through to the house and stayed there in the kitchen with me as she couldn't trust herself to be civil. The bar staff had all been briefed on what was expected of them, so finished their general clearing of the bar and said goodnight. Dad leaned on the corner of the bar while Harry, supped his pint and asked Dad how things were going. Dad told him things were going well, steady weekdays and busy weekends. He didn't ask Harry in return or offer any further conversation. The message was clear and understood. He finished his pint and said goodnight. He never came back to the Unicorn again as long as Mum and Dad owned it.

On the second day of the Easter holidays, Suzanne came round to call for me. She stayed for a couple of hours, providing some wonderful light relief before going home for her dinner. She invited me to go round to her house the next day. She was standing just behind me in the hall when I leaned into the kitchen to ask Mum. 'No! Definitely not,' was the reply. Suzanne was welcome to come back and stop in with me round our house but I was going nowhere. She came back a couple of days later and Mum let her in before going through to the bar. Suzy was on her way to meet her cousin, they were going ten pin bowling and asked if I wanted to go. I didn't bother asking and just told her to have a good time. After she'd gone, I was suddenly angry again, angry with everyone and everything. I raged against my pillow in an attempt to let out some of my frustration but was soon overcome with tears and sobs. When Mum called me down to ask if Suzanne wanted to stay for a bit of dinner she wanted to know what on earth the matter was. I told her there was nothing the matter. I loved being locked up in the house all day and every day and no, Suzanne did not want a bit of dinner as she had gone bowling and actually I didn't want any either so was it alright for me to go back to my cell now? That was the first and last time my mother slapped me, hard across my face. It frightened us both into silence as we both stared at each other before I turned and went back upstairs.

The last four months of year three at Hill Topp went by without further significant incident. I was allowed to go to Suzanne's house a couple of times for an hour after school and her parents took the two of us to the cinema for her birthday. It was a Saturday night in May and Jane was also invited. Suzy's Mum had gone to Lodge House in person to ask but was told it was completely out of the question. She was still under some sort of curfew and not allowed anywhere.

The first week of June brought the end of year exams and although I'd worked hard in class and studiously done my home-work, I still found them hard. As I sat in the school hall, my mind became mush and I struggled to recall much of anything. My panic just increased as I glanced around to see every other head bent and pens being worked frantically. I took a deep breath and re-read the question again slowly, trying to stir what I'd learnt back to a reachable section of my brain. I knew I needn't worry about getting a top place that year.

Jane was still under the 'care' of Lodge House curfew hating it. She hadn't mentioned the male supervisor again and when I asked her, she just said it was sorted and changed the subject. She'd continued on her irritating rather than disruptive behaviour in class and would spend most of her time in lessons looking out of the window. Even art and needlework could not tempt back her interest. It wasn't that she was sullen or troublesome; she was just not entirely with us. Its classic text book stuff I know, an idiot could tell what was going on now but back then she was just labelled as trouble. The general attitude of the grown-ups around us, the guardians of our innocence, was summed up when I overheard the school secretary say to the headmaster,

"Well what can you expect, with her background? The apple doesn't fall far from the tree. The whole family is rotten. I don't even know why she's still allowed to come to this school."

It was a Thursday dinner-time, the week after the exams. I'd tripped and banged my face on a doorway as we were walking out of the dining room. Miss Tempest had seen me and glided quickly across. My nose was bleeding heavily and she produced a handful of tissues from nowhere and dismissed the gathering throng of pupils jostling for a look. Telling me to keep my head back she started to lead me along the corridor to the offices when someone called,

"Miss, Miss, Joyce Cooksey is being sick in the girls cloak room!"

Giving an exasperated sigh she told me to go the secretary's office and ask her to clean me up before going back towards the cloakroom. The door was open, showing an empty office, so I hesitated, unsure what to do. Hearing the secretary's clipped voice, I realized she was in the headmaster's room where the door was ajar. I didn't hear all his response as he spoke in a low voice but what I thought I heard was something about '*not wanting all this unpleasantness in school again.*' And '*the girl is obviously lying*'. I knocked on the door and the voice stopped as a very flustered school secretary opened it quickly. Taking in my bloody face and shirt she cried out,

"My goodness Kimberly, what on earth's happened to you? Have you been fighting?" Always looking for the bad in everyone.

It was a few weeks before I found out what the head and his secretary had been talking about. We were into July, with only another week to go before we broke up for the summer. Class 3B was assembled in our form room just before the dinner break to be given our exam results and a summary of our yearly report. As expected, I hadn't done too well, although better than I thought. English and history were fairly positive, maths was positively terrible and everything else just less than average. My totals were accumulated at the bottom along with my position in the class, 15th, so very much mid-table and very much destined for 4B. I heard a crackling of paper beside me as I saw Jane screw up her result sheet and stuff it in her bag. I touched her arm and she moved her head to look at me and I saw a glimpse of despair before the hardness came back. She shrugged me off and said we'd talk about it at dinnertime.

Sitting on the steps to the science labs in our regular haunt, she gave me the balled up paper and I smoothed it out. On every one of her exams, she had been marked with nil.

"This can't be right, it's a mistake," I said staring at zeros.

"No, it's not!" Then she told me what she'd done.

She hadn't planned it but the first exam was English and we'd been asked to write an essay about Wuthering Heights. She'd written her name and the date and was just staring at the paper when the thought struck her that this would be a good time to tell someone about what was going on at the home, so she wrote an essay about that. She did something similar in the history exam that afternoon but actually went into a little more detail. She said she'd been sure that the following day something would be said but nothing happened and so on the Tuesday she did the same again. In maths and science she just wrote one line statements and added the number of times each thing had happened and how many other girls were also being assaulted. She'd been so sure that the school would report this and get it stopped, but it seemed they had decided to do nothing of the sort.

"On the last test, Friday morning, Geography, I just put '*my name is Jane Schofield and I am not a cock teaser and I do not want that fuckin' dirty bastard Alan Jackson touching me up every chance he gets.*' I thought that might make them react," she said.

I was struggling to understand, when I remembered what Mr. Wedaburn had said about not wanting unpleasantness at the school. They'd not reported it, refusing to believe her. I asked her again to let me tell my parents. My Mum would know what to do. She refused saying that it wouldn't help and anyway they had her marked down as a lying slut. I tried to refute this, sighting their cold shouldering of Harry but she was having none of it.

"Come on Kimmy, you know that's why they've kept you locked up for so long, to keep you away from me. They hate Harry for bringing it all up and want to believe it was all lies but they're taking no chances, just in case."

Saying goodbye at the school gates on the last day of term, I gave her the phone number of the pub, asking her to ring me if there was any chance of her being allowed out. She said she would and squeezed my hand before crossing the road to get into the waiting car.

The summer of 1971 was a relatively warm one and I spent a fair bit of time with Suzanne, a friend my parents approved of. I was finally allowed out on my own again but generally only went to the library or Suzanne's house. There was no family holiday that year but I did have a week in Sheffield staying with Aunty Shirley and Uncle Bill. I was excited at the prospect of a week away and at the much needed change of space. Dad dropped me off on the Monday morning, refusing a cuppa as he needed to get back. He gave me two pound notes and told me to behave myself. Because he didn't come in, he wasn't aware that Alison was in disgrace having been found in the park, off her face on cider two nights before. If he'd known, he would, I'm sure, have bundled me back in the car and taken me home. Alison giggled when she regaled me with the story. One of her so called friends had phoned her house, telling her Mum that she should come and get her, as she was so drunk she couldn't stand up and was being sick by the swings. This particular friend was just jealous because Ali had got off with a lad they both fancied. Her Dad left the house immediately and found her lying on the grass at the side of the playground. She had vomited most of the cider and her tea all over her clothes and hair. There was another burst of giggling from her at this point before she continued her narrative. Aunty Shirley had put her in the bath to clean and sober her up. That was when she discovered two massive love bites on her neck.

"She went mental when she saw them and gave me a right slap but I said I was sorry and it was only because my mates had dared me to drink the cider and the love bites were a dare too. I told her that Gillian had done them and I'd given her one as well. I swore on my life that there hadn't been any boys there." She paused for a delighted laugh at her own ingenuity and guile. "And they believed me!"

She was sorry I had come this week as Mickey, her new boyfriend, was away on holiday. Again I wondered about Alison's stories and thought that perhaps the marks on her neck might really be a dare with Gillian.

The 'Alison is in disgrace' phase only lasted until after dinner on the Monday when she asked if she could show me round the village. As long as we took Mark was the response along with a 'Stay out of trouble!' Mark was as pleased to come with us as we were to have him and as soon as we were out of sight of the house, he sloped off to go and call for his mates. Alison immediately took a packet of cigarettes from her bag and offered me one. I shook my head, so she shrugged and struck a match to light one for herself.

"What if someone sees you and tells your Mum?"

"What if they do?" She was totally unconcerned. "Where do you wanna go? We can go to the rec for a bit see who's there."

"Rec?"

"The recreation ground, like your park but better."

I don't know about better but it was certainly bigger. We spent most of the afternoon there and she introduced me to a group of five girls who were hanging around the sports pavilion. She said they were her friends but they didn't seem friendly. They were mostly my age or older and all smoked constantly and talked about the boys who were playing football. I noticed without comment that they practically ignored us, although Ali didn't seem aware of this. After a long half an hour, one of them suggested going down to Woollies to see what they could nick. Alarmed, I glanced at Alison who smiled and said we needed to get off as well. We walked back via a transport café which Alison insisted did the best milkshakes. The milk was warm and powdery and actually made me feel sick.

"I normally come here at night," she said with her conspiratorial smile, "There's usually bikers here, Hells Angels and that!"

Finishing my disgusting drink - years of indoctrination about never leaving food or drink - we finally got back to see Aunty Shirley dancing around the house with her Hoover. She had the radio on really loud and was singing along to Tom Jones telling us that 'it's not unusual'. I couldn't compute this scene with any description I had heard from my parents. According to them Uncle Bill led her a merry dance and made her life a misery. She looked far from miserable to me. After tea that day, I asked her if we could go into the centre of Sheffield on the bus the next day. She winked at me saying,

"Course you can love but best not tell your Mam eh?"

We caught the bus into Town and wandered around the shops for a couple of hours, had our dinner in the Wimpy and caught the four o'clock bus back. Aunty Shirley and Uncle Bill took the three of us ten pin bowling the next day and ice skating the day after that. Uncle Bill went out to play darts most nights and Aunty Shirley played board games with us. Alison insisted on being Miss Scarlet when we played Cluedo and was really rubbish. Mark insisted on being banker in Monopoly and embezzled money quite brazenly, although neither mother or sister seemed to notice, but it was still fun. I didn't meet any more of Alison's friends until the day before I went home. It was Saturday and Ali had been going on at length about the youth club disco in the scout hut which happened every week. I was unsure about what to expect, my knowledge of discos being a little tarnished. But I needn't have worried. It was very well run and controlled by a team of adults who stood no nonsense. There were only about six or seven boys to about thirty girls and they were mainly Mark's friends who stayed in a little group snorting with laughter or running up and down and sliding across the floor. We danced, avoiding rude little boys and filled ourselves up on crisps and cola before being picked up at ten by Aunty Shirley who walked us home. The next morning after breakfast, she again reminded me that it was probably best if we didn't let on to Mum and Dad about our solo outings, even the disco.

"I know your Mam is a bit funny about you going out on your own," she said. "She's always been a bit over-protective. She were the same with me growin' up but it's only cos she cares about you." I nodded agreeing it was best for all concerned that I didn't let on; after all I was good at keeping secrets.

Chapter Twenty-eight

In September, my fourth year at Hill Topp began but there was no sign of Jane. At first break, I went to the staff room to speak to Mr Lloyd. He said that she was living at the other side of Leeds now; it was impractical for her to still attend the school. Struggling to fight back tears, I went back to the form room and slumped in my seat next to Suzanne. She was reading a book about French grammar in preparation for her second year of evening classes.

"Jane's left the school. She's not coming back."

"Oh! Well perhaps she's got a new foster home, somewhere nice."

"Then why didn't she phone and tell me?"

It was a question I wondered about all day. I was sure that she'd have let me know if she could, so thought she must be in trouble. I was still thinking through possibilities as Suzanne and I walked home. She asked,

"Is your phone in the house or the pub?"

"It's in the pub, behind the bar but there is an extension in the house."

"Look Kim, I'm not being funny or anything but would your parents have told you if she'd phoned?"

I was about to say of course but the words froze in my chest. I ran most of the way home and charged into the house, slamming the door and throwing my basket down. Seeing the downstairs empty, I stomped upstairs and knocked loudly on the bedroom door.

"Mum, Dad are you awake?"

"We bloody well are now!" Dad's voice, "What's up?"

They were both fully dressed while having their afternoon nap.

"Did Jane call me during the holidays?" I demanded.

"Kimberly, what on earth do you think you're doing bursting in here shouting?" Mum's voice was sharp and angry and I knew. Taking a step forward I looked past Dad, directly at her, and repeated the question.

"Did Jane call me?"

"Just who do you think you are talking to?" she countered, her anger increasing, "Get out of this room now or I'll..."

"You'll what?" I cut her off, "Slap me again? Lock me up for another year while you pick and choose who I can talk to?"

"Go to your room Kimberly, NOW!" Dad was on his feet in front of me.

I threw myself on my bed as my anger collapsed and I sobbed into my pillow. Through my blubbering, I could hear their raised voices as they went downstairs. After the obligatory cup of tea and nicotine infusion, Dad shouted for me to come down. I sulkily stood in the doorway, looking over at them sitting at the table, cigarette smoke mingling with the steam from the mugs of tea. I folded my arms and glared at them with my swollen surly eyes but said nothing.

"There was a phone call from Jane," Mum began, "couple of weeks ago."

"When?"

"I don't remember when it was, a while ago. She asked to speak to you but I told her you were out."

"But I wasn't out was I?"

"Me and your Dad think it's best if you and Jane aren't so close."

"Well you've made that perfectly clear. Did she leave me a message?"

"No." She took a drag on her cigarette. "She gave me a phone number for you to call her back."

I opened my mouth to ask for it but she shook her head saying,

"I didn't write it down. Anyway she said to say she was only there for a couple of days so it wouldn't be any use now."

"Right, now you say you're sorry to your Mam for the way you spoke to her." Dad picked up his mug as he spoke.

"But I'm not sorry," I said, "And you're right it's no use now and I'll never forgive you for this."

I turned and went back up to my room. I expected being shouted back or followed and grabbed but there was nothing. Feeling the after-effects of the adrenalin rush, I put the radio on and lay on my bed staring at the ceiling.

All the anger and frustration of the last six months had finally been let out and aimed directly at Mum. I knew this was unfair but I couldn't be sorry for what I'd said. A bad situation now seemed unbelievably worse because they didn't like my friend. No, it was worse than that, they had liked her. They just didn't like what other people said about her.

It took much longer to get any normality back in our household after that. The next day, Mr Lloyd told me that he'd spoken to the children's home to be told that Jane was now living with her grandparents in Middlesbrough. There was no telephone number but he gave me the address so I could write to her. I wasted no time in putting pen to paper and Tuesday 7th September 1971 was the start of our written communications. Jane's response came on the Saturday morning and after reading it through several times before replying, I put it in my dressing table drawer where, over the months, a substantial pile of our letters grew. Her words were full of humour and warmth. I thought she was happy.

Her new school was quite close so she didn't have far to walk. The teachers were ok but spoke in the same stupid accent as the kids. There were a few girls that were alright but no Kimmy. She was very happy to have heard from me and when I wrote that I never got her message, she replied that I shouldn't be hard on Mum, she was just scared, and who could blame her; growing up was hard. I told her about life at Hill Topp, about how Miss Aveyard was practically wearing a black armband now her star pupil was gone. I informed her that Sharon was in 4A but not very popular with any of the girl in the class but temporarily very popular with the boys as she worked her way through them. I mentioned Eric Moody breaking his leg on the cross-country and the games teacher thinking he was putting it on until he started crying for his Mummy. All these missives were written in an uplifting and chatty style, each of us painting an entertaining portrait of our coping without each other; a good deal of rose-tinting going on.

My relationship with Mum and Dad got better after my Mr Hyde incident. They were delighted when I said I'd like to learn the guitar with Suzanne and bought me one immediately. I was allowed to sleep over at Suzanne's occasionally, after we had been to the pictures, running the gauntlet of Joey the manic budgerigar. Dad offered to collect me from the drama club and other places but stopped insisting. It was a fine line well-drawn. They knew about my contact with Jane and on days when the postman arrived after I'd gone to school, I'd find the letter propped up against the clock when I got home. I never told them anything about the contents and they never asked. I put a tiny piece of cotton across a corner of the top envelope when I went out and checked it when I came home. It was never disturbed and always lay in the same squiggle but I continued to do it; I was my father's daughter regarding trust.

The downside of this was we felt the distance that had grown between us and it hurt. We'd never been a demonstrative or tactile family. In fact I struggle to remember many cuddles from them as a child. So it wasn't that outwardly our interactions changed but it was like an invisible force-field had come down between us. They were at a loss to understand how their pliable and well-mannered child had become this willful stranger. For my part, I felt their disappointment in me constantly which only made me more determined and fed my hormone fuelled angst.

At the end of October, I got a Saturday job at a hairdressers on Bramley Town Street. It was the first time in ages I saw a real smile on

Mum's face. She thought I was finally coming round to the idea of leaving school and becoming a coiffeur. Although I didn't mind the job and loved earning money, the thing that my time at 'Curl up and Dye' taught me was that I absolutely hated hairdressing. The job also provided me with a new friend, a girl called Elizabeth who was the full-time apprentice. She was a year older than me and had wanted to be a hairdresser ever since she was born, she claimed. She had short (bottle) blonde hair and lots of make-up. I liked her from instantly. Holidays and boys were just about the only thing she ever talked about, she was good fun and always nice to me. I told Suzanne about her after my first week and after listening to my description of Liz and what we had talked about in-between my shampooing, making tea and sweeping the floor, she smiled and nodded.

"Yes, that's absolutely right," she stated quite simply, "she was born to be a hairdresser and you weren't."

A new year started and towards the end of January, we were treated to a visit from the careers officer. Assembled in the hall we sat in our rows and listened while a bored and disenchanted middle-aged man talked to us about the importance of sitting our GCE and CSEs. He stood in front of us, disappointment and resentfulness personified, and said,

"Some of you here are quite bright. A's and B's, I'm sure I don't need to tell you that these examinations are important to your future, even the girls in these groups. You'll have a chance of snagging yourselves a better paid husband if you have these exams behind you. There may even be one or two of you in the C group who should consider staying on and trying to better yourself."

He went on to tell us that we were the last year that would be allowed to leave school at 15. From then on every child throughout England would be made to stay on and sit these examinations and so anyone foolish enough not to take the opportunities offered would be forever competing against better qualified young people for jobs.

"Of course," he went on, "I know some of the girls here are just looking for a little job to tide them over while they get married and start having babies, in which case a factory or shop work will suit you fine, so you shouldn't waste yours or the school's time in staying on."

As Suzy and I walked home that day we talked about who we thought should go and get themselves a factory or shop job and how the whole of the D group must feel terrible. They had been so irrelevant they weren't even mentioned.

"Seriously though Kim," she began, "it is important and just the start of doing what you want to do. You could go to University if you wanted." I was smiling as I thought about this all the way home.

That night, I saw the spark of hope Mum had been holding on to die as I gave her the forms to sign, committing myself to stay on at school and sit my O levels.

"But you've been really enjoying your little job," she said, giving herself a few more seconds to cling to hope, "and you've made new friends."

"And I've discovered that I'd hate to have to do that job every day of the week."

"But we'd buy you your own shop." Her voice was almost pleading.

This was a tone I hadn't heard from her before and my resolve wavered for just a second before common sense returned and I stuck to my guns.

I wrote to Jane that night telling her about the careers officer and his disparaging remarks and how what he'd said had confirmed my resolve. I was going to stay on and there was a chance, if I did well, I could stay on another two years and do A Levels. I was so full of my bright and hopeful future, I poured it out in an epic letter that ran to six pages. Her reply came four days later, only one sheet, one side. Her resolve had not been broken either. She was leaving school at the end of June and was already looking for live-in nanny positions.

Chapter Twenty-nine

Jane left school and her grandmother's house at the end of June, 1972 and moved in with the Goldberg family in Allwoodley, a north Leeds suburb. At fifteen she had her first job as nanny to their children. Mr Goldberg was a Rabbi and he and his wife had a three-year-old son and a six-month-old daughter. Our correspondence continued as we shared glossed-over highlights of our changing lives. Even though now she had moved back to Leeds, neither of us suggested meeting up, the letters seemed to suffice. I think we knew that our mutual pretence only worked in letters.

At first Jane seemed to find the Jewish traditions a good source of witty material for her missives, caricaturing and mocking their rituals and customs. In particular, she singled out Mrs Goldberg and her mother-in-law, who lived just a street away, for particularly cruel ridicule. Their overbearing personalities and constant nagging were exampled in various anecdotes which had me in stitches. Although always light-hearted, I wondered if her humour was a disguise and I supposed she was finding it hard to settle into this life. From what she wrote, I could tell she enjoyed caring and playing with the children but could sense her uncertainty. As the weeks went on the mockery receded and in its place, I found warmer and kinder descriptions of the matriarchal household. The longer she was there the more she started to understand and even respect their culture. In particular these women's overwhelming love and passion for protecting their family. All that said, she still got the odd jibe in about the two Mrs Goldbergs and their propensity for guilt and chicken soup.

A year later, she was still with the Rabbi and his family and excited about going with them on holiday. That same summer I sat my GCEs and got A's in all but the maths where I scrapped a C. I'd worked hard in preparation and was still harbouring thoughts of university. Mr Lloyd and Miss Tempest were encouraging me to stay on and take A Levels and even Mum and Dad seemed pleased with my academic success. On the Saturday morning, the day after I got my results, I heard Dad telling Sally that he always knew I had brains and that of course I took after his side. An hour later, I overheard Mum telling her that she wouldn't be at all surprised if I didn't end up with a really good job, as a secretary or something. After breakfast, I went to finish getting ready for what I'd said was a shopping trip to Leeds. I was going into Town but not for shopping. This week instead of a letter, Jane and I were going to meet; our first face-to-face meeting in over two years. I should have been really looking forward to it but this meeting had been arranged quickly and I wasn't going on my own. In the time we'd been writing to each other, Jane hadn't mentioned her Dad or David once and I had no idea what had happened to either of them. Harry having remained *persona non gratis,* there were no late night updates and there was an unspoken agreement that none of that sorry tale was spoken about. Even as the letters continued and were placed on the mantelpiece for my collection, there was no further acknowledgement given to them. My parents stuck rigidly to the 'no questions asked' policy.

Suzanne had overheard her parents talking about Don some months before. One phrase she heard clearly was, 'Ten years isn't long enough for what he did.' From this, we guessed that whatever Don had been charged with, he'd been found guilty and was now doing his time. So when Lorraine Brookes, now a third year, approached me that week on Wednesday morning, I was completely taken aback.

"Hi Kim, David asked me to give you this and say you can give your answer back to me."

I took the letter and nodded in an effort to disguise my confusion.

"So I'll catch you at dinnertime then, for the reply?"

"Yes," I nodded as she walked off.

I read the note as I walked back to the form room. Suzy was already there having a tidy up of her desk and bag. I sat down next to her and started to re-read the words again. Just one of the brilliant things about my flame haired friend was that she never pried. She smiled lightly at me before continuing her task, leaving me to mine.

Dear Kimberly,

I need to see our Jane as there is something I have to tell her. I know she doesn't want to talk to me but this is important. I know she left the children's home and went to live with Granny and Grandad but they won't tell me where she is now. I'm sure if she kept in touch with anyone it would be you. I promise I don't want to upset her. I would also like to know if she is alright and happy.

Please will you let me know how I can get in touch with her?

Yours Sincerely,

David.

I pulled out a sheet of paper from the back of my geography exercise book and wrote my terse reply.

Dear David,

If you want to tell me what you want to tell Jane about I will pass it on.

Yours Sincerely,

Kimberly.

Lorraine sought me out the next day, to deliver another note. It basically asked me to meet him at Bramley Town End at half past five that evening. He didn't want to write down what he needed to tell Jane but would tell me so I could decide if I'd let him know where she was. He wasn't asking for or expecting a reply and said that he would go to Town

End and wait there anyway.

After reading this one, I went to find Suzanne to ask her opinion on whether I should go or not. Suzy nodded solemnly as I told her of the two notes and said she had no idea why I was even asking her. We both knew I'd be going as I would die of curiosity if I didn't, she was right of course. After getting home from school I changed into my new self-purchased Lee Cooper jeans and purple smock top and sauntered off towards Town End Road. David was already there, standing in front of the old Clifton cinema building which now presented itself as a do-it-yourself centre proudly named Forest Products. Struggling for the right expression, I approached, remembering how I used to be scared of him. Appearing a fair bit older than his seventeen years, he seemed nervous and after greeting each other we crossed the road and started to walk towards the bench in front of the Boys Brigade Hall. Chatting as we walked, he asked me how my exams had gone and what I planned to do next. He seemed genuinely interested and I found myself telling him about my ambitions. He nodded and said I should do it, I was obviously clever enough. I asked what he was up to and he told me he'd left school and had a job at the Midland bank. He was still living with the Woods but planned to move out when Keith went to University next year. As we sat on the bench he asked,

"So, how is she?"

"I haven't seen her for two years but we write to each other every week. She says she's happy."

"Don't you think she is?"

"I think she's happier than she was in the home," I said pointedly.

He sighed deeply and sat back on the bench. The silence grew between us but I remained sitting, eyes focused on the road, waiting for him to say something. I suppose he was looking for the right words, but he gave up and he blurted out,

"Dad's dead!"

I turned quickly to look at him. His face looked pained and eyes moist. I opened my mouth to speak but he held up his hand.

"He died in prison on Monday. It was sudden, a heart attack they think but they have to do an autopsy so it's not confirmed. Granny and Grandad have been told but they've said Jane is better off not knowing. They won't tell her and Grandad says they didn't want anything to do with him while he was alive so they won't be burying him."

"Oh my God! So what'll happen?"

"The prison will sort it out, pauper's burial or somat."

"Oh my God!" I repeated, lost for words.

"He was a bastard and some of me agrees with them, not to tell her, but I know she'd want to know. She should decide if she wants to go to the funeral for herself."

"Will you go?"

Shrugging, "It's stupid I know after all the things he did. I think he probably murdered me Mam as well, but yeah I'll go. I think I have to even if it is just to be sure he's really dead!"

He rubbed the side of his temple and sat forward again.

"The man who phoned me said they'll put a death announcement in the paper once the inquests done, with the date of the funeral. So I'm worried that she might see it or someone might tell her. I don't want her to find out like that."

I agreed to ask her if she would meet him or let me give him her address and left him sitting there while I walked home. As Don had already been dead three days I didn't think there was time to write to her. Jane hadn't given me the phone number, so I rang directory enquires from the phone box on the way home and after jotting down the number called it straight away. One of the Mrs Goldberg's answered and after the initial surprise that I was calling to speak to Jane, got her to the phone. The call was brief; she was in the middle of getting the children ready for bed. I told her I'd just seen David and he wanted to see her to pass on some family news. She didn't question how I'd seen him or what the news was but said she had Saturday afternoon off and could meet me in Leeds. David could come and tell her his news but only if I was there. It was a long time since I'd heard her voice but she sounded different. I imagined her employer standing close to her making her self-conscious but even so, her voice was barely recognisable. I went home straight after the call. Mum and Dad were both in the pub, so I made myself some toast which I took into the bar to eat. The egg shell carpet was now a permanent fixture in our relationship. Mum asked if I'd been out with Suzanne,

"No, I just went for a walk up to Town End. I'm just eating this then I'm going to Michelle's for an hour but I'll be back by eight."

I watched Mum glance across at Dad. They'd both met Michelle, who had only moved to the area a year ago, when she had called for me. They were unimpressed with the amount of make-up she wore and her short skirts but had learnt enough not to express this out loud. I smiled as I saw their restraint and softened a little.

"Shall I to come and give you a hand later?"

"That'd be good. Sally's not working tonight," Dad nodded with an overenthusiastic smile.

I shoved the last piece of toast in my mouth, smiled back and left.

I'd planned to go round to Michelle's. She'd started at Hill Topp at the start of our exam year. Despite her glamorous appearance, she was actually quite bright. Her ambition was to get a good office job where she would meet her future husband and live happily ever after as a wife and mother to four wonderful children. Maybe she wasn't really that bright. Having achieved excellent grades in all subjects she was looking for a job and had been for an interview at the Yorkshire Post that afternoon. I wanted to hear all about it. But first I needed to go to David's foster home.

"Hello, you must be Kimberly," the lady of the house said warmly as she opened the door. "I'm Janet; come on in David's expecting you."

Leading me into the dining room where David and Keith were sitting at a large oak table with papers and books strewn in front of them.

"He's helping Keith with his personal statement for his University application," she said in voice filled with pride. "I'll leave you to chat," she said, closing the door behind her.

I didn't get to Michelle's that night, instead I stayed at the Wood's house being entertained by the boys. After telling David about my arranged meeting and his inclusion, Keith spent the next hour regaling me with stories of how University can change your life. David said very little and after about fifteen minutes excused himself. It was only when Janet came in and asked if I'd like a tea or coffee that I realised it was ten past eight. Explaining that I needed to get home, Keith said he'd walk with me as he wanted some chocolate from the off-license. As we got to Unicorn he brushed his fingers on mine and asked very casually,

"So do you fancy going to the pictures or something?"

"Like on a date?"

"Yes, exactly like a date." He was facing me now.

"Oh well, yes I would like to go out sometime." I smiled at him.

"Great. When?"

"How about Sunday afternoon we could go for a walk?"

"Yes, Sunday, a walk that's a great idea, shall I call for you?"

"Ok, we have our dinner late so make it about three."

And giving him a quick peck on the cheek I ran happily across the car park and through the house door.

The next morning David was at the bus stop already and gave me a smile as I approached. We didn't speak until the bus arrived when he held out his arm saying, "After you."

After paying my fare I went upstairs and he did the same. He took the seat next to me near the front.

"So you're going out with Keith then."

"Yep, that's the plan."

"Let's hope Harry Henshaw's son can keep his fists to himself this time."

He said it to the back of the seat in front without so much as a glance at me. I was instantly nervous of what else he might say, so I said quickly,

"He's moved away, I heard, and good riddance!"

"Yeah I heard that too," he gave a forced laugh, "seems Harry wouldn't have won Dad of the year either!"

I'd heard via Suzy, that Chris had joined the police as a cadet and had gone to Sheffield specifically so that he didn't have to work anywhere near his Dad and so he could leave home.

There'd been no hesitation in deciding where we would meet. It had to be The Golden Egg cafe. Seeing that Jane hadn't arrived yet I went to sit in one of the window booths, just like old times. David had just gone to the counter when she came in. Walking straight across to me our arms flung themselves around each other. Blinking back tears as I hugged her tight, I whispered through her hair,

"I have missed you so much!"

She pushed me away so we could look at each other and smiling, she replied.

"Of course you have and I've missed you."

I watched her take a couple of blinks herself as she drew away and walked across towards the counter but only far enough to get her brother's attention.

"You getting the drinks in David?"

"Yep, what do you want?"

"Same as Kim if she's having banana milkshake."

She shuffled up next to me in the booth as we waited for him to bring our shakes. He'd got himself a frothy coffee and sitting down opposite us he smiled at his sister.

"You look good our Kid. Enjoying the job?"

She didn't return his smile or answer his question.

"So what's this family news then?"

He lowered his eyes and inhaled before nodding an acceptance of her animosity. He took a sip of the milky bubbles of his coffee and, placing the mug down carefully, began to tell her about Don. She listened carefully, making an exasperated noise at the news that her Grandparents were not interested in burying their son, but saying little else. When he'd finished his missive she thanked him for telling her and asked if the Woods had a phone. She wrote the number down in a little notebook and told him she'd phone him on Monday teatime to find out where and when the funeral would be and then dismissed him. As he left the cafe, walking away without a backward glance, the enmity went with him, her smile returned and I had my best friend back. Just for a second I thought about telling her how well David had done at school and his job but I was too scared it would chase away her smile. Instead, I asked her how it was going with the family and what she normally did on her days off. We talked through a second milkshake as she told me that she'd been doing a course in childcare at college. The Goldbergs were paying and she was really enjoying it. She loved the children who were exceptionally well behaved and so cute. I listened to more tales about how the Rabbi was this revered and important man who everyone looked up to in public but how he was scared to death of his wife and really hen-pecked in private. She asked about me and I told her about my plan to go to Uni, about Suzy and other bits from school and finally I added that Keith had asked me out.

"He seemed alright the couple of times I met him," she mumbled not looking at me.

"He is. He's really funny as well. He's going to Uni next year if he gets the grades." I was aware that I sounded giddy and that her smile had waned.

"Well don't let him break your heart before he goes. Do you fancy a trip to Woollies?"

It was like we'd never been parted, so easy and comfortable. When it was time to get our separate busses she said,

"I was scared of us meeting up but it's actually been great."

"Me too!" I half laughed half choked in relief as she voiced my thoughts.

"Shall we do it again then?"

"Absolutely!" And we had a big fierce hug before she had to run for her bus.

Chapter Thirty

Keith called for me on Sunday afternoon as I was finishing the washing-up. I'd told Mum that he was calling for me and we would be going out for a walk. It's quite strange as I think back to how calm I was. Let's make no mistake here, this was a big deal, a boy calling for me. Mum got to the door first as I quickly dried my hands. Hearing Keith's voice, I nearly fainted as Mum was asking if he'd like a cuppa.

"Maybe when we come back," I said, grabbing my cardigan and ushering him outside.

Calling over my shoulder that I didn't know what time I'd be back but I wouldn't be late, off we went. Walking across the car park, his hand brushed against mine and turning on to the main street he asked where I'd like to go. I shrugged and said I really didn't mind and our fingers brushed again before fusing together.

"Let's go to the park," he said and we walked, slightly swinging our clasped hands. I felt a brand new infestation of butterflies swarm around inside, making me so giddy I couldn't help but laugh out loud. When we reached the gates of the park he bought us a 99's from the ice cream van and we chatted easily about our likes and interests. His infectious enthusiasm for just about everything had me completely mesmerised. After we left the park he asked me if I wanted to go to his house to play a board game.

"I love board games!" I exclaimed, "What shall we play?"

"How about Scrabble?"

"Brilliant!" I said quickly, "I love Scrabble."

I'd never played Scrabble and had no real idea how to play it but thought, well it's letters and words – how hard could it be? Arriving at his house, his Mum, *'please call me Janet'*, gave us a warm welcome, offering tea and cake; homemade of course. It became apparent quite early on that I hadn't played Scrabble before and had no concept of strategies required to win. Relying only on the luck of tiles, I was easy prey for Keith's master moves. He was not someone who subscribed to allowing opponents a fighting chance, so he beat me soundly on all three games we played and the start of my Scrabble tuition began.

Jane and I continued our letters on a weekly basis but despite mentioning it and both saying how we must, we didn't plan to meet up again. She told me about her father's funeral in one letter but only in passing.

'Dad's funeral was last Wednesday. Mrs. Goldberg took me but didn't come in for the service. There were only seven of us there and four of them were undertakers! It only took an hour so I was back in time to take the kids to the park.'

She didn't mention David, so I had no idea if they spoke or planned to keep in touch or who the other person was. I kept her up to date with what was going on with me and Keith and she seemed pleased for me. For his part, whenever I saw David at the Wood's, he never mentioned or asked about Jane.

On our second date, a trip to the cinema, I knew I had to ask the question.

"So do you still go fishing down at the canal?"
We were sitting on the top deck of the bus after he'd come to call for me.

"Now and again," he began, turning away from the window to look at me. "Why, do you want to come?"

"Maybe," I began with a laugh, "as long as I don't have to sit near the maggots."

"It's just me and David that go though. We don't see Paul Turner anymore if that's why you were asking."

He looked flushed and suddenly I was embarrassed about what he might have heard about me and why he thought I was asking. I was trying to think of something to say that would make it ok but was lost for words, still feeling the warmth in my cheeks.

"He left school last year, not sure what he's doing but we weren't ever really friends. I always thought he was a bit of a tosser".

I laughed and nodded.

"I think you're right, he was. I'd like to come fishing one day if we can take a picnic."

I didn't ever go fishing with him but over the next twelve months my Scrabble playing improved and our relationship was easy and fun. Mrs Wood seemed to like me, which was an added bonus. She was very pretty and had been a librarian in her younger days. Mr Wood also approved of me, once he had heard of my plans for higher education. He was a professor at Leeds University and very much the intellectual. My parents liked Keith and fell over themselves to make him welcome whenever he came round. They didn't know his parents but I'm sure they'd asked someone, probably Sally, about them. She would have undoubtedly told them that they had provided a foster home to Jane's brother. However, this was never mentioned.

At the end of August, just before we went back to school, Keith passed his driving test and a week later he took me to The Coniston Restaurant in Farsley for a meal. Walking in I began to feel self-conscious, it was so posh I hardly dared breathe as we were shown to our table. Cut glass and candles adorned the whitest linen and heavy, highly polished cutlery framed the place settings, it was so beautiful. The Coniston had a reputation for good food and fine wines at top drawer prices. It was owned by a local businessman who I knew vaguely from his occasional late night drinks at the Unicorn. The meal was wonderful and we had three courses, which I struggled to finish but my upbringing wouldn't let me leave a morsel. Our conversation had been easy and vibrant throughout the feast and only stopped when the bill came. Keith raised his eyebrows as he glanced down at it and I said that he must let me pay half, which he immediately refused saying it was his treat. I smiled but noticed him getting a bit flustered as he fumbled in his jacket pockets.

"I just need to pop outside," he began, "I must have left my wallet in the car."

After a few minutes he came back looking wretched.

"Kim, do you think you could pay. I must have left it at home. I'm so sorry I'll pay you back tomorrow."

I couldn't help giggling as I pulled the bill towards me.

"Of course," I started to say as I looked at the bill. I felt my cheeks burn. "Oh lord, I haven't got that much with me," I said in a loud whisper.

We both stared at each other for a second and it almost broke my heart to see his normally happy face looking so forlorn. I looked round and seeing our waitress over at the small bar talking to a man in a suit I stood up quickly.

"Don't worry I'll explain," I said and walked as casually as I could towards them. As I got closer the man gave me a huge smile.

"Hello, It's Kim isn't it, how are you?"

Relief swept over me.

"Hiya Ken. I'm alright thanks. I've just had one of the best meals of my life."

"Ah that's good to hear. Is it your first visit?"

"Yes but I know it's not going to be my last," I beamed at him. "But there's just a small problem. We've realised we didn't bring enough money with us. We can pay some of it but will it be ok if we go home to fetch the rest?"

The waitress looked from me to him and over at Keith who was trying to look anywhere else but over at us. Ken Maddon returned my smile.

"Come and introduce me to your young man," he said, moving round to my side of the bar and walking towards the table. I followed and as we got there Keith stood up. Ken held out his hand and I said,

"Keith, this is Mr Maddon, Ken, he's a friend of Mum and Dad's. Ken, this is Keith Wood, my boyfriend." A little gurgle of pride popped through my oesophagus as I used that word.

Ken picked up the bill and said that as long as we promised to come again, this meal was on the house. Pulling up a chair he chatted with us as we enjoyed a further complementary coffee. When he heard that Keith would be 18 the following month he told him he had a treat in store as he'd then be able to sample my Dad's excellent ales. As we left, he again shook Keith's hand and asked me to give Mum and Dad, who were apparently the salt of the earth, his best wishes. As Keith drove me home I smiled as I glimpsed at my boyfriend in profile. I felt a warm fuzziness of contentment wrap itself around me. That was the first time in my life that being the landlord's daughter had made me happy.

That was the night I was supposed to lose my virginity. We'd talked about it, very sensibly and planned carefully. I'd gone to the family planning clinic in Leeds who had given me six months supply of the pill and we had waited the two weeks for it to get into my system. The expensive romantic meal was supposed to be a prelude to having sex on the back seat of Keith's little Austin 1100. But the best laid plans and all that. It didn't happen that night, for three reasons. Firstly, we were both so full of the delicious food, we felt uncomfortable sitting up let alone cramping up in the back of the car. Secondly, Keith was still mortified about forgetting his wallet and thirdly, we both decided that we wanted our first time to be a bit more special. So when he suggested we waited a little longer, I was only too happy to agree. Instead, we went back to his house, his parents and David were out so we played Scrabble for an hour before he took me home. Dad ribbed Keith for weeks after that about him forgetting his wallet but he took it in good part. We did go back to the

Coniston a couple of times afterwards but we didn't attempt to factor it into our physical intimacy schedule again.

It was the Monday after our romantic meal that I did finally surrender my virginity. It was the middle of the afternoon and it was in Keith's bed. His Dad and David were at work and his Mum was in Ripon visiting her parents. We'd been in the middle of a game of Scrabble when Janet left, telling us to help ourselves to the cake from the pantry or biscuits from the cupboard. She'd also made some comment about us enjoying the last few days of the holiday before we went back to school. We'd exchanged quick and furtive glances at each other and telepathically transmitted that we intended to.

I'd like to say it was wonderful and that the earth moved and we melded into one astonishingly sensual being but I can't. I'd thought that I would experience immense pleasure but actually it was terrible. It was painful and uncomfortable as he slid his erection into my unmoist vagina, and sharply brought me out of any semblance of desire. Instead, our brief foreplay ended with a sharp sting and burning as he thrust his way inside me. It was the first time for him too and I knew he was nervous, so I tried to smile through my pain and disappointment. I'd read enough magazines to know how fragile the male ego was. I'd also read that the first could be painful but I wasn't expecting it to hurt so much. We'd had several very passionate sessions in Keith's car, fumbling inside each other's clothing, it had been hard to disengage our mouths and pull apart. I thought our passion would fuel our intimacy and that I would love it, so the disappointment stung along with the physical pain. I also knew enough about human biology to realise that once Keith had ejaculated it was over. I bit back my feelings and smiled at him as he searched my eyes and asked if I was ok and if I'd enjoyed it. It had not been what I expected; no orgasm or feelings of deep emotion, just a searing pain and a few spots of blood but I answered with the affirmative to both. It was true, I was ok, now it had stopped and I had enjoyed our intimacy. My smile got bigger as a thought struck me – I was no longer a virgin and next time it would be better, I was sure.

An hour later I kissed him passionately as we stood in the kitchen before going home on my own. Walking into the house, I was amazed that everything seemed perfectly normal. Mum and Dad were in the living room

"You alright love?" Mum asked with a smile.

I had been convinced all the way home that they'd be able to tell instantly that I was no longer virgo intacta. It must be written all over me. I was sure they would notice that I was no longer a child but a sexually active woman. But they didn't. I got ready to meet Suzy after tea. We were going round to Michelle's to hear about her job at the Yorkshire Post. Throughout the evening I wondered if perhaps my friends might notice a difference in me, see me as a little more womanly but of course they didn't. Michelle was animated as she told us about her job. How great it was, the responsibility, and the people she'd met and of course the £23 a week she was earning. I still had my Saturday job at Curl up and Dye where I got £3.50 plus tips. Tips on a good week could be another £1.50 but were usually around £1. Not that money was an issue for me, I only had to mention that I liked something and my parents would buy it for me. It was more the independence of earning my own money that enticed me. Suzanne was impressed that all new office staff got free touch-typing and shorthand lessons and there was a social club that arranged monthly nights out. It all sounded very grown-up. After giving her glossy presentation of life after school, she looked delighted with herself. Looking at her beautifully painted fingernails, she gave me a sideways look and mentioned that they would be taking on more office juniors in January if I was interested. She went on to tell us about the print rooms full of great looking lads, training to be compositors. This apparently was highly skilled work that was rewarded with excellent pay. She already had her eye on one of the second year apprentices who was drop-dead gorgeous and had his own car.

As Suzy and I walked home she asked, "Are you changing your mind about doing A levels?"

"I don't know," I found myself answering honestly, "I'm just thinking that another two years of school and then another three at Uni, well it's just starting to seem like too long before I can be like Michelle."

"What – you want to be like Michelle? Bloody hell Kim what's got into you?"

"No that's not what I meant. I just mean she's earning a good wage and has a job where she meets new people and she likes it and can make decisions about what she wants to do. She's a grown-up."

"Actually she gets more like a little girl wanting to play Mummy's and Daddy's every time we see her."

"Maybe she is but at least she's in control. I'm still a schoolgirl and I might not even get in to University."

"What rubbish, course you'll get in."

It was quiet in the bar when I got in and Dad was on his own. He said Mum wasn't feeling too well and so was in the house. I went through to find her asleep on the sofa with the TV playing to itself. She woke up when I turned it off and I made her a cup of tea. She looked really pale and had been dribbling on the cushion. Handing her the mug, I noticed how thin her arms were and wondered how I'd not noticed before that she'd lost so much weight.

"Are you alright Mum?"

"Oh aye, just got a bit of a headache and I've not been sleeping so well. I'm off to the doctors tomorrow so I'll get some sleeping pills an I'll be right."

She placed her mug down on the radiogram as she got up and switched the TV back on.

"So what shall we watch?" Glancing up at the clock she added, "Look at the time it's nearly nine o'clock. There's a film on after the news."

A week later I went back to school to start sixth form. There were only sixteen of us staying on from our year, ten boys and six girls. It was only the second year the school had offered A Levels and the upper sixth consisted of only a further eleven making us an elite little group with our own common room. Despite my earlier concerns, I was quite excited to get back and looking forward to some in-depth reading and studying. As I walked through the school gates on the first morning, a member of the lower sixth, I felt like the bee's knees. The feeling didn't last long.

It was over a month before Keith and I tried again to have sex. Funnily enough, I never remember either of us trying to pretend it was any more than that. There was no talk of *'making love'*. Instead, it was more like an exercise or practical biology experiment. For me it was only better in the fact that it didn't sting so much and there was no blood and I'm not convinced he enjoyed it all that much either. Not that there was any discussion during or after the event but there was a definite cloud of disappointment in the air. After this our penetrative sexual encounters happened only rarely and I found each of these melding liaisons equally disappointing and was generally relieved when we parted after just a kiss and a cuddle.

Two weeks in to the term and Keith got a provisional acceptance at Warwick, his first choice University, if he got his predicted grades. On the advice of his teachers and father we decided to only see each other at weekends, leaving us both plenty of undistracted weekday evenings to work hard. Suzanne also said this was a very sensible plan and anyway the evenings were getting darker and colder, so it was much better to stay in and swot up. Mum, still looking a bit rundown but claiming the pills were definitely helping her sleep, announced she was giving up smoking. She managed almost three weeks, during which time she was irritable beyond belief before she cracked. The end of her resolve came in the middle of the night and hearing someone moving around downstairs, I found her sitting at the kitchen table in a fug of nicotine.

"I'm just having the one," she declared as she caught sight of me.

"I know," I smiled at her and made us both a cup of tea before we went back to bed.

I hadn't been sleeping all that well myself and it wasn't because I was reading into the small hours. Having always been an avid reader I'd been looking forward to doing a much more in-depth study of books, poetry and plays. But actually, I wasn't enjoying it all and the tedium of the books we were covering was disturbing my rest. Only five weeks into the course and I was bored to tears with King Lear and Wuthering Heights and hating the poetry. I had a deep sense of dread as I glanced at my alarm clock knowing another school day would begin in just four hours.

Chapter Thirty-one

On the Saturday of Keith's 18th birthday, after finishing work at the hairdressers, Gwen the senior stylist put my hair up for me in a French pleat. I hardly recognised myself in the mirror as she sprayed me with firm hold lacquer. She could see I was impressed,

"You should have your hair up more often, it suits you. If you'd come and work here properly instead of filling your head with books, you could be doing it like this yourself."

Mum and Dad were gasped when they saw it. Dad took a picture of me and Mum standing in the bar when I'd finished getting ready.

"My duchess and my princess," he said quietly to himself as he took another two just to be sure he got a good one.

The Woods arrived to pick me up as they were taking us for a meal. David had also passed his driving test in the summer and was allowed to borrow Keith's car so that he could come along and bring Mandy, his girlfriend. She worked with him at the bank and lived in Armley. She seemed very grown-up although she was the same age as me but the thing that took my breath away was her coat. It was a three-quarter length Coney fur and was absolutely gorgeous. She talked about her job quite a lot and her nights out with her best friend who she shared a flat with. My mind immediately flew back to the plans I'd had with Jane and nostalgia filled me up along with my Chicken Maryland. A couple of times during the evening I glanced across at Janet. She looked lovely as ever, calm and composed, almost regal until I saw a look, a suggestion of a raised eyebrow from her husband as more wine was offered. A small

---

frown washed across her face, momentarily but was quickly banished as she put her hand over her glass and shook her head. Smiling brightly at the waiter, her composure returned and her husband nodded his approval.

When they dropped me off that night, I had all sorts of things going through my head. Telling Mum and Dad I'd had a good time but was really tired, I rushed up to my room and got out my Basildon Bond notepad to write to Jane. After reading it through it was suddenly clear what I needed to do.

On my way home from school on Thursday I bought a copy of the Evening Post. Michelle had told me the day before the advert would be in for office junior positions to start in January. It took me well over an hour to write my letter of application but I enjoyed it much more than anything I had written for my studies. I had stamps already, so I posted it that night. While writing my application, I'd tried to impress the person that would read it and in doing so had completely sold myself with how good it would be working there. It took them nearly ten days to get back to me with an interview date which was just a couple of days after that. On the week before Christmas, in a new skirt and jacket, I sat before Mr Ward-Browne the Head of Personnel and after half an hour of answering questions, was offered the job.

The next day was the end of term and the end of my schooling. Mr Lloyd said he wasn't surprised at all, he'd seen my heart wasn't in it. Miss Tempest gave me a hug and told me to let her know how I got on and Mr Wedaburn shook my hand and sent his regards to my Mum. Although I was excited and happy and in no doubt that I was doing the right thing, I still struggled not to cry as I walked home. Mum and Dad were really pleased, Mum still clinging to her new dream of me being a secretary, but Keith thought I must have gone mad. He was actually quite angryt, which I'd not expected. Even Suzy was pleased for me saying she knew I'd be successful whatever I did. Along with the Christmas cards that year, I got three others congratulations me on my new job, from Jane, Suzy and surprisingly my cousin Alison. Mum had obviously shared my news with the family. A week later, I heard Ali's news. She too was leaving school. Her new job was to be a fifteen year old Mum.

Not wanting to let them down over the busy Christmas period, I'd worked my last shift at Curl up and Dye on Saturday 29th which was a fun but emotional day. I got five pounds in tips and a vanity case filled with hair spray and toiletries and was told not to be a stranger and to visit regularly to get my hair done.

I started my first proper fulltime job on Wednesday 2nd January. I was one of six new starters, all girls, being inducted into the working world of Yorkshire's National Newspaper. After watching a short film showing how important the two daily broadsheets were, not only to the region but also to the whole world, we were given a tour of the building and different departments. I was in complete awe as I followed the small group around with wide-eyed incredulity. Our tour started in the iron framed glass reception, from where we climbed the stairs to the belly of the newspaper above. Going through the double doors at the top of the stairwell I almost gasped at what I saw.

"This is our editorial department or newsroom as the sub editors like to call it." Our immaculately dressed female guide told us.

The cavernous and windowless chamber was a sight to behold. It buzzed with the noises of fluorescent lighting, air conditioning and industriously busy people. The sounds of telephones ringing, of clickety-clacking typewriters and the booming of male voices echoed around the futuristic concrete walls. In weeks to come I would discover the reporters who worked there were not impressed with these surroundings.

"A newsroom, a window on the world, without any windows!"

There were tiny skylights way above the clouds of nicotine and suspended strip lights but the stark, intimidating atmosphere was completely untouched by the outside world. We walked quickly down the carpet tiled central aisle of the room as our leader pointed out different sections of the paper. The photograph and cuttings library, the sub's desk, competitions and readers offers, I remember hoping I wouldn't have to remember all this. The open plan arrangement was mesmerising as we filed past, catching snatches of instruction and communication from the busy journalists and their minions. Nearing the other end, towards a further set of doors, our guide turned around and pointed up to a mezzanine floor that covered about a quarter of the room.

"That's where all the back copies and archives are kept. We have copies dating back to when the paper was first founded in 1754."

From her tone we knew we should be impressed and made the appropriate noises as we moved on and down the stairs to the back of the building.

"This is the press and printing floor. It's where all our highly skilled compositors and typesetters work and where we produce the hot metal for printing."

Following her along the stone floor, looking to our left and right we saw vast machines and rows of benches with metal frames on them. A few men in blue overalls were scattered around, mostly with their heads bent towards their work and paying us no attention. We stopped for a moment and our guide explained it was quiet now as the print runs hadn't started, allowing us to appreciate the marvellous scene before us. Sternly, she told us that should we ever be required to come into the hall during a print run we were to wear a pair of the ear defenders situated just outside the door. I turned to look back at the door and jumped as I heard a voice just behind me say,

"Hello Kimbo, long time no see."

I didn't get a chance to respond or even close my mouth, as I turned to see Paul Turner. He smiled and waved as I was ushered along in our walking crocodile through the machine room and out into the distribution hall at the end. The rest of the day was taken up being shown how the post room was run. We would all work there to gain a better orientation of the building until a position was found in one of the departments. At half past four, we were all taken back to Personnel where we were introduced to Mike Thorne who was 'the father of the chapel'. Mr Thorne, or Mike as we were told we could and should call him, was our shop steward and representative of our trade union, the National Society of Operative Printers and Assistants.

"Or NATSOPA," he added, pronouncing the acronym as a word affectionately.

Yorkshire Post newspapers was a closed shop employer; he explained, and in order to work there, we must join the union. Handing out the forms for us to consent to membership and for our subs to be deducted from our weekly pay, he talked more about the importance of his role. We learnt that NATSOPA worked closely with the National Union of Journalists to ensure good working conditions and pay. There would be a union meeting once a month and we would have to attend or would be fined. Wording to this effect was on the forms we were signing. As we were all 'just young lasses' we could, if we liked, take the form home and show it to our Dad's but they had to be back the next day filled in and signed. Deciding that I was perfectly able to fill a form in myself, I did so, signed it with a flourish and handed it in on the way out. Only two of the others wanted to take their forms home for discussion with their Dads. The next day, these two were sent straight to personnel but only one of them came back. The other girl, whose father was 'opposed in principle' to the trade union movement and told her not to sign, was sent home and we never saw her again. At the end of my first day, I stood at the bus stop feeling grown-up and excited. It had been a shock seeing Paul in his blue boiler suit with his blonde curly hair and sparkling eyes. Mid-smile at the memory, I stopped myself sharp. He wasn't someone I was going to have nice warm thoughts about. He'd been the catalyst for a horrible phase in my life. He also bore some responsibility for Jane being sent to bloody

Lodge House.

"Bastard!" I said to myself as the number 14 bus pulled up at the stop and I climbed on board.

Dad was in the bar when I got home but Mum was in the kitchen. She made me a cup of tea while I told her about my day as she got on with making me steak and chips. She made lots of noises of approval and interest as I told her about what I'd seen and done. Although the thing she seemed most impressed with was that there was a tea lady who came around twice a day. Keith came round that evening to see how it had gone and we sat in the taproom bar. The first thing I told him was that I had seen Paul. He nodded.

"Yeah, I heard he's a printer or something." He made the occupation sound somehow dirty.

"So you knew he was working there?"

"Well sort of. Somebody told me but I didn't know if it was true," he said defensively. "So what did he have to say for himself?"

"I didn't speak to him; just saw him as we were passing through the print room."

Our conversation moved on to the unions and the closed shop arrangement. Keith said this was outrageous and went on at great length about how the union's had way too much power. I nodded in what I thought were appropriate places but actually thought he was being a bit simplistic in his argument. Having done a term of social and economic history, I knew that this power of the working classes had not been won easily. Although I was aware that it was all far more complicated than our naive assumptions, I didn't want to explore them now while Keith was in this haughty and slightly condescending mood. I changed the subject as soon as I could and told him about the tea lady with her big trolley full of biscuits, buns and beverages. He too seemed to find this impressive, although did suggest I didn't partake too regularly as he wasn't sure he'd like me as much if I got porky. He was laughing as he spoke but I thumped him on the arm anyway.

"You're not likely to get fat though, looking at your Mum," he nodded over at her. "You've got her genes, so you'll get better looking and slimmer the older you get."

Within the week, I settled easily into my nine to five routine, starting touch-typing lessons two afternoons a week. Dad was really impressed that I was given this training in work time and being paid to better myself. I told him that this was probably agreed by union negotiations as part of fair and better working conditions but I didn't say that to Keith. I was assigned to sorting and franking post for the first week and didn't get out of the mailroom except for the dinner break. On the second week I moved on to delivering and collecting. Excitedly, I set off with the postal trolley and a girl called Carole. She'd been doing this job for the past month but had just secured a job in one of the departments. It all went smoothly through Editorial, Personnel and the Management Suite as we made our way through the building. However, when we entered the print and press floor, we were greeted by whistles and calls of 'hello darlin's' and 'nice pair of legs luv' at us as we walked down the aisle. Carole's cheeks turned a bit pink but she said nothing. Eyes forward, we quickened our step towards the foreman's office. She knocked once on the half open door and walked in. The man at the desk smiled as she put down his post and picked up a couple of assorted brown internal envelopes from a red basket.

"Hello Mr. Harding, this is Kim. She'll be doing the post from today."

"Hello Kim," he smiled at me, "don't mind that lot they're more to be pitied than feared." He laughed and I managed a smile in return.

Paul was standing in our path as we came out and stood with his arms folded across his chest.

"You alright Carole? I thought you were starting in Sports today?"

"No, that's tomorra," she began, "This is Kim, she's new. I'm just showing her the post round."

"Me and Kim are old friends, aren't we Kimbo?" he said winking, "We've got loads of catching up to do. What dinner break you on?"

"We're on twelve to one," Carole answered for us both.

"Great, see you in the canteen then." Beaming he walked away.

"How do you know Paul?" she asked me as we made our way through to distribution.

"We used to hang around together when we were kids," I replied picking up the post for the next department.

I tried to tell myself that 'catching up' with Paul over my chicken salad and chips would be just a way of finding out what had actually happened after the disco incident. I was also interested to know if he was still friends with Chris. The fact that I'd felt the tingle of excitement on sight of him was something I was trying hard to ignore. I didn't see him as we entered the large canteen but was too scared to look around. I followed Carole to order and pay for my food before sitting at an empty table. Michelle walked in and, spotting us, waved and came over with her packed lunch of Ryvitas and cottage cheese.

"Just one more day Caz," Michelle smiled, "How you finding it in the mailroom Kim with the old witches?"

Michelle was referring to Mrs Bennett and Mrs Gordon who ran the postal department. They'd worked for the newspaper for many years and had little or no patience for the young and flighty girls sent to work in their domain. When not being referred to as old witches or hags, the pair were merged into one entity and called 'Gordon Bennett'.

"I'm enjoying it and so far I've not been noticed by the old bags."

"Well will you look at this, my three favourite girls all together and waiting for me. I must have died and gone to heaven!"

Paul had appeared from nowhere and placing his mug and plate of sausage, beans and chips on the table, he sat down next to Carole and opposite me. As he forked up a large cluster of chips he asked,

"How's that lovely cousin of yours Kimbo, little Alison?"

"She pregnant actually."

"Fuck a duck!" he spluttered choking on his mouthful, "It's nowt to do with me, I haven't seen her for yonks!"

He reached out to take drink from his mug of tea, looking amused.

"How's your mate Chris?" I asked, "I heard he's joined the police."

"Yeah I heard that an' all, think he moved to Sheffield." Spiking a piece of sausage he asked, "Hey, it's not him that's knocked up your Alison is it?"

The thought hadn't occurred to me and was obviously absurd, Sheffield was a big place, but his suggestion unsettled me. He was still laughing as he chewed his processed meat.

"Who's Chris?" Michelle asked.

"Chris Henshaw, he was in the year above us at Hill Topp and Paul's best friend." I stated.

"We were mates when we were kids but we had a bit of a fallout, couple of years ago," his eyes were on mine as he spoke, "and we didn't get on much after that." He held my gaze until I looked away first.

Michelle asked him where Trevor was. Trevor Gates was an apprenticed compositor in his last year. He was the one that she'd set her cap at. However, rather annoyingly, he already had a girlfriend of three years who worked in Debenhams. But since the Christmas party, when he and Michelle had a bit of a snog in the lift, things had changed and he'd asked her if she fancied going out with him. Michelle was trying to find out from Paul if Trevor had finished with the other girl, or if he was just hedging his bets.

"I dunno, do I? Lads don't talk about that sort of stuff. "

"Surely he wouldn't have asked you out if he hadn't dumped her," Carole offered.

"There you go," chuckled Paul. "Carole's right, what bloke would do that?" And putting his knife and folk down he asked, "Anyway Kimbo, you still going out with Woody?"

Chapter Thirty-two

1974 was a good year for me. It had its ups and downs but the majority of the time, I was in control and my transition from school to work felt seamless. I kept in touch with Suzanne and we went into Leeds on Saturdays quite often. I asked Jane to meet us several times but she was never able to make it. Occasionally, I worried she'd moved on with her life and I didn't fit anymore but we still wrote regularly and her letters were still warm and chatty, so I brushed the thoughts aside. I'd had a vague idea that while I was still at school she thought I was a bit childish, so I was disappointed she still seemed reluctant to meet up. I can be a bit dense sometimes; the real reason for her keeping me at arm's length was obvious if I'd thought about it.

When I got home on the evening I'd had the canteen catch-up with Paul, Keith called round. It was an unplanned visit and I was jumpy and a little defensive. I didn't tell him about speaking to Paul, telling myself it was a harmless exchange, so there was no reason to mention it. He didn't stay long and our conversation seemed a bit stilted and littered with long silences. I claimed a headache and tiredness to get him to go so I could think through what I was feeling. The fluttering wings started in the pit of my stomach as I remembered the way Paul had looked at me across the table. I hadn't asked him how he knew about me going with Keith, I'd reverted back to being gauche and tongue-tied for the rest of dinner time as the other three chatted away happily. Once my brain finally regained control of my senses, the break was over and it was too late for me to ask the million questions ticker-taping through my head.

The next day, I looked for him while I did the post run. He was at the far end of the print room, head bent and engrossed in his work. I spent a while outside Mr. Harding's door, resorting the mail on the off chance that he would look up so I could smile but he remained absorbed in his compositing. I went for dinner with Carole and Michelle again at the same time and scanned the bright room for his blonde curls but there was no sign of him. My excitement was overtaken by disappointment which remained all day. At five o'clock, I walked towards the bus stop, bundled up in my warm coat, scarf and gloves, mulling over why I'd allowed myself to read so much into that look. I saw him leaning casually on the bus shelter, the collar of his long black Crombie coat turned up and his hair glistening from the street light above his head. As I got a bit nearer, I saw his smile and butterflies again swept the euphoria through my bloodstream.

"I thought I'd get the bus home with you, we've got some unfinished catching up to do."

The bus came round the corner at that moment and we climbed on board along with the others waiting at the stop. He followed me upstairs and sat next to me near the front. I was by the window and hugging my canvas bag tightly in an effort to stop myself from shaking. It obviously didn't work.

"You cold?" he asked.

"A little bit," I managed to say, swallowing hard and not daring to look at him.

He squashed in closer to me and put his arm on the back of my seat. I turned to look at him and our heads were inches apart.

"So this is nice," he said, voice full of laughter and I smelt the beer on his breath.

"Have you been to the pub?"

"Yeah, I'm on 8 to 4 this week so I had to do something to kill the time waiting for you."

The Rising Sun just down Wellington Street, towards the city centre, was a watering hole favoured by the majority of Post employees.

"So how did you know about me and Keith?" I asked.

He said he'd seen him with David back in the summer down at the canal and he'd told him then. I was surprised.

"He never mentioned seeing you," I said and Paul laughed.

"Well he wasn't that friendly and he was actually warning me off."

"What? Why would he do that?"

"Why do you think?"

I looked out of the window, unsure what to say, so I said nothing. Prodding my arm with his free hand he asked,

"So, what you been up to since I last saw you?" His voice was light and playful. I finally remembered my prepared script and took a deep breath,

"Well I spent a little time wondering what on earth really happened that night at Pudsey baths, then I wondered why you and Chris told his Dad those awful things about me and Jane that got her sent to a children's home."

"Wow!" he held up his hands, "I can help you with the first bit but the second bit had nothing to do with me."

He told me the fisticuffs continued outside the swimming baths before they were pulled apart by a group of passing blokes who knew Chris. They told Paul to scarper and held on to Chris, asking what was going on. He said he was only too happy to scarper and ran all the way home. Unfortunately his mother was in the kitchen when he came in and was apoplectic at the sight of him.

"Stupid bastard had broken my nose and dislocated my jaw. Took months till it was right," he said with feeling.

"He was certainly annoyed with you that night," I confirmed.

"I know and I'd told him earlier that I was thinking of asking you out. He said you wouldn't be interested but he wasn't bothered anyway as he was going out with Maureen."

"So why did he go so crazy?"

"Well it's not like we've ever talked about it since but I guess he just didn't think I stood a chance with you."

"Ok. What happened afterwards?"

"It's a long story," he began and I listened while he explained.

His mother was so worried about his injuries that she'd dialled 999, told the operator her son had been assaulted and insisted on an ambulance. He started off telling his mother that he had been attacked by a couple of lads he didn't know but once the police constable arrived at the hospital he had to fess up. While he was waiting for an x-ray of his jaw his mother used the hospital pay phone to call Mrs Henshaw to let her know what her son had done. Paul didn't know if Sergeant Henshaw heard the news via his wife or from the station but the next he knew, Harry turned up by his bed. He made it clear to Paul and his mother that no one was going to be accused of assault. Chris, he informed them, was in an equally bad if not worse state and there were witnesses to prove that Paul had started the fight.

"Mum was furious but she knew as well as I did we stood no chance against Harry's law. She'd been best mates with Sadie Henshaw for years but they've never spoken since."

He told me that Harry asked him what the fight was about, insisting he told him he hadn't got the faintest idea. He tried to claim that he was just standing there minding his own business when Chris had started laying into him.

"Harry just looked at me with that hard stare and a scary smile and told me I was talking out of my arse but not to worry, he'd get to the bottom of what happened and I better watch my step."

"Bloody hell!" was all I could manage.

"Then all my mates turned their back on me, even Kenny. I don't know what Chris told them."

He paused for a sigh.

"As far as you were concerned, I thought that I'd better let things die down a bit before I saw you again when I got back at school it got worse."

David had followed him in to the toilets on the morning break and just gone 'mental' at him.

"He was yellin' at me that I'd caused shit loads of trouble, shooting my big mouth off about you and Jane. He wouldn't let me get a word in edgeways. I thought I was in for another good hiding even though I had this cage thing round me jaw. Keith was with him, I think he was a bit worried an' all but in the end he just punched the bog door at the side of my head and walked off."

"Then what?"

"Then I kept me head down till I could leave school and start me apprenticeship at the Post. I knew then that whatever Chris had told his Dad was bad and that you'd think, like everybody else, that it were me."

He rubbed his eyes and I turned slightly towards him.

"Course, then I heard about Don Schofield getting put away. It all seemed a bit useless after that. What exactly am I supposed to have said anyway?"

"It doesn't matter now, but it certainly caused a chain reaction."

"Just cos of a couple of slow dances and a snog!"

"It was two snogs."

"Ah, you remembered!" His arm along the back of my seat dropped forward and he gave me a hug before taking his arm back and feeling in his pocket. Taking out a packet of mints said,

"I'll have to suck these all the way home otherwise I'll get an earful from me Mam about drinking. Do you want one?"

We companionably worked our way through half the packet while chatting about life in the concrete bunker, as the Post building was known. When we neared my stop he stood up.

"See you tomorrow then Kimbo," he said as I squeezed past him.

"Quite probably," I replied with a smile.

I did see him the next day and most other days but we only exchanged a Hi or a smile. It was almost two weeks later when we got the chance to speak again on a morning post run. I'm pretty sure he'd been waiting for me as almost as soon as I came through the large double doors with my trolley, he was at my side. He gave me his cheekiest smile and asked me if I fancied going down the road to the pub after work.

"Not a date or anything, you know I don't want to get thumped again, but if you fancied it we could just have quick drink or something?"

I said I had to get home that night but maybe another time, perhaps next week. I was giving myself time to get my house in order. I'd told Jane in a letter written the night after the bus ride home all that Paul had told me and asked her for her thoughts. In her return letter she agreed that he'd been stitched up by Chris, who she reminded me was just a chip off the old block.

On the second Saturday in February, Keith and I went for a walk over Post Hill in the afternoon and I attempted the 'It's not you it's me' speech that I'd read about on the Cathy and Clare pages of Jackie. Despite my best attempts, he didn't take it too well and I didn't feel I'd let him down easily. In fact it was quite horrid and I felt terrible. At the end of my speech, I saw tears in his eyes as he said, rather gallantly,

"I really can't bear to watch you walk away from me, so I'm going to turn round and count to ten. If you're still there when I turn back I know we still have a chance, if not well…"

He turned around and I walked away quickly, without looking back.

Mum and Dad were astounded when I told them I'd finished with Keith and their bewilderment manifested itself in a sulky annoyance with me. They couldn't comprehend and I knew I'd never make them understand. Keith had been my 'go to relationship'. He had swept into my life at a time when I needed someone to be more than a friend. I was flattered by his interest in me and liked to be included in his family life. I'd never thought it was forever or anything and I hadn't meant to hurt him but he was only a stepping stone for me. He'd been the catalyst for me to change my life. I couldn't tell Mum and Dad any of this; even if I had the words. So my parents, who'd met in their teens and had never really been apart since, dealt with it in the only way they knew how. After Mum yelling that I was throwing away probably the only chance I'd have of marrying a decent lad, they gave me the silent treatment again.

As their displeasure was so clear and defined, I was smart enough to not mention that Keith had been replaced, almost as soon as the '*Kim's boyfriend*' role became available. I'd already told Suzy about meeting up with Paul and his version of events, so it was no surprise to her when I dumped Keith. But she did suggest I leave a gap between relationships to give myself time to take stock. I of course ignored that and on the way home from my break up with Keith, phoned the Turner household. Luckily, Paul answered as I wasn't ready for a run-in with his mother. I told him that if he wanted to ask me out for a drink again, I could accept now without any risk of him being thumped. He laughed and thanked me for letting him know and said he'd bear it in mind. Not meaning to sound too callous but wanting to keep the record straight, the hardest part of my break up with Keith was trying to keep the smile off my face when I got home to tell Mum and Dad.

Although we started going out in mid-February, it wasn't until my birthday on the 20th March that I told my parents I had a new boyfriend. It was a Wednesday night and we'd planned a trip to Leeds for a steak dinner at the Berni Inn. I told them, as he told his parents, that we'd met at work which technically wasn't a lie and that seemed to work with three out of the four of them. There was no fooling his mother. I was waiting in the bar at 7pm when he came in wearing a black velvet jacket over his blue and white checked Ben Sherman shirt and black corduroy trousers. I thought he looked amazing and I fought to control a whoosh of adrenalin. I introduced him to the welcoming committee and he stepped forward and held out his hand to Dad.

"Hello Mr. Asquith, pleased to meet you," he said with probably more confidence than he felt.

Dad took his hand and shook it firmly while giving him one of his looks. He said nothing but nodded. Mum was a little more friendly as she called from the far end of the bar.

"I'm sure we're pleased to meet you an' all as long as you make sure you have our Kim back here before eleven."

"Yes," he nodded at her with his easy smile, "I'll make sure she's home at a decent time......"

Sensing he was going to attempt some joke or funny line, I linked arms and spoke over him that we'd see them later and pulled him out the door. The week before we'd been at Michelle's house on the Saturday night while her parents were out. It was a small gathering rather than a party, consisting of three other couples beside Paul and me. Towards the end of the evening we found ourselves alone on the sofa. Michelle was upstairs with Trevor and one of the other couples was on the floor behind the sofa pursuing intimate explorations of each other. I had no idea where the other two were. At first I'd thought Paul's long kissing and his caressing hands very exciting but was starting to feel a little uncomfortable and the situation was fast becoming far from romantic. I could feel his breathing becoming fevered and suddenly thought the whole thing seemed grubby. I leapt to my feet saying I needed a glass of water and shot into the kitchen. Paul followed me and immediately apologised, saying he was happy that I wanted to wait and that he would prefer to make my first time special. There was a little voice in my head that said it would be better to let him assume I was still intact, so I just smiled and we agreed we would wait.

When we got home from my birthday meal that night, well before eleven, Paul had kissed me, very passionately, behind the car park wall.

"Oh God Kim, I am so hard! I don't know how much longer I can wait."

My response was just a small giggle as I pulled away and led him to the pub door. He stepped far enough into the bar to wave at my watchful parents before taking his leave after a peck on the cheek. The only comment Dad made about him as I passed, was that he needed a good haircut. That from my Dad was acceptance verging on praise.

Chapter Thirty-three

A couple of weeks after my birthday, I was introduced to Paul's parents. Mike seemed nice enough, a tall stocky man with dark hair who kept his own council and smiled warmly at me. Beryl was a different kettle of fish. I'd been asked to tea and Paul came to meet me off the bus. Walking along hand in hand, I felt his grip tighten as he exclaimed,

"Oh fuck!"

"What's up?" I asked, looking around.

Ahead of us a woman was standing by a car, her hand on the handle of the passenger door but making no effort to open it. She just stood frozen, staring at us. It took seconds to register it was Sadie Henshaw. Horror on top of horror, Chris got out of the driver's side and walked round the back to stand next to her. Paul let go of my hand and put his arm around me as we carried on walking. Just before reaching the car we stepped off the pavement to cross the road and Paul nodded saying,

"Alright Chris, Mrs Henshaw?"

I kept my gaze on the road in front of me but heard no response as we headed towards the Turner's house. I hadn't realised I'd been holding my breath until I exhaled in an audible moan when Paul closed the garden gate behind us, giving me a quick squeeze.

"Don't worry about them. Come on, let's get inside."

Beryl had clearly made up her mind about me and no amount of smiling could cover it up. I think Mr Turner's genuine smile actually made her dislike of me worse. Her opening gambit was,

"At last we get to meet you. We've heard so much about you. Come on in and sit down. I'm Beryl and this is Mike," she nodded at her husband, before continuing her management of the meeting.

"Paul, put the kettle on and make us all a nice cup of tea."

I followed her in to their sitting room and sat awkwardly on the edge of the sofa while she began her interrogation. Where was my family originally from, had my parents always run pubs, what did I do in the evenings while my parents were in the pub and finally was my Mum still friendly with Harry Henshaw? The last question was said with great implication that made my cheeks warm. She didn't wait for a response, not really wanting one. Seeing she'd got a reaction, she stood up quickly, saying she'd better see what Paul was up to. He was as much use as his father in the kitchen. Mike seemed to relax as she left the room and started to ask about what I did at the Post, which was a nice distraction. Shortly after we'd finished our cups of tea, from the best china, the back door opened and slammed announcing Russell's arrival home from the football. This sparked Beryl into immediate action, standing up and announcing we could now have our tea. We went through the frosted glass door to the dining room and a table set for five. Over the meal, Paul mentioned I had just started driving lessons. Beryl was sprinkling salt over her meal as she made the observation,

"I don't understand why girls want to learn to drive. I've never bothered and I get around alright."

"That's because I drive you everywhere," Mike said, not looking at her.

"That's because we go everywhere together," she said sharply. "Anyway you don't take me everywhere. Since our Paul's passed his test, he's taken and collected me from the hairdressers every week."

An uncomfortable silence followed, broken by Russell telling his Dad and brother about the finer details of Leeds United's excellent win that afternoon. Paul had already told me that since passing his test, his driving had only amounted to chauffeuring his mother around. He was still working on both of them to be allowed to occasionally borrow the car, which his Mum seemed reluctant to allow. After eating, there was a further half hour of uncomfortable conversation until Paul and I left to walk back to the bus stop. I was worrying about the way Beryl had asked about Mum and Harry. She had meant to make me feel uncomfortable. I tried to voice my concern,

"I don't think your Mum's very impressed with me."

"She's only just met you. She's always a bit wary of folk 'til she gets to know them. Anyway, she knows that I like you so she'll like you as well. That's how it works int it?"

I let it go, realising that he either hadn't noticed or didn't want to acknowledge his mother's hostility.

The rest of that year me and Beryl rubbed along, just about tolerating each other, which was relatively easy because I made my visits to his house rare and far between. I told Jane about our first encounter in my next letter. I explained in detail about the meal which, to my horror, was a preloaded plate of small pink prawns and salad. Everything on my plate was in separate sections, two large lettuce leaves, four slices of cucumber, a spring onion and a chopped up tomato. There was also a mound of something that looked like sick but was apparently Heinz Vegetable Salad. It was my worst nightmare. How could she have possibly known that prawns were the one thing that was guaranteed to make me gip? I know I should have said straight away that I had a problem with the maggot-like crustaceans but I didn't. The plate was placed in front of me in a flourish that suggested that the boat had been well and truly pushed out. A glance at Paul's delighted face confirmed that this was a special tea in my honour, so I struggled to get them down my throat, thankfully without throwing-up. This was only achieved by coating them in salad cream and interspersing each mouthful with big bites of bread and butter. Jane's return missive told me she'd enjoyed hearing about my encounter and added a few of her own observations and comments about Beryl Turner and her long suffering husband. She said I should ignore her hostility saying that she would never like any girl that Paul brought home. I took a lot of comfort from her letter.

It was a week after having been formally introduced to his family that we had full intercourse on his single bed. Saturday night and his parents were out, Russell was in with us and we had, at my request been playing Scrabble. When it was his turn, Paul stood up and said,

"Me and Kim are going upstairs for a bit to listen to some music; I'll have my go when we come back."

"Oh right, well make sure you have the music loud then, I don't want to hear you havin' it off!"

I don't know what he did or didn't hear, I was too busy trying to control my excitement and fear. Excitement at the impending intimacy and fear that he might realise it wasn't my first time. If he did notice my hymen not being intact, he hid it well behind his enthusiasm. There was a great deal of foreplay, much more than was necessary I remember thinking, and the act was over pretty quickly. He didn't ask me if I'd enjoyed it, he just rolled on to his back and addressed his bedroom ceiling.

"That was fuckin' amazing!"

I said nothing but turned on my side and nuzzled up to him. He turned and with a look of total contentment, smiled before kissing me deeply.

At the end of the summer I met up with Jane again, at the Golden Egg. She was just back from a holiday with the Goldbergs and really tanned. As I arrived first, I witnessed the heads turning as she walked in. She radiated a childlike innocence in her petite but curvy frame and as she approached me in her confident easy swish of a walk, her lovely face broke into a warm angelic smile.

"Hey you!" she said.

"Hey yourself!" I smiled back, my eyes welling with tears.

"What?" She raised her eyebrows as I continued to stare at her with my wide grin.

"I'm just so happy to see you, it's been ages."

"I know," she began looking suddenly serious, "but it was difficult before..."

"I know," I cut her off; "it was hard for you because I was going out with Keith and the David connection. I understand."

"Yeah, I know it's stupid but I just need to put all of it behind me now. I can't have our David trying to pal up with me." The smile returned, "I'm getting somewhere without any help; I've got no family now."

I raised a very theatrical questioning eyebrow at her and she laughed, "Cept for you of course!"

I reached out to take her hand across the table and squeezed it. "But you're still in touch with your Granny and Grandad though?"

Shaking her head she wrinkled her nose. "No, I'm not." Before giving my hand a return squeeze and taking hers back, to push her hair behind her ears. We talked through two milkshakes and a frothy coffee, catching up with the finer details of what we'd been doing. She'd done well at college and gained two qualifications in childcare and had started a business course, her plan was to start her own nursery. It had been Mrs. Goldberg's idea as Jane was, she told her, a hard worker and could really do something with her life. She'd told her she wanted to see her succeed and was paying for the business course.

"She doesn't expect me to stay much longer, says I'm far too smart to be the hired help."

Her tales of the recent holiday convinced me she'd had a great time. The children were much easier this year and they'd shared a villa with another family, who had their own nanny, so she'd had someone to spend her time off with. For a couple of hours we sat chatting and laughing and feeling totally relaxed. It was wonderful. It's a marker in this story of how little either of us needed to make us happy and stands out of the hazy facts because of it. I told her about my efforts to learn to drive and how I thought I'd never do it and about how well it was going with Paul, despite his mother and that we were planning a weekend in Blackpool with Michelle and her boyfriend to see the illuminations.

"Blackpool!" she grabbed my hands, "it was so brilliant. If ever I'm feeling a bit fed up I just say Blackpool to myself and it brings it all back."

When we left to go our separate ways we hugged on the pavement with the ferocity of unbreakable friendship and promised each other that we wouldn't leave it so long till our next meeting.

After two failed attempts, I finally passed my driving test on 30th September. To this day I am not sure how I managed it. Dad was astounded after taking me out the day before to see how I was getting on. He'd said in his calm and matter of fact way that I had no chance but the experience of another test would be good for me. His wide eyes looked massive in his pale face when I got home having passed. Looking at the piece of paper which stated I was a competent driver who had scored only one minor, he shook his head and lowered himself on to the chair arm. Mum was all smiles saying how great it was that Dad could now have a drink when they went out and I could drive them. A week later Dad bought me my own car and I had my first motorway driving experience a couple of days later when Paul and I went to Sheffield to visit Alison and her baby daughter. I'd wondered how Ali would be with me turning up with Paul but there was no problem. She was so wrapped up with four-month-old Melody, named after one of the angels in Captain Scarlet, her memory of Paul seemed to have completely disappeared. Steven, Melody's Dad, had just joined the army and talked excitedly about them getting married as soon as Alison was sixteen. He'd just been told he'd be based at Catterick and would qualify for married quarters. Shirley and Bill had been great, he told us, but they were really looking forward to getting a place of their own. The new Grandparents were equally as besotted with the baby and obviously much taken with Steven and his plans. Before we'd set off Mum had said,

"The pair of 'em are soft in the head, shouting about it and telling everybody! They should be ashamed of themselves."

Looking at the family tableau before me, I knew my Mum was completely wrong. On the way home we stopped off at Woolley Edge service station and had a mug of powdery hot chocolate.

"Is Ali's Mum really your Mum's sister?"

"Yes, why?"

"I can't see your Mum being that happy if you'd got knocked up."

"She wouldn't, but then I wouldn't be that stupid."

"That's good to hear," he replied laughing. "Anyway I think your Alison and Stevie boy are a good couple and will probably be really happy."

I agreed he was probably right.

As the summer came to an end, Mum and Dad decided that not only was Paul a suitable boyfriend but they'd really started to like him. So much so that they arranged for the four of us to go to Batley Variety club to see Shirley Bassey. I had the afternoon off work to get my hair done and I'd bought a long black halter-neck dress. It had all the foundations of a great evening but was flawed by two significant incidents. Firstly, Paul got very drunk trying to match pint for pint with Dad and during the break between the support act and the headliner, he started telling them how he'd fancied me from the very first time he had seen me.

"Course it was Chris that actually saved her life when we were at the tannery," he let them know, "That's why he was such a prat at the baths that night," he slurred "but she was never interested in him and he couldn't take it."

Luckily the lights went down and Shirley came on and gave us her all. Paul sat back in his seat and held my hand smiling like an idiot, oblivious to his gaff, but I'd seen the look my parents had exchanged as they'd registered the information and knew we'd be having words later. The other thing which put a damper on the night out was that it took place on November 5th, Paul's nineteenth birthday. The fact that he'd chosen to spend his birthday with me and my family was an abomination to his mother. Even though she had nothing planned, Beryl was incensed at my parents presumptuousness. As I was still underage, I was the designated driver for the night and pulling up outside the Turner household, I saw her formidable figure standing in the window. She stood, arms crossed over her chest, highlighted in the large picture window, leaving no doubt of her displeasure. It was almost 1am but every light in the house was on; even though it was a week night. No one was sleeping in their house until Paul was home and had been interrogated about the evening. I drove off as soon as he staggered out of the car while shouting his thanks and waving enthusiastically. The next day at work he told me she'd been livid he'd come home in such a state and she'd called me a trollop. To this day I'm not sure why he told me that, it was hardly likely to help in our relationship and my rare visits to his home became rarer still as I gave her a wide berth.

The day after Shirley Bassey, I got up and went off to work before Mum and Dad were up but when I got home, Mum was sitting at the kitchen table waiting for me.

"So what was it like in the old tannery building then?" she asked in a fairly reasonable tone. I sat down on the sofa with resignation.

"It's a dangerous place," I began, recalling what I'd spent the day rehearsing, "and I found that out on the one and only time I went there."

"What did he mean about this Chris saving your life? Is this Harry's son Chris?"

I looked at her levelly for a second wondering if now would be a good time to tell her the truth. She folded her arms betraying her irritation. I took a deep breath and told her. I'd wanted to show off to Alison. She'd so much more freedom than me and was allowed to go out and do stuff. It was a spur of the moment idea to go in and look round but one we as soon as we got in. I'd tripped and almost fallen into an old dying pool and caught my leg in some old machinery. Paul and Chris had come along in the nick of time to get me out.

"Nobody saved anyone's life but Chris Henshaw never stopped pestering me after that. He kept asking me to go out with him and I kept saying no, I was too young, and I didn't fancy him anyway. The last time he asked me was that Christmas when I got mumps. That's why he told his Dad all those lies about me and Jane."

"Well not all of it was lies," she said evenly.

"You just don't get it do you?" Despite my efforts at calm and controlled, my voice had risen, "It was ALL lies and Harry bloody Henshaw is a cruel and vindictive arsehole who did everything he could to destroy Jane's family."

I stood up and despite knowing that swearing wasn't going to help, I was unable to control my rage. I started to walk past her but she stood up and grabbed my arm. Her eyes were sparking with a matching fury.

"That man did not get sent to prison just because Harry or his lad told some lies about him. He did some terrible things to that little lass and thank God he was made to pay for it."

The clock on the mantelpiece ticked out the seconds as we stood, eyes fixed, inches apart. The move was simultaneous as our love overruled everything else and we grabbed each other in a hug. Half an hour later as I made myself some cheese on toast, we chatted about the night before, all unpleasantness put aside. Just before she left to go into the bar she asked me how Jane was getting on. I told her she was doing well, working as a nanny and going to night school. Mum nodded her approval through the mirror as she finished applying her lipstick.

"No more secrets, Kim," she said, without looking at me.

"No more secrets," I echoed, looking at my fingernails.

Turning around she leaned forward and kissed me on the forehead before smiling as she went through to the bar. It was a little while before I realised we were both lying.

Chapter Thirty-four

The trip to the Blackpool illuminations didn't happen as Michelle and Trevor split up the week before we'd planned to go. Paul told me that Trevor had got back with his previous girlfriend but not to let on to Michelle. I was annoyed that he'd told me and we had a bit of a row about it and he said I was unreasonable. I wanted to retaliate that I was sick of other people's secrets but held my tongue and settled for sulky silence. He softened a bit and said that now we were a couple, we should tell each other everything. I said Michelle was my friend and she would ask if I knew if he'd gone back to his ex and I'd have to tell her. Why couldn't I lie, he wanted to know. It wasn't like it would be a bad lie, just one of those little white lies to make life easier. We'd been having this discussion over egg, beans and chips in the canteen and were in stalemate when Trevor came over with his tray and sat down with us. I glared at him, pointedly placed my cutlery down, got to my feet and left the canteen. Paul later told me that Trev had been annoyed; realising that he'd told me and felt sure I'd tell Michelle. Finally, I thought, he gets it. Some snippets of information are best kept to yourself.

Christmas that year was wonderful. When he picked me up for the work Christmas party, I fell in love with him all over again. He stood there in his new three piece suit, his golden curls framing his face and his blue eyes sparkling. Even Dad made a comment,

"Good suit lad, you've scrubbed up nicely, still need a haircut though."

New Year's Eve, I helped Mum and Dad behind the bar while Paul drove his parents to a party in Armley. He returned to nurse a pint or two of shandy in the tap room until the clock struck midnight when we had a

New Year kiss before he went off to pick them up. I didn't see his parents through that festive season even though I was asked, via Paul, to go to Beryl's famous Boxing Day buffet. I'd declined, saying we had family visiting. He asked who it was and I said it wasn't anyone; I just didn't want to go. I smiled and said it was just one of those little white lies to make life easier.

January and February of 1975 were particularly cold ones with several days of heavy snow. I remember this because I have some photographs of Paul and me standing beside a massive snowman we built in the car park. Dad took them and there's one of me and Mum too. She'd come out for the photograph but not before putting on her lipstick. She didn't like the snow and would normally not set foot outside the door but was keen to be included in the record of this epic snow sculpture. The date on the back is February 9th, 1975. It was a Sunday afternoon and taken just before we went to the park, with the wooden sledge that Dad had bought the day before. Mum and Dad went back inside for their Sunday afternoon nap. Two weeks later, I collected the developed film from the chemist and saw what I should have seen months before.

They were both in the bar when I got home with the pictures. I had looked at them as I walked back and the ones of Mum took me by complete surprise. I went over to the bureau and rooted around for more photographs of Mum. I was laying them out on the table when they both came in. Dad went straight to fill the kettle but stopped when he saw what I was doing.

"Oh, you collected the film," he said unnecessarily. Mum came up at the side of him and the three of us looked down at the images of her. She was virtually fading away before our eyes.

"No more secrets hey Mum?" I said without looking up.

Over the inevitable cup of tea, she talked while I listened and Dad pretended to read the paper. She had Addison's disease, which is a rare, chronic condition brought about by failure of the adrenal glands. It had been diagnosed nearly two years ago and, she assured me, was being managed well. She would need to take steroids for the rest of her life but as long as she did she'd be fine and could live a normal life. I was terrified and my fear became a bubbling anger of guilt and frustration.

"But you don't live a normal life!" I yelled at her petulantly, "And you're clearly not fine, look at you, you're disappearing in front of us."

Dad looked up, his glasses on the end of his nose and I could see his eyes glistening.

"Don't exaggerate Kim. I've lost a bit of weight but that's not such a bad thing."

She stood up and smoothed her hands over her hips in a ridiculous gesture, her smile faded and she sat back down.

"I get a bit tired which is bloody annoying but then I'm not the spring chicken I was," she tried a laugh but no one joined in.

Dad explained their five year plan which we were already two years into. The Unicorn had been a good business for them, although hard work. Another three years would see them right, then they'd sell up and do something else. A little shop maybe, or a cafe or something, where they had their evenings free and less hassle. It was all thought through and I wasn't to worry. Mum gave me a hug before getting up to peel some potatoes, letting me know the discussion was over.

The next day in my dinner break I went to the library in Town. I'd checked with the Yorkshire Post internal library for a medical dictionary but there wasn't one. Sarah, the girl in charge asked me what I wanted to look up.

"Addison's disease? Oh yeah, that's a nasty illness, JFK had it apparently."

Leeds's central lending facility had several big tombs of medical information and I was late back to work as I had a compulsion to read everything I could about it. Thinking I would find some miracle cure the doctors hadn't thought of or something that would make it better. I knew that I could help her in other ways, so from that weekend onwards, I worked behind the bar every Friday night and Sunday afternoon. She still wanted to do the Saturday nights, even without G and T's, she said she needed a big night to get dressed up for. When I wrote and told Jane about it all, she wrote me the most amazing letter back. She had obviously also researched the illness and talked positively about the prognosis with just the right amount of candour and a good measure of positive humour.

In March, Mum and Dad arranged another trip to Batley Varity Club. This time it was to celebrate my eighteenth birthday and they arranged a mini-bus. The trip was the week before my birthday but the day before Jane's. When Mum had suggested it, I'd said this was good planning and I could give her the present I'd got for her on that night. I phoned her two weeks before to tell her about it. I could tell by the split second of hesitation that she wasn't going to come. It was the older Mrs Goldberg's macramé evening and she had to babysit. She was of course devastated to miss the evening but we would have another night out soon and celebrate both our birthdays. I asked her if she had any plans to do something on her actual birthday. Again, there was that pause that unnerved me before she answered that the two Mrs G's were cooking her a special meal that night and she might even be allowed some wine but she supposed it would be an early night, changing the subject she asked about Paul and who else was going on the trip.

The outing consisted of Mum and Dad and a couple of their friends, Suzanne and her new boyfriend, Carole and two other girls from work, Michelle and Trevor, who had just got back together, and Paul. Everyone had a good time and I discovered I quite liked vodka and lime and on the way home back there was even some singing. I knew Jane would have enjoyed the evening and felt a twang of sadness because she'd missed it. The next day I decided to drive over to Allwoodley to see her and give her present. I arrived at to the Goldberg's at 8pm thinking that the family would have finished their meal and the children would be in bed so, I might get invited in. That's not what happened.

I parked on the road just in front of the driveway to the large white detached house. Clutching Jane's present and feeling a bit giddy, I rapped on the impressive oak door with the cast iron lion's head knocker. The door was opened by a large Jewish woman I knew instantly. An awkward self-consciousness swept through me as I felt, rather than saw, the scrutiny of her gaze. Her smile came nowhere near her steely calculating eyes as she raised a perfectly plucked eyebrow. I introduced myself and asked if I could speak to Jane. Her gaze softened a little as she informed me that Jane had gone out for the evening with her friends, to celebrate her birthday. Something far more cutting than confused embarrassment filled me as I stammered out my apologies for disturbing her and thrust the wrapped gift at her before retreating down the drive. Back in my car, I took control of myself, driving away quickly, wanting to get home and work out why my best friend had lied to me. I didn't work it out and she didn't explain.

She phoned the next day while I was at work and left a message with Mum, saying thank you for the present, sorry that she'd missed me and that she'd write and let me know when we could meet up. When her letter arrived on the Saturday, she made a two line reference to her birthday. A girl who worked as a nanny to another family had suggested going to the pictures. It had only been decided that afternoon and she'd not enjoyed herself. I felt relief wash over me as I read it and decided nothing had changed, but it was another four months before we met up again.

She wrote at the end of June asking if we could meet in Leeds and maybe have lunch at the Wimpy bar. By return, I said absolutely and commented on her use of the word lunch, asking if she'd turned posh. Telling me she had other commitments for the next couple of weeks, she suggested the 20th July as her first free Saturday. I didn't comment in my letter back but was surprised by her having 'commitments'.

On the way to our meeting, it occurred to me I had no idea what she'd been up to over the last year and as soon as I saw her I knew something had changed. Her hair was a different, she'd had a fringe cut in, making her look younger, but it was more than that. After our initial greetings and giving our order to the waitress, I said,

"So what's been happening with you? You look.........different."

"No flies on you Kim." Her voice was light and warm and full of amusement, "So, what do you reckon it is then?"

"I don't know it's like you... like you're lit up. It's......" I stared at her looking for the words. She just sat there with her happiness radiating out of her like a force field - and I knew.

"Oh my God you've met somebody!"

She had indeed met somebody, a man to be exact and I don't use that word lightly. As she started to tell me about Matthew, I was beaming back at her, enjoying her happiness, nodding and smiling. But a few minutes, after our bottle of Coke and curly sausage meal arrived, my smile became strained. Matthew was not only twenty years older than her, he was also married. I struggled to eat much of my fry up but Jane's appetite was solid as she munched her way through the plateful. I was just getting my head around the fact that her first ever boyfriend was a man almost as old as my Dad, with a wife and two children, not much younger than her, when she dropped the real bomb shell. She leaned forward and put her hand on mine and announced with a huge grin,

"But the best news of all is I'm pregnant!"

I couldn't speak. I leaned back, heavily against the red plastic chair. I couldn't compute what she was saying with how happy she looked. How could she think this was good news? It made no sense. I managed to ask her,

"What on earth are you thinking?"

She laughed, pushing her empty plate to one side and ploughing on with her deranged cheerfulness, waving her hand to dismiss my concern.

"It's all fine, in fact it's bloody marvellous. He's offered to leave his wife, but I've told him there's no need. He's sorting me out somewhere to live and he'll support me and the baby when it comes. It's all ok, really!"

"How far gone are you?"

"Four months, I'm due at Christmas – double celebration!"

Her elation was indifferent to my concern. Shaking my head I admitted,

"I don't understand."

"I know you don't and I'll try and explain but I just want you to be happy for me even if you don't get it. That's really important to me Kim."

Her explanation was simple. She wanted a baby, a child of her own and the support of someone who cared for her. What she didn't want was all the messy stuff of living with a man, with his wants and demands. Matthew was an attractive and very wealthy man who had never been a faithful husband. He thought he'd seduced a young and innocent girl but the reality was Jane had stage-managed it all. He and his wife were friends of her employer and he had great standing in the Jewish community. He'd cried when Jane told him she was pregnant, fearing his philandering was finally to ruin him and destroy his marriage. She'd been wide-eyed and retained her role as a naive little girl, those large brown eyes on her pretty elfin face mesmerising and convincing. She subtly took control, allaying his fears and giving him the perfect solution. If he found her somewhere to live and supported her, she could be his port in a storm. He could have her and keep everything else.

"I have to tell Mrs Goldberg tomorrow that I'm leaving. She knows I have a boyfriend but thinks he's from Bramley and I'm sure she's noticed my growing waistline, she doesn't miss much."

"I don't know what to say."

"You don't need to worry about this Kim. It's all working out."

Sitting on the bus on the way home I tried to make myself be happy for her, as I'd told her I was, but couldn't lose the feeling of foreboding. Her happy news was another secret she asked me to keep, just for a little while, until she was settled. I ran through all the confidences she'd shared with me and felt the weight of them. I thought of Mum and Dad's reaction when they found out she was having a baby and what Paul's witch of a mother would say. All the old stuff would probably come up again and Beryl's sharp and acid tongue would be working overtime. She'd no doubt take every opportunity to make Paul see what a slag Jane was, and me too by association. Remembering what she'd endured and my part in her being sent away, I recognised my selfishness. Maybe it would be alright. Perhaps this Matthew would support her and she would have this perfect life, the one she dreamed of, but I seriously doubted it. Whatever happened she was my best friend and I owed her the unquestioning loyalty she'd always given me.

Chapter Thirty-five

As it transpired, loyalty and friendship was all Jane needed from me. Matthew provided her with a little back-to-back terraced house in Stanningley and made sure she was alright financially. She left the Goldberg's house in mid-October when she was seven months pregnant, with a leaving present of a cheque for £25 and a bag full of beautiful baby clothes. Mrs Goldberg had not needed telling that she was expecting but had been amazingly kind about it. I'd told Paul, with Jane's consent, of her predicament but had left out the part about Matthew's age and marital status. Paul borrowed his Dad's car, with the pretext of taking me to Sheffield, but after picking me up we drove to Allwoodley, to pick up Jane and all her things. After an emotional farewell from the Goldberg mothers, we took her to her new home where Matthew was waiting with flowers and champagne, so we go in. Just before we left he held out his hand to Paul and thanked him warmly for bringing Jane to her new home. I noticed Paul trying to see over his shoulder and thought he was being nosey but on the journey back he asked me,

"So what's with the Dad then, bit weird him being there?"

Realising he thought Matthew was the Dad of Jane's bloke, I decided not to correct him. It was actually the only time we met him and Paul never realised that he was the father of Jane's baby.

For the rest of her confinement, Jane lived happily in her small stone house. Paul and I were regular visitors and helped with general decorating and preparations for the baby. I didn't tell my parents about Jane being pregnant straight away. I'd planned to pick my moment. One night, as Mum and I were watching television, she asked why Jane hadn't been round, now she was living locally again. I realised that she might be worrying that Jane felt slighted, which was a reasonable assumption, so reasonable in fact that I knew I needed to tell her. I gave her the edited version – she'd been going out with someone who had scarpered when he found out she was pregnant.

"So how's she managing, money wise?"

"She got some money from when her Dad died," which was a lie, "and her boyfriend says he'll help when the baby's born, " which was true.

"Yes, well he might be saying that now but there's some as don't do what they promise. Ee that poor lass, whatever next?" she asked no one in particular, shaking her head sadly and asked, "Why didn't you tell us she were in trouble?"

"Because of all that stuff Harry Henshaw made up about her and I thought you'd just think the worst."

"Come on Kim give us some credit. All that business with Harry were awful, all those lies! Me and your Dad have spent hours talking about that poor lass's home life but we always liked her and nobody could blame her for what happened. She should be given a chance but now she's gonna be saddled with a bairn."

"She's happy Mum, about the baby I mean, and she thinks she's better off on her own."

"Aye, well I can understand her thinking like that after all she's been through. Any road if she needs any help, you know, money wise or owt, you let me know."

I assured her I would but knew that Jane was doing alright '*money wise*' and had plenty of help. Matthew visited her every week, bringing her a wad of cash and a bottle of wine. She put the money in her tin by the bed ready to be allocated to her living costs and bills. She was quite the little house manager. The wine she saved for Wednesdays when I went round on my own and we had our girlie chats. Well before it was frowned on to drink while pregnant, Jane discovered she had a taste for good red wine. On one of these lovely evenings, as she worked her way through a bottle, I plucked up the courage to ask her if she was still sleeping with Matthew.

"Oh he never stays over;" she giggled. "He always goes back to the dreadful Hannah!"

"You know what I mean," I insisted. "It's just, you know, him giving you money and stuff. If you're having sex with him, well I don't know it seems a bit....well...a bit...."

She was suddenly sober and seriously annoyed.

"What Kim? What does it seem? Like I'm a prossie?" Putting her glass down on the coffee table she sat forward, her eyes flashing. "Well it's what I've been doing for years, according to half of Bramley anyway."

"I didn't mean that, course I didn't." I left my chair and went to sit next to her grabbing her hand. "I'm sorry, it was a stupid thing to say."

She gave me a hug, picked up her glass again and leaning back told me about Matthew's visits. He arrived at five every Tuesday tea time and stayed until just after eight. After doing little jobs like changing light bulbs or putting up shelves, they sat on the sofa drinking tea. He chatted about his week and asked about hers and her prenatal appointments. He'd recently taken to stroking her bump and putting his ear on her belly. He liked the decorating she'd done and would inspect it and make a list of other things she needed for the house. At half past six he would walk round to the Chinese takeaway round the corner and buy them dinner, which was always the same, sweet and sour pork with special fried rice and barbequed spare ribs.

"I'll swear he enjoys eating pork much more than he's ever enjoyed sex. His face is in some kind of rapture."

"But he's Jewish."

"Well that's the point you idiot! He's not allowed it so it's like the forbidden fruit. He says his family would be more horrified at that than they would about him and me. Anyway, we hold hands for a bit after that on the sofa and then he goes home."

"Seriously, that's it?"

"Seriously, yes that's it. I am no longer his type."

"What do you mean?" But I knew the answer even before I asked the question.

"He's only turned on by innocent little girls," she said casually before going on, "He hasn't wanted to fuck me since I told him I was pregnant. Instead, he treats me like a princess, his way of easing his conscience. This place is where he can be someone else for a bit. It's like a playhouse for him and he can easily afford it. It's perfect for both of us."

"Do you love him?"

"Course not! Anyway, I don't really know what love is but I know he cares about me and he'll look after me and I'm happy with that." She leant forward to top up her glass and suddenly remembered. "Oh and he's getting a telephone put in for me to call you or an ambulance when my little lump decides it's time."

The phone was put in the following week which was just as well as Jane's little lump decided not to wait until the expected date to arrive.

It was a Tuesday only a couple of weeks later and I was late home having missed my normal bus. It was really cold and even though the bus was crowded, the open platform kept the cold air circulating. It was gone half past six when I got in and had just filled the kettle when Dad burst through the bar door.

"Kim, Kimberly, quick come and get the phone!"

On the other end of the line Jane was calmly counting the minutes between her contractions and wondering if I'd like to take her to the hospital. Less than forty minutes later, I was approaching Leeds General Infirmary with Jane and my Mum in the back of my car. Mum was holding Jane's hand and doing the breathing with her as the contractions were about four minutes apart. I stopped outside the main doors to let them out before going to park the car. When I got inside Jane was in a wheelchair and Mum was informing the receptionist that she needed examining immediately. A nurse came along and joined the receptionist in attempting to placate her, saying they were quite busy and there was no rush, Jane's delivery was far from imminent.

"And how do you know that?" Mum demanded.

"She's not due for another ten days," the receptionist said with a 'So that's that' shake of her head.

"Oh right, and in your obviously extensive experience you've never heard of babies coming early then," Mum countered.

"Please!" Jane yelled as she pushed herself up from the chair, "Please, something's happening!"

As her waters broke over the floor in front of her, Mum's 'I told you so glare' at the receptionist was fabulous. The nurse burst into action, whisking us off to the labour ward.

I got to stay with her throughout the two hour delivery, holding her hand as she fought to breathe through the contractions, wiping her face with a damp cloth and stroking her hair. The word wasn't used so much back in 1975 but I can only describe the experience of watching my best friend give birth as awesome. She declined all pain relief and I could only marvel as I watched her dig deep into limitless hidden strength, never once complaining of the obvious pain. The final push was through gritted teeth and a hand squeeze so strong I felt sure my bones would break. Her tiny frame became rigid with effort as she found the reserves to expel her red, blotchy and beautiful daughter.

Rachael's birth is recorded at 10.05pm on Tuesday 16th December ten days earlier than predicted and a healthy weight of six pounds five ounces. Mum and I left just before eleven and Jane gave me Matthew's office phone number to call him as soon as possible the next morning. I left her tired and sore but looking ethereal in her contentment.

I made the call as arranged and told Matthew that he had a daughter.

It was a brief conversation and he only asked if Jane was alright before thanking me for my call. When I went to the hospital after work, she lay in her bed in the shade of a massive bouquet. He hadn't been to see her; they had agreed he wouldn't, but they had discussed names. Matthew had asked that if it were a boy would she consider Daniel and if it were a girl he liked Rachael.

Picking a name was the only involvement Matthew was to have in the baby's life. He was not named on her birth certificate and his only contact with her was on the normal Tuesday night visits. But he did buy the little terraced house and have it signed over to Jane a month later and set up a trust fund for his newest child. I was standing in the small sitting room with Rachael in my arms, marvelling at her perfectness, when Jane told me this. Since the baby had arrived I was spending a great deal of time with her. Paul had joined the squash club in Armley and played three or four times a week, so I spent those evenings with Jane.

"There's something I want to ask you," she began, "I don't want you to answer straight away I want you to think carefully about it."

I sat down in the armchair facing her as Rachael's little fingers folded round one of mine. She told me that given her circumstances, Rachael's parentage and because she didn't believe in God, she wasn't having her christened but if she had, she would have asked me to be her god mother. Instead, she wanted me to be legal guardian. She'd discussed this with Matthew who agreed it was the sensible thing to do. If anything happened to Jane, she wanted to sure that Rachael would be cared for by someone who loved her and that she would not end up in care. It was out of the question that Matthew would be able to, although he would make sure she was provided for. I said I didn't need time to consider it, I would be delighted and Rachael would always be loved by me.

The start of 1976 was a not a very happy one, even though it had held such promise. Just minutes past midnight on New Year's Eve, it all started to feel wrong. Little did I realise that it was just the start of it.

Paul and I were going to a fancy dress party at the squash club to see in the New Year. Paul was a frequent patron but I'd only been in once and wasn't impressed. My visit had been on a Saturday afternoon when I'd met him there, after a game. We'd had a quick drink in the bar before going into Leeds. The woman behind the bar, who was around Mum's age, was quite off with me. Nothing I could put my finger on but definitely giving me the impression I wasn't welcome. The other customers were all male and so I thought it might be that this woman liked being the only female and resented my intrusion. I'd not suggested going again and Paul didn't ask me to. I worked on Christmas Eve and Christmas night along with Mum and Dad and so I'd only seen Paul on Boxing Day afternoon when I'd been unable to avoid his mothers famous Boxing Day spread.

New Year's Eve was meant to be our big night out and Paul was up for it. We'd been to a shop in Bradford and hired fancy dress clothes, I had a French maid's outfit and Paul had a batman costume. He'd been allowed to borrow his Dad's car and when he came to collect me, Dad made him get out of the car and come in the bar to take a picture of us. Just before he let us go on our way, he told him that he better make sure he stuck to two pints if he intended to drive me home. Paul grinned and replied he'd be on pop for the whole evening so not to worry. Dad had already given me a fiver to pay for a taxi if I needed one, which I'd tucked away in my bra. We got to the club about half past eight and were given our complimentary glass of fizzy wine. Paul gave me his and said he was off to get a coke, leaving me with someone called Howard who I had a vague memory of meeting before. He made a bit of small talk, asking about my job and how long I had been going out with Paul but it was all a bit stilted. I began to feel nervous and before I realised it both glasses in my hand were empty. Howard reached behind him and got me another one after taking the empty ones off me, asking me about the pub and what it was like growing up there; he certainly seemed well informed. As I finished the third glass of fizz, I was trying to scan the crowded room to see where Paul was but all I could see were lots of elaborately dressed people who were either drunk or getting there. The music got louder and I shouted to Howard that I should go and look for Paul just as Batman appeared in front of me.

"God it was murder getting served," he said passing a tall glass to me with his left hand while retaining the pint of bitter in his right and taking a big mouthful.

He introduced me to a lot of people, as I sipped the large vodka and lime he'd given me. I was starting to feel relaxed and a bit giggly as the binge drinking began to take effect. We had a couple of dances and a couple more drinks then I went to find the ladies, leaving Paul chatting to an older couple. Coming back and manoeuvring through the crowded bar area to where I'd left him, my path was blocked by a small circle of people performing some sort of group hug. Pausing to allow them to finish I heard a voice off to my left and turned quickly to see Cat Woman talking animatedly to a scantily clad policewoman and a pirate. I didn't recognise the womanly curves, accentuated by the tight fitting leather cat suit, the pulled back hair and masked eyes gave away nothing but the voice was unmistakable.

"Sharon?" I exclaimed.

She stopped mid-sentence and turned.

"Oh Hi Kim, Paul said he was having to bring you along." She pointedly looked me up and down asking, "Did you come straight from work?"

The policewoman gasped and then muttered something to her which I didn't catch.

"It's ok Karen, me an Kim are old friends," she laughed. "She knows I'm only having a laugh." Turning slightly she added, "Lovely outfit, French tart, it's so you!"

"Thanks," I said managing a laugh, "and the cat-suit certainly is a perfect choice for you too." I could feel my cheeks burn and fixing a smile, I started to move away.

It took me a while to find Paul who was chatting to a group of older men at the side of the dance floor. By the time I got to him I was blinking back tears.

"Hey what's up?" He put his arm around me and pulled me slightly to one side.

I told him and he gave me a hug telling me he'd seen her there the week before. She was going out with someone on the squash team. He hadn't known she was going to be there but I shouldn't let the silly bitch get to me and we needed another drink. I asked if he would be ok to drive home and he said drinking actually sharpened his senses and he was only having one more anyway. After another drink, things did seem better and I started to enjoy myself. There was a lot of dancing and singing and general joviality and the time seemed to dissolve in the boozy atmosphere. Suddenly, someone started the countdown to midnight. I'd been waving my arms around on the small over-crowded dance floor with a girl named Julie. Paul was talking to her boyfriend. The music stopped as everyone joined in the countdown. On hearing Nine, I look over to Paul but he's gone. The large amount of alcohol in my bloodstream fuels my panic as Eight is shouted and the urgency of finding him increased. I push my way through the throng. Seven, I edge past Julie, reunited with her boyfriend. Six, I stop, blocked by a group of people in a shoulder-locked embrace. Five and Four, I maneuver round them, bumping straight into Howard who puts his hands on my shoulders to stop me. Three, I shrug him off, ignoring what he is saying to me, Two, I glimpse the back of the caped crusader just ahead and open my mouth to call to him. One, I see arms going around his neck and, as the cheer of 'Happy New Year' goes up, my voice is frozen in my throat. Batman and Cat Woman are engaged in a passionate mouth to mouth gesture that I know wasn't a first kiss. I won't say the sight of Paul and Sharon playing tonsil hockey sobered me up but it did spur me into action. I managed to find my coat and feather duster in the pile of garments by the entrance and get out through the door before either of them came up for air. I noticed Howard watching as the door closed behind me and I turned in to a cold and frosty night. I ran down the small street toward the main road and a phone box, which was out of order. Cursing out loud but then gratified that this annoyance topped up my anger, keeping the other feelings locked down. I started walking along Stanningley Road and had got quite a way, muttering to myself about how stupid I'd been not to have realised why Paul had been spending so much time at the club. I'd just reached the start of the dual carriageway when a car pulled up at the side of me.

"Are you alright love?"

My initial panic disappeared when I saw the female officer getting out of the police car while the male driver remained inside. It's funny how it's always that question that breaks down resilience. I sobbed out my story, none of which was very coherent but she nodded a few times before helping me into the car and asking me where I lived. Mum and Dad were still turfing out the punters as the car pulled into the car park. Thanking my police escort profusely, I almost fell out of the car and clumsily staggered towards the house door.

I managed to get in to the house and wash off the rest of my mascara just before Mum and Dad came through. They both looked really tired and didn't spend too long asking me about my night. I said I was tired too, so we all went off to bed. As I switched off my lamp, I glanced at my alarm clock; it was ten past one.

"Happy New Year," I said quietly and even though I thought I wouldn't, I fell into a deep and dreamless sleep.

Chapter Thirty-six

Paul was on the door step at 10am the next morning and I was ready for him. I didn't want Mum and Dad knowing how I'd got home or the reason I'd walked out of the club. I opened the door and pushed him away, my car keys in my hand.

"Don't say anything," I warned, "Just get in the car."

I drove up to the park in a silent car, both of us looking ahead. As soon as I stopped he turned to me,

"Kimbo, I'm sorry. I was really pissed and you know what a slag Shaza is. She was just on me. I was so worried when I couldn't find you."

His words tumbled out as I sat stock-still watching a bird hop along the stone wall ahead of me.

"How did you get home?" He asked.

Turning to look at him I saw his unsure smile and his eyes, still blue but cloudy and framed with red thread hangover veins.

"How long?" I asked.

"What?"

"How long have you been two-timing me with Sharon?"

"I haven't, it was only a kiss we'd all had a bit to drink and it was New...."

"For fucks sake Paul! Do you think I'm that stupid? Either tell me, this minute how long you've been screwing her behind my back or get out of this car now!"

And even though he did tell me; it was all her of course, he'd been helpless to her charms, a victim really, I still made him get out of the car and I drove away. Seeing him in my rear view mirror with his words still echoing in my head, my anger bubbled over with a righteous outrage.

"Well if you hadn't been spending so much time with Jane or working at the Unicorn, it wouldn't have happened..."

It was difficult at work the next day but being Friday, I got through it by counting down the hours to the weekend. He engineered the crossing of our paths a couple of times and tried to speak to me. He was insisting he was sorry, that it was just sex, that it meant less than nothing and that he'd never see her again but I told him to leave me alone. I convinced Gordon-Bennet that I wasn't very well towards the end of the afternoon and they let me leave half an hour early, so I got on the bus without seeing him. I managed to force thoughts about him out of my head and replaced them with memories of the week in Blackpool with Jane. When I got home, I was smiling and looking forward to the start of my shift. Mum sat on a stool in the corner for a little while but had to take herself off to bed just before ten. It was a fairly quiet evening and although Dad and I chatted between customers, he didn't mention New Year's Eve or Paul. I'm fairly sure they knew something was up but decided ignorance was the best policy for the time being.

The next day, I helped Dad sort out the draymen and once Sally arrived to start her cleaning, I went to see Jane. She let me give Rachael her bottle while she sorted her washing and opened a tin of tomato soup as I told her what had happened, adding other stuff I thought or guessed. My boyfriend had told me that Sharon had been going to the squash club since September, when she'd started working behind the bar. Claiming she'd thrown herself at him and that he'd resisted for ages before finally succumbing, he admitted he'd started having sex with her just before Christmas. However, he assured me it was nothing. She'd literally flung herself at him and it had only happened three, maybe four times at the most. I didn't believe him. I started to remember bits of conversations and a change in him at least a month before that.

"Well he's always been a bit of lad as well you know," Jane observed.

"Yeah, I know but I thought we were settled, you know I thought we'd get married and do the happy ever after thing."

"Happy ever after isn't the end of a story though is it? Real life's full of pain with everybody out for themselves. Don't matter what you do, it'll always end up shit."

"That's not true; it doesn't have to end up shit!"

"No you're right it doesn't but in general - life is shit. Being nice and good gets you nothing and nowhere." Her voice didn't raise an octave but the emotion was scarily intense.

And I knew she was right. I also knew that my anger was fading and giving way to the pain of betrayal. This coupled with the humiliation of my ignorance was really hurting.

"I hate that!" I burst out, emotion pricking at eyes, "I wanted the fairy story, I want the happy ever after!"

"Right and which fairy story do you want then?" she asked, taking Rachael from me and placing her over her shoulder, "Cos from what I remember they're full of evil bastards and girls don't usually get a very good deal in most of them or didn't you notice those bits?"

It stopped me short and I knew where her thoughts were and suddenly felt ashamed of my self-pity. The coward in me instinctively drew back. Continuing this conversation would open up a whole pit of horror that I wasn't brave enough to look into. I got up to serve the soup. As we ate, she suggested that I didn't tell Mum and Dad yet. I should give myself some time to think.

"Nothing's perfect Kim, you just have to decide what you can put up with. You always knew he was a player and he probably won't ever change but maybe he's still your Prince, I mean if there'd been another chapter in Cinderella, we could have discovered that after the confetti blew away, HRH Charming was screwing around an all."

Years later, I did a bit of research and read some of the original versions of these faerie stories and the dark tales appalled me. Forget the Disney sanitised glitter and sparkle and good always finding a way. In the real versions of these yarns, you'll find rape, incest, necrophilia and torture. Most have no happy endings; they are just brutal lessons in mortality. The handsome prince is generally little more than a sexual predator or paedophile. As I drove home, my thoughts were full of the modern day fairy story of Jane's life.

By the Sunday afternoon, I'd decided that I needed to look for a new job. I couldn't stand seeing him every day. Having realised this, the last semblance of control evaporated and I shut myself in my room to wallow in self-pity. I was still sobbing into my pillow at half past five when Dad called up that Paul was here. He had his Dad's car and asked me if I'd go for a drive with him. Dad gave us both a funny look, blatantly aware that there had been some fallout and asked,

"Well Kim, do you want to go with him?"

I knew if I said no, Dad would tell him to clear off and he would never be welcome again.

"Yeah, I'll go out for an hour with him." I said and because I didn't like the alternative and maybe Jane had a point about the devil you know, I took him back.

For a little while things went back to normal. Sharon disappeared as quickly as she'd returned and I tried to put her out of my mind as Paul and I got back on an even keel. In June, we got engaged and had a bit of a bash at the pub. Alison and her new husband came and Jane was also there having left Rachael for the first time with a babysitter. There were a few people from work, including Michelle and Carole and it was lovely to see Suzanne. She was using it as her chance to say goodbye, as she was about to go and work in France. It was a lovely evening; even Paul's mother was relatively pleasant and chatted amicably, albeit after several gin and tonics, to my parents. She also returned a smile and said hello to Jane when she arrived although I'm not sure she knew who she was. At the end of the evening makin my way up to bed, I thought back to the start of the year and decided that despite how it had begun things were turning out alright after all. Completely unaware that another one of those set markers plotting my life was about to thrust its way into the story and before the sun came up over the pub car park my happiness and optimism in the year would all but be gone.

The darkness of my room told me I hadn't been asleep long, just long enough to disorientate. Blinking and rubbing my eyes while wondering what had woken me, I could hear Dad's voice, raised and panicked. I shot out of bed and along the landing towards their bedroom. The light was on and he was standing at the side of their bed in his pyjama bottoms with phone receiver pressed to his ear. I heard him saying that he needed an ambulance just before he thrust it at me, pulling the base off the bedside table and as I took it he fell to his knees and began to stroke Mum's still and grey face. I've no idea what I said to the operator but apparently, I managed to give her our address and twenty minutes later was letting the two-man ambulance crew in through the house door. I must have told them about the Addison's as the guys were asking me about her medication in upbeat calm voices, assessing and managing the situation. After giving her an injection they put a comatose Mum on a stretcher and carried her down to the ambulance. With lights flashing and sirens blaring, they whisked her to St James Hospital. Realising quite quickly that Dad had gone to pieces, they talked mainly to me. They took him, after he had put some clothes on, with Mum in the ambulance but told me to follow in the car once I'd got dressed. I called Sally first and despite the early hour, she answered immediately; she'd heard the sirens. She came round just as I'd finished getting dressed and drove me to the hospital. After delivering me to the side ward where Dad had set up vigil at Mum's bedside, she went off to get us some tea.

I found a staff nurse who told me that Mum had suffered an acute adrenal crisis and fallen into a coma. The initial injection of steroids given by the ambulance crew had helped but she was still not fully conscious and so was being treated with intravenous and intramuscular medication. She said the doctor would be back to speak to us soon and tell us what would happen next. Dad lifted his head as I walked towards the bed, his eyes leaking a lifetime of silent tears he tried to speak.

"She knows I'm here Kim, she squeezed me hand. She's gonna be alright."

I could only nod as I pulled up a chair at the side of him and put my hand on top of his. We sat, not speaking, hardly moving, just willing her to open her eyes. When the doctor came, he told us much the same as the nurse but added she was comfortable and not in any pain. He insisted that we went home; promising they would call us if there was any change. I sat in the back of Sally's car with Dad who could not stem the flow of his tears and didn't seem to care who saw.

It was two days before Mum came round and another two weeks before she came home. Her attack had been brought on by stress and fatigue which was all the motivation Dad needed and the Unicorn was put up for sale the day before she came home. I'd already worked my one weeks' notice at the Post and so was working full-time in the pub. Mum had been horrified when I'd told her but I explained it was only a temporary thing, for a month or two till the pub was sold, and anyway I'd been getting fed up at the Post and needed a change. I still went to Jane's most Wednesday and we drank wine and talked about shopping trips and days out, once Mum was back on her feet. Jane had plans to go back to work the following year. She was sure she'd be able to get a job at one of the nurseries or playgroups where she would be able to take Rachael with her. Her long term plan was to start her own, maybe even more than one. That was what her college course had been about. I didn't doubt for a moment that she'd succeed.

Dad had been worried about how long it would take to sell the Unicorn but his fears were unfounded. The success of the business they'd built up was well known and the price he was asking went up drastically when three different bidders wanted it. The move in September from the licensed premises to the three bed-roomed pre-war semi at the other side of Bramley was doubly stressful for Dad and me but we pretended that it wasn't, for Mum's benefit. Number twenty-two Whitecote Gardens had been newly decorated and the carpets and curtains came as part of the deal. It was a good house and I knew Mum and Dad would be happy there. When she saw it for the first time she decided that she and Dad were going to finally stop smoking as the beautiful white ceilings were going to stay white and not take on the nicotine hue of everywhere else they'd lived. Dad agreed whole-heartedly but didn't manage to stop permanently, but he never smoked in the house again. On completion day, I saw Dad physically relax in the knowledge that they had a nice home and a fair bit of financial security and Mum was doing great. While we were in the kitchen making tea, he went for a walk down the garden, to survey his estate and fill his lungs with smoke and tar.

Paul had been astounded when I told him I'd resigned from the Post, saying I should've asked if to take some time off unpaid. I'd explained the uncertainty of how long it would take to sell the pub and Mum's illness but he still didn't get it. I think he knew that there was another reason I wanted to leave. Jane's words about him always being a player had echoed around my head since she'd said them. After I'd agreed to marry him, I asked Michelle if she thought he was a player. Her response of 'Is the Pope a Catholic?' was not what I wanted to hear. I found myself being put out at the way he looked at and spoke to other girls and work seemed full of so many of these little incidents. I'd witnessed the laddish behaviour and he'd often regale me with his anecdotes of cheeky or suggestive comments he'd made to so and so and how she'd loved it. Even though it'd always been like that, it hadn't bothered me until we got engaged. So I would most probably have left anyway even if Mum hadn't got ill. Maybe the changes in my home life made me a little more conscious of how unsure I was about my status as fiancé or about marrying Paul. But I decided not to tell anyone how I was feeling and just see if not seeing so much of each other made me feel differently.

My next job was with the Yorkshire Electricity Board, in a department called Field Activities, which I started at the end of September. I'd had an interview two days before the house move and was offered the job a week later. These offices could not have been more different from the modern Yorkshire Post bunker. They were old, brick built and had drafty metal framed windows and giant radiators with two settings, off or inferno. There was a constant damp smell and strip lighting which was almost always on the blink, but I absolutely loved it. My job was to prepare paper work from the non-paid accounts and take it to the magistrate's court to obtain warrants. I also got to accompany Reggie Kent, our head electrician, and the police when they used the warrants to enter people's houses and cut off their electricity supply. Paul said he thought it sounded like a terrible job but he was wrong, it was brilliant. His complete inability to understand my enjoyment of the job or even be interested in it did nothing for my hopes an improvement in my feelings for him. So when he began to talk about setting a date to get married the following year I went with the age-old adage Dad swore by; when you don't know what to do, the best thing to do is nothing. I evaded the question, saying we should think about it in the New Year.

Mum inviting Jane round to ours for a special tea to celebrate Rachael's first birthday. Paul was doing something with his Dad so it was just the four of us and the birthday girl. Mum was baking up a storm while I went to collect them. As we walked into the dining room I could hardly believe my eyes when I saw the table set for four with a high chair at the end. Jane and I looked at each other and exclaimed at exactly the same moment,

"A high tea!"

Chapter Thirty-seven

A New Year began with Paul and me having a couple of drinks at the local working men's club with Mum and Dad. It was 1977, the Ford Fiesta went on sale and my parents bought me one. It was white with black plastic trim and I thought it looked really sporty so I called it Billy, after Billy Whiz from the Beano. In February, Fleetwood Mac released their seminal album Rumours and a bit nearer home, West Yorkshire police finally realised, after victim number three, Irene Richardson, that they had a serial killer on their patch. The Yorkshire Ripper, as he became known, was a topic of conversation everywhere in the first few months of that year. My parents constant worry about me being out in the evenings suddenly didn't seem quite so paranoid.

Towards the end of February, while Jane and I shared a bottle of wine one Wednesday, I asked her if she had any photographs of Matthew with Rachael. She shook her head and said,

"No, I didn't think that would be a good idea."

I nodded, thinking of his other family and the secrecy, but she went on to tell me that she hadn't seen him for a while anyway.

"Oh really, has something happened?"

She seemed a little surprised at my reaction and shrugged before wrinkling her nose,

"No nothing's happened, it's just better that he stops coming now before she gets too attached to him."

"But doesn't he want to see her grow up?"

"Quite probably but I certainly don't want that."

"What? Why wouldn't you?"

"Don't be so naive Kim," was all she said and changed the subject.

She had a job at a local playgroup and she was due to start after Easter. Her plan, she went on to tell me, was to work there for a year, two at the most, before starting her own. She had an account with the Leeds Permanent Building society with an allotted amount of money, which I guessed had come from Matthew, specifically for this venture. She had even earmarked the small church hall in Farsley that would be ideal as it was already being used by Brownies in the evenings. I'd known about her master plan for her own playgroup for some time, so it wasn't news to me but suddenly something was news. My eyes widened as I listened to her talk confidently and coolly about this business venture, straight after her telling me that Matthew was dismissed. Before I could stop myself, the words were out of my mouth.

"Was this always your plan? Did you ever even like Matthew or was it always just about the money?"

I don't know who was more surprised by my question. I flinched as much as she did. She looked directly at me, eyes ever so slightly narrowed and I stared back. She blinked first. Sighing, she said,

"I gave him what he wanted and I haven't taken anything from him he wasn't happy to give." When I didn't reply she added, "I didn't take his reputation or spoil his 'happy family man' image." A brief pause before she continued, "Happy ever after isn't the same for everyone."

She got up and went to the kitchen to fill the kettle. The conversation was closed as far as she was concerned and I pushed my half a glass of wine along the table towards her empty one. Leaning back on the sofa, I closed my eyes and tried to imagine what the effects of her childhood had done to her. I knew I would never get close to knowing how much she'd suffered and I also knew that although she still might look young and malleable, she was anything but. She kept the hardness hidden but my lovely friend was not someone to be underestimated. The rest of the evening was a bit stilted and I got up to leave as soon as I'd drunk my tea. At the door, she hugged me and said,

"Don't be mad with me Kim or disapproving, I really haven't done anything bad."

I hugged her back and said sorry for being judgmental, adding that she had Rachael and a plan for the future and as her friend, her bestest friend, I was happy for her. I had tears in my eyes as I spoke into her hair. As we pulled apart she wiped the tears away, kissed me gently on the lips and opening the door on a cold and frosty evening said, "Good Night Kimmy, drive carefully."

She started her job on Monday 3rd May and was an instant success. It was part of the deal that she could take Rachael with her so it was a perfect arrangement. The owner of the business told her she was a natural, both in handling the children and the mothers that dropped them off and offered her extra days. The playgroup was term time only and ended with the start of the school holiday in mid-July. At this point, Jane started working on one of the summer play schemes organised by St Peters church. Although this was really poorly paid, she said it was all good experience, both for her and Rachael, in dealing with children from different types of backgrounds.

"Rachael loves the singing and the Rector comes along and bangs his tambourine. I have an idea he's trying to save my soul," she laughed.

The weather that summer was fairly kind. There were street parties at the start of June to celebrate twenty-five years of Queen Elizabeth II's reign. I split my Jubilee afternoon between two. First, I sampled the amazing spread Mum and the rest of the ladies from our cul-de-sac laid on and the last hour helping Jane tidy up after her party at the playgroup. That evening, as Paul and I sat at the bar in the White Horse, he asked me again about setting a date for getting married. I told him I'd like to wait until next summer as I wanted to be twenty-one when I got married. He seemed happy with this and said he'd tell his parents that we were thinking of a June Wedding.

I was starting to really love my job and doing well and for the rest of that summer my little world plodded along amicably, although in the wider world a dark shadow was descending. At the end of June, sixteen-year-old shop assistant Jayne McDonald was found murdered in what was becoming a sickeningly familiar manner, bringing the tally of suspected victims of the Yorkshire Ripper to five. As Jayne wasn't a prostitute, suddenly the fear of the boggie-man became even more real. All females were now potential victims. I started going to Jane's straight from work, drank only orange or blackcurrant squash and left as soon as it started to get dark. I still took wine with me, it was part of the routine but Jane drank the whole bottle herself now. After I'd gone she continued playing records on her newly acquired stereogram but with the doors all double locked.

In July the Ripper made a mistake. He was interrupted in his assault of a woman in Bradford; his victim survived and there were witnesses to him fleeing the scene.

"It'll only be a matter of time 'til they get him now," Dad said with confidence as he read the newspaper report a day or two later. I smiled and nodded. He just wanted this maniac caught and taken off the streets so folk could feel safe again and he didn't have to worry himself sick every time I left the house. It's bizarre I know, but I shared his belief that the police would catch this man. I shared his faith in right and wrong and a conviction that West Yorkshire's law enforcement was on the side of right and so would prevail. Jane wasn't so convinced. She said that Harry Henshaw must be gutted her Dad was dead cos no doubt if he wasn't, the bent bastard would be trying to pin the murders on him. The week after she'd made this observation and three glasses into a bottle of wine, she shared her new theory with me. Could Maggie have been one of the Rippers earlier victims she wondered?

"I know it was a long time ago but he could have started attacking women years ago and it's only just now that they've realised they're connected."

When I mentioned that her mother's body hadn't been found, she stiffened and sensing her annoyance I shrugged.

"But you're right; maybe he hid the bodies when he started his killing spree."

"Yes!" she exclaimed, "Now though he's more daring, leaving them to taunt the police and let everyone see how clever he is."

In mid-August, Paul and I babysat for her one Friday night, while she went for a night out with the other workers and mothers from the playgroup. We arrived at six thirty and I bathed and fed Rachael while Paul drove Jane to the meeting point at seven, where a coach was waiting to take them to Wakefield Theatre Club. They had until midnight to enjoy the music, dance, drink warm red wine and eat chicken-in-a-basket. Paul was due to pick her up again at 1am. That is more or less what happened and she had a great time, even if we didn't.

Paul was in a funny mood all evening even though he'd been fine with the arrangement when I'd first asked him. He'd been ok when Jane was around but as soon as he got back from dropping her off, he slumped on the sofa. I'd brought Rachael back downstairs and was looking at a book with her on the beanbag. He was annoyed that she was still up, clearly wanting to have a bit of nooky, as he called it, and turned on the TV quite loud. When I asked him to turn it down, he got angry and said he was off to the pub for a quick pint and would be back in an hour when 'hopefully the sprog' would be in bed. It was nearly eleven before he came back. I'd been getting worried that I might have to call Dad to collect Jane and had been hovering over the phone when I heard him coming up the path to the house. Once inside, he was full of remorse at his behaviour. Work had been a dog that week; his boss was a dick and had made some big thing out of a stupid nothing that had gone wrong. I listened to him talk, mainly to assess how drunk he was. He wasn't slurring his words but when he cuddled up to me and started to kiss me, I could taste the beer on his breath. I offered to make him a coffee but he said that wasn't what he needed. Half an hour later we were eating cream crackers and cheese after which, I watched a black and white film while Paul dozed on the beanbag, until it was time for him to collect Jane.

On the morning of 17th September, I was still in bed reading when Dad called up to say Jane was on the phone and as I got to the bottom of the stairs, he put his hand over the receiver and whispered,

"She sounds right upset."

Giving me the handset, he went into the kitchen and shut the door.

"Hey what's up?" A massive sob followed by, "He's dead Kim. I can't believe it, he's dead!"

I felt panic surge through me and took in a deep breath before speaking.

"What? Who's dead? Jane, calm down and tell me."

"It's Marc, he's dead. A car crash, I can't believe it, oh my god I love him so much..."

Her voice trailed into further weeping. I was blinking away my own tears as I thought of her on the other end of the line. I started to ask,

"Marc? Who do you mean, who's ...?" The penny dropped.

I tried for a few moments to console her but ended the conversation telling her I'd get dressed and be over to hers in about an hour. As soon as I'd replaced the receiver, Mum very casually came out of the kitchen to ask if everything was alright.

"Yes its fine, Jane's just a bit upset about Marc Bolan, she's a big fan."

And it was true, Marc Bolan had been Jane's one and only crush that I could remember. The only pinup she'd ever put on her wall and was fifty percent of her record collection and now he was gone well before his time. When I got to her house, she'd pulled herself together a bit but looked the saddest I'd ever seen her. I put Rachael in her pushchair and took her to the park to give her some time to have a bath and pull herself together. The truth was that I needed a bit of time to process what was going on. The whole situation seemed incredulous. After all that had happened to her, everything she'd gone through, why was this upsetting her so much? I'd thought she'd made herself untouchable to this sort of emotion and yet here she was breaking her heart over a glam rock star dying when his purple Mini hit a tree. She was much better when I got back a couple of hours later and even managed a smile when she opened the door. After making her some dinner we sat quietly in the lounge and listened to The Slider, his best album according to Jane, while Rachael had her nap. She was almost her old self after that and when I suggested a drive up to the new supermarket in Pudsey, she jumped to her feet.

"Oh yes, let's go up now. I can buy some wine."

The status quo returned and our routines resumed. Summer was completely displaced by cooler autumn winds blowing in from the east, bringing us misty evenings, brightened only by the orange street lights. The Ripper struck again with his fourth murder of that year and the sixth one to be linked by the West Yorkshire Constabulary. This time he'd struck in Manchester which had everyone in and around the Leeds area breathing a sigh of relief and silently hoping he'd moved on.

It was a Tuesday afternoon, the first day of November, when the next small pebble started an avalanche that engulfed our lives. I'd been out with the disconnection team for most of the day and just got back to the office. There was a message on my desk asking me call someone back urgently. My heart was drumming in my ears as I instantly recognised the number. I screwed up the scrap of paper as I dialled. Jane answered the phone after the first ring.

"Hello," not upset, just distant and cool.

"It's me, what's wrong?"

"Please can you come round, I can't tell you over the phone."

"Of course I will, I finish in half an hour I'll come straight up to yours. Are you ok? Is Rachael ok?"

"Yes we're fine, just come round soon as you can." And she hung up.

I finished off my work and checked that everything was up to date. I called to tell Mum I wasn't going straight home. I was trying to pretend that everything was ok but I'd heard something in Jane's voice I'd never heard before. Swallowing my concerns, I smiled, saying my goodbyes to my colleagues and headed off to my car. She opened the door before I reached it and hurried me inside. I stepped into her little living room and was instantly cheered by Rachael's shriek of delight in seeing me and her attempt at my name.

"Kin Kin Kin" she intoned in giggly squeals.

"Hello my special girl!" I responded scooping her up and pulling her to me so I could take a deep breath of her clean, talcumed scent. Jane had gone into the small kitchen area and was filling the kettle. I sat on the floor with Rachael on my lap and started to make a tower of plastic beakers, our favourite game of build up and knock down.

"So what's up?"

"This!" She handed me a folded up piece of paper. I opened it and read the *'Dear Jane'* before skimming down the neatly written words to the signature at the bottom – *love Mum xx.*

"What?" I yelled, "Where did you get this?" My voice so sharp Rachael jumped a little, plastic cup in hand, looking at me uncertainly. Jane crouched down beside her and taking the cup from her, placed it carefully on the tower.

"It came in the post this morning." She spoke calmly and kept her face set in a reassuring smile for her daughter. I got up from the floor and sat on the sofa to read the letter through.

Dear Jane

I know you will be surprised to hear from me after all this time but I think the time is right now and I really want to see you again. It has taken me a while to find you but I was determined to do it. Now you are all grown-up I want to see how you are and tell you why I had to go away when I did. I have got your address and phone number but thought it would be best to write to you so it would not be such a shock. I am coming to your house on Friday 4ᵗʰ November in the afternoon at about half past one. I can't give you my address or telephone number just now because my new family don't know anything about my past so I will just come on that day and at that time. If you're not in I'll know that you don't want to see me but I hope you do.

Please don't tell your brothers yet as I don't think I'm ready to see any of them just yet.

Love Mum xx

Looking up from the carefully formed words written in blue biro, I shook my head. It barely seemed credible and turning it over I asked,

"Have you got the envelope?"

She pointed to the little side table by the chair and I picked it up. It displayed Jane's name and address written in the same neat but not quite joined up writing, an eight and a half pence stamp and a post mark.

"Blackpool, it's post-marked Blackpool!"

"Yeah," she managed but her voice was faint.

Rachael had lost interest in the cup tower building and was sucking her left thumb while twirling the fingers of her other hand in the hair curl just behind her right ear. She looked on the verge of tears. I picked her up as Jane said,

"Will you come round on Friday?"

"I wouldn't miss it for the world." I said enthusiastically feeling a buzz of excitement. Finally I was going to meet the infamous Maggie Schofield, Jane's missing Mum, it was so extraordinary and I let out a laugh. I could see Jane didn't appear to be quite as thrilled, so I muttered a sorry and offered to go to the chippie to get us some tea; the irony of this errand wasn't lost on either of us. I was back in less than twenty minutes, not that either of us ate much but we did talk. If this woman really was her mother, the truth was, she'd walked out on her family, of her own free will but more importantly, she deserted Jane. She'd chosen to run away and start again. To turn her back on the little girl who she'd left to a life of certain abuse. Suddenly I wasn't so excited about seeing her either.

"Maybe she didn't run away though," I tried, "Maybe she was kidnapped as you thought, and was brainwashed or lost her memory or something."

She looked at me through narrowed eyes confirming my theory as ridiculous.

"Or maybe she was abducted by aliens." She said coldly. "I know her life was shit and that Dad knocked her about but he loved her, he really did. It was her leaving that made him change."

I didn't trust myself to say anything. I was scared to even look at her. Very softly she said,

"If she hadn't gone, none of it would have happened."

As I drove home later that night I thought about a housewife, battered one too many times, closing the door and turning her back on her home and her children. And with that one act of self-preservation she'd condemned my friend to years of abuse and an irretrievable loss of self.

Chapter Thirty-eight

I told my boss I had a doctor's appointment on Friday saying I'd skip my dinner hour on Thursday to give me a two hour lunch break to cover it. This would mean I wouldn't have to cancel either my morning court visit or the 4pm disconnection planned for Friday afternoon. The planned disconnection was of a very nice five bed-roomed house near Roundhay Park and the home of the Barrington's. This was one of the eight out of ten disconnections that never happened but was scheduled every quarter. Mr Barrington believed delaying payment until the very last minute was good business practice. He habitually ignored three red demands, waiting for the disconnection letter. This gave him the day and time we'd be arriving with a magistrate's warrant and a police officer to force entry, if required, and disconnect his electricity supply. I'd no doubt in my mind that he would be waiting for us with the full payment, in cash, of the outstanding bill and equally certain we would be back doing the same thing at the end of next quarter.

I agreed with Jane not to tell anyone about the letter. I suggested it could be someone playing a sick joke but she disagreed. She was certain that in three days time, she would see her mother again; the woman everyone had been telling her was dead for the last eight and a half years.

I had one of my rare visits to the Turner house the evening before but was more than a little distracted. Paul's parents and brother were out and I was sitting on the sofa with him, in front of the TV, drinking tea. I was semi-listening to him telling me, in great detail, how the entire workforce of Yorkshire Post Newspapers had almost been brought out on strike because the canteen had run out of chips during a dinner break. I was wondering why he thought it was so funny. To me it seemed absolutely ridiculous that the paper might not come out because somebody miscalculated how many potatoes to cook. Still pondering on this, I missed how the strike had been avoided and was suddenly back in the room as he casually mentioned that Trevor had asked him for a game of squash, the next and did I mind.

"Why should I?" I shrugged

"Well you know, she might be there. I won't talk to her even if she is but I've not played for ages and I miss it."

It was written all over his face that it wasn't just the squash he was missing. So I smiled and said yes he should go, I would go round to Jane's. We were going out on Saturday night to celebrate his birthday, so that was fine with me. He grinned from ear to ear and took my mug off me and suggested we went upstairs. I told him my period had come early which killed his mood. We had a bit of a kiss and cuddle but I could tell his heart wasn't in it and mine certainly wasn't. I left shortly after and was home before ten.

The next day I drove straight from having my warrants signed at Leeds Town Hall, to Jane's house and got there just after one. She'd made us cheese and tomato sandwiches, sliced corner to corner, and I ate mine while she gave Rachael her dinner. She'd only been back from the playgroup about ten minutes and the detritus from the meal preparation still littered the work top. She had thought hard about how she wanted to conduct herself on this meeting with her Mum. She explained that she wanted me to be behind the door to the stairs, which she planned to leave ajar, so I could hear the conversation. This was a first meeting and so much had happened that she wasn't sure how it would go. She explained quickly that she didn't know if she was going to let 'this woman', her words, see Rachael. So she needed me to stay out of sight and comfort her if she woke and only to come out if she called me. I glanced over at the child who looked like she might fall asleep in her rice pudding; Jane followed my gaze and smiled.

"My little lady has had a very busy morning haven't you beautiful girl?" ruffling her hair before refilling the spoon. Rachael gave her a beaming smile before wrinkling her nose and very forcefully saying 'No', closing her mouth tight shut and shaking her head. Putting the spoon down in the dish, Jane swept her up out of the high chair.

"Right, let's get your face wiped and nappy changed and then you can have your lovely sleepy time."

"No!" repeated the child again, obviously pleased with her new word as she rubbed her bawled up fists in her eyes.

Finishing my sandwich, I took my plate in the kitchen and I filled the kettle. Leaving it to boil, I quickly wiped and tidied away the high chair just inside the cellar door, rinsed and put away the Peter Rabbit bowl and spoon and glanced around for any further evidence of a child. The kettle boiled and I poured the water on the teabags as Jane came back down stairs. As I handed her the plate with her uneaten sandwich, she walked past me towards the window, putting the plate on the window ledge as she looked out,

"I can hardly believe this is happening," she said.

"I know it's crazy. But at least you were right. You always said she was still alive."

"I stopped believing that ages ago." Her words were quiet as she looked pensively out of the window. I knew where her thoughts were, had known since I read the letter. There was a sentence that stuck out which I knew had hurt her; *my new family don't know anything about my past.*

"It's probably best if you go up and check on Rachael now, then you can sit on the stairs and listen." I noticed the wistfulness had gone now and she was back in control.

"Ok." I took a sip of my tea before placing the mug next to the chopping board in the kitchen.

I was bending over Rachael's cot when I heard the knock and was so concerned with not making a noise that my progress to the bottom of the stairs was slow. Therefore I've no idea what passed for a greeting between them. The first thing I heard as I sat down on the third stair from the bottom was an unfamiliar voice saying,

"Well this all looks nice, you've certainly done alright for yourself."

Jane's response was a bit muffled and I heard the tap running, she was filling the kettle. I leaned forward a bit as I heard the woman ask,

"So do you live here on your own?"

I didn't catch a reply, if there was one. I only heard Jane ask her own question.

"How did you find me?"

"Oh well, now that IS a story."

Her voice told me she'd moved across the room towards the door and I held my breath until I heard her sit down heavily on the sofa.

"Well it weren't easy I can tell ya. I wrote first off to your granny up in Middlesbrough, I said I was a cousin and looking for Maggie's family. Didn't want to let that old witch know I was alive. She never liked me you know. Any road she wrote back tellin' me as she couldn't help, more or less told me to bugger off, saying she'd no idea where you and your brothers were but the old bitch did tell me that Don was dead."

"Did she tell you how or where he died?"

"No, but I'm sure I can guess, either got killed in a pub fight, finally picking on somebody his own size or his liver gave up."

"Do you take sugar?"

"Two love. So anyway, knowing he was dead, I came down here a month ago and went over to Armley Heights. There's another family living there now but they weren't very helpful either. Thanks."

She paused and I heard a mug being placed down on the side table.

"No, they were no bloody help, I even took a chance an' went into Old Hargreave's shop to see if I could find out from that old nosy parker what had happened to you an' your brothers, but it's new folk in there now."

Another pause as she must have taken a sip of her tea but still no comment from Jane.

"So, I was waiting for the bus back to Leeds when I saw the phone box over the road. I thought maybe one of your brothers might have a phone and it would be in the book."

In the next pause, I could hear the clock on the mantelpiece ticking. Jane remained totally silent. Maggie went on,

"Any road, there were no book in there and the bloody box'd been vandalised! As I come out this woman says to me, it's terrible what kids do round here, smashin' up things and I tell her I was just looking for a phone book to look up an address. Then she tells me I should try the library as they keep copies there for all over Leeds, or I could just phone directory enquires if I had a name and the area."

She noisily slurped her drink before asking,

"You haven't got any biscuits have you? I had some sarnies on the train down but that were ages ago."

"I've got some digestives."

"Chocolate?"

"No just plain."

"Oh well, a couple of them will do I suppose," spoken with a sigh, "and another cuppa love as well for your old Mam!"

The image I'd built up of Maggie crumbled away as I listened. The more I heard the less liked this woman. I heard the tap running and Jane raised her voice asking her to continue her story.

Maggie told how she'd caught the bus back to Leeds Station and train home to Blackpool. She mentioned at this juncture that she lived in a guest house on the front with her boyfriend, Lance, and his two children. Oblivious or insensitive, she broke off her narrative to give Jane more details about her 'new family'; John was 10 and Jacqueline 12, she'd brought them up *like her own* for the past eight years. For the first time since she arrived, I could hear something like softness in her voice which only seemed to intensify the irony. There was a pause as she must have started eating her digestives, perhaps lost in thoughts of her acquired children. Still Jane said nothing. I was trying to imagine where she must be sitting and how she must be feeling. With a contented sigh, Maggie returned to her narrative. She'd tried Blackpool central library but although they had directories that covered the Leeds area, they were all about ten years old. So she tried calling directory enquiries who confirmed that there were several Schofields listed in the Leeds 12 and 13 areas but none with the initials I, K or D. As a last resort, she wondered if there was one with initial J to be told that there was but it was Leeds 28.

"That's when I had to be a bit clever," she said, with delight at her own cunning. "I put on the crocodile tears and told her I was trying to find me kids that had been taken away from me. Told her you were me baby and I hadn't seen you for nine years. She said the number was for a Miss J Schofield and she weren't supposed to give out addresses but she felt sorry for me so just this once, she'd make an exception." Another pause, probably waiting for Jane to congratulate or make some approving noise.

I could imagine her cool gaze as I heard her words.

"Very clever."

"Yeah I know. I told you, I were determined to find you."

"Why?"

"Cos you're my little lass an I always meant to come back for you."

"Why did you wait so long? In fact why did you leave me in the first place?"

Even someone as thick-skinned as this woman, couldn't mistake the hostility in her voice.

"I had to go, I just had to get away, he would have killed me if I'd stayed, you know what he was like!"

"Yes I knew what he was like but why didn't you take me? How could you leave me, knowing what he was like?"

"I'd no choice. I couldn't make a new life for me self with you in tow, it were impossible."

"Make a new life for yourself! Well I'm so glad it all worked out for you, so why are you here now?" She was not quite shouting but there was no doubting her rage.

"Look, I expected you to be a bit upset, I should have tried to find you earlier but things were going well for me and I wasn't sure 'bout how Lance would feel if I told him, but I'm here now." In a surge of annoyance, she added, "I went to a lot of trouble to find you."

I steeled myself for Jane's reply. I expected an eruption but instead she asked,

"So how did you do it? How did you disappear without a trace?"

"Well that were quite easy actually. I'd planned it for ages see."

I moved to the bottom of the stairs to make sure I heard all of what she said next. I was finally going to hear Maggie's exposition on how she just disappeared into thin air.

After leaving the house to collect the fish and chips, she'd walked quickly through the passageway between the houses, in the opposite. This route took her onto the ring road where she got on the number 17 bus to Leeds city centre. There, she got a train to Liverpool and stayed there for one night in a B&B to get cleaned up before getting an early train to Blackpool, where she door-knocked her way into a job as a cleaner in a small guest house. She also got a job as a barmaid. She stayed in a hostel for the first two weeks until she was offered a box room at the hotel she cleaned at, in return for helping with the breakfasts. She told the owner, Lance, who was a widower, that her family were all dead and that she'd been living hand to mouth for some time and just needed a break to start again. Lance had two small children and was struggling to cope since his wife's death a year earlier. Maggie soon progressed from paid help to godsend as far as he was concerned; at this point, she mentioned again how much she loved his kids.

Going back to her escape as she called it, she'd been planning it for well over a year, squirreling away all the copper she could and scrimping and saving to build up a secret store of cash. She'd stolen money out of Don's wallet on more than one occasion and knew that Kevin had been beaten for it. Occasionally, she'd even taken the odd pound notes out of Ian's jeans when he'd come home drunk. She'd not actually planned to go until nearer the summer but a particularly brutal encounter the previous weekend had tipped her over the edge and she felt she just had to go. She was wearing two dresses, a skirt and a pair of trousers and had two more tops, underwear, soap and a flannel in a carrier bag. That, and the forty-two pounds in her purse, was all she left with.

"So why now, why come back now?"

"Like I said, I always meant to come back for you."

"But why now?"

"Well Lance wants us to get married, he's wanted it for a bit really but I knew I couldn't course, still being married to your Dad but he kept going on so I started thinking that maybe as we'd been apart for so long he'd divorce me. Thought he might have found himself another woman by now. So I tried to get in touch."

"And Gran told you he was dead, so why are you here?"

"Jane, don't be like this I've explained what happened, I'd no choice. I had to go and any road you've done alright for yourself, I mean nice little place like this, good furniture an all. Did your Dad leave you some money?"

"What?"

"Well I mean, he was always a tight old bastard but I knew he must have had some money somewhere, not that I could find it, but I knew you was his favourite."

"This is about money!" She was shouting now, "You cow, you fucking cow!"

Behind me, I heard a yell from Rachael and climbed quickly upstairs to sooth her before she started to cry. I heard Maggie ask who else was in the house as she must have heard my footsteps on the stairs but I didn't hear a reply. Once in the bedroom I could hear the angry shouting coming from both of them as they moved around. I plucked a very distressed Rachael out of her cot and was pacing around the bedroom wondering what to do. The shouting got louder and I made out a few words here and there. I heard Jane call Maggie an evil witch and Maggie retaliate calling Jane a stupid little girl who didn't know anything about what she'd had to put up with. The real reason she didn't take her with her was she was too much of a Daddy's girl. I heard Jane shout or rather scream something and Maggie also made a noise that could have been a scream, then there was silence.

I walked to the top of the stairs still holding Rachael. I glanced at Jane's bedside clock and saw that it was gone quarter past two. I needed to think about leaving soon. I walked down the stairs as quietly as I could, Rachael nuzzling on my left shoulder, all the time listening but hearing nothing but the baby's breathing. When I got to the door I pushed it slightly and peered round. Jane was sitting on the arm of the chair just in front of the kitchen doorway. Her mother lay just in front of her sprawled awkwardly on the floor, partly on her side, with blood pooling in front of her. Rooted to the spot, I managed to turn my gaze back to Jane. She was holding the bloody knife loosely in her hand as she sat staring at what she had done.

"Jane!" I gasped.

She looked up, surprised to see me. I carried Rachael over to the sofa and placed her carefully down. Taking the knife out of her hand, I stepped into the kitchen and dropped it into the sink.

"I've killed her," she said in a quiet, almost matter of fact voice, "and I'm not sorry."

Chapter Thirty-nine

Crouching down, I put my fingers on her neck, feeling for a pulse. The blood pool was increasing and I had to move to avoid it running into my shoes. As I got up Jane grabbed me by the arms,

"She's dead, she's definitely dead isn't she?" panic in her voice. Nodding and freeing myself from her grasp, guided her into the kitchen.

"Yes, she's definitely dead so we need to keep calm and think about what we'll tell the police. Let's get your hands clean first though."

Perhaps it was the adrenalin shooting through me, or maybe it's part of the natural human desire for self-preservation but I was unbelievably calm. I ran the tap and pulled her hands under the flow, rubbing mine over hers, rinsing off the blood. My mind racing to process what had happened and come up with a believable scenario, one we could explain to the police, one that wouldn't end with Jane in prison. There had to be one, I just needed to think of it. Suddenly I realised, this was it; the moment had come for me to step up to the plate. A ridiculous trickle of excitement dripped through me, boosting my serotonin levels. I needed to come up with a plausible reason for this woman being dead on the floor of Jane's living room that in no way left her culpable. But of course there wasn't one. Even without her family history there could be no version of events that would exonerate her once the full story came out. The water was still running over our hands, cascading on to the knife, when we heard a noise behind us. I thought for a moment that I'd made a mistake and Maggie wasn't dead. We both turned quickly and saw Rachael coming towards us. There was one of those frozen moments when neither of us moved. We watched her tiny bare feet paddling through the congealing blood, lose purchase with the floor and fall over. She started a high pitched scream, calling for her Mummy as her little hands flailed in the thick red puddle. Jane lurched forward and snatched up her child, pulling her into a tight embrace and began to sob.

"I'll go to prison. They'll lock me away for this. God Kim, I couldn't help it. She didn't come back for me, she was just looking for money." Her voice was rising and her words spilling into one another.

"Don't panic, we can say it was an accident, somehow she fell on the knife, let's just calm down a minute and think."

"She didn't fall, I stabbed her, I stabbed her twice. I did it to shut her up. She's a selfish, self-centred bitch, she was never my mother, and I hate her." Slightly calmer, she said "She'd no right to come here and say those things."

I moved closer and pulled her away from the body to stop her from stepping in the blood but said nothing. My mind racing again, *Come on, come on, I have to think of something, I have to sort this....*

"Oh God what have I done? If I go to prison, they'll take Rachael away. Kim don't let her go into care, oh God, God..."

"No one's going into care or to prison," I said with more certainty than I felt, "You go upstairs and clean yourself and Rachael. Get out of those clothes and bring them down here with hers. I'll start to clean up here."

She did as I asked her which gave me some time to think. I looked down at the slender well-dressed woman lying dead at my feet. How could this hard faced woman whose voice I'd heard, be the mother that Jane had missed and longed for? And just as that question formed, it unlocked something and a part of my brain clicked open with the answer.

There was a sweet metallic smell in the room and I knew I had to move quickly. I glanced at my watch, it was twenty to three. I needed to leave by quarter past to make the Barrington disconnection. I went upstairs and asked Jane for a couple of sheets. She'd washed and changed Rachael, who was sitting bemused and very still, watching her Mummy slowly, stripping off her clothes. I told her to hurry up, to put Rachael back in her cot and come down and help me. I took her clothes and the sheets downstairs with me. I put the clothes in the washing machine and switched it on before getting on my hands and knees to set about wrapping up the body like a Mummy. I stuffed newspaper over the wounds in an effort to stop anymore blood escaping. This seemed to work but I needed something to make the binding secure. I was opening and shutting drawers and cupboards in frustration when I glanced out of the window at the washing line. I went out into the yard and, using the same vegetable knife Jane had sliced the tomatoes with before stabbing Maggie, I cut it down at both ends; I didn't have time to waste untying it. Back inside I was crouching over the body-sized package, tying the sheets in place when Jane came back.

"What are you doing?"

I didn't look up from my task.

"This woman disappeared nine years ago so we're going to make her disappear again."

"What are you talking about?"

"We'll dump the body somewhere where it won't be found for awhile. Your neighbours, are they in during the day?"

"What?"

"Are your neighbours likely to have seen her arrive or heard the shouting?"

"No, I think Mrs Frost at that side is in hospital and the couple at this side will be at work. What do you mean dump it, where will we dump it?"

"I don't know yet, I'm still thinking."

"Ok but what about when she's found and they work out who she is."

"How can they? She disappeared all those years ago. She's somebody else now with nothing to do with you."

"She's got a new family."

"Well then that will be the body they find, whoever she made herself. The police decided years ago your mother was dead so this can't be her."

There was a silence as we looked at each other and let my plan sink in. She nodded her head slightly and said,

"My mother died years ago."

I pointed to a pile of black bin bags I'd brought in from the kitchen.

"You need to help me do this now. We need to cover her with these."

She dropped to the floor at the other side of the shroud, pulling the bags towards her. We used six of them, bending, forcing, pulling and tying. Turning the white cadaver shape into a large but slightly less body-like black parcel and we used an entire roll of tape to secure the bundle.

"I've got to go in a minute so you have to be strong for a little while."

Her eyes looked panicked but I held up my hand, continuing firmly,

"I have to go back to work. We have to try and be as normal as possible. I'll come straight back after, then later tonight we'll take the body somewhere and dump it."

She was staring at the large twisted, plastic shape in front of her and I saw her face starting to crumble again.

"Jane!" I shouted grabbing her arms and giving her a shake. "Are you listening to me?"

It did the trick. The two of us carried the body over to the cellar door and put it at the other side, just at the top of the steps. All the time we were heaving the dead weight I was talking to her, telling her how we were going to sort this.

"Right, tell me again what's going to happen next?" I said sternly as I started to straighten up my clothes and picked up my bag. She stood in front of me looking more focused but her voice was still flat.

"You are going back to work and I'm going to carry on cleaning up."

"Good, that's right, what then?"

"You'll be back here at about six and you'll stay with me tonight. Later, we'll take her to your car and put her in the boot without anyone seeing us and drive her somewhere where we can dump her."

"Right," I nodded.

Before I left, I hugged her and kissing her on the side of her face, telling her it was going to be ok. As I walked to my car, I was buzzing. I calm and in complete control but there was also something else; I was the strong one sorting out the problem. I was doing this to help Jane, I was the only one who could help her. I was empowered by this thought. Driving to the appointment, I processed why I was so calm. I'd just seen something terrible, a woman stabbed, a dead body right there at my feet oozing blood. I should've been horrified, appalled, afraid even but I was none of these, I was animated and pumped with adrenaline; I was happy.

As expected Mr Barrington was waiting behind his door for our knock. He took great pleasure in counting out the £79 all in one pound notes and 88 new pence into my hand as I stood on the doorstep with my entourage. He said very little but faced us with what I would now call a supercilious smirk; what I called it then was a stuck-up and ugly phizog, but not to his face. The transaction took just over fifteen minutes and once complete, the prick, as Ron Kent referred to him, also not to his face, wished us all a good evening and our little group departed in the three vehicles parked on his drive. It was a twenty minute drive back to the office and once there, I took the money over to the accounts department before going to check my desk. It was just before five and as I moved bits of paper and forms around, to give the appearance of work, I was racking my brains to try and think of somewhere to dump the body. Post Hill came to mind, there were some thick wooded bits there near the bottom where it probably wouldn't be found for ages but it would be tricky to get her down there, it was a long way from the road. Gibson's tannery would have been the perfect place to dump her, in the bottom of that large soaking tank, there would be some poetic justice for me in that. Maybe the certainty I'd felt at the time about her body being dumped there had really been some sort of premonition. But the building had been demolished for the extension the Gamble Hill estate. There was still some scrub ground around there but it was a bit exposed and would be hard to get to without being seen. So where else was there? I liked the idea of putting her in water. Yes, that was a good idea. I'd read somewhere that when drowned victims were not found straight away they became unrecognisable because of the way the water bloated and degraded them. There was the big expanse of water on Butt Lane, but again it would be exposed and someone might notice us parking up and throwing a large body-shaped thing in the lake. Then it came to me, the perfect place to dump her. Later that night me and Jane would take Maggie fishing.

I got back to Jane's just after 6pm and she opened the door before I knocked. As I crossed the threshold, the whiff of bleach hit me and stepping inside, I saw the massive wet stain of it just outside the kitchen doorway. Rachael was strapped in her high chair at the far side of the room with an assortment of toys. She was quiet and not looking too happy. Seeing me, she held out her arms and called out hopefully, "Kin, Kin!" I walked across and ruffled her hair.

"Hello my favourite girl," bending to kiss her before turning to Jane. "Well that's definitely got rid of the blood."

"I'll take the carpet up tomorrow and bleach the floorboards," she was staring down at the wet colourless patch. I glanced at her hands, red and sore, she rubbed them together and sighed.

"Is this really going to work Kim? Will we get away with this?"

"Yes of course we will as long as we're careful. I have the perfect place to dump her."

"Right," she said nodding her head but not sounding convinced. She went to the sofa, picked up a black leather handbag and handed it to me. "Here have a look."

Opening the bag I glanced inside before tipping out the contents on the sofa next to Jane. A comb, a handkerchief, a purse a chequebook and a piece of Basildon Bond paper, like the one the letter to Jane had been written on. It had Jane's address and phone number and underneath was David's name and an address in Armley. I opened the purse to see two five pound and four one pound notes and an array of silver and bronze change. In the wallet section at the back was a picture of a young boy and girl smiling happily at the camera, John and Jacqueline no doubt. So sweet that she carried their photo around with her, perhaps she'd intended to show it to Jane? There was also a screwed up bus ticket and a return train ticket to Blackpool. I opened the chequebook that apparently belonged to a Mrs Margaret Elizabeth Brayburn. I noticed Jane watching me.

"Well the Margaret Elizabeth is right, maybe she married this bloke she's been living with."

I put the money on the side table before taking the chequebook, tickets and photograph into the kitchen and put them in the big pan on the stainless steel draining board. With the box of matches from the side of the cooker, I set them alight. Jane came up behind me and we stood in silence watching the flames take hold and after an initial high surge, flicker into flimsy black flakes. I ran the tap on the residue and filled the pan before taking it out into the yard and pouring it into the roots of the privet hedge.

"Do you fancy some fish and chips?" she asked me as I came back in and, nodding at the money on the table, "Well it is Friday. And Maggie's buying."

I looked at her and saw the fear and vulnerability had gone. She'd forced the trepidation, along with her anger, back down inside her. She was back to being the person she had to be.

"Yeah, why not? Do you want to go and get them?" I smiled, glad to have her back.

Chapter Forty

It was surprisingly easy to dump a body without being seen back in 1977 and was ridiculously straight forward once we'd agreed on the site. It seems incredible that two twenty-year-old girls managed to get a body out of a house, carry it down the footpath to a car parked on a main road, shove it in the boot and dump it in the canal without anyone noticing. But we did it and It all went completely to plan and without a hitch – well almost.

We only had to worry about the neighbours on one side, the young couple, but Jane was confident they would be going out, as they did every Friday, and wouldn't be home until the early hours. I thought the fates were definitely with us as their house was the only one whose window we would have to pass carrying our cargo; all we had to do was wait for them to go out. We ate our fish and chips with attempted gusto and a good deal of salt and vinegar, straight from the paper. At first the smell of hot grease and acetic acid masked the lingering bleach but soon began to combine, creating a sharp and sour aroma curbing our appetites.

"I think I might buy myself some flowers with the rest of the money," Jane mentioned and I nodded saying that was a good idea.

At seven o'clock, Jane took Rachael upstairs for her second bath of the day before putting her to bed. I sat downstairs, looking at but not watching TV. I could hear Jane as she read her daughter her favourite bedtime story. The Tiger Who Came to Tea was one of the last gifts that Matthew had given his daughter. I am sure he would have loved to see how much she loved that book.

At eight-thirty we heard the slam of the neighbour's door and a stealthy peek out of Jane's bedroom window confirmed that they had left the house and were standing at the bus stop. We watched until we saw them climb on board the green bus that would transport them to Leeds city centre, before bringing Maggie out from behind the cellar door. She felt markedly stiffer than when we'd put her there, making her easier to carry. Maybe it was the rigidity of the corpse or perhaps we'd finally developed some panic but as we got her near the front door, the bags started to tear where we gripped them.

"Let's put it down here on the rug," Jane said, "It'll be easier to carry it out if we roll it up in that."

Noticing that Maggie had now lost all her humanity, I side-stepped and we deposited our cargo on the brown and beige hearth rug. Once rolled up, our burden much easier to carry and within minutes was safely shut in the boot of my car. I got in the driver's seat while Jane went back to the house and emerged a few moments later with a sleeping Rachael wrapped in a blanket and a carrier bag hooked on her wrist. I drove down Stanningley Road and towards Whitecote Gardens for the next bit of the plan. Dad was having a couple of pints with the bloke from next door at the Barley Mow while Mum was having a quiet night watching TV. She got up quickly, looking worried as she saw Jane follow me with Rachael in her arms. I launched into the planned story. Jane was feeling really unwell; she'd been sick and had a severe pain at the right hand side of her stomach. The pain had been on and off for two days but the diarrhea and sickness had just begun today and was getting worse so I was taking her to the hospital. Mum nodded saying she did indeed look pale and unwell. Ten minutes later Jane and I were back in the car, leaving Rachael in Mum's care, driving the two miles towards Rodley and the Leeds and Liverpool canal. Passing the Barge pub we turned right at the roundabout towards Horsforth. Less than half a mile on this road, just after the bridge, we turned left down the gravel slip road which brings you directly to the canal towpath. It was now nearly half past nine and I let out a large sigh of relief that there were no other cars. This was a popular spot with couples for clandestine meetings but on this Friday, at this hour, were completely alone. I drove the car in a big circle so that the back was nearest the path and as close as I could get to the stretch of the canal that went under the bridge. I noticed the moon as we got out of the car. A full moon was four days away and a half buried memory of some pointless trivia sprang to mind, wasn't November's full moon called the Mourning Moon?

"We need something to weigh it down," Jane told me as she stepped over to where the grassy bank edged the sides of the bridge. We grabbed at handfuls of rocks and stones and carried them under the bridge before opening the car boot. Awkwardly, we grappled with the package, still wrapped in the fireside rug, manoeuvred it out and were soon standing under the bridge with it at our feet. Rolling it forward out of the rug, we put as many rocks as we could in the holes of the black plastic before rolling it into the water. After the initial splash, there was a gurgling as the body seemed to float a little just beneath the surface. We held our breath and watched bubbles of trapped air rise and break the tension, making a slight hissing sound as the dark water soaked through the holes into the sheets and around the fleshy remains. I reached out and felt for Jane's hand as a swathe of larger bubbles popped to the surface and with a whoosh and a sigh, Maggie was gone. Finally daring to breath, I turned to Jane who was still staring down into the blackness. I pulled on her hand and she turned her head towards me and smiled a soft "Thank you".

Fifteen minutes later, we were stepping back into her house. It felt cold and seemed strangely empty and my teeth started to chatter as we rinsed the soles of our shoes under the kitchen tap. I was shaking quite violently and I knew it wasn't just the cold. The gravity of what we had done was beginning to dawn on me as I stared at the running water. Jane put her shoes on the floor and turned off the tap before taking my shoes from my frozen fingers and pulling me into an embrace. I could feel the emotion pulsing upwards, looking for the release valve behind my eyes. I choked back the beginnings of a sob as she whispered through my hair,

"It's alright, it's fine, we did ok." She pushed me away a little and leaned in, our foreheads touching, she looked deep into my eyes for a second before leaning in further and kissing me gently and lovingly on the mouth. My reaction was instinctive and I kissed her back. She put both her hands on my face as she drew herself away slightly and smiling said, "Come on." Taking my hand, she led me upstairs.

She ran a warm, bubbly bath and without narrative or instruction, we took off our clothes and climbed in. There was no shyness or hesitance, only a reciprocal tenderness as we washed the events of the last few hours from each other's bodies. After gently towel drying, we slipped into Jane's bed, our hair still damp as we wrapped our bodies around each other and kissed deeply. She as always, was my teacher and guide and reverting back to my role as follower, I was the eager schoolgirl wanting to learn and full of desire. I was happy to be lead and my easy compliance felt like bliss. There was nothing rushed or vigorous about our love making, it was a gentle and tender exploration of each other, with our fingers and our mouths. We caressed and tasted, gliding fingers over expectant skin and moved in a symbiotic cornucopia of pleasure. After almost an hour of this, we lay back facing each other, breathless and smiling. In that instant I felt so much love for her, I thought my heart would explode but instead, the emotional release was through my eyes.

"Hey, what's up?"

"Nothing, I'm just so really happy. I'd never thought about this, that we could be together or that you wanted this. But it all makes sense now."

She traced a finger down my face, following the tracks made by my tears and her smile faulted as a cloud passed over her thoughts.

"I love you Kim. You're my best friend, probably my only friend, and you know me like no one else does."

I could feel a tightening around my chest as I sensed a 'but' coming. She held my face with both her hands and kissed me gently on the lips before pulling herself away and getting out of bed.

"We'd better get back to your house."

Afraid of what she might say if I pressed her, I nodded my head and got out too. I wiped my eyes on my hand and started to dress, aware all the time that the control I'd felt earlier had evaporated in our intimacy. But I didn't care, that intimacy had been so deep and had felt so right, she must feel the same way as me. She had to. She hugged and kissed me once more before we left the house but neither of us spoke until we were in the car. We went through the story we planned to tell Mum and Dad about our trip to the hospital as I drove us back to Whitecote Gardens. I pulled up on the drive sometime after midnight. Mum was in bed but Dad was still up and waiting for us, he claimed he'd been watching TV and had only just turned it off. but his concern was obvious.

"The doctor thinks I've got a grumbling appendix and I'll be alright in a day or two," Jane told him, "Has Rachael been alright?"

"She's fine love," he answered. Addressing me he said, "Your Mam wasn't sure what to do and thought it was probably better if she stopped here as it were so late. So she's put little lass in your bed, she only woke up once but soon went back after a bit of a cuddle and we've been checkin' on her. She's fast on."

After assuring himself that we didn't need anything he went off up to bed and shortly after we followed. Jane kept her bra and pants on and I did the same and we both got into my bed at either side of Rachael. When I turned off the light, I reached across and gently stroked her arm.

"Do you ever get lonely, living on your own?" I whispered into the darkness. I felt her shoulder tense a little then shake and I knew she was silently laughing.

"Oh Kimmy, you're so predictable."

Pushing myself up a little I asked, "What do you mean?"

She answered in a whisper but with an edge to her voice. "No, I never get lonely. I've spent far too much of my life not being left alone, it's brilliant to finally have my own space."

I leaned back into my pillow and let the darkness settle around us again and tried to think of something to say. She must have sensed my discomfort, maybe it was my predictability as in a softer tone she said,

"I love living on my own with Rachael and I don't want that to change."

Reaching across, she stroked my hair and whispered, "Night Kimmy," before settling her arm around her daughter. I lay awake for a while listening to their breathing. I was thinking that even though I was mentally exhausted, there was no way I would sleep but suddenly I was jolted awake with a loud banging at the door. Woozy from the slumber I hadn't realised I'd fallen into, I pulled myself to a sitting up position. My momentum nudged Rachael awake and looking confused she started to whimper. Jane was already out of bed and over by the window.

"It's the police," she said.

I couldn't speak, I just stared at her. Rachael was struggling to get out from the covers and calling for her Mummy. I didn't move or blink, I just stared at Jane. I could hear Dad thumping down the stairs wanting to know who was there banging on his door at five o'clock in the morning and still I didn't move. Jane was cuddling Rachael now, standing at the other side of the bed, rocking slightly and staring back. We heard Dad unlock the door and a loud voice from the past said,

"Hello Ray, I'm sorry it's so late or early even. But we've got some bad news for you. Can we come in?" The loud booming voice of Harry Henshaw was unmistakable.

Jane's hold on Rachael tightend and her eyes were huge with fear. Hearing Mum's voice calling down, asking him what was going on, and Dad's raised, angry question brought me out of my stupor.

"What the bloody hell are you talking about?"

Scrambling out of bed, I quickly pulled on my jeans and jumper. Dad was really losing his temper as I descended the stairs, Mum seemed to be chipping in as well, asking what sort of game he thought he was playing. I pushed open the sitting room door and Harry, who had been trying to explain something, immediately feel silent and gawped at me.

"What's going on?" I asked.

"What's going on is this bloody joker has just woken us up at this god-forsaken hour to tell us another pack of lies!" Dad spat out the words, jerking his thumb at the policeman.

"What have I done this time then?" I asked, praying my voice sounded calmer to them than it did to me.

"Well there's obviously been some sort of mistake," he began, looking a little sheepish, "Have you been out this evening with Paul Turner?"

Both his apologetic demeanour and his question threw me a little.

"No, we weren't seeing each other tonight. He was playing squash."

"Do you know who he was with?"

"Trevor Sedgwick, he works with him at the Post. Why are you asking me this? What's this about?" Confusion was allowing my fear to surface.

"I'm sorry to tell you Kimberly but Paul has been involved in an accident. He's in Leeds Infirmary. There was a young lass in the car with him and his mother told us that it'd be you... We should 'ave checked. I'm sorry Ray, Pam."

I sat down heavily on the chair arm and Mum rushed across to put her arm round me. I didn't speak, so Mum asked,

"How bad is he?"

"He's badly hurt but the doctors are hopeful that they can keep him stable. It was a head-on collision and there are two fatalities from the other car. The lass from the passenger seat, the one we thought was you," he nodded at me, "is in a really bad way."

"It's probably Sharon Weldon," I said flatly and without emotion.

All faces looked at me and I shrugged. I knew I needed to try and reign in the relief that was flooding through me with a wash of near hysteria but I knew I wouldn't be able to pull off the 'concerned and upset fiancé role', so I said,

"He was probably pissed, he's always saying that drinking sharpens his reactions and makes him a better driver. What an arsehole!"

"Kimberly!" Mum said sharply.

"No Pam," Dad held up his hand, "If that lad was driving drunk and caused that accident, he is a bloody arsehole and thank Christ our Kim wasn't with him this time."

Harry and the other policeman took their leave, apologising again for disturbing us. I heard some mumbled conversation in the hall as Dad was showing them out and moved nearer the door to try and hear better. Unfortunately, Mum moved closer to me to try and give me a hug, saying something about me going to see Paul. I was shaking my head and telling her I wasn't interested how he was and had no intention of ever seeing him again. Dad came back in looking like thunder.

"What did he just say?" I asked, feeling heat rising inside me.
Dad said, with a rage in his voice that I'd never heard before,

"He said he were surprised that you'd taken up with Paul Turner," he tried to swallow down a little of his anger without success. "He said it was him as told him all them tales about you and Jane goin' with lads down at the canal, when all that trouble started."

The three of us stayed stock-still for the longest second before I broke the silence.

"Of course it was, I am so bloody stupid, I should have known," and wiping my idiot tears on the back of my hand I stood up.

"Anyway, I'm safe and sound now and everything here is fine so let's get off to bed."

Kissing them both goodnight, I went back up to my room to tell Jane the good news.

Chapter Forty-one

Jane listened as I explained about the mistaken identity and that the visit was nothing to do with us. Muttering something about Harry Fucking Henshaw always being the curse of her life she placed a sleeping Rachael gently back into bed and we got in either side of her. Within minutes I heard Jane's breathing deepen and the next thing I knew, the toddler beside me was poking her fingers in my ear. It was 7 'o clock and Jane was getting dressed. Seeing me awake she said she needed to get Rachael home as she didn't have any clean nappies. An hour later, after Rachael had splattered our kitchen with regurgitated Weetabix and Jane and I had drunk a mug of tea and nibbled some toast, I drove them home. We hugged briefly, a reassuring hug rather than a passionate gesture but our lips brushed lightly at the end of it.

"I'm going to take Rachael for a walk to the shops and then try and get some more sleep. You should do the same."

I asked her if she wanted me to stay and help her tidy up a bit more, glancing at the bleach-stained carpet. She said she'd sort that out but I should get rid of the rug and handbag that were still in the boot of my car. I went the scenic route home via the Working Men's Club on Elder Road. An extension was being built at the back and there were two large skips of rubbish in the car park. I drove down the narrow drive and pulled up by them and after glancing around, took out the rug and empty handbag and tossed them in. Then I performed a perfect three-point turn and drove home.

Mum and Dad were in the kitchen when I got in and looked exhausted.

"I don't know what to say to you love," Mum said wrapping her arms around me. It took a minute before I realised she was talking about Paul.

"There's nothing to say, it's over and I never want to see him again."

Harry phoned late morning after he'd finished his shift. Mum answered the call and handed the receiver to Dad. He wanted to meet him for a pint at the Globe saying he felt bad about what had happened both last night and before and he'd like to bury the hatchet. Dad agreed reluctantly but said he wouldn't go if I didn't want him to.

"I think you should go," I said, "I'd be interested to hear what he's got to say."

Mum gave me one of her sleeping pills and I went back to my bed and slept for three hours. Dad coming home, after four afternoon pints on an empty stomach and closing the front door harder than he meant to, woke me up. I went down to hear the latest completely biased police report. Harry confirmed that it was Sharon in the car. Her parents had eventually been contacted and were now at the hospital. She'd been seriously hurt and hadn't yet regained consciousness.

"Most dangerous seat in the car," Dad observed to no one in particular. These were the days when seat belts were only worn by softies. Paul's blood alcohol levels were well over the limit and he would be prosecuted. Halfway through the second pint, he told Dad about that Christmas five years before.

The following morning Beryl Turner phoned the house. I answered to hear her telling me that it was my duty as his fiancé to go and see her son. I refused; leaving her in no doubt that I was now his ex-fiancé. The next day, she turned up at the house to beg me. She wanted me to go with her and let him tell me what really happened. I told her, leaving no room for ambiguity, that I knew exactly what'd happened. He'd been seeing Sharon behind my back, again. He'd driven his father's car while drunk and not for the first time, and as a result he'd killed someone and he and his floozy were in hospital. I didn't need to know any more, none of it was my concern.

"But he loves you. This other girl means nothing to him, he was only giving her a lift home and he'd only had a couple of pints."

"He clearly does not love me and I'm certain I don't love him," and as I said it out loud I knew it was true, "and you've never liked me. Never thought I was good enough for your precious son, so why are you so keen to keep us together now?"

"That's not true!" her red face contradicting her words. "It wasn't you I was worried about, it was the company you kept. But that's all water under the bridge. He needs you Kimberly and he's been asking for you all night. I promised him I'd take you in with me to see him."

"Well you'd no business promising him that. I'm not going to see him in hospital or anywhere else – Ever!" I pulled off the sapphire and diamond white gold engagement ring and handed it to her. "You'd better give him this back as I certainly don't want it."

I'd an idea that Mum had been listening at the door and smiled at her as she came in to the room. Beryl had started to argue that I couldn't break off the engagement while he was in hospital fighting for his life.

"I think our Kim's made it clear how she feels Beryl, so I think you should go now. You should be sitting with your boy, especially if he is fighting for his life." She held her arm out gesturing towards the door. Beryl stood and Mum added, "Although when I phoned the hospital half an hour ago they told me he was doing well and his injuries weren't that serious. Anyway you should get off now an leave my little lass in peace."

There was something invigorating watching Mum not exactly throw her out, but definitely making it clear she wasn't to bother coming back. I wanted to tell Jane about it. I'd been desperate to see her the night before after Dad had passed on Harry's revelations but when I'd called her she sounded sleepy, distant, and vague. She'd said to leave it until the next day and although I knew she must be tired, her tone unsettled me. I felt Beryl's visit and the formal breaking off of my engagement warranted a conversation with my best friend so I called. Hearing her voice immediately made me smile and relief poured through me as she told me she was just about to call me. I said I had loads to tell her and suggested going round.

"We can take Rachael to the park or something."

"It's a bit cold for the park. Come round tonight, about seven."

"Ok."

I tried not to sound sulky in my disappointment, I'm not sure I pulled it off. If she noticed, she didn't acknowledge it. Instead, she started to tell me that we needed to get hold of David. We had to be sure that Maggie hadn't sent him a letter as well. She'd phoned directory enquiries but there was no number listed for a David Schofield in Bramley or Armley.

"We need to get hold of him, Kim," She said simply.

I knew what she wanted me to say, that I'd call Keith's parents and ask them. I meant to say nothing. I didn't want to call the Wood's home; it would be awkward and painful. There was also a good chance that they wouldn't talk to me but I heard my voice telling her what she wanted to hear. After hanging up, I went to the kitchen to get myself a glass of water, before going back to stare at the phone. I looked up the number, even though I didn't need to. I was stalling to give myself time to get over my disappointment, mainly at myself, but also with Jane. I wanted to go and see her; I wanted her to want me to go round. I could think of little else other than the intimacy we'd shared and the feelings it had aroused in me. That she had neglected to make any reference or suggestion to it hurt me. It was the natural consequence of our friendship and why it had been so special. It was such a powerful revelation to me, surely it meant as much to her. Mum suddenly appeared at the side of me.

"Dinner will be ready in half an hour. Go and tell your Dad and set the table for me will you love?" It wasn't a request.

This was the perfect distraction for me. I would phone the Wood's after my dinner.

Dad was in the garden where he'd been for most of the morning. He'd never been big on DIY or even odd jobs but since leaving the pub he had a lot of time and energy on his hands. He was trying his hand at woodwork and attempting to make a bird table. He'd been working a couple of evenings a week at the Bramley Band Social Club and also applied for a job as a postman, which he claimed, had always been his ambition. This was news to me and I instantly wondered about how he'd manage the early mornings. When I got into the garage, he was standing on his step ladders with his hands up in the eaves of the roof.

"Hey Kim, just in time, 'ere help me get this lot down will you?"
He started to lift out some large basket thing before lowering it down towards me.

"What is it?"

"Fishing tackle and stuff that the folk who lived here afore left."

I took it from him and he continued to rummage, handing me a couple of rods and a fold-up stool.

"I've allus wanted to do some serious fishing," he went on, "Just never 'ad the time afore."

I knew this wasn't remotely probable. Sitting in silence for hours on end in all weathers by a muddy stretch of water would have about as much appeal to him as it had to me. But I smiled, telling him dinner was ready, as he came down the steps. The sight of the fishing equipment brought some different images to my mind. As I set the table, the scene of Maggie's tightly bound body slowly sinking in to the dark water was playing in my head. That was the moment that it finally started to sink in, just exactly what we'd done. I struggled to eat my dinner; even Mum's excellent Yorkshire puddings seemed to turn to cardboard in my mouth. The normal empty plate rule was relaxed and I was allowed to leave most of my Sunday roast without comment. After washing up and helping up the kitchen, I went back to the hall and to the telephone.

Mrs. Wood answered the phone, her friendly tone turning frosty on hearing my voice. I explained that Jane was keen to get in touch with David. She asked why Jane hadn't phoned, letting me stumble over my words trying to answer for a few seconds, before saying she would pass on the message and if he wanted to speak to his sister he would, she was sure, call her. I knew she was aware that Jane had refused his efforts to stay close and that she felt protective of him. She asked me for Jane's phone number which I gave her before she abruptly rang off, her dislike clearly communicated was no less than I deserved. I went upstairs and shut myself in the bathroom and turned on the taps in the washbasin. I sat on the floor and with my head over the toilet and threw-up the morsel of dinner I'd managed to swallow.

When I came downstairs, Mum and Dad were sitting on the sofa watching Sunday afternoon TV. They looked anxiously at me and so I smiled and sat with them a while, eyes towards the screen but seeing only the programs showing in my head. I stayed for about an hour before making them a cup of tea and going to my room with the excuse of a book I wanted to finish. I was just killing time until I could go and see Jane and she could convince me that everything was going to be alright. All the new-found strength and decisiveness had compleatly deserted me.

I got to Jane's just after quarter past seven after stopping off at the off-licence on the way to buy a bottle of Mateus Rosé. I also had a bag with my toothbrush and work clothes for the next day but I left them in the car. My heart was pounding loudly, inciting a growing fear as I knocked on the door. I was terrified that she would be cool with me and I needed her to want me, like I wanted her. I needed to feel that the closeness we'd shared wasn't just a by-product of this new secret. I wanted her reassurance that what we had done was right and our coupling was always inevitable.

Her warm smile welcomed me and once the door closed, she took me in her arms and kissed me fully and passionately. I almost skipped as I went back to the car to get my overnight bag while she opened the wine.

We sat on the sofa sipping it while she told me David had called her. They'd spoken for a good half an hour without him mentioning Maggie. She was beaming. I told her about Beryl coming round, building up to the bit where Mum had practically thrown her out. Endorphins were swimming through my bloodstream with the wine, consumed on a practically empty stomach. I was chuckling as I described Beryl's aggravation and very red face. Jane was laughing as she poured the last of the wine in our glasses and said that she would have loved to have seen that. The mood changed slightly as I wondered, out loud, how Sharon was but Jane said,

"She got in the car with him knowing he was drunk. You pays your money you takes your choice."

"Yeah, you're right, we shouldn't waste time worrying about her."

"And," she said getting to her feet, "we shouldn't waste any time worrying about anything else either. I'm starving so I'm making some cheese on toast. Do you want some?"

While she was assembling our supper, I went to the bathroom and as I climbed the stairs thought about the other thing I wanted to tell her. I played with the words in my head to see how they sounded.

"You'll never guess what Harry told Dad." No! That wouldn't be a good idea; the mere mention of his name would spoil the happy mood. *"I found out something else about Paul"*. Yes, that was a better start, perhaps I could just casually mention that Dad had met up with Harry. No that would still spoil it. I should tell her somehow without mentioning Harry. I was still struggling with how best to do this as I came back down to eat. Handing me the plate with one of her loveliest smiles she said,

"Let's eat this quickly then we can get a bath before we go to bed."

Taking the plate from her and returning her smile, I banished all thoughts of that discussion completely.

Later, as I curved my body around hers, my nipples still tingling as I pressed them to her back, I sighed my contentment and sleepily nestled into her shoulder.

"You are so amazing," I murmured.

"Maybe," she said without moving, "but you really don't have much to compare me with."

I felt a little stir of panic and before I could hold it in check, I asked,

"Have you done this before, with someone else I mean?"

She gave a forced laugh but her body hardly moved before she replied,

"A couple of times."

I knew I should let it go. I should let the sleep we both needed drift over us but instead I pushed myself up on to my elbow trying to look at her face.

"How many times?"

She turned her head slightly to look at me.

"I don't know, I haven't been keeping a record." Her voice measured. I was floundering. This realisation of my naivety jolted me from the comfortable afterglow. Petulantly I asked,

"So have you always preferred girls then?"

All warmth gone from her eyes and with a voice sharp with derision she said,

"You don't get to prefer who you have sex with when you're in care, but in my experience, the females tended not to be quite so brutal."

I felt my cheeks flush with shame as my breath caught in my chest. I tried to speak.

"Oh god, I'm so sorry... I didn't think... I just thought... I mean... it's just... "

"Oh just shut the fuck up Kim and go to sleep!"

She turned her back on me again but this time there was no curve of her body for me to meld against. Instead, I shuffled down the bed and lay, staring into the darkness at the gap between us.

Chapter Forty-two

Driving to work the next morning, I tried to analyse my feelings. When I opened my eyes, there'd been a tingle of joy at the memory of our intimacy, but it quickly dissolved as I remembered the despondency I'd fallen asleep in. The contentment and euphoria of the previous evening seemed to have disappeared. Jane was already up and in the bathroom talking to Rachael. Cautiously, I got out of bed and pulled on the t-shirt I'd been wearing the evening before. I was just picking up the rest of my clothes as she came back into the room. She was wearing only her bra and pants but looked relaxed and smiling. Rachael, perched on her hip, gave a dribbly grin before putting her arms out to me. As I took her, dropping my clothes on the bed, Jane kissed me. It was a light brushing of her mouth against the bottom of my cheek, before she turned to pick up her jeans and shirt, dressing quickly. Hugging Rachael to me, I breathed a sigh of relief, perhaps it was going to be alright.

My optimism increased over the next half hour as we fell into the domesticity of a Monday morning. Readying ourselves to leave the house, eating breakfast and clearing away the evening's debris, effortlessly and cheerful, in what could have been a choreographed synchronicity. I was buoyed by the easiness of it as I asked,

"Do you remember when we were kids and we used to talk about getting a flat together?"

"Yeah, god how stupid were we?" her reply was accompanied by a sardonic laugh. "Thinking that it could ever have turned out like that."

I left a small silence, not wanting clarification but desperate for it.

"It wasn't really stupid," Aware of my whiney note in my voice I still went on, "that week in Blackpool was brilliant."

"Yeah," she said with a brief smile, "but it was a holiday, away from the real world and we were kids playing at being grown-ups."

Her tone was even but I could hear the suggestion of something unsaid, something that I wanted to remain unsaid. Picking up a damp facecloth, I started wiping the baby's buttery fingers. But Jane wasn't finished.

"You were always so desperate to leave home, get away from your Mam and Dad's control and live your own life. Really though you only wanted to go and live with someone else who'd control you. I'm surprised you didn't marry Paul as soon as he asked you."

My heart started thumping in my chest as her words hit home. I couldn't understand why she was trying to hurt me and needed to park this conversation quickly. So I let her words settle into a small silence between us for a few long seconds before changing the subject.

"Shall I come round straight from work tonight?" I was wiping toast crumbs from Rachael's face.

"No, not tonight, let's leave it for a couple of days and let the dust settle." She'd been looking in her bag but glanced up at me. "Anyway you probably need some time to think about Paul and if you really mean it, about not taking him back."

She tilted her head slightly, her eyes wide with something of a suggestion. I felt my mouth open slightly in surprise. My heartbeat had calmed slightly but there was a prickling feeling at the back of my neck. I said nothing and kept my attention and focus on wiping the high chair. Through the corner of my eye, I saw her go back to gathering her things together for her morning at work before she continued,

"It's not like you didn't know he was a player, Jesus he's even got form. He just can't help himself. But it's only sex, it doesn't mean anything. And it's not as if you even enjoyed him fucking you anyway."

Feeling my face flush at her words, I looked over to her. She was looking at me, waiting. The thudding heartbeat came back with such force that it made me blink and I had to struggle to get my words out,

"What? So I should be grateful that he's been shagging Sharon then?"

She held my gaze for a couple of seconds before shrugging, a smile hovering around her mouth.

"Course not, but he loves you and wants to marry you. He can get you away from home and into your own place. Seriously, you could do a lot worse and he might even settle down a bit now. This accident's probably been the wake-up call he needs. You should think about it properly before dumping him."

I nodded, not trusting myself to speak and hoped that my smile remained intact as I started to get my stuff together. We kissed goodbye before leaving the house and she walked off briskly in to the frosty morning. I couldn't help but notice she didn't look back. Rachael, in contrast, leaned out of her pushchair and waved furiously at me until I disappeared into the car. It was only as I sat, waiting for the windscreen to clear, that I allowed the events of the previous thirty-six hours free rein in my head. The disparity between the contentment I'd felt the previous evening and the growing uncertainty was vast. My emotional roller coaster had plunged me into an abyss that was fast filling up with words and scenes but most prominent were the three words that Jane had used that morning. *'it's only sex!'* and they echoed around the chasm.

She'd said it about Paul and Sharon but the way she'd looked at me and her matter-of-factness about me marrying him, dismissing his betrayal as nothing. *It's only sex,* a phrase she'd used before but I knew that this time, her words and delivery had held an ambiguity, meant to unsettle and stir up my insecurity. She didn't want to see me for a few days, she wanted us to *'let the dust settle,'* and while it was settling she wanted me to think about marrying Paul. Her comment that I could do worse had astounded me but then I hadn't told her everything. Even so, how could she think I'd go back to him with his laddish behaviour and selfish approach to everything he did, including sex? She'd been right to say it was *only sex* but the baseness of those words wounded me. It was true I'd found my previous couplings uncomfortable, painful and never over quickly enough and that I wasn't a fan of penetrative intercourse. I considered it something to be endured, a trade-off in the relationship that I'd accepted as the norm. The ultimate pleasure was in the ejaculation and it belonged purely to the male. I knew about female orgasms of course but understood that they were hit and miss and some women never experienced them. I'd thought I was one of those women, not capable of a climax. But now I knew different. I knew that an open sexual relationship between Jane and me was impossible and even any covert arrangement would be difficult. I didn't even know if that was what I wanted but I knew that what we had done felt so much more than *just sex*. Our intimacy was incited by a tender desire and need to demonstrate our closeness. It had nothing to do with the carnal appropriation of my previous experiences.

As my journey to work progressed, I began to think about why I hadn't told her about Paul. That he was not the friend we'd thought him to be. I'd wanted so much to be close to her again and after the worry and trauma of the last few days, those few hours of reciprocal intimacy had soothed me. I craved the feel of her hands on me, feeling her breath on my skin, my ultimate surrender and glorious release. I'd been terrified that mentioning Harry would wreck it all. She would have become agitated and all the horrors would break through and spoil things. She held him solely responsible for all that had happened to her since her Mum left. But things had changed now. Maggie wasn't the loving mother she'd remembered and those false memories surely had been displaced. That cherished image of life before her mother left had been brutally shattered and surely the perception of her childhood could be re-examined. The hero and villain roles couldn't still be that black and white. However, I'd not been prepared to take the risk. I was afraid that re-evaluation would ruin the anticipated sensual pleasures I wanted.

I believed we had something precious, something wonderful and enlightening. But I was waking up to the fact that it wasn't the same for Jane. For her it was payment I'd earned by helping her to conceal a violent crime. My drive to work that morning is another marker plotting the path of the story. In the thirty-five minute drive, I finally acknowledged what was going on. The physical and tactile love, the affection and closeness, it was just my reward for finally stepping up to the plate, by helping her dispose of her mother's body and becoming an accomplice in her murder. I could feel the detachment from Friday afternoon's events dissolving around me. I pulled into the car park of the Electricity Board and parked up. Just sitting, staring down at the steering wheel, trying to shut out this insight, taking deep breaths before finally getting out of the car. The cold air cursed into my lungs as I walked towards the double doors with a determination just to get through the day. I made a start on the normal Monday morning's list of unpaid accounts and corresponding warrant preparations, with unswerving focus. My head bent over my desk giving a clear message to my fellow workers that I didn't want to be distracted. And it seemed to work, all other thoughts were banished even when I ventured briefly to the canteen to buy some soup at dinner time. The afternoon was harder as weariness fuzzied my head but I made it to five o'clock with the minimum of interaction and got back into my car to join the evening ring road traffic. I was home in record time and telling Mum I was tired and had a headache, escaped to the sanctity of my bedroom.

Putting aside my decision not to tell Jane that it was Paul who started the rumours about her and me, I needed time to think about it myself. It all started to make sense now. That's why he hadn't stayed friends with David and Keith. And Chris, the person we'd blamed for it, the person who I'd felt such hatred towards and despised for his lies, well apparently he'd defended us to the hilt. No wonder he'd stared in disbelief when he'd seen me with Paul. He must have thought that I was crazy or stupid even, to go out with him. Dad said that Harry had seemed gutted when he told him about this final fall-out between him and his son and how they'd not spoken in five years. Not since that Christmas Day, when he got home late for his dinner because he'd called into the club, purposely he admitted, to wind up Don Schofield. He'd told his wife and sons as he drank more beer with his heated up turkey dinner that he'd had a nice little chat with Paul Turner the day before and he'd told him the real reason for their fight, which was me. Paul had been looking out for his mate and told him what a slapper I was. That he'd seen me and Jane hanging about with gangs of lads, smoking and having sex, down at the canal most Saturdays. We didn't charge much either apparently. Chris had insisted this was a pack of lies but Harry was having none of it. The ale and the reaction he'd got from baiting Don had fuelled his righteous arrogance. The Turner lad had told him everything. Told him that the fight between them started when he'd tried to tell Chris about what he'd seen that night, which was supposedly me in the back of a car practically naked, with some lad. He'd told Chris not to waste his time on me and that was why Chris had hit him. As Harry had laid this version of events in front of his family at that not so festive feast, his younger son did something he'd never done before, he answered back. Trying to defend my honour, calling Paul a liar, telling his father he was wrong. This outburst only made Harry angrier and more belligerent and so it was inevitable how it would end. Chris, equally enraged, yelled that he thought Harry was a drunken disgrace to the uniform he wore. Harry had leapt to his feet and hit him on the side of the head, knocking him to the floor. Without a word, Chris got to his feet and left the room. Even though it was another five and a half months before he was able to leave school and move out, he never spoke another word to his father. The moment he was able to, he'd joined the police force, deliberately requesting another town so he didn't have to live at home.

To give Harry his due, he admitted to Dad that once he'd sobered up and thought it through, he knew that the Turner lad was lying. By then though, the ball was unstoppably rolling and it all came out about Don *'messin' with his lass'*. He said he felt justified that he'd got him locked up and that he got the *'young un'* to a safe home. As Dad recounted this to Mum and me, I'd interrupted to tell them that the home Jane was sent to had been far from safe. They'd looked at me sharply and for a minute I thought I might tell them. Let them share with me the knowledge of her further and continued abuse. How she'd been raped by the staff members that were supposed to be caring for her - but I didn't. I knew they didn't want to hear it, may not even believe it. That sort of thing was way out of their comprehension. Harry ended the conversation apologising to Dad and assuring him that he'd never mentioned my name when passing on the information. He was keen to explain that he'd never thought of me as that type of lass.

"So are you an' him going to be regular drinking pal's then?" I asked.

"No bloody chance," Dad replied firmly, "I'm particular who I drink with and he were always a self-important know it all." He got up to fill the kettle and added with an undisguised sorrow in his voice, "And all his sorrys have come a bit late."

After a fitful night of half formed images and semi-remembered thoughts, I woke up with a head feeling like it was full of cotton wool, puffy eyes and the start of a cold sore on my top lip. I'd hit my clock so hard when the alarm went off, waking me with a start; it was now in pieces on the bedside table. Dad was on the landing as I came out of the bathroom.

"Bloody hell Kim, you look terrible."

I'd intended to say I was alright, just tired and needed to go to work but instead I heard myself saying,

"I know, I'm just going to get some Paracetamol then I'm off back to bed. Will you phone in at work for me at nine o'clock?"

I drank a large glass of water to wash down the pills and had no trouble getting straight back to sleep, sinking into deep and dreamless nothingness; it was a welcome oblivion. When I got up again it was just gone two in the afternoon. Mum was baking and the house was full of the warm aroma of freshly made scones. Dad was doing an extra afternoon shift at the club and probably forgetting I was there, Mum was singing along loudly to a song on the radio using a wooden spoon as a microphone. She stopped suddenly as I stepped into the kitchen.

"Oh Kim, you made me jump!"

After seeing it was embarrassment that made her colour up rather than any stress to her nervous system, I laughed. She heated up a tin of chicken soup, sat beside me and watched me eat before letting me have one of her still-warm scones with a cup of tea.

"Aren't you having one?" I asked as she watched me eat that too.

"God no! I've put on so much weight since I packed in smoking, I'll be the size of a house if I don't start slimming."

"Shall I have another one then just to help you out like, so they aren't hanging around tempting you?"

"Go on then, you can have one more but don't tell your Dad I let you have two. I'm only letting you cos you're poorly."

She took the kettle over to the sink to refill it.

"It's good to see you looking better. Me and your Dad were right worried this morning. I said we'd have the doctor out if you weren't up by the time he got home."

"I don't need the doctor; it's only a bit of a cold."

"Oh it's a lot more than that, you're proper run down. When you came home from work yesterday you looked like you'd not slept for a week." Sitting down at the table she tried to catch my eye. "I know you're upset about all what's happened but you mustn't let it make you poorly."

I smiled and assured her I wouldn't. I could feel the headiness of the cold virus starting a further battle and I screwed up my eyes in an attempt to stop the surge of mucus to my sinuses. The second scone having lost its appeal, I decided to have a bath and go back to bed. I was laying in the hot water feeling floppy and a bit sick, when I heard the front door open and close, Dad was home. I pulled myself up out of the restorative hot water, my limbs feeling like they were made of lead, got dried and put on the clean nightdress, dressing gown and slippers Mum had put out for me and went down stairs.

"Hey Kim, your Dad's had an exciting lunch time session."

I looked over at him as he was taking his first bite of his uncut, unbuttered scone. He chewed fast and swallowed way too soon in his keenness to tell the tale.

"Aye, I think mebbes I'll be thinkin' again about taking up fishin' down the canal." He paused for a small choking cough which he remedied with a slurp of tea before continuing, "Ken Bentley was in the club tellin' us the police are down there. They've only gone and found a body in it."

I took a step forward to hold on to the back of a chair as I didn't trust my legs to hold me up.

"Wrapped up it were and weighed down so he says, so it's murder. Police are crawling all over the place."

Chapter Forty-three

I thought I'd been so clever with my idea of how to get rid of the body. I'd believed the canal was an inspired solution and that I'd calculated perfectly the risk of it being discovered. I'd used the bit of knowledge I didn't know I had; people don't go fishing under noisy road bridges. It's dark there and the water is generally murkier from the undisturbed mud and slimy reeds, so no chance of it being hooked out. But I wasn't clever enough to see the big picture. To start with, the canal was no way deep enough for anything to stay undisturbed for long and there was the matter of science. Maybe if I'd learned a bit more about biology at school, I'd have been aware of what happens to the human body when life has been extinguished. I might have learned about the putrefaction process and known that after 36 hours, it fills up with gas as self-digestion commences. Knowing this, I might have considered more what we used to weigh it down. Perhaps I would have found something to take with us rather than rely on the few rocks and stones we found at the site. They were just about adequate to sink Maggie slowly from the surface but were nowhere near enough to counter-balance the bloating gasses of her decomposing remains. Apparently, it's a mistake made even by master criminals so I suppose I shouldn't feel too bad.

Once I'd re-assured Mum that I wasn't about to faint, even though the colour had completely drained from my face, I sat down and listened to Dad tell us what he'd heard. Some woman walking her dog, isn't it always, along the canal towpath had seen something floating on top of the water just this side of the Horsforth Road Bridge. This unfortunate dog walker was Nellie Wilson, next door neighbour of Ken Bentley. Once she'd got over the shock and rung the police, she'd been keen to tell all to her neighbour. Ken had seen it as his civic duty to dash straight up to the club to spread the news further. Dad said he didn't know about this Nellie Wilson but he was sure that Ken would be drinking out on the story for years.

"The way he told it, you'd think he were there," Dad laughed, "Well any road, it were wrapped up like a mummy and when she got close to it, her dog Toby, one of them stupid bloody spaniels, started howling like he were demented!"

"Bloody hell!" exclaimed Mum, "Was it a man or a woman?"

"Well nobody's said as yet. Coppers took it off in a big police van. Ken thinks it'll be in tonight's Post, they had a photographer down there."

"It won't be in 'til tomorrow but it'll most likely be on the news on telly, so we might find out then," Mum said, brushing my fringe aside to feel my forehead. "You're still a bit warm Kim, go and lay on the sofa and I'll get you a blanket, I think Scooby Doo's on in a minute."

Dad did his inevitable bad impression, shouting out 'Scooby Dooby Do' as Mum lead me to the sitting room, like the ten-year-old she thought I'd suddenly regressed into. Dad went to get a blanket and two pillows from my bed. I lay, still in my dressing gown, under the thick blanket on the settee in front of all four panels of the hissing gas fire, wondering when those pesky kids would realise that, yet again, that the villain was the caretaker dressed up. The cold virus along with the overbearing heat and stuffiness soon had me lapsing back into unreality. I was half aware of the phone ringing but it seemed far away and I was preoccupied by the vivid scene playing through my head. I was being chased through the old tannery by the laughing policeman from Blackpool Pleasure Beach. His grotesque hilarity freshly painted on his hard white face filling me with dread. I found a hiding place behind a large pile of newspapers but this stupid bloody dog came bounding up to me and started to howl. I screamed myself awake and Mum was there in front of me.

"I'm getting the doctor out, Ray," she told Dad, who was just coming into the room. "She's red hot!"

"Of course she's bloody hot!" Dad shouted, "You've made the room hotter than a furnace, you bloody daft woman."

He turned off the fire and pulled the blanket off me. I felt clammy with the sweat and Mum muttered something about getting me a cold drink as she left the room.

"You were having a proper nightmare there love," Dad said as I sat up and he bent down in front of me, "Not that I'm surprised after what's happened but any road, you'll only ever get in a car with him again over my dead body."

I smiled and asked if Jane had rung as I'd half promised to go round.

"No love but that bloody Turner woman phoned again saying as you might like to know that her lad's home if you wanted to go and see him. Bloody cheek, I told her where to go!"

"He did an' all," Mum confirmed, smiling as she handed me the glass of lemon barley water. I gulped down the drink and went upstairs to wash my face but all the time, that dream was unfolding in my head.

The Yorkshire television regional news was just starting as I came back in to the living room. Mum and Dad were sitting in their two respective armchairs, eyes eagerly focused on Richard Whiteley as he told them the day's headlines, starting with the body discovered in the Leeds and Liverpool canal at Rodley bottom. The coverage didn't tell us anymore than what Dad had heard but there was a short recap by one of their roving presenters, standing in almost the same spot I'd parked my car. A body had been discovered floating just under the bridge by a local woman at 9.30am that morning. The body was that of a woman but cause of death had yet to be established. The police were not releasing any further information other than to say that, because of the way the body was found, they were treating the death as suspicious. Anyone with any information should notify the police immediately and a phone number was displayed on the screen just as our phone began to ring.

I continued to sit on the stairs with the receiver still pressed against my ear well after Jane had hung up at her end. I'd thought, as I picked up the phone, that she'd be alarmed or worried about the news report but she sounded neither.

"Did you see the news about the body in the canal?"

"Yeah, we were just watching it." I tried to sound casual, aware Mum and Dad weren't too far away.

"Exciting eh? Wonder if it's anyone we know," she laughed and changed the subject, "Do you want to come round on Saturday? I need to go to Asda for a big shop so it'd be a help if you could take me?"

"Yeah, I can do that, what time?"

"Come round mid-morning and we can go in their cafe for a milkshake first."

"Ok."

"See you then, bye."

"Bye."

The casual arranging of a shopping trip, letting me know she didn't want me to go round until then, was one thing but her joke about the body had been totally unexpected. Mum broke my train of thoughts by telling me to come out of the drafty hall and would I like a boiled egg and soldiers or rice pudding. Dad said he'd have both. I astounded myself by sleeping well that night but still didn't feel that great. The cold was starting to come out and after evidencing my red nose and streaming bloodshot eyes in the bathroom mirror, I called my boss to say I wasn't well enough to go back to work but would try to get in for Thursday. I spent most of the day tidying my bedroom and reading, giving myself something to do while I waited for the regional news bulletins. Although it was briefly mentioned, the only new bit of the story was that the police still hadn't identified the woman. Thursday's Yorkshire Post scooped the

TV news with its lead story of the autopsy findings. I saw it on my boss's desk as soon as I got in. 'Woman in canal was murdered' it announced.

The other news that hovered around our house that week was neither on the TV nor in the local papers. It was further news of Paul, brought round by Michelle. She called round out of the blue on Friday evening to show me the very sparkly engagement ring Trevor had given her the night before. She was excited and giggly, telling me and Mum how they were not planning on waiting to get married, so I could expect an invite soon. Dad had escaped to the garage almost as soon as she'd arrived, claiming to have 'stuff to do.' Mum had made a massive apple pie that afternoon and Michelle accepted a piece gratefully with her cup of tea.

"That was absolutely amazing Mrs Asquith, fabulous pastry," she said having eaten the large piece. Mum nodded her agreement and asked if she'd like another.

"Well I shouldn't really but it's so lovely, go on then just a small slice."

I'd been surprised at her accepting the pie in the first place, she'd been on a permanent diet ever since I'd known her; always watching her weight. Putting my piece down, I tilted my head slightly and looked at her through narrowed eyes, the question hanging in the air between us. She smiled and nodded slightly and taking advantage of Mum being out of earshot, she ran her hand over her stomach and mouthed, 'three months.' Mum handed her the refilled plate and went back to the kitchen leaving us to chat, although I did more listening than chatting. As she munched her way through her seconds, she filled me in on all the gossip from the Post, who was going out with who and the plans for the Christmas parties and eventually got round to the subject of Paul.

"I'm so sorry for you Kim, you must be devastated."

"Not really, I'm more annoyed with myself for taking him back after the last time."

She nodded sympathetically before asking,

"Did you really have no idea he was still seeing her?"

Her use of the word 'still' and the slight incredulity jabbed at me and I knew that not only had Paul continued cheating on me for the whole year, but also that Michelle and probably loads of other people had known. 'More fool me!' I thought. Nothing to be gained by going there now though so instead I asked,

"Have you heard how he is?"

"Oh yeah, Trev went to see him in hospital but he's home now. He's got some cracked ribs, a lot of cuts and bruises, but he's mostly alright. Course he's bricking himself over the charges."

"So he should be."

"Well yeah, but he's cut up about Sharon as well."

"How is she?"

"She's off the danger list and they managed to save her leg but they couldn't save the baby."

It was like she'd slapped me. I felt the sting in my chest surge up through my neck and throat. Saying nothing and barely moving, I must have been staring at her as the horror registered on her face.

"Oh my God, you didn't know!" she exclaimed, "Oh Kim, I'm so sorry."

I allowed myself to blink and break the surface tension on the film of tears, allowing them to fall silently. She came over and hugged me, saying again how sorry she was. I couldn't move, I just sat rigid until Mum came in; she'd not been out of hearing range. Michelle was stammering an explanation but Mum held up her hand and told her not to worry before taking her to the door.

The local news and speculative gossip around the woman in the canal continued with endless suppositions throughout the run-up to Christmas. The police were still baffled as to her identity. She had no identifying marks; except for a long-time healed broken arm, and no one matching her general description had been reported missing. An artist's impression of her face appeared in the newspapers and was featured on both regional news programs but no one came forward.

"I can't believe," the head of the investigation said to the camera, "that this woman has not been missed by anyone. Someone must know who she is."

When still no one came forward, the case lost momentum. It was generally assumed that she must have been a prostitute, thus giving a brief suggestion that she could be yet another Ripper victim, this was refuted by a police spokesman but this theory still held water with the general public, who continued to speculate. My trips to Jane's house became less and less frequent over the next few weeks. She didn't say much when I'd told her about Sharon having been pregnant and after that she didn't mention Paul again. We got into a routine of spending Saturdays together like we had all those years ago. Instead of a bus ride to Leeds, I'd drive us up to Pudsey, which had its own Woolworths, where we'd usually found something to buy. Then we'd go to Asda's family cafe where we had milkshakes. We didn't play at being grown-ups anymore.

I'd started to socialise a bit more with the girls from work. One of them had asked where my ring was. My thin and worn appearance, coupled with my ringless finger had been the subject of their gossip for nearly a week, so I told all. They were all really lovely and began asking me out on jaunts including joining the newly formed drama group, the Electricity Players, and a trip to the cinema to see a new film that everyone was talking about called Star Wars.

Jane was also making new friends, or perhaps I was just discovering she had other friends. The last Saturday before Christmas, she had a midday tea party to celebrate Rachael's second birthday. She was vague about who else was coming other than four or five of the toddlers from the playgroup and their parents. I arrived just after nine, ready to help her blow up balloons, put cheese and pineapple on sticks and make sandwiches. On the previous Saturday, I'd been in a rush after our day out and had dropped her and Rachael off. So I hadn't seen the plush new carpet until she opened the door to me. She smiled at my surprise and took it as a prompt to tell me that Yvonne, one of the Mums that I'd meet later, was married to a carpet fitter. It was an off-cut apparently and had less than a tenner and about twelve cups of tea. She seemed really animated and slightly giddy, laughing loudly and unable to keep still. Rachael on the other hand was grizzly but perked up a little when I gave her my present - a xylophone.

"Thanks very much Kim, she'll be driving me mad with that for days!" But she laughed as her daughter took the sticks and started to experiment with the sounds. As per some pre-existing agreement there had been no gift from Matthew but instead a cheque for £500.

I met Yvonne and her two daughters Leanne, who was Rachael's age, and four-year-old Amy. I can't tell you why but I hated them all within seconds of them arriving. This woman's well-groomed and self-assured appearance and her semi-posh accent with her perfectly formed vowels grated on me, as did her precocious and spoilt children. She was only three years older than us but seemed so mature and fully-formed, and incredibly patronising. Also she mirrored my dislike, so we mentally circled each other with lightly veiled hostility all afternoon. Nothing specific happened, her horrid children shouted and screeched above the others, they were carbon copies of their Mummy but all three of them, with their showy selfish behaviour made my head pound. Jane seemed oblivious to any of it, so I left well before the party broke up, just as Yvonne's husband Steve arrived with an abundance of wine and beer.

When Mum asked me how the party went, I told her about this awful woman and didn't hold back on what I thought. Mum suggested that there might be a bit of jealousy on my part, about Jane's new friends. Although that made me even angrier, I knew there was an element of truth in what she said.

"You need to let her spread her wings a bit and make friends. You two will always be friends but you have to live your own lives."

Chapter Forty-four

As time passed and there was no more news, I thought less and less about Maggie. There was something far more pressing for me to worry about. Michelle and Trevor's wedding. She brought the invitation round on Christmas Eve and after checking the date, put it behind the clock on the mantelpiece. Christmas was a fairly low-key affair, just the three of us, but we did have a trip over to Sheffield the day after Boxing Day. Alison was there with little Melody who was now a cute little girl of three. Steven, her husband, had been posted overseas for six months so Ali was staying with her parents. She seemed hardly recognisable as the girl I'd known; being a wife and mother suited her well. I commented on how good she looked and Aunty Shirley beamed,

"Yes well she would, wouldn't she? She's blooming!"

"Shush Mum!" Alison said quickly, "Its early days."

I followed her into the kitchen to get the tea, leaving the sisters to begin their squaring, while our Dads attempted small talk. Once out of earshot, I gave her a hug and said it was lovely to see her, blooming or not, and she must keep me informed. She coloured up a bit.

"Kim," she began avoiding my eyes, "I'm really sorry to hear about..."

"Honestly Ali, you don't have to be. I was stupid to ever get engaged to him in the first place. I'm fine."

She nodded and smiled as she turned the cooker ring off under the boiling kettle.

"I know he was good looking but he was always a bit of a wanker. Anyway, can you slice up that egg and bacon flan for me?" She pointed to the kitchen table, "If you can get it into seven pieces that would be brilliant."

Mark arrived just as we'd made the tea, he'd been swimming and we were all astounded to see how tall he'd grown. Mark was clearly fed up with his height being the topic of conversation and moodily grimaced through the rest of the afternoon. Mum and Shirley seemed almost amicable so Dad relaxed and I only caught him checking his watch once. As we drove home, Mum said how much she'd enjoyed it and that we should make the effort a bit more often. Dad agreed, saying that Bill hadn't got on his nerves half as much as he usually did.

"Don't get me wrong, he's still a pain in the arse but you're right Pam, we should get out a bit more."

As I put up the new calendar on the wall of the living room, I stared at the date of Michelle and Trevor's wedding. The nuptials were on 21st January and I wasn't sure I could face going. Four days later she called round to talk about it. The ceremony was at St Peters with a buffet reception in the upstairs room of the Barley Mo and a disco in the evening. Michelle blushed a little and glanced down at her stomach.

"I know I shouldn't be getting married in church but well it's not like I'm showing yet." Mock embarrassment over, she became animated telling me about her dress with cape and fir trimmed hood and how Trevor would be wearing a cravat with his three-piece suit.

"I really want you to come; it's going to be a great day," she said, finally getting round to the difficult bit.

"I know he'll be there but is he bringing Sharon?" I asked.

She nodded and rolled her eyes.

"Sorry, he's Trev's best mate. I know it will be awkward, hard even, but it wasn't you who did anything wrong so you shouldn't be the one to miss out. And you can bring someone if you like."

I smiled and said I'd love to come but needed to think about it, I'd let her know soon. The thought filled me with horror and my instinctive reaction was to get her a nice card and present and stay home. I talked to the girls at work and they suggested finding out who else would be there.

After checking that I wouldn't be the only single female and I knew most of the other guests, including Suzanne, I decided to be brave.

It was a freezing cold day and I'd arranged to pick up Carole so I didn't have to arrive on my own. We got to St Peters only a few minutes before the bride and the church was already quite full, so we sat at the back. I kept my focus peripheral and didn't look around the congregation. Instead, I gave my full attention to the nuptials as they unfolded, needing to blink away tears as I watched Michelle being walked down the aisle by her very proud Dad. After the ceremony we stood around for a short while watching the bride and groom being photographed. Dreading this bit, I kept my eyes fixed on my new shoes and the gravelly path. I knew that Paul and Sharon would be somewhere in the throng but hoped not to see or acknowledge them. Suddenly, a pair or arms flung themselves around me and a flurry of long auburn hair went from one cheek to another as Suzanne exclaimed,

"Bonjour ma belle vieil ami!"

The rest of the afternoon was lovely. I did see my ex with his 'officially new' girlfriend but I needn't have worried as they both seemed as eager as I was to keep a distance. Michelle's Mum gave me a massive hug as we arrived at the reception, telling me I was well shut of 'him' as she gesticulated with her thumb quite openly at Paul. Clutching both my hands in hers she said quite loudly,

"And as for that trashy little tart he's with now, well they deserve each other!" She gave me another big hug and finally let me move along the line. Suzanne, who was just ahead, chuckled,

"Michelle's Mum started on the gin a bit earlier than normal today then. So come on, tell me everything I've been missing. How's Jane getting on?"

Suzy was only back for a long weekend, so I arranged to go out for a drink with her the following evening before she went back to France on Monday morning. I phoned Jane on Sunday morning to see if she wanted to come. Mum had already said she'd babysit but I was also up for taking Suzy round to Jane's with a bottle of wine. As it happened Jane wasn't up for either scenario. She'd '*made plans*' and would catch Suzy next time she was over. I was instantly irritated by this and almost demanded to know what her plans were. Even more annoyingly, she laughed at my churlishness before telling me she was going to her boss's house for the afternoon and evening along with the other people from the nursery. She ended the call saying she'd see me the following Saturday.

In the blink of an eye, January turned into February followed hastily by March and we were turning our clocks forward to welcome British Summer Time. I'd suggested to Jane that we went out on the Saturday night between both our birthdays but she wasn't keen, saying getting a year older was no big deal and she was no fan of night clubs. Instead, we went into Leeds in the afternoon and had a curly sausage meal in the Wimpy followed by ice cream sundaes. I got the bus into Leeds that night with a now visibly pregnant Michelle and four other friends from work. After doing a pub crawl we ended up in Cinderella's where we danced around our handbags until 2am. Dad came to give Michelle and me a lift home, after seeing the other four get in a taxi.

"Did you have a good time love?" Dad asked as I got in the seat next to him.

"It were a brilliant night Mr. Asquith and your Kim is the bestest mate in the world!" Michelle shouted from the back.

Dad glanced across at me as he started the car and I smiled broadly. As the haste of her wedding had prevented her from having a hen night, Michelle spent the whole evening telling everyone that this was her after-wedding hen night. Since discovering her pregnancy, she hadn't been out much at all. They were temporarily living with Trevor's parents while they saved up to buy their own house and she was not enjoying life with her new in-laws. Trevor's mother was not much of a drinker and didn't approve of anyone who was. Michelle had jumped at the chance of a night out and surprised me by asking if she could stay over at mine. It was a good evening and I was a little drunk but had stopped drinking once we got into the club, unlike Michelle and the other four who seemed intent on soaking up as much alcohol as possible. Dad told us to have some tea and toast before we went to bed and suggested I take the washing-up bowl to place at Michelle's side, just in case, and left us to it. We sat up talking for a further hour, munching on thickly buttered toast and drinking a full pot of tea. Again I didn't talk much.

"I really love Trev and it's gonna be brilliant once we get our own house but just now it's bloody awful." She blinked moisture from her eyes and wiped her nose with the back of her hand. "His bloody mother hates me of course, thinks I'm common and that I got pregnant on purpose, well I knew I'd never get that one past her, but she talks to me like I'm a piece of shit and he doesn't say anything. Tells me it's just her way."

I was tempted to pretend that I was shocked at the suggestion that her pregnancy had been no accident but decided I wouldn't carry it off. She knew that I knew she wasn't the sort of girl that left much to chance.

"If we don't get our own place before the baby comes, it'll just get worse."

"Couldn't you live with your Mum and Dad instead?"

"God no, that'd be worse!" She put her cup down and leaned back in the chair, closing her eyes. "Oh God, I don't know why it has to be so bloody hard. It's not like I wanted much, just to get married, have babies and to live happily ever after!"

"A fairy tale ending?"

"Yeah, why not?"

"Because life's not like that and a happy ending is generally a story that's not finished yet."

"When did you get so pessimistic and hard?"

I smiled at her, standing up and holding out my hands to her.

"Come on, we'd better get you to bed and sleep off the gallons of martini you drank. Now, will you be needing the sick bowl?"

We cleaned our teeth, put on our nighties and got into bed. It was very late and our chat over the tea and toast had been enough to sober Michelle in to realising how tired she was. Within seconds of me whispering goodnight into the darkness, I heard her breathing deepen and slow before turning into a gentle snoring.

As the year progressed, my social life became fuller and my new friends spawned even more friends, so I was never short of a something to do. Invites and outings were being planned constantly. There were some single males in our group and I'd been asked out a couple of times but had politely declined, not ready to get back on that horse. Every Wednesday evening, I went to the Electricity Players drama group where I'd rediscovered my passion for the stage. I'd been cast with a fairly big part in a three act comedy scheduled for the middle of May. But we were struggling to find two of the male leads. It was the beginning of April and only the second rehearsal. The first week had seen Frank, the fifty-eight-year-old leader of our little band of actors, reading both the vacant male twenty something parts and we were all quite concerned that he might end up having to play one of them. Jenny, the lady who looked after the props, said there was a new guy started in her office who seemed keen. She'd mention it again and try to bring him along. The following week, I left home late and had to buy petrol on my way, so I was a good half an hour late to the rehearsal. Having run across the car park of the church hall, I crashed through the double doors, spilling out my apologies, when I saw him. He was standing at the front of the stage, book in hand and mouth paused, mid-sentence, staring back at me. It wasn't that it was a bolt of lightning, whistles, bells or poetry; it was more like a sudden recognition, like a pleasant, distant memory. I was instantly confused and also stopped mid-sentence. Other people started to speak and I was aware of someone telling me his name was John and a few moments later, he spoke in a voice I knew.

"Hi Kim." He looked equally confused.

"Do I know you from somewhere?" I asked.

"I was just wondering the same, you look so familiar but I just can't place it."

"Ok come on people we need to get on." Our director stopped further discussions as he introduced Garry and Pete, two other actors he'd recruited. We were jollied along for a full run through. As John and Garry looked a similar age, they took it in turns to read the part of my slightly older brother. We stopped for a break about half way through and the director said he liked the easy banter and timing between John and me and so wanted him to take the part. Over a cup of tea, I managed to find out that he was from Gloucestershire but had recently moved to live near Roundhay Park and tarted working at the North Leeds offices of the Electricity Board. He asked me where I was from, desperate to work out where we knew each other from. I told him I'd only lived in Sheffield and Leeds so there was no connection there.

"Well it's a mystery," I said laughing, "Or perhaps we knew each other in another life."

"Yes, maybe that's it," he nodded and I liked the way he smiled at me.

I was quite disappointed when he didn't come to the pub afterwards for a drink, saying he needed to get home. Jenny came, as always and I made a point of sitting next to her and as I sipped my half a larger and blackcurrant, I casually asked if John had to get home to his wife. Jenny told me I wasn't very subtle and that as far as she knew he wasn't married or going out with anyone. She had an idea he lived with his sister but wasn't sure. He didn't come to the pub the week after either; again he had to get home. The director's panic at the majority of actors still not 'off the book' meant there was no break, so I had no opportunity to talk to him. Finally, on the following week, he came over to me as soon as he arrived and asked if I was going to the pub after we'd finished. Our rehearsal went well and the director commented how animated I was that evening.

"I don't know what you had for your tea tonight Kim but please can you have it again every night until the performances are over?"

After our one drink, my half of larger and blackcurrant and his bitter shandy, he walked me to my car and asked me if I fancied a day out with him over the weekend. He wanted to go to Howarth to see the birthplace of the Bronte's.

"I expect you've been loads of times but I've only been once and it was raining so I'd like to have another look."

"I've never been."

"You're kidding!"

He was astounded but thrilled at the prospect of taking me to act as my guide. I explained about my childhood and day trips and run outs being out of the question, so he made it his mission to take me on various sightseeing tours of my Yorkshire heritage. Our first excursion to the Wuthering Heights of the Yorkshire Moors on that Sunday in May was glorious. John called for me that morning at half past nine and managed a brilliant PR campaign with my parents, accepting the offer of a quick cuppa before we set off. During the day we talked constantly, well I mostly asked him questions about his life so far. I wondered afterwards if he thought at some point I was part of the Spanish inquisition. He told me his parents had split up when he was small and although he hadn't seen his father for over twelve years, when he died the year before, he'd left John his pre-war three bed semi, close to Roundhay Park. That was why he was in Leeds. He was finding out about his father and sorting out his things. John had trained as a teacher and had a job starting at a school in Gloucester in September. His mother had died when he was seventeen so he'd lived with his sister Christine, a midwife and six years older, until he went off to teacher training college. I was a little alarmed at the prospect of him only being around until the end of the summer, but managed to push these thoughts out of my head during the times we were together, although in fact never needed to confront them. The day in Howarth was the start of a wonderful whirlwind romance. John and I were married on Saturday 30th July 1978, just three and a half months after we'd met, at St Peters church with Rachael as my only bridesmaid. Afterwards, there was a buffet reception in the concert room at Bramley Working Men's Club for our fifty guests and in the evening, Mum and Dad continued the celebrations with a bit of a do at our house. My parents loved everything about John, especially his decision to withdraw from the Gloucester school job and take a position at a school in Leeds.

"So you finally found your Prince then?" Jane said as she hugged me outside the church.

I smiled and nodded through my tears. Not only did I think I had but I also thought I had a happy ever after, allowing myself to conveniently forget that this story wasn't finished yet.

Chapter Forty-five

I embraced my change of status from single girl to married woman wholeheartedly. I was like the ugly duckling that had just seen my reflection for the first time and was happily basking in my new-found role. Everyone said married life suited me and it did. I was determined that my marriage to John was going to be perfect, we were soul mates and like swans, we had mated for life. I flung myself into it with a passionate abandonment, keeping the image of the graceful swan gliding majestically through life. However, several significant events taught me that to glide gracefully you need to paddle like mad just below the surface.

My first year of marriage was wonderful and five months in to it I was pregnant. We'd hoped to have a baby fairly soon but were surprised it happened so quickly. My due date was around the beginning of August, just over a year after we got married. I thought I would explode with happiness when we told Mum and Dad, who were equally euphoric. They phoned me every day to check I was eating properly and getting enough rest. Dad thought I should give up work straight away and finding it ridiculous that I continued until the month before. Mum set about knitting a whole layette of clothes, all in white, even though I'm sure she'd never held a pair of knitting needles before in her life. I still have most of those, the bootees, mittens and matinee coat and it fills me with an immense sadness whenever I take them out from the white tissue paper. Mum never got to see her first grandson being carried out of hospital wearing her beautiful handiwork. She died, peacefully in her sleep just two weeks before he arrived. Daniel's birth was an emotional event for Dad and me, having lost Mum so soon before. Her funeral, just eight days before my due date, was almost unbearable.

I don't remember phoning Jane to tell her about Mum but I must have. We called each other rarely by this time and saw each other even less, but she arrived at Dad's two days after Mum had gone. John had been brilliant at sorting out the arrangements, registering the death and speaking to undertakers but had reluctantly gone back to work. He and I were staying at Whitecote Gardens until the funeral. I daren't think about what would happen after that. Opened the door to Jane we both burst into tears at the sight of each other. After a long and consoling embrace, I led her into the sitting room where she immediately went over to Dad on the sofa and hugged him. Eventually, we managed to control ourselves and Jane stayed for the rest of the day until John got back from work. He gave her a lift home while I scrambled about in the kitchen trying to make a meal for us. On the day of the funeral Jane was with us again, helping John support Dad and me through the ceremony. She'd left Rachael with a friend for the day so she could focus on us and, once back at the house, she began offering the sandwiches and cakes she'd made, as well as pouring tea from a permanently full teapot to the thirty or so people who'd turned up. John had suggested we booked a room for after the funeral but Dad wouldn't have it, although to be fair he didn't know what he wanted or even what to do with himself. I remember looking at him standing by the fireplace trying to look like he was listening to Aunty Shirley and knowing he wasn't going to cope without her.

When John brought him to the hospital a week later to meet his grandson, it was a bittersweet moment. I sat propped up in my bed, my body flooded with hormones, watching my father's shaking hand as he reached out gently to touch Daniel's chubby, slightly jaundiced cheek and I thought I would drown in emotions. My beautiful and perfect baby boy, lying in the fish tank crib at my side, wrapped in his blue hospital blanket with his dimpled chin was a source of awe for him.

"Ee she would have loved him Kim, she really would."

"I know Dad and she'd have made the best Nana ever."
John leaned in a bit and pulling back the blanket, picked him up and
handed him to Dad saying,

"I think he's got a look of Pam about him Ray, see, around the eyes."
Dad sat on the visitor chair looking down at the bundle in his arms.

"Aye you're right he has, he's a bonny lad an' no mistake."

There's no doubt in my mind that seeing and holding Daniel lifted his
spirits. On the way home, John took him to the Barley Mo for a couple of
pints to wet the baby's head and for the next few weeks he seemed a bit
brighter. I know how hard he tried to deal with his life without Mum but
I'd always known that my parents functioned as one unit and either
would struggle on their own. He was not just struggling though, he was
missing the mechanics or purpose to go on. As the year moved on he
seemed to withdraw more and more and as Christmas approached I
could see the dread in him at the prospect of this celebration without her.
He called me on a Friday morning in November to tell me he was full of
cold and so I shouldn't bother going round the next day, as I normally did
on Saturdays. He didn't want me or Daniel to catch it and anyway he'd
been off it for most of the week, so he hadn't eaten much and didn't need
any shopping. I got off the phone feeling a little uneasy but had lots of
things to do, so I said I'd phone him later to see how he was. When he
didn't answer his phone, I knew there was something wrong. The official
cause of his death was put down to heart failure but I and anyone close to
him knew he'd simply died of a broken heart. He'd lasted three months
without her.

My second funeral of the year was no less painful but at least I didn't
have Dad to worry about anymore. This time we did hire a room at the
Barley Mo, being the nearest pub to the church and after seeing Dad
safely settled with Mum, John and I drove down the hill to a

professionally catered funeral tea and another round of condolences. Again, Jane was there doing all she could. Rachael who'd started school a few months earlier was being picked up by a friend, so she stayed and helped me get through it. She came back to Whitecote Gardens afterwards and John took Daniel up to bed and left us alone in the sitting room with a bottle of wine. She came and sat next to me on the sofa, put her arms around me and said,

"I'll always love you Kimmy, no matter what, you'll always have me." She kissed me really tenderly on the lips, hugging me and stroking my hair. We sat like that for quite some time, just holding each other. I'd forgotten how she could make me feel. Pulling away, she reached out for our glasses and we clinked them.

"To Ray and Pam," she said, before kissing me again gently and getting up to leave.

I saw that year end with some relief. John and I raised our glasses of Asti-Spumante to the chimes of Big Ben on the television and I cried again. 1979 had seen the loss of both my parents and the birth of our beautiful boy. I looked at John through my tears and tried to voice my muddle of emotions. We talked for a long time about what we wanted for the future, for us and Daniel and it was that night that we decided we would move to Gloucester. I knew John had secretly always wanted to go back and agreed that a fresh start in a new place would be good for me. When I told Jane, she agreed it was probably the best thing for both of us. Our friendship would remain no matter how far apart we were, she assured me, and I remembered Mum saying something similar.

"We won't lose touch. We can visit each other regularly and talk on the phone every week and we could even write like we used to," she said with an assurance in her voice that neither of us really believed.

It took two phone calls and one interview for John to get a teaching post in Gloucester and he was able to start straight after Easter. He'd been happy at the school in Leeds and was sad to be leaving but the headmaster was kind and told him he understood fully and gave him a brilliant reference.

As we had two houses to sell, I was concerned that we wouldn't manage it all by the time John started his new job but our house sold within days of it going on the market and Mum and Dad's only two weeks later. We were packed up and ready to follow the removal men the day after John left his job at the end of the term. It all went like clockwork. We moved into John's old family home with his sister Christine, until we found our own house. There'd been a fairly large sum of money to go with the house that John's father had left him and so with the money from my parent's house as well, we found ourselves very comfortably off. We didn't hurry to find a new one as we both enjoyed living with Christine. She in turn loved having us, specifically Daniel, stay with her. She was brilliant at getting me out and about, making new friends and putting me in touch with other young mums. It made my migration easy and I found myself fitting smoothly in to my new life.

After eight months and just before the end of the year we found our dream home, a house only two miles from Christine which was perfect. On the day we moved in, John insisted on carrying me over the threshold while Christine held Daniel's hand and helped him follow us in. It was a very happy house and our second son Nicholas was born there a year later. Jane and Rachael came to visit just after he was born, their first and only visit, staying for two nights before getting the train back home. John and I took our boys for a visit to coincide with Rachael's ninth birthday, staying for two nights at the Queens hotel in Leeds as Jane didn't have the room to put us up. We went to see Michelle and Trevor the next day before driving home. They had only the one little boy and seemed desperately unhappy, jibing and sniping at each other for the whole two hours we were there. One of her thinly disguised attacks on him was the amount of time he spent at the squash club with Paul.

"And we all know the sort of things you and him get up to there, don't we Kim!"

I asked how Paul and Sharon were in an effort not to get too drawn in. I knew they'd got married and was curious if they had managed to make a go of it. Michelle gave a snort followed by a bitter laugh.

"Sharon threw him out a couple of months ago. Caught him messing around again and decided she'd had enough. He's back living with his Mummy again and screwing anything that moves, when he's not completely off his face that is."

Trevor got up, muttering something about putting the kettle on, and left the room but the look he gave her spoke volumes. It was sad to see them both so bitter. Michelle had definitely not got her fairy tale ending, even having their own rather lovely house hadn't helped. I later realised that this was the very last throws of their marriage. Trevor left her only a few months later for someone he'd met at work.

Despite our best intentions, communication lapsed to almost a silence between Jane and me. The phone calls were not made and the letters never written. We exchanged cards at Christmas and remembered each other's and the children's birthdays but we had busy lives that took all our attention. Time continued to move us on, down roads that were too far apart.

Suzanne was a regular visitor and came to stay with Henri, her fiancé, for a long weekend in the spring every year. John and I took the boys to stay with them in their beautifully renovated farmhouse in Provence which they ran as a B&B. She rarely went back to Leeds now; both her parents had passed away but she did occasionally visit an elderly aunt. She said she found it all a bit stark and harsh, much preferring the rural retreat of her quaint and picturesque auberge.

The clock continued to tick away the years as the children grew and our lives became fuller. I lapped up my new middle-England existence. I'd never gone back to work after having Daniel and found the role of full time housewife and mother wonderful. Throwing myself into the local community, I was usually baking cakes or sorting jumble for some village event or other. The boys and I walked to and from school together every day and we all went swimming on Saturday mornings. It was the idyllic family life I'd dreamed of as a child and there was never a day that I didn't thank whatever force had led me to John and making it all possible.

As the summer ended and the Christmas of 1990 fast approached, John was having a difficult time at work. He'd been appointed headmaster at a school a little further away from home which meant his working day became longer. He was also struggling with a couple of long established staff members. Although they'd not applied for the role themselves, they resented the fact that John had got it. Both were older teachers who had been at the same school all their working lives and they didn't like the change of regime. In turn, John was not impressed with their style of teaching and so battle lines were being drawn.

I decided to invite a few friends round for some mulled wine and mince pies on the last day of term to try and take his mind off work for the start of our Christmas holidays. When I'd first thought of it, at the start of that week, I realised that the last day of term was 16th December and my thoughts turned to Rachael. She was going to be fifteen, I could hardly believe it. I'd already posted a card with a Woolworth gift token, wondering if she spent her Saturdays hanging round the make-up counter. I wondered how she would look and tried to imagine her. Jane and I had exchanged the odd school photograph but the last one I had seen of her, she was eleven and wearing her secondary school uniform. Jane had sent it with a note on the back, *'Do you remember when? No beret with this outfit!'*

The picture was on the bookcase in the dining room and I went to have another look at it. Although outwardly she didn't look too much like her mother, I could see that determined stare and the hint of mischief on her lips. Suddenly, I had a yearning to see them both again. I thought of phoning right there and then but something distracted me and the intention got lost in my domesticity. I thought about it again as I was walking to school to collect the boys and decided I would phone on the Friday to wish Rachael happy birthday.

For the rest of the week, I busied myself getting the house ready for Christmas and preparations for the Friday drinks party, all thoughts of my old friend and her daughter left my head.

John got home a little earlier than normal, just after half past five, looking tired and care worn. Christine had arrived in the afternoon and was busy supervising the boys making a cheese and pineapple porcupine.

"Have I got time for a quick shower before people arrive?" John asked.

"You've time for a long shower or a bath even if you want, I told everyone from six thirty."

"A shower's fine. I just need to freshen up."

Pushing one of the cooling mince pies into his mouth, he went through to the hall and up the stairs. I put another two trays of mince pies in the oven and poured two bottles of red wine into my biggest pan with a sachet of spices, putting it on the stove. Turning to admire the layout of finger food, mostly brought by my sister-in-law, I said,

"That all looks lovely, thank you for your help Christine. Are you okay if I just pop upstairs and tidy up my hair and make-up?"

"Of course. Me and the boys will just sort out the plates and serviettes, then we are going to quickly write our letters for Santa before the guests arrive."

I'd just got to the top of the stairs as the phone started to ring.

"I'll get it," I called down and went into our bedroom to pick up the extension.

"43772," I said automatically.

"Kim, it's Jane."

"Oh Hi Jane, I was going to phone a little later to wish Rachael a happy birthday. How are you?"

"Kim, something's happened. Are you on your own?"

I could hear the shower running in the en-suite and the excited voices of the boys downstairs.

"Yes, I'm in the bedroom getting ready; we're having a few friends round. What's happened? Are you alright?"

"We're fine," she said dismissively, "but Chris Henshaw's just left. He's in CID now and part of some sort of historic case unit."

I felt my chest tighten as my heartbeat struggled to maintain its usual unflustered rhythm. I said nothing, waiting instead to hear what had prompted this visit.

"He came to tell me that they've finally found my mother's body."

Chapter Forty-six

It took a second for what she said to sink in before words began tumbling out of me,

"What? How? They can't have. Did he say? How can they?"
John came through from the bathroom as she started to explain. I wasn't speaking much, just sitting on the bed, receiver pressed firmly to my ear, trying to stem the panic. He started getting dressed, dropping the damp towel at the side of me as he mouthed 'Everything alright?' I nodded and held up my hand in assurance, without making eye contact. He left the room still fastening his shirt and closed the door.

"Listen to me Kim, I am going to tell you what happened and I don't want you to say anything, I just want you to listen. Maybe you could come up for a few days after Christmas and we can talk about it then, but now I'm just telling you what happened. Do you understand?"

"Yes, I understand," and I did, I was being briefed.

Chris was now a detective inspector and when his father retired he'd transferred to Leeds. He explained to Jane that there'd recently been some innovations in forensic science. This meant they could clear up some old cases, especially ones where identity was an issue. They'd used this new science on a body found in the Rodley canal thirteen years before. Perhaps Jane remembered the case? She'd said she had a vague recollection but thought that was a Ripper victim. No, he had told her, the police never linked that body to that inquiry and it had remained a mystery who she was, until now. Although the body had been incinerated years ago, samples had been kept along with clothing, wrappings and ropes. These had been stored in an evidence vault deep below the West Yorkshire constabulary at Millgarth. As part of the clearing up of old unsolved crimes, these samples had been re-examined and details entered into the new police computer database. And they'd found a match, to an even colder case, from 1968 in fact. Chris explained that clothing and artifacts taken from her childhood home, after Maggie had first disappeared, had been kept. These along with medical and dental records meant that Chris could tell her unequivocally that the murdered woman from the canal was Maggie. When she asked how this was possible, he told her this was what he and his team were investigating. He said he'd wanted to come and see her personally to let her know. He couldn't begin to imagine what it must have been like, all those years not knowing what happened to her Mum.

"There was something in the way he said that Kim, like he were trying to trip me up or something."

"Why would he do that?" I asked

"Because he's an arsehole just like his Dad and he's trying to stir up trouble."

"So what did you say?"

"I asked him if I was supposed to be grateful for this. For him coming round to tell me that all those years of his bastard Dad persecuting my family were a waste of time, she'd just run off like Dad had always said."

"And what did he say to that?"

"He said that his Dad were a wanker," she laughed.

He'd told her he didn't think much of how Harry had behaved in and out of uniform and that he'd not had a particularly distinguished career. However, one of the few good things he had done was to secure the box of evidence that had led them to this discovery. Jane parried that he'd only done that with the hope of being able to pin something on her Dad and Chris agreed. He told her he was ashamed of Harry and it had taken a long time to shake off the legacy of being his son.

"He said he was sorry for the way things turned out. He was bloody sorry! I asked him how sorry he was for telling his Dad all that stuff about me and you, all that stuff that pushed my Dad over the edge and got me put in care."

She said he seemed really upset and swore that he'd never said a word to his Dad about either of us.

"Said that the lies were someone else's. But then he would say that wouldn't he. I know it was him and he's still too much of a coward to admit it."

"Jane I need to talk to you about all that..."

"Never mind that now Kim, just listen. You need to take this in, ok?"

"Ok."

Once she had confirmed to him that she'd had no contact from Maggie since the day she walked out, she asked him if he'd spoken to any of her brothers. He was planning to see David the following day but had wanted to tell her first. Kevin was at Her Majesty's pleasure during most of that time, although they would be checking with him and they were still trying to trace Iain. At this point, he'd made a half-hearted, bad taste joke about him having pulled the same trick as Maggie and disappeared without a trace.

"I just looked at him and shook my head so he got all flustered and said he didn't mean to cause offense." She started laughing. "I don't think he has his Dad's nasty streak but he's still a bloody Henshaw."

"So have they any idea what she did after she'd run off?" I asked.

"Apparently not, he seems to think that Iain is the key to it, being only a year or so after she'd gone that he took off. They're thinking that's what caused the fight between him and Dad cos' he knew where she was."

She paused to give me a space to comment but I couldn't think quickly enough.

"Right," was all I managed.

I tried not to be hurt by her sigh before she continued,

"He asked if I remembered anything about the night Dad beat seven bells out of him or if I'd heard any arguments between them before. I said no but it was something I'd wondered about myself."

She laughed again, leaving another pause and I heard the chink of glass on teeth before hearing her swallow.

"Are you on your own?" I asked suddenly.

"Yes of course, why? Oh right, well I needed a drink after he'd gone and I always like a glass or two of wine before I go out on a Friday night."

"Well don't drink too much." I have no idea why I said that, it just came out.

"Why? In case I spill the beans?" This time her laugh was much harsher, "I know the role of my mother has been vacant for ages now but I'm not actually looking for a new one."

"I just meant..."

"I know what you meant, sorry." A deep breath before she continued in a friendlier tone. "I've turned into a bit of a bitch lately. Anyway, here's a newsflash for you. Just as he were leaving he asked me, all casual, like he'd just thought of it, if me and you were still in touch."

"What did you say?"

"I told him you were alive and well and living the dream in Gloucestershire with your perfect husband and two point four children and that we spoke occasionally. He said to say Hi."

"Is he based at Millgarth?" I asked.

"No, he's at Dawson's Corner, handy for the inquiry. You're not thinking of phoning him are you?"

I laughed, remembering how she'd always said I was transparent.

"No," I replied with what I hoped was conviction. "Did he say he'd come back?"

"Said he'd keep me in the loop, I expect our David will be on the phone after he's been to see him." She sounded like she'd lost interest now. "So anyway, we'll talk again after Christmas right?" I nodded a redundant confirmation of my agreement and she rang off.

After washing my face, I looked at my reflection in the bathroom mirror. I was a grown-up now, with a husband and children. I'd found a role and I had made it my own. I was a good wife and mother and I wasn't going to let something from the past come back and spoil it.

Our family Christmas was an idyllic and joyous occasion but I was a distant spectator to most of it, unable to free myself from the echoes of the past. John was aware of the official version of Jane's growing up; her mother disappearing, her father being a bit of a wrong 'un who died in prison but not the abuse she'd suffered, familial or institutional. Although I'm sure he was aware of something nasty in the woodshed, I loved him even more because he'd never asked. He understood immediately, without question, when I said I needed to go and see her. He insisted he was happy to have time on his own with the boys, even though we both knew he needed most of his free time to prepare for the inevitable staffroom battles ahead.

It was still dark when he carried my overnight bag to the car, on a Saturday in the first weekend in January, 1991. Kissing me and giving me a really tight hug before whispering '*safe trip, call me when you get there*', I set off on my first ever solo pilgrimage back to Yorkshire to re-visit some old wounds. Normally when driving the boys around, we listened to the radio and sang; on that dark and frosty morning I didn't feel like doing either. The night before, John had expressed concern about the drive, I was quite nervous about it too but keen not to let him know this.

"I'll be fine. I'll stop at the services a couple of times and if I set off early, I won't see much traffic."

Feeling wobbly, I glanced through my rear view mirror and saw him and Nicholas waving from the front door step. Fixing a smile, I raised a hand in return and set off through the village, towards the M5 trying hard to concentrate on the road and not let my mind stray into the past.

As the sun rose over my horizon and miles clocked up, I began to relax a little. With the two planned stops, I expected the journey to take about four hours, getting me to my first destination by mid-morning. Feeling a lot more confident than I'd expected I decided I didn't need to stop on the M5. Instead I pulled into the Leicester Forest services on the M1 to phone John from the payphone and update him on my progress. Getting back in the car after my comfort break and conversation I was feeling slightly buoyed and turned on the radio and found myself singing along.

The miles seemed to be dissolving quicker and it was hardly anytime at all before I was exiting the motorway. I felt a small panic as I turned on to the outer Leeds ring road and as I drove under the footbridge where Jane and I used to meet, the dark bird of suppressed memories beat its wings. Taking in a deep breath, I began to steel myself for the covert meeting I had not disclosed to anyone. Turning right at the Dawson's Corner roundabout, I diverted from my route to Jane's house and took the first left turn, up Cote Lane and the driveway of new Pudsey police station.

Chapter Forty-seven

The officer on the desk took my name and, confirming my appointment, asked me to take a seat. I sat and began to examine my fingernails, trying to keep calm as I heard him phone through to announce my arrival to Detective Inspector Christopher Henshaw.

"Kim!" He was walking towards me with a broad smile which went all the way to his warm brown eyes. "It's great to see you, how are you?"

I was conscious of where we were and of the desk sergeant watching our exchange but Chris seemed oblivious and as I stood up, he hugged me like the long lost friend he was.

"I could hardly believe it when I got your message," he hugged me again repeating, "It's really great to see you."

"I'm just on my way to see Jane, she's told me about her Mum."

"Yes, it's terrible," as if he'd suddenly remembered who he was. He stiffened a little. "Do you want to come through to my office?"

I followed him through the double doors and down a corridor to a medium sized room with his name on the door.

"Impressive," I murmured with a nod.

He grinned and asked if I'd like a tea or coffee. I declined as he closed the door behind us and stood by his desk awkwardly for a second before sitting on one of the chairs in front of it and blurting out,

"This is a bit of a spontaneous visit; I didn't tell Jane that I was coming. When she told me you were involved in the investigation, I thought you might want to talk to me," I paused and allowed myself a big smile, "and I thought it would be good to see you again."

He returned my smile as he moved across the room and perched on the window ledge, tilting his head slightly as he spoke,

"It's been a long time."

"It certainly has," I replied quickly unnerved by the intensity of his stare. "You've done well," I nodded at our surroundings.

"Career wise, yes, I have. Unfortunately, my personal life's not been quite so successful."

"I'm sorry to hear that."

"Oh you don't have to be. I'm being over dramatic. I'm actually a living cliché; the ambitious policeman who put his job before his marriage. Luckily we didn't have kids so it wasn't too messy."

"Sorry," I said again helplessly.

He laughed with affectionate humour.

"There's no need. Anyway I understand you're very happy, you certainly look good on it."

I felt myself blush and I confirmed I'd been very lucky. A brief silence fell around us as he held my gaze for a few seconds. I had to look away briefly before I could tell him what I'd come to say.

"I wanted to see you to tell you that I know that it was Paul who caused all that trouble with Jane and her Dad and not you and that I'm sorry for ever thinking it was you. I should have known you would never have done that."

He sighed loudly and closed his eyes rubbing his temples as if banishing a train of thought and muttered,

"Thank you," before asking, "Did he tell you?"

"God no, you must know he would never have done that."

He nodded at the truth of that. I started to tell him about the night that his Dad had turned up at our house with news that I'd been in a car crash with Paul. He didn't interrupt, letting me tell my story, nodding occasionally but not filling any pauses in my narrative. He was a good listener, I thought, and probably the good policeman he'd planned to be.

I made no mention of Jane or of the alibi we'd prepared. He raised his eyebrows when I said that Dad had met with Harry the next day and when I told him what his Dad had said, he nodded and looked really sad. I let the silence surround us, feeling I needed to prove I wasn't afraid of the stillness.

"Did you know he was messing about with Sharon?"

"Probably, well he did have form."

"He always was a bit of a tosser, thinking he was God's gift," Chris snapped.

"Why did he do it though, tell Harry those things?"

He sighed deeply, tilting his head back as he looked up to the ceiling, like he was making his mind up about something. Shrugging he said,

"It's a long sordid story but what the hell. There was so much subterfuge going on then. You might as well know."

I opened my mouth to say something, unsure that I wanted to hear it but he held up a hand and said quickly,

"Dad was having an affair with Beryl Turner."

"Bloody hell!"

"Yeah, I know; quite the Don Juan my Dad."

"Did you know?" I asked

"Not at the time although I'm pretty sure Paul knew. Probably loved that bit of knowledge," he said bitterly.

"Probably," I agreed.

"Anyway, after the fight Beryl was furious. Paul had told her I'd just started on him for no reason..."

"Well..."

"Yes I know I shouldn't have hit him but he knew how I felt about you and he had that smarmy, self-satisfied grin on his face. God, I wanted to kill him!"

"That was his natural expression," I laughed, hoping to soften the memory.

He laughed too.

"I suppose it was. Anyway, she dragged him round to our house and made a right scene. When Mum tried to defend me she just went crazy, tellin' Mum that she had no idea about anything, she didn't even know that her and Harry had been having an affair for years and it was only because of his job that he didn't leave her."

"What a cow. Your Mum must have been devastated."

"Yeah, well Beryl always had a nasty streak to her and don't get me wrong, Mum knew Dad was unfaithful and slept around, well everybody knew. But she'd thought Beryl was her friend. That was the killer for her." A big sigh deflated him before he gave the pretence of shrugging the memory away. "As it turned out the lovely Beryl was using your Mum as a smokescreen, suggesting to my Mum that she was his latest bit on the side."

"Bloody hell! Well that explains why your Mother never took to me."

"I'm sure he fancied your Mum so he would have probably played up to her suspicions."

"Well I can tell you quite categorically that..."

"No, I know and I'm not suggesting that anything happened, from what I remember of your parents they never left each other's side anyway. I knew there was never a chance of that." He leaned back a bit and opened his palms toward me as he said, "Basically, Dad was a bully who slept around and Paul was a scheming selfish bastard who was always looking to stir things up but always making sure he was ok."

"What do you mean?"

"When he saw how big a deal our fight turned out to be his thoughts were all about keeping himself squeaky clean, so he had to dirty the rest of us. His mother would have encouraged him as well no doubt."

I shook my head with sorrow and disbelief.

"And of course, that whole me going out with Maureen was his idea, he told me it would make you jealous, but then to break up with her just before the play," a big sigh, "Well he was the one with the experience of going out with girls, had them falling at his feet, so I thought he should know. Course I realised straight away I'd behaved like a prat and that it had the complete opposite effect. I told you I wasn't that bright back then. Took me 'til the Christmas disco to realise he'd got his eye on you."

"But after Christmas when it all kicked off, you knew we thought it was you that told your Dad those things, why didn't you say something?"

"The damage was done and I knew that Jane would never believe me over him. He always had a way with the lasses." He laughed ironically as he added, "Must be those big blue eyes."

So much was suddenly falling into place. Paul's charm only worked on '*us lasses*', his mates and school friends were not so gullible. They all knew him as a fantasist and manipulator who would bend with the wind to keep himself popular.

"Keith really hated him. He once said it was a good job he wasn't that clever or he could have been really dangerous. Anyway, after that Christmas nobody spoke to him again, that's why he left school. It cost him all his mates."

"It cost Jane a lot more," I said, keen not to talk about Keith, another area of my past where I hadn't behaved well, "She still thinks it was you though."

"I know and she certainly didn't try to hide her feelings either."

"I didn't tell her after I found out, I don't know why. I suppose I was scared of dragging it all up again." I could feel my cheeks burning with my admission.

"I doubt it would have made any difference to how she feels about me. I'll always be guilty by association. Harry was a vicious old bastard."

I said nothing, knowing that it would be senseless and insincere to dispute that. He filled the silence between us by testing me,

"I was a bit surprised with Jane's reaction, when I told her about her mother."

"Really what do you mean?"

"Well I would have thought after all these years of uncertainty, she would've been a bit more, well glad to finally know what happened."

"What? You mean after her family was broken up, her childhood destroyed by a false accusation made by your Dad, you thought that you calling round, out of the blue to say 'hey guess what it turns out your Dad didn't kill your Mum after all' you thought she'd be, what – grateful?"

He held up his hands in a gesture of surrender.

"Yes of course you're right. In hindsight, I should have let someone else go round and see her," he lowered his head, "It's all a bit too personal for me."

Again the silence rested on us and again I waited for him to break it. He took a deep breath,

"But I was even more surprised at her attitude to her Dad."

I looked up sharply as he went on,

"I mean, he was abusing her and for God knows how long," he held up his hand to stop me from commenting and looked me very directly in the eye. "Oh I know she denied it but I've spoke to the other guys who went to their house that morning. There really is no doubt about what they saw AND the medical evidence confirmed it. So there's a bit of me that wonders why she never told anyone and why she wasn't relieved when Don was locked up."

I took a deep breath and glared back at him as my anger flared.

"If he was abusing her and I still don't believe it," I lied, "she clearly didn't see it that way and you clearly don't have a clue about what happens to girls who have already been labelled as promiscuous when they are in care."

We stayed eyes locked and mouths set for a few seconds. I felt him trying to read my mind, watching for my body language to tell him something. I sat rigid, hardly daring to breathe. Finally he said,

"It's a wonder she survived at all. Thank God for you eh Kim?"

"Yes, it is a wonder, a miracle even but she did more than survive. She's living a good life now and bringing up her own daughter and the last thing she needs is you and your storm troopers raking up the past."

His expression changed suddenly and the warm smile he'd greeted me with returned. His forehead furrowed a little as he dipped his head slightly and fixed his brown, widely dilated pupils on me and I heard his young teenage voice again.

"I'm just trying to put right some of the damage that Harry did. I want to give them some answers. I will find out who killed Maggie. I owe Jane and David that much."

I smiled at him before shaking my head slightly but only managed to say,

"Oh Chris..."

He shrugged and rubbed both his hands over his face as if wiping away his emotions. The policeman's voice returned as he asked,

"What do you think happened to Maggie?"

I paused to give myself full recall to the lines I'd rehearsed.

"When I first met Jane, Maggie had been gone about seven months and the circus was still going on around her house. You know, visits from your Dad and his buddies trampling around, digging up the garden. She told me she knew her Dad hadn't killed her but she also knew her Mum wouldn't have gone off and left her. Her only theory was someone had kidnapped her, bundled her into their van and made off with her."

I paused there to wait for a reaction. He was still playing the policeman, leaving the silence for me to fill so I went on,

"As the years went by, that's what got her through, thinking Don had done nothing wrong and her Mum was the victim of some random stranger."

"Well she was certainly someone's victim."

"Yes, eventually, but the news you took to Jane's door was that her mother had abandoned her. She'd gone off and turned her back on all of them. She'll struggle to come to terms with that."

"Yes," he said pensively and nodding his head slowly. "Yes, I suppose you're right."

He was mid-shrug when he looked directly at me as if something had just occurred to him. Oh he was good, I'll give him that but I knew a performance when I saw one.

"Do you think Iain knew where she was?"

"I've no idea. He frightened the life out of me so I kept well clear of him."

"But Jane never said anything about why he'd cleared off?"

"No. She knew there'd been a fight but Don wasn't the sort to take people into his confidence. She'd no idea what it was about."

"Well it's a possibility we're considering at the moment," he paused, "But one thing's for sure, Maggie didn't get her new life for long. Looks like she swapped one abusive partner for another." He took in a big breath and added, "I'll keep this case as a priority, and I won't give up on it."

Shaking my head and looked directly at him.

"You always said you never wanted to be like Harry so don't make this your personal crusade. His obsession with the Schofields cost us all so much, don't take on his legacy."

"I won't, that's not what I meant. I just want to be able to tie this up and find Maggie's killer. Surely Jane wants to know what happened to her?"

"I'm not so sure."

"Well, I'm trying for a slot on Crime Watch," he said with hint of pride.

I felt like our conversation needed to end. I'd run out of my prepared script, so I glanced at my watch.

"I'd better go. Jane will be wondering where I am."

We stood up at the same moment and he asked if I'd got time to have a drink with him before I went back home.

"I don't think so. I'm only here for a flying visit, I'll be going home tomorrow and want to get back before the boys' bedtime."

He looked like that was what he'd expected me to say and nodded. I felt the relief and adrenaline I always felt when I thought I'd pulled off a good performance. He blurted out,

"Do you ever wonder if things had been different, if I hadn't been such an idiot with Maureen, that maybe you and me – well, if it could have worked out?"

"Oh Chris, you and me could have been great together or we could have been a complete disaster. It's sad that we'll never know but that ship sailed ages ago, no point dwelling on it. We both have very different lives now. You probably wouldn't have such a successful career ..."

He cut off my ramblings with a cliché of his own.

"Too much water under the bridge eh?" This was an analogy that made me a little uncomfortable, so I kissed him briefly on the cheek as he stood motionless then he opened the door and walked me back to reception.

Chapter Forty-eight

Jane had moved a mile or so up the road and her home was now a semi-detached dormer bungalow in a lovely area called the Chatsworths. On a corner plot, giving her a good sized, neat garden and surrounded by a high privet hedge it was a picture of middleclass respectability. Over the years, she'd dabbled with relationships but none of them had been serious enough to hold her interest. Her friendship with Yvonne had ended abruptly and although she told me very little about it, I knew her well enough to work out what had happened. Yvonne and her husband split up shortly afterwards and both moved away.

Standing in the open doorway as I parked my car on her drive, Jane's smile was warm and welcoming. My heart physically sped to a skipping rhythm at the sight of her. My return smile erupted into a spontaneous laugh that made my eyes moist. After a fiercely warm hug, I looked at her properly. No one would guess that she was nearly thirty-four, she still looked like a teenager. Dressed in jeans and a baggy jumper, her slender and shapely frame was still apparent and her overall attractiveness accentuated by her mane of long curly hair. I moved forward to hug her again, telling her how amazing she looked. As I held her, perhaps a second too long, I could feel the reticence which wouldn't have been perceptible to anyone who didn't know her as I did. And I knew it for what it was. A calculating hardness as she weighed up the situation. I opened the boot, getting out my overnight bag and the two bottles of red wine I'd brought with me. Handing her the plonk, we moved inside and she placed them on the worktop and began to fill the kettle. I glanced round the kitchen making complementary remarks about her home as she set about making the tea.

Rachael was suddenly in the room and walked over to give me a more reserved but far warmer embrace. She'd grown into a chubby and self-conscious girl with a reluctance to smile because of the train track braces. She'd always been a bright and intelligent child and had become a quiet and studious teenager. As she stepped back from our greeting a spontaneous smile lit up her face and her prettiness shone through. Her Jewish heritage was visible but not prominent and I couldn't help but notice her resemblance to the father she no longer remembered.

"Aunty Kim! I'm so glad you're here. Mum really needs someone her own age to talk to," she said with an edge I knew could spell trouble.

"Take Aunty Kim's bag to the spare room Rach," her mother said, not turning around.

"I can take it if you just point me in the right direction," I said, but in reality the spare room wasn't hard to find, having an enamel plaque stating 'Guest Room' on the door. Rachael followed me in and looked quickly around as if checking that it was appropriate.

"So what are you up to at the moment Rachael? Have you decided what you want to do after school?"

Over our mugs of tea, she told me she was thinking of studying medicine but hadn't fully made up her mind although she would be going to university. Her mother had told her that I could have gone to Uni; apparently I was certainly clever enough. She wanted to know why I hadn't. I told her that the draw of working in an iconic new building and earning a proper wage became too great for me to resist. Jane said very little as her daughter and I chatted amiably.

"Do you regret that you didn't go now?" Rachael asked.

"Not really. Well only for the social aspect perhaps. When John talks about his time at Uni it's all about the bands he saw, the parties he went to and endless drinking sessions," I said with a laugh.

Rachael also laughed but Jane gave a little snort as saying,

"Goodness Kim, my daughter would hate that sort of thing. She seems to be totally opposed to having any sort of fun."

Rolling her eyes, Rachael sighed and as the conversation continued it became clear that, although there was a great bond of love between them, there was little understanding. Jane was frustrated that her daughter took everything seriously and didn't want to behave as she thought normal teenage girls should. Rachael in turn disapproved of her mother's lifestyle, suggesting she drank too much and was frivolous in her relationships. She felt her mother should be looking for someone to settle down with and not going to nightclubs with girls half her age. Jane had achieved her ambition and ran her own nursery and playgroup. Now five years in, she had a staff of four working for her. All women, three of whom were a similar age to her but one of them, Julie, was twenty and Jane's new best friend. There was a picture of the two of them on the fridge door held in place by a magnetic alphabet letter. They looked the same age and very drunk. Putting her empty mug down on the carpet in front of her, Jane started to tell me about a night out she'd had with Julie, boasting about the amount they'd drunk and how she'd no idea how she'd got home. I wasn't sure if it was me or Rachael that she wanted a reaction from but I didn't take the bait. I just smiled and shook my head slightly in what I hoped was a *'what are you like'* way.

"She's a nightmare," her daughter confided in me later. "I don't know how she'll manage when I go to Uni."

There was a casserole in the oven for later, Jane informed me, and I bit back a smile when she called it dinner instead of tea. It was scheduled for six but the wine was open a good hour before. She was well into her second glass by the time the three of us sat down to eat at the glass-topped table. The meal was good, although I noticed Jane hardly ate any of it. Instead, she made easy conversation, mainly asking about John and the boys and encouraged Rachael to tell me about things she'd been doing. Once I'd cleared my plate, Rachael asked if I'd like a coffee. She'd planned to go and spend the night at a friend's house so I told her not to worry; I'd sort some out later and reached for the new bottle of wine Jane had just opened. After pouring a glass and taking a sip, I stood up and started clearing the plates.

"Oh leave that, I'll do it in the morning," Jane smiled not moving.

"It'll only take a minute to clear up a bit. Why don't you put some music on?" I said, continuing my task.

She got up smiling and took her glass and the bottle through to the sitting room.

"Ok I've got just the thing, a mix tape from my latest admirer," she laughed.

I scraped the plates over the bin and put the remaining casserole in a Tupperware container. Running some water, I started to wash-up as I heard the tones of Gloria Estefan sing 'I can't stay away from you'.

"Good choice," I said as the song finished and I stepped into the room.

Jane was sitting with her legs tucked under her on her Chesterfield sofa, grinning like a Cheshire cat. I turned the music down a notch and she let out a little chuckle but didn't complain. Instead, she started to tell me about Gavin, the latest in a long line of suitors. He was an estate agent with a big flash car, sharp suit and highlighted hair. Her description of him made him sound dreadful and her laughter suggested to me that she thought so too.

"First time he came round while Rachael was here was hilarious," she laughed, "I thought she'd lose her eyes up in her forehead she was rolling them at me so much."

"She's not impressed then?"

"God no, it was a real problem for her. She's desperate for me to settle down and stop running around embarrassing her, always on at me to find a nice man. So when I introduced her to Gavin, having told her that I thought he could be the one, she almost choked on her tea." Finding her story highly amusing she threw her head back chuckling, "And he's got these really terrible false teeth. God they're massive, hardly fit in his mouth and he's generally very pleased with himself so they're always on show."

"So do you actually like him?"

"Jesus Christ course not, he's an arsehole."

She emptied the last splash of wine into my glass and got up to get another bottle. After she'd filled her glass and topped up mine I asked,

"Has Rachael ever asked you about her Dad?"

"No, not really. She's always known he wasn't around for long and that he wasn't the love of my life or anything." She took a sip and stared off into the middle distance somewhere. "I've never really kept much from her, well apart from the obvious." This time she gave a small tinkle of a not too genuine laugh, before taking another sip.

"Have you told her about your family history, about how you grew up?"

"Well let's see, she knows that I was abandoned by my mother, that my elder two brothers were thugs and worse, that they were always in trouble with the police, but luckily they ran away from home quite early on," a pause for a mouthful of Merlot, "And she knows that her grandfather was persecuted by the police and eventually framed and locked up in prison where he died a lonely death, while I was passed around children's homes full of nastiness and cruelty."

"Well I suppose that just about covers it," I said taking a rather large sip of my wine.

I decided that was probably the best time to tell her that I'd been to see Chris. As I expected she was annoyed.

"What on earth did you do that for?" A flick of suspicion crossed her face. "What did you tell him?"

I recounted our conversation, finally telling her what Harry had told Dad about Paul. I also gave her my post event analysis, how we'd all been deceived by him. I saw from her face she wasn't happy to accept this as her truth.

"It doesn't matter who it was, it happened and he's still guilty by association."

"Just because of Harry? Oh come on Jane, you of all people should know that people aren't responsible for what their parents do."

"That's a bit below the belt Kim!"

"I know, I'm sorry but come on. People shouldn't be judged for their parents' mistakes. If we have to be judged, it should be on our own actions."

We both looked at each other, calculating and apportioning our mistakes perhaps? Suddenly she laughed and raised her glass to me.

"Well said Mrs Middle England."

I shook my head but smiled back and raised my glass too before taking a sip as she went on.

"So tell me more about your life. Still living the dream, shopping in Marks and Sparks, doing your Am Dram and throwing dinner parties?"

The frostiness in her voice could have chilled the room but I chose to ignore it. With a nod and a laugh I said,

"Ah yes, all of the above. I am indeed the poster girl for the stay at home mother. I even do batch baking and yoga!"

Her face softened as she sniffed her annoyance back and washed it down with a large gulp of wine.

"You did the right thing moving away, I should have done the same when I had the chance. Matthew owned properties in York. That's where he wanted me to go." Another mouthful of wine, "She'd never have found me if I had."

"From what I remember of the woman Maggie turned into, I think she would have found you anyway."

Talk turned back to Chris and my conversation with him. I'd been dreading telling her about his ambition for a slot on Crimewatch but she was jubilant at this news.

"It means they've got nothing!" she exclaimed, "So we're safe." She leapt off the sofa to clink glasses with me this time.

"I suppose so but what if her family from Blackpool recognise her? They must have reported her missing and that's the main aim of the program, to jog people's memories."

I noticed she flinched when I used the word family and I felt my cheeks flush a little at my tactlessness. My defense as always was to leave a silence, to wait for the ball to come back to my court. Jane eyed me sharply, despite the alcohol, before saying,

"Well yes let's hope that her '*family*' don't see it. But what if they do anyway?" She got up and took my glass from me.

"As far as I know there's no pictures of her. We were never the happy smiling posing type of family. Maybe my Gran had some of their wedding. I don't remember seeing any but they would have been thrown out when she died..." She paused as a smile danced on her lips, "so any reconstruction can only be done on descriptions." Her smile reached her eyes and an expression I hadn't seen for a long time. "They've got nothing; we can sleep easy in our beds..." She leaned forward and took both my hands and pulled me to my feet, "and talking of beds..."

I woke up the next morning just after seven, alone in her bed. I could hear the shower running in her en-suite as I slowly took in where I was. Looking round the semi darkness I could make out my clothes in a heap by the door. I got up, picked them up and moved quickly down the stairs of the dormer and into the main bathroom. After showering, I went into my allocated bedroom and dressed. When I came out she was in the kitchen making coffee.

"Morning," she said with a smile, "Did you sleep well?"

"Yes thanks. Did you?"

"Like a baby. Coffee?" she nodded to the filter machine dripping its aromatic darkness into the glass jug.

After a leisurely breakfast of cornflakes, bought especially for me, followed by bacon sandwiches, we got in her car.

"I'm taking you for a tragical history tour," she laughed as she indicated left out of her drive. I smiled at her; it was so good to see her in this buoyant mood. As she drove, she told me Gavin wanted to take her to New York for her birthday. She'd planned to dump him straight after Christmas but he'd mentioned this birthday treat so she'd decided to hang on. *'Well I'm not going to turn down a free holiday am I?'* I suggested that he might have got the measure of her and would continue with planned gifts and holidays until he finally got a ring on her finger.

"Don't be so ridiculous Kim. Marriage is for mugs, no offence."

"None taken," I laughed.

As she indicated left and started to turn up Hill Top Road, I felt my eyes moisten as a spontaneous squeal of giddy delight burst past my wide smile. She stopped the car and turned slightly, "So this is where it all started." Reaching in the back she grabbed at what looked like a piece of felt and tossed it at me saying,

"I got you this; you don't HAVE to wear it."

We got out the car and walked towards the high, chained gate and I put on the beret.

"It looks just the same," I said, taking in the wide gates and the broken chain link fencing.

"They're planning to close it," she said wistfully, "Apparently, we're not producing enough kids to fill it." Turning to me she said, "You look mental in that hat, but you can keep it on if you stick with me."

Next we went to Bramley Park. Full of nostalgic *'do you remembers'* and *'oh what abouts',* we walked around the perimeter of the Sunday League football match, linking arms as we evoked all our happy memories, glossing over and ignoring others. We had a quick go on the swings, white knuckles gripped as we leaned back as far as our arms allowed, swinging our lower legs back and forth in a manic rhythm, whooshing higher and higher, laughing like the children we should have been. Once back in the car she pushed a cassette from her coat pocket into the machine as she pulled away from the curb. Marc Bolan was singing about 'Hot Love' as we passed the flattened buildings that had once been the Thrift stores and the old off-licence. The telephone box where we had spent so much time and money on dial-a-disc remained forlornly like a determined beacon to our past. She crossed the carriageway to pull into Back Lane where she performed a two point turn to park facing the Unicorn. It wasn't yet eleven and wasn't open so we didn't get out of the car. The music changed and Steve Wonder's voice evoked the tears as he sang 'Yester you, yester me, yesterday.' We said nothing at all until the end of the song when she asked, "You ok?" I nodded as the Archie's filled the car with the bubble gum pop of 'Sugar Sugar' but as the car sped towards Armley Heights Drive, the joviality of the song seemed bizarre.

Although she slowed down as she passed her old home, she didn't stop. I noticed the large overgrown hedge had gone and the doors and windows had been replaced. No one who didn't know would guess at the darkness that had been hidden within those walls.

She turned into Whitecote Gardens but I knew this was just a slight detour. After pausing only slightly in the cul-de-sac, where I could see a different front door and not so tidy garden, we continued our excursion down the hill toward the canal. I don't remember the music for the rest of the trip. I hardly remember getting to the slip road but suddenly we were there, stopped in a very similar place to where we had parked thirteen years before. We got out in silence and walked down to the towpath looking down it towards the bridge.

"I don't feel anything," she said, "not a thing. It could just all have been something I watched on TV. What about you?"

I could hardly take my eyes from the spot. The dark water still and glass like. I managed a small shrug.

"Yeah, I know what you mean," I managed.

A pebble hit the surface making me jump and Jane launched a second one before brushing dirt from her fingers.

"Come on, it's too cold to hang around here. Let's get back home for a cuppa."

When we got back, via Jane's old Stanningley home, Rachael was in and peeling carrots. I declined the offer of staying for their Sunday roast dinner explaining I needed to get back to give John some time for his preparations. In reality I wasn't sure I could keep up the pretence much longer. We'd said what we needed to say and we were both satisfied that our secret was safe and that our sleeping dog would be left to lie. We said our warm goodbyes after coffee and biscuits and I was on the road home by half past twelve.

Chapter Forty-nine

The mystery of what happened to Maggie Schofield was never solved. No one ever worked out what happened to her between leaving her home in 1968 and turning up stabbed and trussed in the canal in 1977, despite a Crimewatch appeal. And so her killer remains at large. There was no reconstruction, just some footage of Armley Heights and an artist's impression, based on Jane and David's memory of her appearance. The piece ended with some shots of the canal and description of the clothes she'd been found in. I watched it with John and the boys and expected a call from Jane afterwards, but none came. The earth continued to rotate in its normal axis around the sun and the years continued to pass.

Rachael grew from the serious and studious child into an eminent academic. She did study medicine but chose a research career, becoming a professor of human biology at Leeds University, where she could keep an eye on her mother. She married another academic in a small, non-religious ceremony in the summer of her 30th year.

John and I went along without our boys and I was shocked to see how thin Jane looked. It had only been a couple of years since we'd seen each other but the change was astounding. Most of her curves gone and her face was thin and lined. All the childlike innocence had vanished and she looked ravaged. I tried to talk to her but she was having none of it. Instead it was Rachael who told me the following morning. It was cancer, diagnosed early in the New Year and the prognosis wasn't good. The happy couple were not having a honeymoon as their nuptials were nothing more than a legal confirmation of their relationship. Bizarrely,

Jane left shortly after the ceremony for a week of sunshine in Majorca with her latest squeeze. Rachael and I met for coffee before John and I went home. Jane had made her promise not to tell me until after the wedding and was refusing to discuss it with her or anyone. I phoned her the day after she'd got home from holiday but she was still dismissive of her illness.

"No point in wasting time on all that now. When are you coming back to see me?"

I spent a week with her in September helping her finalise the sale of her business and sort out her things.

"I need you to help me put my affairs in order," she'd said with a chuckle, "I don't want Rachael finding my hidden bottles of vodka after I've gone."

She wasn't kidding about that either. I poured at least three bottles that had been secreted around the house, down the sink.

"It turns out I'm more like my mother than I knew," she said with a shrug as I held up the last bottle that I'd found under the sink behind the washing powder.

"You are nothing like that woman!" I snapped, the strain fraying my practical calmness.

I went back for a weekend in November. She was on a good deal of medication by then but still insisted on having a glass of wine, to toast our friendship, on the night I arrived. We played our game of nostalgia tag, taking turns in airing our rose tinted memories. All the dark areas banished, emitted by an unspoken agreement and we didn't mention any of her family. It was a lovely evening but when she began to struggle, I made her some hot chocolate before helping her to bed. Tucking her in, I lay down next to her, on top of her quilt and stroked her thinning hair for a while before she fell asleep. Then I crept into the guest room where I cried myself to sleep.

Suffering a little the next day, perhaps because of the wine, she seemed even frailer. The morphine was making her woolly and confused. Rachael had come over and was making some soup as Jane and I sat in her kitchen. She was talking about Mrs Silverberg and how like a mother she'd been. A cloud passed across her face and she suddenly said,

"I don't regret what I did Kim. She was a wicked old bag."

"Mum!" Rachael turned from stirring the pan, "That's no way to talk about anybody."

"You didn't know her, thank God." She screwed up her face as if trying to remember something and the darkness passed and she smiled and nodded at her daughter, "You'd have liked Mrs Silverberg, she was lovely."

"Blimey, make your mind up, you just said she was an old bag."
I saw Jane fighting to understand as the painkillers clouded her thoughts.

"It was all a long time ago," I said, "That soup smells lovely Rachael, what is it?"

I visited her again shortly after Christmas. She was in a hospice and I'd been told she was rallying a little, although that was hard to see. She was tired and vague but seemed really happy to see me. Although she could walk she found it exhausting, so I pushed her around the grounds in a wheelchair as she insisted she needed some fresh air. Asking me to stop by one of the benches she asked,

"Do you think I've been a good mother, Kim?"

"Of course," I replied immediately, "What a ridiculous question, Rachael is testament to your parenting skills and a real credit to you."

She smiled, looking satisfied.

"I did a better job than Maggie."

"You did a brilliant job, despite Maggie," I corrected.
She lived another twelve weeks before dying 1st March 2005, just short of her 48th birthday.

I was surprised to see Chris at the funeral. He was outside the crematorium as John and I arrived. I introduced him as an old school friend and after a few moments of polite conversation, we moved on to speak to Rachael.

"Hello Kim, you know Uncle David of course."

I did a double take just before he leaned in to give me a hug. I managed to murmur,

"Yes of course, how are you David?"

He winked at me, reaching out to shake hands with John.

"I'm good thanks Kim, you must be John."

I was still a little confused. I had no idea Rachael knew David but their easy body language told me they'd known each other a while. Suzanne was there too, still living in France and still a breath of fresh air and common sense. She was advising Rachael on the benefits of buying property in France as an investment as well as being a bolt hole. There was an old farmhouse not too far from them that was just about to go up for sale. Noticing that John seemed really interested in what Suzy was telling Rachael, I stepped away towards the buffet where David was standing alone.

"You've hardly changed at all," he said as I approached, "it's incredible."

"I could say the same about you."

I told him I hadn't realised that he and Jane were back in touch with each other. He laughed.

"Well that's my sister, she did like her secrets."

After my call to the Woods back in 1977 they'd stayed in touch and had become quite close, he told me. I commented that I really was surprised as she'd never mentioned him to me, but then there was so much she didn't tell me in the later years.

"Perhaps she wanted to keep us pigeon-holed," he suggested, "or maybe she thought you knew enough of her secrets already."

I looked at him closely and he held my gaze for a second before picking up a plate of sandwiches and holding them out to me. I shook my head and reached for a cup of tea instead. Smiling, I asked him how he was doing. He was still happily married to Mandy and it was her and their two grown-up daughters who were responsible for the fantastic spread we saw before us. I commented on the sumptuous and appetising array and was starting to tell him about Blackpool high teas when I remembered something else. I picked up a cupcake from the fine assortment and held it up to him.

"Oh my goodness, butterfly buns. This really brings back memories."

Telling him about the baking day and the cakes we'd made and what his sister had told me of how she'd baked cakes with her Mum and the happy memories she had. He let me finish before tilting his head to one side and with a sad resigned smile he said,

"Ah if only that were true, Maggie never did anything like that with any of us."

I looked at him sharply.

"She wasn't a nice person. In fact she was a nasty, selfish and hard woman who loved her drink. After she'd gone, when the police searched the house they found bottles of booze stashed everywhere. No wonder we were always hungry, there was never any food in the house."

"But..." I began, "I always thought, from what Jane said..."

"Jane knew exactly what she was, even at her young age. And she knew Maggie hated her. She'd slap her for no reason or pull her up by the hair. Not while Dad was around though, she was cleverer than that."

I stared at him with my mouth open.

"She was jealous of Jane, there's no other way to describe it. She resented how Dad doted on her. She never bought her anything. All her clothes were cast offs from the neighbours. Did she really never tell you any of that?"

"No," I shook my head, "never. This is incredible, she was distraught at losing her, we had a scrapbook full of newspaper cuttings, she was...oh god...I don't know."

I was lost for words. He shook his head and smiled.

"She was good at creating her own reality my sister, but I think she needed to be."

"This is crazy, it's turning everything on its head."

"Maybe, but it's ancient history, all in the past where it should stay." He stepped a little closer to me and turned us both slightly away from the rest of the gathering. "All that stuff Kim, it's done and no one can undo it, so it needs to be left alone." He nodded over at Chris chatting to Suzanne and John at the other side of the room.

"He apologised earlier for not being able to give us any answers about what happened to Maggie. I told him, Jane and me, we didn't care what happened to her. She was a nasty piece of work who met a sticky end." He gently squeezed my arm, "Nothing to do with any of us."

He held my gaze for a second and as I took a deep breath and smiled and asked, "Do you want some more tea?"

John drove me to Hill Topp after we left. No longer a school, it was now very spacious council offices surrounded by well maintained metal security railings, but the building still looked the same. I got out of the car and stepped towards the fence, holding the felt beret in my hands like prayer beads. John stayed in the car, pretending to look at the AA map. The gates were locked with a new looking padlock but I didn't need to go inside. I leaned against the bars looking for the spot by the playground where we'd lined up that day. As my tears flowed freely, my eyes caught the ghost of a memory. Two young girls, meeting for the first time on the cusp of adolescence and finding a friendship so strong it would not be broken, even by death. Clutching the hat tightly to my mouth as a sob burst its way out, I pressed my forehead against the metal as I saw them smile at each other before filing forward and into the school.

ABOUT THE AUTHOR

A.K.Biggins grew up in Yorkshire and has been penning stories and tales all her life. Having reached a significant age she decided to see if anyone else might be interested in her scribblings. After completing a Creative Writing course at Bournemouth Arts University and Novel Writing course at the Faber Academy she dared herself to show and tell. Losing Jane is her first novel.

31063300R00253

Printed in Great Britain
by Amazon